FEAST OF
BONES

Non-fiction books by Daniel P. Bolger

AMERICANS AT WAR, 1975–1986
An Era of Violent Peace

DRAGONS AT WAR
2-34th Infantry in the Mojave

FEAST OF BONES

a novel

Daniel Bolger

PRESIDIO

The views expressed herein are those of the author and do not purport to reflect the position of the United States Military Academy, Department of the Army, or Department of Defense.

Copyright © 1990 by Daniel P. Bolger

Published by Presidio Press
31 Pamaron Way, Novato CA 94949

Library of Congress Cataloging-in-Publication Data

Bolger, Daniel P., 1957–
    Feast of bones : a novel / by Daniel P. Bolger
        p.   cm.
    Includes bibliographical references (p. 355)
        ISBN 0-89141-370-7   90B 3376
        1. Afghanistan–History–Soviet occupation, 1979.1989–Fiction.
    I. Title.   1995
    PS3552.058464F4   1990
    813'.54–dc20   89-70971
                                                        CIP

Maps by Valentine Typesetting

Printed in the United States of America

*For the cadets of the United States
Military Academy at West Point,
classes of 1987, 1988, 1989, 1990, 1991,
and 1992—warriors all*

CONTENTS

AUTHOR'S NOTE

Many of the situations and characters described in this book are based upon careful research into the recent history of the Soviet Union. Actual Soviet units, military commanders, and political leaders play their parts in operations and events that closely parallel historic developments. Although the 688th Guards Air Assault Regiment served in Afghanistan during the period of this story, the activities of its reconnaissance detachment are strictly fictional.

I have taken certain liberties with Russian names and titles to make the story more intelligible to English-speaking readers. Anyone who has ever read *War and Peace* knows the difficulty with Russian names. A Soviet soldier can be identified by rank, first name, patronymic (father's name), and surname. Soviets distinguish between guards ranks, as in their air assault forces, and regular ranks. I have avoided this cumbersome distinction and simply used standard titles. Also, Russians traditionally employ diminutive names (Misha for Mikhail, Sasha for Aleksandr) between friends, and sometimes call people strictly by their patronymics ("dear Ilyich" for Vladimir Ilyich Lenin). I have stuck with full names for clarity.

In a similar vein, I have used the colloquial Western names for certain socialist countries, such as East Germany rather than the German Democratic Republic. This should avoid understandable confusion among American readers, but they should be aware that Soviets would never employ these "bourgeois" names.

Finally, I have employed typical Russian expressions whenever appropriate, but have occasionally substituted equivalent English colloquialisms. With regard to the use of profanity and obscenity, readers should be aware that a certain amount of earthy language is endemic to soldiers worldwide, and that Russians, in good socialist fashion, actively attempt to exceed these norms. If anything, I have toned down the more graphic figures of speech.

Within the obvious constraints of fiction, I have tried to reflect the Soviet military experience as realistically as possible. In addition to the books noted in the bibliography, I am indebted to the following individuals for their kind assistance, suggestions, and ideas: Douglas Boltuc, James Breckenridge, Daniel Burghart, David Isby, Charles Jacoby, David Lamm, Michael Mellor, Ralph Peters, and Steven Zaloga.

PROLOGUE
The Desantniks

The wolves conjure the tempest in the ravines.
The screeching eagles call the beasts
to the feast of bones.

from *The Lay of the Host of Igor,* a medieval Russian tale

The little pass bore no official name. It had never needed one, because the smugglers who used it over the centuries knew where to go. It was not as if such passages were in short supply in the rugged Hindu Kush. On a summer day, even experienced mountain men might well have avoided this particular tortuous, rock-strewn gully, which meandered southwest from the grim hovels of Chitral, Pakistan, into the equally squalid hamlets of Afghanistan's devastated Kunar Valley. On a dark winter night when wind-whipped clouds blotted out the pale moon, only desperate men with sure feet dared to test the rocky, narrow path.

Harsh elements conspired to delay travelers bold enough to traverse the ravine. Stygian shadows shrouded the broken ground. The welcome glow of human settlements did not penetrate into this remote crack near the roof of the world, nor could the weak light of the December moon and stars filter through the thick, woolly banks of restless, mottled snow clouds that raced across the peaks of the Hindu Kush. Only the feeble phosphorescence of a shallow blanket of dry, sifting snow served to outline the pass and its steep ramparts. Jet-black lumps of exposed boulders and the equally inky depths of yawning crevices broke the dreary pallor. Thin crusts of brittle, snow-covered ice disguised potholes and cracks all along the twisting cut. Although the gusts of snow flurries sometimes tapered away, the frigid temperatures insured that the path remained half buried and uncertain.

With vision greatly impaired, wayfarers might naturally try to depend upon their hearing. Here again, the unforgiving mountain night offered little assistance. Along the uneven bottom of the pass, fitful northeasterly breezes rattled loose stones and drove occasional icy needles through the gloomy defile. Hundreds of meters up, roaring wind blasted above the upper reaches of the jumbled ramparts that formed the contorted passageway. The steady rush of moving air combined with the intermittent grumble of distant avalanches to create an ambient noise level that dulled and confused the ears. Only a discerning listener could distinguish the muted sounds of gunnery emanating from the embattled Afghan Army fire base at Barikot, fifteen kilometers south in the wide Kunar Valley basin.

Blinded and deafened by the cruel environment, resolute hikers relied upon balance and touch to guide them. Of course, the same brutal conditions that rendered movement so difficult made a snowy mountain night perfect for those who preferred to be neither seen nor heard. Thus, just past midnight on 23 December 1984, a half-dozen bundled men and their two reluctant, overburdened mules made excruciatingly slow progress as they picked their way down the crooked trail. Constrained by the jumbled rock slides to either side of their route, the men led their animals in a single file.

At odd intervals, the mules balked when the big, dark crates on their backs thwacked heavily into protruding rocks. The men cajoled, cursed, and slapped the rumps of their unwilling charges. Now and then, the mules felt nudges from the butts of the wicked Kalashnikov automatic rifles carried by each member of the tiny midnight caravan. About four kilometers ahead of them, fellow guerrillas of the Afghan National Liberation Front waited at the gully's end, high on the east wall of the main Kunar Valley. No doubt Mujaddidi and his rebel leaders would be quite happy when they opened these important shipments.

The six escorts hurried along as best they could, spurred by familiar images: the cheering heat of their friends' huts, the warmth of hot tea gulped from brimming cups. No lazy Russians dared stir from their warm fire bases to bother with such a small, seemingly insignificant group. So believed these veteran *mujahidin*, especially their leader, Sayed Ismail, deputy commander and logistics chief for the National Liberation Front, the band that controlled Kunar Province. Ismail had used this favorite, insignificant passage a hundred times over the past four years, always around midnight when the weather was bad. Tonight the snow ended a little too early, but Ismail remained confident that the cold and darkness would keep his adversaries well away.

He could not have been more mistaken. Between the two mules and their linkup point, squirreled into well-built sangars and camouflaged listening and observation posts, sixty-one hidden *desantniks* and eleven Pathan scouts of Reconnaissance Company, 688th Guards Air Assault Regiment, waited in ambush.

Captain Dmitriy Ivanovich Donskov's three white-clad platoons deployed athwart the little track. The 1st Platoon manned three security outposts 800 meters to the east, well up the flanking rock faces. One squad set up on each side of the trail. A few hundred meters north, the third squad surveyed a secondary approach route that fed into the main defile behind the 1st Platoon's positions. West of 1st Platoon, 2d Platoon formed an L-shaped chain of squad positions along the south side of a rather straight segment of the gully, where the far side was especially sheer and the two-meter-wide trail lacked any semblance of cover. Two squads held the base of the southern wall, planted in the rock work within ten meters of the footpath. The third squad actually blocked the route and would fire directly northeast, up the throat of the pathway. This constituted the ambush kill zone. Finally, 3d Platoon secured the western approaches to the ambush site, with squads on either side of the track. A third squad waited almost 800 meters farther down the trail to ward off any mujahidin coming northeast to meet their supply mules. Established two days earlier, the entire array of recon units was tied together with well-buried field wire telephones and backup R-114D radios. It seemed like a standard ambush, right out of any basic infantry exercise.

But this ambuscade was anything but routine. First of all, Soviet Army reconnaissance units do not normally conduct fighting missions, unless absolutely necessary to gather vital information. In this case, the effort revolved around an attempt to capture the valuable

Sayed Ismail alive. Handed over to the vicious attentions of determined GRU interrogators, Ismail would only too gladly reveal the logistics network that laced the Kunar Valley and sustained the stubborn National Liberation Front guerrillas. When Donskov's parent 688th Guards jumped off for its planned Kunar offensive in January, the regiment hoped to descend in force on the key nodes of rebel resistance rather than flail impotently at a vague, half-seen enemy.

Donskov's determined quest for information led to the second major difference between this undertaking and most Soviet efforts in Afghanistan: These paratroopers knew exactly what their foe was doing. Over a period of four and a half weeks, the nine recon squads and company headquarters had gradually infiltrated the eastern Kunar region. The tough, well-trained desantniks marched an average of almost a hundred kilometers while gathering extensive information on mujahidin activities and searching diligently for any enemy logistics kingpin. Brief, well-practiced communications procedures allowed Donskov to feed his squads into the mountains one by one, then assemble them once he discerned a useful pattern. March divided, fight united; the principle had served the Mongol Tatars well, and now it served a Russian as he maneuvered against the Tatar residue of Afghanistan.

Donskov never expected to pinpoint the wily Ismail himself, but the rebel leader proved to be a frequent traveler in the 1st Platoon zone. It appeared that the proud National Liberation Front deputy commander enjoyed making personal trips to the American CIA depot at Chitral, Pakistan. Given the small size of two previous shipments, Donskov guessed that Ismail was delivering some key "goodies." Unusual devices might interest the higher directorates of the GRU, but grabbing those items promised little for the 688th Guards. Donskov needed Ismail himself. So the captain and his troops paid more attention to the pattern Ismail established than to the potential nature of his activities. Every ten to twelve days, the National Liberation Front logistics chief and a few chosen men used the small pass to ferry two mules from Chitral to the Kunar Valley, crossing the border around 2300 under cover of snowstorm and completing the trip before dawn.

Donskov had drawn his company together as Ismail's next usual transit day approached. He placed his units for optimum fields of fire and camouflage. The commander insured that platoons could rotate their paratroopers into selected nearby caves to warm up, clean up, eat, work on weapons, and sleep while the company readied its ambush positions. Small outposts and roving patrols fanned out to provide warning of potential interlopers while the company created its snare. In his usual exacting way, Donskov rehearsed his prisoner snatch team, inspected weapons, and circulated throughout the defile as his men prepared for action.

Once nightfall came, the company went to full alert. The rest plan helped the recon soldiers pay attention as they settled into their fighting holes and waited for the mujahidin. In his shallow shelter in the 2d Platoon zone, Donskov lay on the chill rocks, his ear pressed to a field phone. He had a good feeling about the mission. It just might come off.

Hours passed. An early evening snow squall blew west, no doubt pushed by the torrents of cold air cascading off the main Hindu Kush range to the north. Donskov fidgeted in his position, noticing as he did so the spectral figures that comprised his headquarters: his radioman, artillery officer, air controller, aidman, political officer, deputy commander, and company sergeant major. These men propped themselves silently among the fractured rocks around their commander. The waiting was bad enough; the cold merely deepened the numbing tedium. So Donskov shivered and the minutes crawled.

"Wolfpack Leader, Gray One. Movement on the primary trail. Party of six armed men and two loaded mules heading toward you. Passing my location now." The sergeant's distant, whispered tone reverberated in Donskov's ear as he shifted the black plastic telephone against his numb head. So 1st Platoon saw them. Donskov checked his watch; it showed eighteen past midnight. Good—the bastards were punctual as ever.

"This is Wolfpack Leader," responded Donskov. "Confirmed. Continue mission."

"Exactly so!" rasped the tinny voice. Donskov smiled inside at the standard Soviet Army affirmation; a mere "yes" would not do for the greatest army in the world. The incongruous thought passed as he heard Corporal Padorin ring up Black Leader, 3d Platoon, and insure that Lieutenant Lebedev had monitored Gray One's warning. Beside Padorin, Donskov saw his deputy commander, Senior Lieutenant Yegorov, signal to the nearby 2d Platoon leader, hulking Lieutenant Popov. A certain wave of Yegorov's hand prompted big Popov to respond with a thumbs-up and a wide grin visible even in the prevailing gloom. Donskov estimated that the enemy would be in the kill zone within twenty minutes.

The clicking of the phone ringer jarred his thoughts.

"Wolfpack Leader, Gray Three. Movement on the secondary trail. Four armed guerrillas headed toward the trail junction. Moving fast, your way. Passing me now," said the squad sergeant.

"Confirmed," answered the company commander, obviously distracted by this unforeseen development. "Continue mission."

Donskov barely heard the sergeant's assent as he considered the altered situation. He knew immediately that this meant trouble, and saw with crystal clarity and rueful hindsight that his well-crafted plan included a huge, gaping flaw. This is what comes of spending too much time perfecting a razzle-dazzle prisoner snatch, Donskov told himself. The veteran commander winced at his neophyte mistake: He had assumed what the enemy *must* do, rather than account for what the foe *might* do. Now he and his men were stuck with a half-assed plan, and Donskov could blame only himself.

True, the 1st Platoon watched both the main route and the smaller branch, but the juncture lay in the unseen half kilometer between the outposts and Donskov's main kill zone. He had no idea if the guerrilla quartet was racing to warn Ismail's team, if these new participants represented a hostile mujahidin faction intent on waylaying the mules for their own purposes, or if the second bunch was even aware of Ismail's approach. He calculated, without much doubt, that the smaller group would reach the track connection before the two-mule supply caravan. Then what? Without surveillance on that key spot, Donskov had no way of knowing.

Donskov's faulty deployment limited his options. If 1st Platoon fired on the foursome, the shots would alert Ismail and negate the ambush. Should he order the Gray Three squad to pursue the new players, the noise might alarm the quarry, and this move guaranteed an open route for any other rebels using the secondary path. If he did nothing, the two guerrilla outfits seemed certain to join up, with unpredictable results. How did he miss the obvious importance of the trail junction? Could he salvage this one?

Then he knew, as a clear alternative coalesced. He snatched the field telephone handset and twirled the ringer knob. "All stations, stand by. Gray Leader, this is Wolfpack Leader," said Donskov quickly. Lieutenant Savitskiy answered immediately; the other two platoons also chimed in.

In a few short sentences, Donskov rapidly sketched his scheme. He ordered Savitskiy to lead his Gray One squad down the main trail, behind the mule team. Gray Two was to stay in place and watch the path to the northeast. He also told Gray Three to stay put. He held his other two platoons in their positions, to see what Savitskiy turned up.

Perhaps Savitskiy's patrol might give away the whole show, but Donskov needed to know what happened when the two mujahidin forces met. He knew that the shrewd little lieutenant would bring along his Pathan scout to translate any snatches of conversation that the followers overheard. Unfortunately, Ismail's party was down-wind from Savitskiy and his squad, which made detection of noise from the trailing Russians all too likely. Oh well. It had been a good idea. Donskov knew his Clausewitz, and having neglected the friction of the battlefield, he was undergoing an unwelcome refresher course. The glum commander turned to shoulder his radio and wait for a report from the mobile patrol.

Nothing happened for five minutes. The wind moaned, and Donskov scanned the kill zone idly, lost in thought. His trained eyes just barely made out the irregular humps that he knew to be Popov's 2d Platoon ambushers, still hoping against hope to carry out their tasks. The captain sighed. Maybe, somehow, things could sort themselves out. What if the mujahidin groups were out here by mere coincidence? . . .

Brilliant silver flashes bloomed suddenly to the east, and then the scarlet radiance of a red flare drifted over the pass, followed within seconds by sounds: the steady ripping of an AKD on full automatic and a few throatier pops from a venerable AK-47. In less than a minute, the firing died away, the flare burned out, and the darkness closed in again. Donskov did not wait for a report.

"Yegorov, take over here. Padorin will stay here with the main commo set and phone switchboard. I've got my radio, and I'm going to the trail junction. Oleg Danilovich!"

"Comrade captain!" answered big Popov, keyed up by the nearby gunfire.

"Hold your men here. Warn them that the sergeant major and I are going east on the trail. I'll radio you before we come back. Standard recognition signals."

"Exactly so!" replied the excited lieutenant, who immediately began whispering and gesticulating to his squad sergeants.

"Sergeant major!" hissed Donskov, standing up, AKD rifle at the ready across his chest. He tightened the straps on his radio pack as he stretched and got ready to move out.

Red-haired, broad-shouldered Company Sergeant Major Rozhenko also stood up, his AKD autorifle loose in his right hand. "Ready, comrade captain!" said Rozhenko.

It took Popov about two minutes to be positive that his three squads expected their captain's departure and would not treat Donskov to any other unpleasant surprises this evening. Satisfied that the kill zone was safe, the captain and his sergeant major set off, striding purposefully despite the layers of warm clothes that bulked out their white coveralls. Donskov's ungainly R-114D transceiver bounced on his back as he threaded his way through the rocky ravine bottom, followed closely by Rozhenko.

The two had barely turned the bend just past the easternmost 2d Platoon paratroopers when Donskov's radio crackled to life. "Wolfpack Leader, this is Gray Leader. Over."

"This is Wolfpack Leader. Send it," grunted Donskov as he pumped his long legs across the slippery, rocky track.

"This is Gray Leader. Contact report follows: The smaller bandit unit attacked the other at the trail junction. No Gray element fired. Three of the Ismail force are dead. One wounded. One of the smaller group is wounded. Ismail escaped, apparently up the secondary route. You need to come to the trail junction immediately. Over," finished Savitskiy, who sounded a bit shaken.

"This is Wolfpack Leader. I'm en route; expect two from the west, standard recognition procedures. Break. Wolfpack Base, Wolfpack Leader," breathed Donskov as he pressed along. Right behind him, puffing Sergeant Major Rozhenko listened keenly to catch the radio traffic.

"This is Wolfpack Base. Monitored your last. Gray Three reports by land line that he has two men in his zone, heading toward the border. He requests permission to engage," concluded Yegorov.

Ismail was getting away; should the desantniks kill him? Shooting to wound at night hardly seemed likely, even for an expert sniper. Besides, Donskov wanted this one alive. He deliberated a few seconds. The 1st Platoon leader and a squad already held the trail connection. This served to cover both the primary and secondary approaches, and thereby obviated Gray Three's early warning role. Right. Donskov knew what to do.

"This is Wolfpack Leader. Tell Gray Three do not engage. Allow the bandits to move through, then initiate pursuit to the border. Tell Gray Three to maintain radio contact and report when the enemy stops or the enemy crosses the border, whichever comes first."

"Exactly so," intoned Yegorov. Savitskiy came in to note that he understood his third squad's new mission. Donskov wondered what waited at the path intersection as he clambered across rocks and sidestepped holes. Rozhenko, like any good senior noncommissioned officer, gave voice to his commander's concerns. "This is bound to be strange, comrade captain," opined the Ukrainian. "It's been that kind of night."

Donskov merely nodded.

Ten minutes later the duo reached the vicinity of the trail crossing. I anticipate a sentry about here, thought Donskov. Best to be careful on a dark night that has already belched out more rebels than anyone wanted to meet. The captain held up his right arm in front of the sergeant major. Breathing heavily, both men knelt down on the right side of the gravelly trail. They streamed sweat, their overwhites stiffened at necks and wrists with a sheen of frozen perspiration. Steam wafted from their exposed skin. I should have stripped off some of these layers, Donskov told himself. Just what I need – a little frostbite to top off a shitty night.

It took only a few seconds to detect the tiny white spark of the 1st Platoon outpost, to the right and low, barely visible among the dim, snow-rimmed rocks. Satisfied, Donskov palmed his penlight, thumbed the red filter into place, and pointed it at the sentry. He pumped twice on the switch – two reds. The alert soldier responded immediately with two white blinks. Donskov and Rozhenko stood up, relaxed a bit, and walked forward the hundred meters to the sentinel. As they came abreast of him, the private on duty looked up at them. "Very weird tonight, comrades," said the young soldier. "Very weird."

The two leaders nodded and walked past the paratrooper, around a huge boulder, and into the trail crossing. There, Donskov saw two crumpled mule carcasses and three lumps of rags – dead Afghans. This tableau, barely visible on the uneven track, seemed all too familiar. One of the mule's crates lay upended and shattered, with dark pipes spilled onto the snow pathway.

He did not see the other crate, or the wounded men the lieutenant reported, but he suspected that they could be found inside the tight cluster of Afghan Pathan tribesmen and a few desantniks, all huddled around the base of the gnarled rock piling that formed the intersection. One short soldier turned as Donskov approached; the captain instantly recognized his 1st Platoon leader, reliable Savitskiy. The lieutenant went toward his commander, with a dark-robed Pathan tagging along. Donskov did not recognize the scout as one of his company's auxiliaries.

"Who's that guy with the lieutenant?" asked the ever-curious Rozhenko.

"I guess we'll see," Donskov retorted. Rozhenko stood by to find out.

"You're not going to believe this one, comrade captain," said Igor Petrovich Savitskiy, who looked for all the world like a bandy-legged, muscle-bound troll, especially when he was wrapped in cold-weather gear and swathed in snow whites.

"Well, Igor?"

"This officer demands to speak to you," said Savitskiy. He indicated the very average Pathan at his side, who looked like a common hill tribesman, not any sort of Afghan Army officer.

"My papers," announced the ragged specimen in perfect Russian. The man produced a small, dark folder. Donskov quickly illuminated it with his penlight. The beam revealed enough: Committee for State Security, KGB. Great—this character is a damned Chekist. Rozhenko backed away. Donskov could guess the sergeant major's thoughts, something like, better leave this for the officer types.

"I am Captain Kazakov, KGB. Why have you interfered with my mission here?" asked the disguised officer. The irritation dripped from his voice.

"Well, I'm Captain Donskov, Recon Company commander, 688th Guards Air Assault Regiment. I could ask you the same question," retorted Donskov. He stood almost a head taller than the KGB officer, and despite the dark of night, the airborne captain was close enough to look Kazakov dead in his flat eyes. Both men stared at each other in silence for almost a minute. Then Kazakov spoke.

"Your desantnik hooligans damn near compromised an important task, from the Center."

"My paratroopers have been operating in these mountains for more than four weeks. We have no knowledge of any other efforts cleared for this area," said Donskov quietly. People who knew him understood that this level, emotionless tone often presaged an ugly outburst.

"Do you think we routinely clear sensitive undertakings with run-of-the-mill Soviet Army clodhoppers?" asked Kazakov. "The Center assured me that your zone of reconnaissance lay to the south of Barikot, not up here."

"The company received verbal orders authorizing an extension of our zone almost three weeks ago, straight from Colonel Leonov, the regimental commander," stated Donskov directly. He seethed, but kept a civil tongue.

Despite Donskov's annoyance, Kazakov's sentences registered. A KGB man in native Pathan dress on a vital assignment somewhere up the rectum of Afghanistan signified only one possibility: Osnaz. The Russian acronym stood for directed operations, and Osnaz outfits represented the elite of the state security forces. Donskov knew that these chosen Chekists handled critical political missions like assassinations, kidnappings, important document thefts, destruction of rebel media organs, spectacular terror displays, and other strikes aimed to discredit or erase rebel civil leaders. The recon commander had often worked around Army Spetsnaz, military special operations units that served the GRU, Soviet military intelligence. Although trained, organized, and often employed in ways similar to Osnaz, these elite soldiers restricted their efforts to vital military targets. Ruthless and determined, Spetsnaz still functioned under army orders. Osnaz, in contrast, answered directly to the highest party officials.

Since the "Center" meant Moscow, Donskov tried to guess what Kazakov was doing in this dark Afghan gorge. Asking him seemed a waste of time; a paratrooper captain had no right to know such a thing, and posing this kind of question only brought unwelcome inquiries from KGB types. So Donskov tried another tack. Despite all of his instincts, he maintained an outward calm.

"I assume since you stated that your mission was 'damn near compromised,' it nevertheless succeeded," Donskov remarked. Kazakov gave no indication one way or the other. "I'll take that as a yes," Donskov concluded. He went on, his face impassive. "My unit is involved with an ongoing task. Do you require any assistance, or may we proceed with our efforts?"

"I require no further assistance, although I appreciate the first aid your men rendered to one of my people. The best thing you could do would be to move out of this area so that I can complete my duties here. Is that possible?" asked Kazakov.

"We'll be on our way within the hour," said Donskov. The Osnaz officer nodded.

"Just for purposes of coordination, of course," replied Kazakov, "but might I know the nature of your mission in this particular valley?" Even in the prevailing gloom, the KGB captain showed plenty of his gleaming teeth as he feigned innocent interest. His expression resembled the leer of an intent crocodile.

"No, that's none of your business." Donskov returned an equally acidic smile. Kazakov's eyes hardened.

"You can count on negative comments in my report," warned the Chekist in an ominous tone. The KGB people forever said such things, much as traffic policemen say "mind your speed" or teachers warn "there may be a quiz soon." Donskov had much more serious concerns than this old line.

"We've done quite enough to fuck up each others' show tonight," said Donskov with finality. "Frankly, I really don't care what you report. If you and your friends don't leave this location quickly, you'll have some unpleasant company. Then you won't have to bother with a report, and your family can soon expect a nice pension." With that Donskov faced away from Kazakov, who sputtered and waved his arms in response.

"Yes, get the hell out of here, Donskov! Take your damn blue beret hoodlums and leave. You and your entire chain of command can expect a negative report. I promise you!" threatened the Osnaz leader. But the discussion had already evaporated.

Donskov ignored Kazakov and strolled about ten meters down the main trail. He waited for Savitskiy to join him. Rozhenko, who wisely had missed the entire dispute by talking to paratroopers on local security posts, returned as he saw that his commander was ready to issue orders.

"What is to be done?" asked the 1st Platoon leader in perfect earnest. Savitskiy realized only as the words left his lips that he had inadvertently given the straight line for one of the Recon Company's blackest jokes, a jest that dated back to the summer, back to a smoking bomb crater on the bloody road to Ali Khel.

"Put an end to the third period," retorted Donskov.

"You always say that, comrade captain," said Savitskiy.

"What else can I say? Let's get out of here. Maybe Gray Three has some good news for us."

❖❖❖

"I still can't believe we got into this situation because the KGB wanted to catch a bandit with a box of British missiles," said Company Sergeant Major Rozhenko to his officers.

The political officer continued: "The really ridiculous thing is that Akbar spoke with that Pathan guide with Kazakov—you know, the guy that took an AK round through the hand? Well, he turned out to be rather talkative. They'd tracked Ismail all the way from Chitral because Kazakov thought the rebels picked up Blowpipe antiaircraft missiles. Our beloved highest organs in Moscow would have traded their left nuts—"

"As if those flaccid, ancient turds needed such personal hardware!" interjected Yegorov with a snort. Hearty laughter followed. When it died away, Senior Lt. Andrey Viktorovich Zharkowskiy, deputy commander for political affairs, resumed his story.

"Yes, you know those old bastards wanted something marked 'Short Brothers, Ltd., United Kingdom' to toss on the negotiating table in Geneva. Our friendly Chekist Kazakov must have been pretty disgusted when he found only good old Russian Strela missiles. I wonder how he even caught Ismail—chasing the mujahidin blindly down a parallel defile hardly seems like good tactics. Anyway, he got what he was chasing, even if it wasn't what he wanted."

"Even the KGB cannot hide from you scoundrels," laughed Donskov.

"Comrade captain, we are after all a *reconnaissance* outfit," said the political officer with mock gravity. Donskov could not ask for a better political deputy.

Slightly built, with razor-sharp, dark features and a mind like a steel trap, Zharkowskiy functioned as the recon company's political officer in a rather unique sense. Rather than bore busy desantniks with tedious Marxist-Leninist claptrap, Zharkowskiy enthusiastically embraced the role that Donskov assigned him. He gathered local intelligence, controlled the company's section of Pathan scouts, assessed the political makeup of enemy tribal units, and recommended courses of action based upon his findings. The political officer also coordinated unit propaganda and deception efforts. It hardly seemed standard, but Zharkowskiy disliked standard behavior anyway. "I'm an unreconstructed relic of the civil war, when commissars meant something," he liked to say.

As Donskov explained it, recon units had no intelligence officers, but the party had blessed them with a man schooled in manipulating human minds. Refocusing his training from the Air Assault Forces special faculty back in the Novosibirsk Higher Military Political Combined Arms School, Zharkowskiy endeavored to mold and confuse Afghan thinking. Thanks to a natural gift for Central Asian languages courtesy of a childhood in Tashkent, he was good at it.

The command group sat relaxing under low banks of scudding gray clouds. Waiting out the hours of weak daylight, the headquarters was sheltered from the wind under a chipped trapezoidal overhang. By Donskov's reckoning, they were within a few hundred meters of the Pakistani border, burrowed into the last decent covered terrain. Around them, the three platoons formed a rough triangle, tucked into several fractures and hollows with minimum security awake.

Tonight promised a second chance at Ismail, a rare thing in combat. With only a few hours till dusk and action, and having already snatched a short stretch of dreamless slumber, Donskov sat awake now, waiting, as always. The military has made me good at waiting, he thought. While the time passed, he talked with his equally keyed-up subordinates. In the back of his mind, he reviewed his new plan, listening with one ear to the usual round of his command group soldiers' talk about women, drinking, and outrageous army experiences.

The third squad of 1st Platoon, dogged Gray Three, had done their duty superbly. While Donskov and Kazakov were sparring at the trail junction, the stealthy paratroopers had set off to trace Ismail up the secondary path. The three young conscripts, led by twenty-year-old Sergeant Motvilas, stuck with Ismail as he ascended the little passage through the jumbled outworks of this tongue of Hindu Kush. It took hours to traverse the two kilometers to the border and open land.

When the ground crested, Motvilas and his soldiers saw that their ravine opened into the sloping flank of the high, wide north-south valley formed by the Chitral River, a tributary of the Kunar. With the ashen glow of dawn brightening the woolly clouds in front of them, the airborne squad observed Ismail and his associate scuttling down the broad incline. The Afghans crossed the pathetic string of rusted, staggering barbed wire that marked the Pakistani boundary.

Wriggling like snakes, the air assault men occupied vantage points and watched in the faint light. Ismail and his companion entered a small, single-story log cabin in a snow-covered meadow within a hundred meters of the border fence. The hidden soldiers observed six armed Pakistani Frontier Corps troops on guard around the building. Later, in the gray glow that passed for the full light of a midwinter day, the squad saw the signs and flagpole that marked a border station. Ismail did not emerge all day. Evidently he was resting, secure either in the belief he had not been followed or the trust that the Soviets would not dare cross into Pakistan.

Sayed Ismail guessed incorrectly on both counts, of course. Donskov did not think twice about violating the border. If this did not constitute legitimate hot pursuit, then what did? Buoyed by excellent reports from his vigilant squad, he had moved his company as close as possible by dawn, and settled them into positions. With the help of his key leaders, he crafted a simple, clever plan to storm the building and secure the guerrilla supply officer.

Zharkowskiy and Donskov agreed that Ismail would most likely stay in the border post until nightfall, probably using the radio to send a report to his National Liberation Front fellows. Whether he intended to go back to the town of Chitral or try another entrance into the Kunar Valley, the Recon Company wanted to make sure he never made it. Dusk seemed the time to act.

At Sergeant Major Rozhenko's suggestion, the plan included a ruse, but did not depend upon it. Zharkowskiy's Pathan scouts, playing the role of harried mujahidin, would emerge from a rock pile about 200 meters south of the border post. To add realism, Oleg Danilovich Popov's 2d Platoon would put in an obvious appearance chasing the "enemy" force. This ought to draw the Frontier Corps men out of their log cabin and into the firefight.

Though he was tempted, Donskov rejected the idea of letting the company's loyal Pathans make a nonchalant, routine approach to the border station, followed by a sudden grab for Ismail. The scouts could handle it, but it posed big risks. Not only would such an unexpected arrival violate usual guerrilla methods, thereby alerting Ismail and his Pakistani cohorts, but any conversation beyond the most casual exchanges would expose the recon Pathans as Safi tribesmen not native to the Kunar Valley. Donskov chose not to rest the fate of the mission entirely upon his willing Pathan auxiliaries. They had a big job, and Donskov knew that they could portray convincing bandits from a distance. He integrated this useful ability into a scheme that fully employed his company's many other powers.

The deception tied into the rest of the tactical concept. Popov's airborne men planned to use the false engagement to rain smoke grenades from the platoon's six BG-15 launchers. This handy attachment mounted directly under the AKD assault rifle barrel, forward of the curved magazine. Fired by a separate trigger, the launcher could loop a 40mm grenade out to 300 meters or so. Alternately, a man with a mounted BG-15 still had full capability with his AKD. With an ample selection of high explosive, smoke, and flare rounds, these potent devices provided two baby mortars for each recon squad.

In Donskov's plan, grenadiers "shooting" at Zharkowskiy's Pathans would actually drop a good amount of smoke on the *north* side of the building. The rest of the troopers planned to aim very high, creating a racket rather than friendly casualties. Squad snipers, however, received orders to shoot only to kill against Pakistanis or any other parties that returned fire against 2d Platoon. New thermal scopes on the accurate SVD rifles enabled the air assault snipers to see through darkness and smoke; strips of special thermal imaging tape on the straps of each Soviet's fighting harness served to distinguish friends from foes. Popov's paratroopers, sorely disappointed the previous night, certainly anticipated a big role in this mission.

With the fight to the south perking and the smoke all over the north side of the objective, Donskov and a squad from Savitskiy's 1st

Platoon hoped to close in from the north. The sturdy cabin would cover them from stray friendly fire, and the smoke should choke off vision from the building's one north-facing window. Once Donskov seized Ismail, he planned to fire a green flare to tell Popov's men they were clear to finish off any Pakistanis or Afghan rebels still on their feet.

The scheme also had a more conventional variant, and 3d Platoon filled the main role in that case. Deployed directly west of the cabin, Lt. Pavel Nikolayevich Lebedev prepared to provide a base of fire against the enemy if the trickery miscarried. They also readied to generate the required smoke, and Donskov's snatch squad would still be able to approach from the north, perpendicular to the line of fire. Of course, Lebedev's men would have to shift their efforts south during the actual prisoner seizure.

Finally, the company command section and the remaining two 1st Platoon squads provided flank and rear security for the raid. Steady Senior Lt. Kliment Ivanovich Yegorov personally handled the security and 3d Platoon base of fire. As deputy commander, he wielded the authority to determine if the ruse had failed and the secondary plan need be employed, with or without Donskov's yellow flare to signal "alternate plan." Flares can fizzle and commanders can get killed, but Donskov trusted Yegorov's intuition and initiative. He'd know what to do.

All the men knew their tasks, and equipment was ready. Donskov spent the last hour before dusk circulating among his platoons, drawing strength from his cheerful paratroopers. Good men, all of them, he told himself. When the light finally began to fail, he crawled on his belly up to the 1st Platoon observation post and spent ten minutes scanning the objective. A thin spiral of white smoke wafted out of the chimney and then blew away on the gusting east wind. Nobody came outside. Almost time, he knew–almost ready for battle at last. Donskov cradled his AKD as he came down from the observation sangar. Nearby troops swore later that they had glimpsed fire in his dark eyes, but perhaps it had been just an illusion of the approaching evening.

❖❖❖

Everything started in accord with the script. Sped by the spattering of AKDs on automatic, Zharkowskiy's Pathans tumbled out from among their chosen boulders. An RPK-74 machine gun opened up, spraying green tracers a bit too close to the scampering Afghans, who turned to shoot back with their own autorifles. Zharkowskiy, arms trussed as if captive, stumbled along on a hemp rope behind Abdullah, the leader of the scout section. Burly Abdullah pulled the political officer out from between the rocks and down the snowy incline. Besides justifying the vigorous Soviet pursuit, the "prisoner" setup made Zharkowskiy readily available if necessary to issue commands to the demonstration force.

Just as the recon Pathans reached the vestigial string of boundary wire, Popov's paratroopers came into clear view of the cabin. Three squads of 2d Platoon soldiers stood, knelt, or went prone on the wide white slope, their barking weapons flashing brightly in the growing darkness. Two white-suited air assault men and one Pathan "died" dramatically as the violent firefight built into a steady, hammering din. Able grenadiers started to shoot their crucial eggs of smoke toward the cabin, where, in obvious disarray, two half-dressed Pakistanis with rifles emerged from the door on the east wall. The pair aimed their weapons toward the Soviets but did not fire. Zharkowskiy's Pathans kept up the show, alternately shooting back or turning to cross the ineffectual wire line. Already, thick grenade smoke built up on the south side of the structure. A few BG-15 smoke rounds began to impact north of the border post as the deception element brought the bound Zharkowskiy roughly across the wire.

Donskov watched all of this from his jump-off point. So far, so good. He saw two more Pakistan Frontier Corps men appear from the cabin and stop next to their mates. All four looked back into the open door, obviously waiting for instructions. The bright yellow light from the station outlined the confused border guards all the more starkly now that the full depth of the December night had descended all around. Thick smoke boiled up as Popov's grenadiers dumped round after round onto the cabin, almost half of them neatly placed on the important northern flank. Within minutes, Donskov could no

longer see the Pakistanis. Oh well, I hope my snipers have those bastards, he thought as he stood up, shifting his AKD to his left hand
and waving his right arm forward. Sergeant Motvilas and his three
men of 3d Squad, 1st Platoon, stood up with their commander.
These toughs had stalked Ismail to his lair. Fittingly, they were chosen to make the snatch.

"All stations, Wolfpack Leader. My element is moving now,"
Donskov said, clipping the radio mike to his hood as he and the
snatch team moved forward. He heard his subordinates affirm his
message: Yegorov and Lebedev with the base of fire, Popov busy in
his grandiose diversion, and Savitskiy in the thankless but vital security role. Zharkowskiy did not answer; the confusion ensuing south
of the frontier building was evidence enough that he and his men
were fully employed as ordered.

The five paratroopers ran clumsily through the dry, ankle-deep
snow. The tough mountain grass beneath the powder felt as brittle as
straw, and Donskov slipped twice as he led the soldiers toward the
log edifice. He homed on the diffuse yellow nimbus hovering in the
midst of the drifting smoke curtain; that was the open door, and
inside would be Ismail. Overhead, Donskov noted the regular snap
of 5.45mm Soviet bullets zipping over his head, and prayed that
Popov's desantniks kept their barrels high. With weapons held
ready, the captain and his men plunged into the smoke.

"Go for the yellow patch, men! That's the door!" roared Donskov. It couldn't have been more than ten meters away. The reek of
cordite stung his nose and eyes; he tasted the usual ashy tang of
chemical smoke. A smoke grenade burst just behind him and he
heard Sergeant Motvilas grunt, "Fucking own shrapnel." Closing in.

Although he could not see them, Donskov could hear the
Pakistanis firing back with AK-47s, the Kalashnikov's harsh, metallic ripping as distinctive now as when he had first heard it back in the
Voronezh DOSAAF a million years ago. From among the blathering
border sentries came a wet sound, a choking sob, and then the gur-
gle of a man with a punctured lung sputtering pink foam into the bitter cold night. Obviously, the 2d Platoon snipers were at work.

The smoke grew especially dense in the still air right near the building. "Go for the light!" ordered the captain. To his left, he saw the indistinct form of a private and heard him saying something into the noisy smoke cloud, something like "what's up!" Donskov looked up, but saw only more obscurity as the private pulled up next to him, repeating "what's up!" Donskov looked directly at him as he spoke again, then finally understood: "Watch out!"

A shuddering impact upended Donskov, knocking him to the ground; he lay there staring up into the blowing smoke and random patterns of wild green tracers. Something big temporarily eclipsed the saffron glow of the doorway, so close he could have touched it if he hadn't been sprawled flat on his back. Oh shit, I'm hit, thought Donskov. Right next to him, he heard Motvilas saying, "That's him! That's him!"

"Get him, get him!" said another Russian voice, and Donskov climbed unsteadily over trampled snow and mountain grass, turning toward the sound of his men. Broken shards of his R-114D radio tinkled off his back as he regained his footing. Okay, okay, I'm up– nothing major loose, broken, or leaking he assessed silently. His head began to clear, and he heard Motvilas's grating Lithuanian-accented speech: "All right, gag him, Aksakov. I don't want to hear any more of that gibberish. Zhelskiy, check on the commander. He went down near the cabin."

"No, I'm here," said Donskov weakly, dreamily, as he walked out of the dissipating smoke and came upon Motvilas and his three men, kneeling in a circle. They worked busily around a twisting, jerking figure pinned to the frozen field.

"We've got him, comrade captain," said Motvilas simply. Donskov nodded. "Are you all right?"

"Yes, fine," said Donskov, actually almost believing it. Young Zhelskiy's eyes widened as he looked at his commander. "What is it, Zhelskiy?"

"Comrade captain, somebody blew the shit out of your radio!" said the private. So that was it; well, better that than my back. The sounds and sights of battle faded in; he heard rifles cracking, heard the intermittent snick, snick of bullets passing over.

"He came out shooting, comrade captain," explained the sergeant. "Winged you, damn near ran right over you, and headed out at a run. But Aksakov here, well, you know, he was the fastest man in Gorkiy back in secondary school. He ran him down."

"Just like a damn rabbit!" grinned Aksakov.

"That was that," finished Motvilas. Donskov took it in. Right. Good, Ismail taken. Have to get the company back under control, finish off the Pakistanis, and get out of here. The shattered radio would not help.

"Right. Good job, men! Hold here, and stay down. I've got to wrap things up, then we'll let the company sergeant major deal with this guy," said Donskov, indicating the well-roped form of glaring Ismail. He turned around toward the cabin.

The smoke was blowing away, but the sound of gunfire still rattled across the open field. Someone fired from within the structure, and Donskov could see corpses outside. Better the radio than me, but I need the radio now, thought the commander. With a start, he recalled the signal flare. He pulled the tube from his right cargo pocket (remember, green right pocket, yellow left pocket). With one fluid motion, he shot it up, a little hard green star drifting against the dome of twirling smoke and racing mountain clouds. Within minutes, most of the fire had died away.

Donskov dropped to the prone and watched the end of the engagement. He could not see it, but his ears told him that somebody in the border station continued to fire from the southern window. Six motionless bodies lay dumped in front of the building's open door. The lights had gone out, and once the floating green flare died, gloom engulfed the cabin.

From the south, two of Popov's RPK-74 light machine guns chewed back at the structure. Now and then, Donskov recognized the deeper crack of an SVD sniper rifle. Give him an RPG-18, urged Donskov uselessly, as if telepathy might help. The single-shot, throwaway, unguided antitank rocket probably would never stop a tank, but this little killer could make short work of the recalcitrant Pakistani in the cabin. The RPKs kept chattering, interspersed with single SVD rounds. Finish this guy, Oleg. We've got to move on.

A tremendous whooshing sound split the night, followed by a

bright orange eruption that blossomed wildly through the doors and windows of the stricken border post. If that's an RPG-18, then someone at the factory tripled the warhead charge, thought Donskov in wonder. The enemy fire stopped, as did Popov's shooting. For the first time all night, Donskov heard the keening mountain wind.

Curious, he got up and walked to the battered log building. As he approached, he saw the large frame of Popov and one five-man squad coming from the south. The commander and the other paratroopers reached the blasted station almost together. Wind already whistled through the shattered window frames.

"So you got Ismail, eh?" asked Popov. Donskov nodded. Through the wreckage of the doorjamb, he watched small flames lick the inside of the gutted, bullet-pocked station. The captain had no interest in seeing the gory, shredded remains of the last defender. A pair of efficient privates went inside, searched the building quickly, and emerged. With understatement, the desantniks reported all clear. At the officers' feet outside the cabin, the Pakistani corpses lay stiff, their clothes rippling in the same gusts that flapped the dark flag around its splintered flagpole.

Once the two paratroopers finished their survey, Donskov borrowed Popov's radio to order movement to the rally point back on the Afghan side of the border. Meanwhile, the search squad began to set thermite grenades to immolate the frontier site and thereby finish this night's work. Only a few bones might withstand the heat of the fire about to be set. Air assault forces, especially recon units, always covered their tracks.

Popov turned to Donskov. "Some wood chip did a nice number on your backpack radio, comrade captain."

"Yes. Sergeant Motvilas thinks it might have been Ismail. Anyway, I feel lucky, you can be sure of that," said the captain.

"A better night than last, eh?"

"Yes, I'll say. Let's get going."

"Exactly so, comrade captain," retorted Popov, who spun to return to his deployed platoon.

"One question before you go, Oleg."

"Comrade captain?" he said with a half turn.

"What the hell did you shoot into this building?"

Popov's face broke into a wide smile. "You remember those Strela antiaircraft missiles that Kazakov took? Well, we borrowed one. You just never know when things can come in handy."

Undeterred by the black night around him, Donskov idly pulled a cleaning patch through the barrel of his AKD as he sat in the center of the company perimeter. He listened as Corporal Padorin sent the radio message to regimental headquarters that reported Ismail's successful capture. The response came back amazingly clear, given the number of retransmission stations between the Pakistani border and the regimental base camp back near Kabul.

"This is Eagle Base. Confirmed. Expect extraction first light tomorrow. Landing Zone Seven. Personal for Wolfpack Leader. Prepare to copy urgent message from Eagle Leader."

That seemed odd. With a quizzical tilt of his head, Donskov picked up the handset himself.

"This is Wolfpack Leader. Standing by for message. Over," said Donskov wearily. He was not looking forward to a long night march to the helicopter pickup zone, but at least the company had Ismail and they were almost on their way out of this biting cold and these eerie mountains.

"This is Eagle Base. Message follows: Wolfpack Leader to report immediately, say again, immediately, to Eagle Leader upon return. Personal reply required. Over."

Donskov hesitated a second, lost in concern. This did not sound good. But the old habits took over. Mechanically, by rote, he heard himself reply: "This is Wolfpack Leader. Understood. Over."

"Eagle Base. Out."

"What's that all about, comrade captain?" asked Rozhenko, genuinely worried.

Donskov shrugged. "Pissing off Chekist pukes, crossing into Pakistan, deviating from established norms, all-around bad attitude—who the hell knows?" he muttered dejectedly.

"You will, soon enough," said Zharkowskiy with his usual wicked smile. But for now, as always, all Donskov could do was wait.

PART ONE

A Most Dangerous Man

Our brave army captains were swaddled
under trumpets, were raised under helmets,
were fed at lance point. . . .

from Sofoniy of Ryazan's *Across the Don*, a medieval Russian tale

Chapter One

The Tatar Yoke

"Into the corner! Pack it in, scum!"

Sergeant Tobulkhin hissed as he spat out the words. The tough little Asian stood just inside the open doorway, his stout legs spread and arms folded across his broad chest. His hard black eyes narrowed to slits above his high cheekbones. A thin sheen of perspiration glistened on his flat nose.

In front of him, thirty-three sweating cadet recruits jostled and pushed to fit themselves into the corner of the barracks storage room. A good-sized desk might have fit into the area now clogged with frightened young men. The nervous recruits tried hard to close in even tighter, regardless of the stifling heat of the summer night. With their newly shaved skulls, vacant eyes, and shapeless faded khaki summer work uniforms, each man looked exactly like the other. So much the better! For the first time in their short lives, these once cocky youths tried mightily to be anonymous, amorphous, unseen, unnoticed, unremarkable.

"Too slow!" rasped Tobulkhin. The muscular sergeant motioned harshly with his right arm.

Like younger wolves in the wake of their pack leader, three junior sergeants appeared from the doorway behind Tobulkhin. With arms outstretched, the men rushed at the knot of cadet recruits. They jabbed and punched at those unfortunate enough to be on the outer rim of the compacted mass; the trio leaned and grunted, smashing the already tight group against each other. Fedorenko, the skinny Ukrainian junior sergeant, smirked crookedly when he shoved at the recruits. His uneven yellow teeth gleamed as he buried his bony left shoulder in the chest of an unlucky man in front.

Within a minute, the junior sergeants pulled back, satisfied.

"Brace up," Tobulkhin growled. "Eyes front, shitheads."

He stood silent, a menacing, eerie presence in the glow of the few barracks' fire-exit lights. The cadet recruits stood steady, dripping grime on each other as they waited in their gloomy corner. The seconds crawled by.

The tinny crash of a fist on a metal wall locker shattered the humid night air.

"Welcome, turds, to 1st Platoon, 3d Company, Cadet Recruit Battalion of the 106th Guards Air Assault Training Division. I am Sergeant Tobulkhin, your drill sergeant. It is my duty to make soldiers and cadets out of you scum. My squad leaders . . . "

The three underlings sprang forward on cue. They bounced to stiff attention, their light blue airborne berets perched jauntily atop their ramrod frames. Tobulkhin continued in his low, measured speech.

"Junior Sergeant Gorinas, 1st Squad," said Tobulkhin. The wiry noncommissioned officer with the sandy little mustache slapped his thighs.

"Junior Sergeant Fedorenko, 2d Squad," intoned the platoon sergeant. Fedorenko's thin thighs resounded with sharp claps.

"And, of course, Junior Sergeant Ryzhov, 3d Squad," concluded Tobulkhin. Ryzhov slapped his legs and smiled. Although his wide face, red hair, and ruddy skin gave him a friendly, open look, the reptilian coldness of his piercing blue eyes suggested otherwise.

The three squad sergeants wheeled and disappeared from the room as soon as the introductions were finished. Tobulkhin eyed his charges, then spoke.

"My junior sergeants and I don't give a shit about where you are from or what you have done. Komsomol awards, DOSAAF training, party membership, father's rank, mother's connections—these things mean nothing to us. Airborne officers are made from only the best. For every one of you here cringing in the corner, two others were turned away during the preliminary examinations. Some of you assholes think that admission alone qualifies you to wear the blue beret and lead men like myself and these junior sergeants. I assure you, right now you couldn't even lick up our piss without written directions."

Tobulkhin stopped for a second. None of the recruits moved. The sergeant mused a bit and lowered his head. When he talked again, his voice was almost a hoarse whisper.

"Are you close enough, girls? Tight in? Nice and friendly? To be an airborne man, you must trust your fellow paratroopers as much as yourselves. An airborne officer leads by force of personal example, pulling a collective that instinctively trusts his will. But first, you need to learn what trust means. You have to understand why the unit always comes first. You think you are tight now? Before I'm through with you, you'll be even closer. My duty is to train you, to discipline you, and to break you. I intend to weed out the weak. These men around you, stinking in your nostrils and pressing their hot bodies to you–they are your only comrades. Rely on each other, or you will never make it."

Again, the sergeant paused. A thick miasma of human odors permeated the room and hung like hot steam in front of the small fire safety lights.

"Historical battalion norms indicate that one of every three cadet recruits fails to complete the six-month indoctrination period. Some of you are no doubt certain that I will be forced to carry you along to keep within these statistical guidelines. That might have been true in the circle jerks that pass for DOSAAF units or in some pussy Suvorov prep school. But these are airborne norms, scum. The goal here is to eliminate the useless, not pump out fat bodies. As a good socialist, I always exceed norms. For example, last summer thirty-four started in my platoon; thirteen remained by December. I intend to be more selective this year."

As Tobulkhin halted again, his eyes narrowed. His thick right arm stabbed forward, aimed like an angry Kalashnikov rifle, at a squat, puffy-faced cadet recruit just behind the stolid front rank.

"You! Are you tired, scum? Have I bored you?" purred Tobulkhin.

"Comrade sergeant, Cadet Recruit Verkalov requests permission to make a statement," said an unsteady voice. It emanated from a pasty visage that betrayed a person about to pass out.

Tobulkhin barely nodded, fascinated with this pathetic, quavering specimen.

"Comrade sergeant, I need fresh air."

"So you do, brother. So you do," muttered Tobulkhin. He reached in and grabbed the sagging recruit by the scruff of his collar and flung the stumbling laggard through the door. From outside came muffled voices, scuffling feet, the sound of a bucket of water splashing, grunts, and then wet, moaning sounds and the unmistakable spattering of vomit on a hard floor.

"Any other scum need air?" queried Tobulkhin. The coagulation of recruits stood like stone. "Think hard about what I've said about sticking together. Not one of you can do this alone. Enjoy the rest of your evening, turds." The tough sergeant turned on his heel and strode out of the storage room.

The young men stood packed in the corner. Sweat ran in free rivulets down noses and off ears. It leaked down the inside of loose trousers and squished in new boots. Stray drops burned the eyes; salt tinged swollen lips. The platoon sweated as a group, sharing their disgusting secretions to form a real socialist collective, all right. Jammed together like cordwood, eyes stinging, muscles cramped, the recruits became brothers in sweat. If Tobulkhin and his henchmen lived up to first appearances, the blood would certainly come later.

Outside, they heard miserable Verkalov whimpering, then the sound of heels scraping on the floorboards as he was dragged off. Nobody dared to move. About five minutes passed, or was it fifteen, or thirty? Who could tell? The room clouded with fetid breath thick enough to feel. The air itself became a physical thing, a wool blanket smothering the taciturn block of new men.

Without warning, Junior Sergeant Fedorenko burst into the room, shouting in his nasal voice: "Get to your racks, scum. To your racks! It's 2310! You're all late for bed check!"

With an audible sigh of relief, the cadet recruits sprang apart and surged for the door. A steady, shuffling tramp reverberated in the storage space as the exhausted men swarmed out through the narrow doorway. They left behind a slimy, warm film of perspiration, which shimmered in the weak illumination like the trail of a massive slug.

Thus ended "personal time" on 1 June 1974, Reception Day for the Ryazan "Lenin's Komsomol" Higher Air Assault Command School. Like his three-hundred-odd fellows, Dmitriy Ivanovich Donskov wondered just what he had done to himself. Nobody really slept that first night, their restlessness sharpened by a giant, shrieking thunderstorm, which raged across the cantonment not long after midnight. Even for good atheistic Komsomol types, it hardly seemed a favorable omen.

When the baleful, naked yellow bulbs flicked on at 0400 the next morning, Verkalov was gone, his bedding rolled up, his name tapes missing, and his equipment locker bare. It was as if he had never existed, and as far as the platoon was concerned, he had not. Verkalov had shown weakness at the outset; his will had failed. Perhaps he would excel sorting socks in some Rear Services depot. But he would never wear the sky blue beret and blue and white striped sailor's undershirt of a VDV man.

As for Donskov and the thirty-one others who stuck through the Tobulkhin platoon's long first day and fitful first night, the second morning began with tumult in the platoon bay. Leering like a jackal, Junior Sergeant Ryzhov created a discordant, hellish military tattoo, pounding on metal trash cans and smacking wooden bunks. Just for effect, he dumped over one set of racks and sent both reluctant occupants sprawling onto the gritty wooden floor slats.

"Physical training at 0500, ladies," bawled Ryzhov. "I want this floor scrubbed, racks broken down, and the shitters shining when you roll out for this morning's festivities. Or else."

Ryzhov stalked out, leaving the recruits to organize themselves. For a minute or two, the bald youths stood still in the stark light, confused in the absence of abuse. Then one man, broad-shouldered Krylov, sat down on his rude wooden lower bunk.

"Well, just fuck it."

Involuntary laughter, a gale of mirth, washed over the platoon. Krylov had captured the mood of the moment, and others soon joined in with their own remarks.

"Brothers," said dark Shuvali, "they never treated us like this in the Strategic Rocket Forces! I made corporal after thirteen months–"

"And now you're going to scrub latrine holes just like the rest of us!" interjected Yerementsev, a former engineer from a Belorussian motorized rifle division. Everyone laughed again, more nervously this time. The clock on the wall showed 0411.

Something had to be done with the barracks. Ryzhov had given no instructions, just threats. Slowly, Yerementsev, Shuvali, and a few other experienced conscripts meandered to the storage room. From the old green cabinet, they began to hand out rags, brooms, mops, buckets, and cleaning powder, although without any apparent organization. Men started to roll up pallets, push dirt across the floors, and sort the cleaning rags. No one was bold enough to attempt cleaning the latrine. Instead, a constant trickle of recruits wandered into the latrine to relieve themselves. Those who could shaved. Everyone did something, in an uncertain and fumbling manner. Everyone, that is, but Krylov. The strapping civilian, fresh from his tenth grade of secondary school in Leningrad, lounged on his bunk and kept talking.

"Hey, I've heard about this fucker Tobulkhin," said big Krylov. "He's pure Tatar, right out of Genghis Khan's hordes, you know? A Komsomol mate of mine from back in Leningrad told me that the airborne cadets call him 'the Tatar Yoke.' "

Laughter pealed across the barracks. Encouraged, Krylov went on: "Yes, it's bad enough we're in Ryazan–"

"No, we're in this shit hole camp *outside* Ryazan," corrected Shuvali as he wiped idly at a screened windowsill.

"All right, outside Ryazan, but still damn close to the first Russian city sacked by the fucking Tatars. And now we've got some damned throwback, some slant-eyed, skillet-headed leftover, here to lay waste to our asses. Oh, we're in for it, friends, I tell you–"

Krylov stopped, his commentary broken by a shadow across his bunk. Tall, thin, ungainly Donskov stood blocking the light, absently fumbling with a damp mop. Donskov said quietly, "Hadn't you better lend a hand?"

Krylov sat up and laughed heartily. "Who are you? Some damn Chekist or Komsomol cheerleader? Hold onto your ass, there, uh–"

"Donskov."

"Yes, Donskov. There will be plenty of shit for us all to suck. Do you think we can please Tobulkhin and his hounds? Hell, no! So why bust our ass? Today will be a nightmare no matter if we sponge out the pissers or not. So sit down, friend, relax," finished Krylov, who settled back.

Donskov hesitated, then spoke again: "Are you going to help?"

"Eat shit, Chekist!" bellowed Krylov, who rolled onto his pallet and feigned sleep. Donskov shrugged and began to mop the wooden floor. Around him, others followed Krylov's lead, muttering "he's right" and "tell him, brother."

By 0450, the barracks were tidied up but by no means clean. Except for Donskov, Shuvali, and a Muscovite named Glazov, all lay sprawled on their rolled up sleeping pallets. Some snored raggedly. Others talked in low tones.

Shuvali mopped near Donskov, and whispered to him. "You just wait, Donskov. The sergeants will find out who slacked off and punish them. We'll be glad we followed orders."

Donskov replied uncertainly, "But the platoon barracks are not clean."

Experienced soldier Shuvali merely grinned and said with an expansive gesture, "And these men of leisure will pay for it, brother." He went back to his mopping. Donskov looked around; the unkempt barracks promised trouble.

Glazov emerged from the latrine. He, too, looked worried. "I need some help in here. The mildew–"

The barracks door slammed open. Gorinas and Fedorenko blew in, clapping and whistling. "Outside, formation! Outside, ladies. Get going, assholes!" The squad leaders hollered and banged on wooden bunks. The bald, shuffling platoon members crowded through the door into the gray misty June dawn. Shuvali, Donskov, and Glazov frantically put the cleaning materials back into the battered cabinet. The three then raced out the swinging door and took their spots in the formation.

In front of the platoon, Tobulkhin faced the assembling unit. The Tatar frowned, bare-chested, his khaki trousers and combat boots tight on his muscled body. All of the recruits were dressed like-wise as they fell in, took interval, and stood at attention.

"Report," said Tobulkhin.

Each squad leader reported "all present." The late Verkalov went unmentioned. As Junior Sergeant Ryzhov finished his state-ment, the voice of the company sergeant major boomed from the pla-toon's left: "Report!"

Tobulkhin and the two other platoon sergeants responded in turn: "All present!"

On a nearby telephone pole, a cluster of loudspeakers crackled to life. A gravelly voice intoned: "Stand by for morning colors!"

The company sergeant major ordered, "Present."

"Present," echoed the platoon sergeants.

"Arms!" barked the company sergeant major. In the dim light, almost a hundred cadet recruits snapped their right hands to their foreheads as the loudspeaker crashed into the reveille bugle call. On a distant pole, the blood-red USSR flag went up. Had any recruits dared to let their eyes stray, they might have seen the crimson stan-dard floating like a wraith above the opposite row of wooden platoon barracks. When the tinny notes died away, the company sergeant major turned about and directed: "Order."

"Order," said Tobulkhin and his two counterparts.

"Arms!" thundered the company sergeant major. "Take charge of your platoons and carry out the morning physical training program!"

"Exactly so, comrade sergeant major!" shouted the three pla-toon sergeants.

The sergeants exchanged salutes, and Tobulkhin turned to face his men. "Ryzhov, check the condition of our scums' quarters."

"Exactly so, comrade sergeant!" and Ryzhov was off. To their rear, the platoon heard the flimsy barracks door squeak open and slam closed. They continued to stand at attention. Already the air dripped humidity. To their left, urged by cursing noncommissioned officers, the other two platoons opened ranks to begin stretching prior to calisthenics. But Tobulkhin stood impassively before his men and waited for Ryzhov.

The screen door banged, and the recruits immediately saw Ryzhov glide by, headed for the front of the formation. The junior sergeant centered himself on Tobulkhin. When the smaller man nodded slightly, Ryzhov rendered his report.

"Barracks hygiene unsatisfactory, comrade sergeant. Three urinals not cleaned. Shower block mildewed, heads unshined. Two toilet bowls not cleaned, two others unsatisfactorily cleaned. Latrine floors dirty and scuffed. Bunks not aligned. Equipment lockers not uniformly arranged. Barracks floors clean but not polished. All but two windowsills not cleaned. Six racks with pallets still rolled out: Amelko, Vostrov, Krylov, Pavlov, Sudets, and Chernykov. Storage room floor filthy. Cleaning equipment cabinet not properly arranged. Ceilings dirty. Light fixtures—"

Tobulkhin held up his left hand. "Enough. Take your post."

"Exactly so, comrade sergeant," and Ryzhov hustled back to his third squad leader's spot, a ghost of a grin still playing on his lips.

The platoon stood at attention. The 2d Platoon marched past on their way to the obstacle course. With their arms swinging, they sang about the sorts of things that once happened in the basements of Stalingrad. The 3d Platoon still held their position, bombarded by a crescendo of profanity as they did push-ups. But Tobulkhin made no move to begin training.

"Unsatisfactory," he said. "You want to be officers and you cannot even clean up after yourselves. You had one hour to complete your task. If you were ignorant conscripts, I and my junior sergeants would have showed you exactly how to sweep, mop, and clean. But I made an error—I thought you were intelligent men. I forgot for a moment that you were scum."

Before the men could absorb this, Tobulkhin's head straightened and he ordered: "Open ranks, march."

The 1st Squad took two steps forward, 2d Squad took one. This left two paces between each silent line of cadet candidates. Tobul-khin checked each rank as the men aligned themselves on the three junior sergeants, planted like stanchions on the right of the squads. When he was satisfied, Tobulkhin spat out, "Ready, front!" Again, the recruits stood at attention. The Asian platoon sergeant paced softly before the platoon and spoke.

"Some of you did your duty. Most of you just fucked off. There is no place in the airborne for an officer who does not do his duty. Now, who tried to assert strong positive influence on this collective? Who did his part and wants to be spared a ball-busting mass punish-ment session? Identify yourselves by taking one step forward."

Swarthy Shuvali in 3d Squad immediately stepped up, as did Glazov in Donskov's 1st Squad. Donskov felt his stomach churning, but his mind clicked like a switch. He knew what to do. The platoon failed; he was part of the platoon. He did not step forward.

"Only two right flanker activists in this collective? I remind you that future officers do not lie. Before a cadet court of honor, lying is a dismissal offense. Any others?"

Donskov remained rooted to his place.

His decision was not simply a gut reaction. A detached portion of Donskov's brain, which Marxist-Leninists would call his "objec-tivity" and some might label perception, detected something that confirmed his choice. Tobulkhin had asked who "did his duty," "did his part," and, most importantly, "wants to be spared" the inevitable retribution. He never really asked "who cleaned up?" Thus, Donskov could remain in ranks without fear of any honor implications. Tobul-khin probably intended this.

Donskov calculated that the platoon sergeant did not especially care who cleaned and who did not; undoubtedly, no effort this sec-ond day could have pleased the Tatar. Despite fatigue, Donskov smiled inwardly at the cunning of the ploy. By simply leaving the pla-toon on its own with a task, Tobulkhin had allowed the natural slackers, solid workers, and self-promoting tattletales to show them-selves. Had Donskov known that Junior Sergeant Gorinas had main-tained clandestine surveillance during the entire cleanup hour, he would have been even more impressed.

But in any event, Donskov recognized the trap that had been set. It disturbed him that he saw the scheme so clearly, and troubled him even more that he choreographed his own response so absolutely. By not coming forward, he proved solidarity with his new platoon mates, demonstrated commitment to the collective over the individual, and, if discovered, showed his sergeants that he was a motivated worker without a streak of sycophancy.

So things would appear to anyone except Donskov, who knew his own heart. It all revolved around making the proper impression, not just on superiors, like a crude bootlicker, but on everyone. Somehow, it would have been purer, more proper, to stand fast because he truly believed in what he did, not simply because he knew that such action could not help but improve his stock among the recruits, or even with Tobulkhin. Yet this act would define Donskov in a certain way, and from that time on, people would expect similar things from him. So be it, thought the tall young man. I cannot go back now.

In any case, Donskov derived great delight from his rapid estimation. He felt for the first time since his arrival at the training camp that he understood and could, to some extent, control his surroundings.

While Donskov determined his course, the Tatar platoon sergeant walked directly to Glazov. "What did the others do while you worked, Cadet Recruit Glazov?"

"Mostly, they just rested, comrade sergeant," Glazov answered.

"And you?"

"I did my duties and attempted to rally the collective," stated Glazov.

"Very good, Glazov. Return to your rack. You are excused from formation," said the sergeant. Glazov clicked his heels and departed.

Sergeant Tobulkhin next approached Shuvali. "What did the others do while you worked, Cadet Recruit Shuvali?"

"Many lay on their bunks, comrade sergeant. Some cleaned their personal areas," reported Shuvali.

"Any particular idlers?" asked Tobulkhin softly.

"Yes, comrade sergeant. Cadet Recruit Krylov proved to be recalcitrant. He cleaned nothing," uttered the little Georgian recruit with finality.

Tobulkhin did not pursue the Krylov matter. Instead, he asked another question, a query that froze Donskov's spine when he heard it. "Who else did his duty that has failed to step forward?"

"Comrade sergeant, I would rather not say," parried Shuvali.

"You *will* say, you little shit!" screamed Tobulkhin, his face looming nose to nose with the now-trembling Shuvali.

"Cadet Recruit Donskov did his part, comrade sergeant," said Shuvali.

"Good, Shuvali. Good. Now return to your rack. You are excused from formation."

Shuvali raced away like a shot from a cannon.

Donskov knew what was coming as the platoon sergeant moved toward him. The little Tatar's statuesque, weightlifter's chest heaved as he halted before Donskov. His obsidian eyes glared up at the gangling recruit.

"You! Report on your activities during the cleanup period this morning!"

"I failed to do my duty, comrade sergeant."

Tobulkhin snorted. "Your comrade Shuvali says otherwise. Explain."

Donskov chose his words carefully. "Cadet Recruit Shuvali is mistaken," he said. "The barracks are not satisfactory. Therefore, the collective has not done its duty. The specific role of individuals is irrelevant."

"Oh . . . " drawled Tobulkhin. "So we have a damned nobleman here, sacrificing himself for the poor little peasants! Well, Donskov, the Great October Revolution put paid to the asshole nobility in the motherland. You'll be sorry, prince. When I ask questions, I want straight answers. Fall out with Junior Sergeant Fedorenko for punishment detail! Scum Krylov, join the fucking prince. You two will enjoy what Junior Sergeant Fedorenko has in store for you. As for the rest of you swine . . . "

The platoon sergeant raved wildly, his almond skin almost purple as he shrieked venomous insults. Yet despite Tobulkhin's screeching volume and violent gestures, Donskov noticed a flicker of definite interest, even approval, around the Asian's dark eyes. It seemed out of place in the explosive tirade, but it unmistakably occurred even as Donskov and Krylov ran to join loping Fedorenko.

The platoon's physical regimen that morning caused two cases of heat prostration during the fourth turn through the two kilometers of walls, windows, rope climbs, jumps, and overhead ladders that made up the urban warfare obstacle course. The rest of the day proved no easier. Tobulkhin used every free second during the day's close-order marching drill for remedial push-ups, leg lifts, high-stepping, and other insidiously repetitive exercises.

Donskov found ample cause to regret his deliberate silence, just as Krylov learned the price of lassitude. Fedorenko's whining, obscene insults spurred them to the punishment area. The subsequent two hours of calisthenics in the sawdust pit tortured already tired muscles into involuntary contractions. Between lengthy periods of exercise, Fedorenko made the duo carry a massive log through a nearby swale oozing with grease from the motor pool. The gooey slime coated the men; its pungent stench brought dry heaves from their tumbling stomachs. Fedorenko capped the punishment detail with a breathless five-kilometer sprint. On a normal day, Donskov could have raced five kilometers and barely broken a sweat. But this evil day, he could barely place one leaden, weaving foot in front of the other.

The two missed breakfast and staggered back to the barracks just in time to fall through a fast shower, draw their inert, heavy training Kalashnikovs, and roll out for marching drill. The constant sets of calisthenics caused Donskov to pass out once in the early afternoon; a bucket of warm, rust-tinged water brought him around. Somehow, he pulled himself upright and returned to formation. The rest of the afternoon drill passed in a hot red haze, like a dream of endless burning.

Late that night, just before he crashed into a dead sleep, Donskov heard someone remark casually, "Glazov and Shuvali are gone." So they were, their areas swept as clean as if the two recruits had vaporized. Donskov registered the information in his tired brain, next to the image of Tobulkhin's approving eyes, and Krylov's thanks for standing by him. Donskov knew that he had chosen correctly. Satisfied, he dropped into a snoring slumber, only to be blasted awake at 0400.

Yes, the second day was worse than the first, and the third worse than the second. But Donskov and his comrades improved even while each passing day became harder. The weaker ones left like thieves in the night, unseen and unlamented. For the remnant, after awhile the pain and discomfort of training and discipline seemed customary, and proper, and expected. Like tobacco or alcohol, grueling military training is an acquired taste, and equally addictive for those who earnestly serve their unpleasant apprenticeship.

To his chagrin, Sergeant Tobulkhin delivered twenty-one new cadets to the Ryazan school faculty on 15 December 1974. Despite the avowed best efforts of Tobulkhin and his minions, this number included Dmitriy Ivanovich Donskov.

Little round-faced Demidkov emerged from the room looking flustered. Nervous perspiration left a stray wisp of blond hair glued to his forehead. "It's a real grilling, Dmitriy Ivanovich, a trip to the damned sausage factory."

Donskov nodded and said, "Did you do well?"

"Who knows? I'll graduate, and I'm still breathing," muttered Demidkov. "Isn't that good enough?"

"I guess so, " Donskov concluded. Demidkov shook his head once and then walked briskly away, his boots clicking on the brilliant light blue tile floor. Alone in the hallway now, Donskov turned to face the door marked "Examination." He hesitated slightly, squared his shoulders, and knocked twice.

"Enter," came the sharp command from behind the thick wooden door. Donskov twisted the knob and swung open the door. The cadet stepped in and marched directly to a spot centered on a long, dark wooden table. Thanks to many hours on the drill field, Donskov faced left crisply and slammed his heels together to create a resounding smack. With appropriate flourish, he saluted the center of five officers, none other than the commandant himself, the hard-bitten General Major Chikrizov.

"Comrade general, Cadet D. I. Donskov reports for examination."

Chikrizov, a spare, sinewy man of medium height, returned the cadet's salute with his characteristic sharpness. The general's penetrating brown eyes glowered from under his crew cut, and Donskov felt like he was being X-rayed. A few seconds passed, then Chikrizov worked his strong jaw and spoke: "Stand easy, Cadet Donskov."

The cadet relaxed slightly, but did not vary his steady gaze or shift his feet much. This is no time to get comfortable, thought Donskov. He quickly surveyed his inquisitors, and found little surprising about the lineup.

Before him, resplendent in dress uniforms, sat five officers of the Military Council of the Ryazan "Lenin's Komsomol" Higher Air Assault Command School. These men held the final authority over Donskov's impending graduation, promotion to lieutenant, and initial posting in the Soviet Army's VDV—the Air Assault Forces. On the polished tabletop, ready for reference by any or all of the five, lay a series of thick folders that delineated Donskov's academic grades, physical fitness, military training, disciplinary performance, political activism, and general suitability.

The choice of the fivesome was no accident. Rather, these men reflected the most basic power relationship in the Soviet Union, the mighty triangle of the army, the party, and the KGB. Designed by the energetic Leon Trotsky in the dark days of the civil war, the system evolved when desperate Bolsheviks found themselves forced to rely upon former Tsarist officers to lead the new Red Army. The bloody turmoil created by foreign interventions and renegade White Army generals was bad enough, but the great Lenin and his principal lieutenant, Trotsky, dreaded a military counterrevolution almost as much as they feared the White forces ranged against the new Red state. Thus Trotsky insured loyal performance among the converted Tsarist leaders by assigning party commissars down to company-level units. Uniformed Bolshevik representatives such as Josef Stalin shared authority with the traditional chain of command. The resultant dual command guaranteed unit adherence to party goals and reduced concerns about disloyal Tsarists in the Red Army ranks.

But the clever Trotsky did not count on the commissar program alone. With Lenin's assent, Trotsky allowed Feliks Dzerzhinskiy's

Cheka secret police to infiltrate spies and snitches into every unit, to provide a clandestine assessment of Tsarists' reliability and serve as an alternative means of central control should the uniformed commissars fail. With armed, suspicious party commissars at their elbows and an unknown number of watchers among their rank and file, former Tsarist officers proved to be quite energetic in carrying out party directives. True, Red Army units moved slowly and reacted clumsily, but they followed their orders. The disjointed Whites enjoyed no such certainty in their efforts and lost the war.

The visible commissars and invisible Chekists remained a feature of the Soviet Army, ever present to guard against some Bonapartist attempt to hijack the revolution. The ouster of Trotsky and ascent of Stalin did not curb this gnawing concern about possibly disloyal officers. Indeed, the paranoid Stalin slew thousands of his best commanders during the ghastly waves of purges prior to the Great Patriotic War. Only the mortal peril of German invasion in 1941 reversed the hysteria about army reliability. During and after the Great Patriotic War, the power of commissars receded, and the new generation of Soviet-trained officers gained and exercised full command authority over their units. At last, the victory over the Nazis appeared to quell party fears of a military takeover.

Yet the controlling levers were not dismantled. Commissars became known as deputy commanders for political affairs, but despite their nominal subordination to the appointed army leaders, these party functionaries stayed in place at every echelon down to company level. Their mission unchanged despite numerous alterations in their agency's title, Chekists still burrowed and reported from every corner of the mighty Soviet Army. These informers worked under the auspices of the KGB Third Chief Directorate. References to superb officer performances in the Great Patriotic War did not overturn the entrenched system; in fact, when war hero Marshal Zhukov questioned the need for these strictures in 1957, Khrushchev sacked him. In short, the two nonmilitary struts of the old power tripod still passed judgment upon the character and actions of every potential or serving military officer.

Young Donskov knew only portions of the history of these

things, partly from his own training and mostly from barracks talk. He certainly expected and understood, however, the day-to-day presence and activities of the control mechanisms. Like almost all Soviet professional soldiers, he resented the implications of the party and KGB surveillance, but he knew no other system. Donskov expected to confront the faces of the local tripod in his graduation interview, and like his fellow cadets, he had mentally rehearsed the answers necessary to satisfy simultaneously the discordant needs of his society's jealous masters.

Along with the commandant, Donskov faced the deputy commandant, Colonel Kavskiy, seated at Chikrizov's right hand. The deputy functioned as the school's chief of staff and overall dean of cadet education. Kavskiy and Chikrizov represented the interests of the Soviet military.

Nervous, fast-talking Colonel Nekrasov, the deputy commandant for political affairs, sat to Chikrizov's left. He, of course, stood for the party's interests in Donskov and his classmates.

On the far right, in the fascist camp, appropriately, thought Donskov, perched Colonel Belov. Ostensibly the chairman of the department of foreign languages, Belov in fact represented the interests of the ubiquitous KGB, Donskov suspected. With his wide posterior, narrow shoulders, and bulbous head, Belov looked exactly like any other college professor, distinguished only by his ill-fitting uniform. Nobody would think him to be a spy, which is why most of the cadets assumed he was one. Belov had an incredible tendency to appear on the rolls of every committee of consequence at Ryazan, and although foreign languages might be important, having a KGB man in the crucial slots seemed to provide a more likely explanation.

The fifth participant, on the far left, was friendly Major Avidze of the Cadres Section, who served as the council's recorder. The Cadres Section handled all cadet and school faculty personnel transactions and maintained the voluminous files and statistics that fed the appetites of the Soviet Bureaucracy. Like his classmates, Donskov could recall numerous times when the Georgian major had gone out of his way to cut through snarls of red tape on behalf of the cadets. Of the five officers, only Avidze really knew Donskov in any personal sense, thanks to the major's involvement in the notification process when Donskov's mother had died the previous autumn. Donskov felt comfortable with the affable Georgian. Major Avidze, of course, was in fact the KGB agent in place. Colonel Belov was simply Colonel Belov.

Donskov analyzed the panel in seconds, which was a good thing, since Chikrizov did not allow him much more. "Colonel Kavskiy?" said Chikrizov, glancing at the gray-haired officer directly to this right. With that the deputy commandant cleared his throat, opened a folder, adjusted his reading glasses, and began the interview.

"Cadet Donskov, your academic record here has been exceptional. Indeed, you have equalled the best marks compiled in the brief history of this higher command school. With all grades reported, you stand first in a class of two hundred and two. With regard to performance in specific subjects, I note a grade of . . . "

Donskov already knew all of this, and so did everybody else in the room, no doubt. But the Directorate of Military Educational Institutions mandated that "each cadet be personally examined by the school's military council before approved for service as an officer," and thus the officers listened to the formulaic recitation of Donskov's qualifications. Avidze's bulky tape recorder whirred softly as the brown tape spooled through, absorbing Kavskiy's comments. The officers looked faintly bored. Well, they should have been, given that Donskov amounted to just the thirty-first cadet of more than two hundred to be similarly scrutinized, and obviously, his positive attainments made the decisions largely perfunctory.

" . . . with an unqualified recommendation for designation as the first honor graduate, general high military honors in promotion to lieutenant, and assignment in accord with his preference statement," finished Kavskiy. "Have you anything to add, Cadet Donskov?"

"Not at this time, comrade colonel," answered Donskov. What the hell was he supposed to say—what a good boy am I? Hearing the litany of his achievements, the cadet experienced more than a little embarrassment. I don't take praise well, Donskov said to himself. I don't take criticism well, either, but I don't expect much from this crew.

"I have no further remarks at this time, comrade general," said Kavskiy.

Chikrizov nodded and said, "Colonel Nekrasov?"

The deputy commandant for political affairs paused briefly before beginning. He held up a single page of translucent paper and stared at it steadily as he spoke. The knot in his throat bobbed up and down jerkily with every phrase.

"Yes, now, Cadet Donskov, a most impressive academic and military record, most impressive. In party-political development, that is to say your progress along the challenging road of Marxism-Leninism, you have met the demanding requirements – and might I say, most handsomely met requirements – to become a full member of the Communist party of the Soviet Union. Cadet Donskov's sponsors included . . . "

Donskov's face displayed nothing, but he knew that Nekrasov's rambling would eventually lead to minor complaints about his ideological development. He expected some niggling criticism of his decision to allow his Komsomol membership to lapse, and he counted on remarks about his rather lackadaisical attitude toward party work. Donskov was hardly unique in these moral-political shortcomings, and he knew from talking to fellow cadets that Nekrasov would wander far and wide before getting to the uncomfortable issues.

" . . . dedication that I am convinced is no accident, because this young Communist was raised in a loving Leninist household in Voronezh. I'd like to remind the council that Cadet Donskov's father served as an activist in the Voronezh electrical construction efforts . . . "

And, added Donskov mentally, as a rifleman in the vast 1944 Rumanian offensive and the final wretched street battle for Berlin. He barely recalled his father, who had died in a power station accident in 1961 when Donskov was only four years old. He remembered his mother saying that his father was among the soldiers who actually seized the fascist maniac Hitler's personal bunker, but as he grew older, he discovered that every veteran of the Berlin campaign claimed that same honor.

Still, Donskov believed the story, and he knew for a fact that his father had fought in the Nazi capital. A photograph in *The Final Storm* actually showed his father's squad of the 150th Rifle Regiment in action; his mother had a copy signed by the local party secretary. When young, Donskov had spent hours closely studying indistinct features of the youthful soldier sprinting past a burning assault gun. His mother patiently replied to his many questions as best she could. Of course, she said nothing about his father's party work, and Donskov doubted that it constituted anything beyond the barest cooperation of any decent Soviet citizen.

" . . . younger brother Mikhail and younger sister Sofia are diligently, and might I say successfully, engaged in party-political work in pursuit of their degrees at the university in Voronezh. They were undeterred, I tell you, undeterred by their mother's death last September . . . "

Mikhail seemed sure to be the local party organizer, and Sofia's writing talents promised a career with one of the many Voronezh party-sponsored newspapers. Donskov always thought himself unlucky to have lost his father so young, and one might have figured that his mother's death should have been more traumatic than it turned out to be. She had spent herself raising her three children, and Donskov did not consider it purely coincidental that her death by lymphatic cancer came the same year that her youngest child Sofia entered the university. As much as Donskov felt the loss, the passing of his mother severed his last tie to dreary old Voronezh. With his siblings safely in the warm folds of the vast party organs, Donskov considered himself free of family obligations, and fully ready for military service.

" . . . and yet I must ask, even with these many fine political efforts to your credit, why you have chosen to forgo your Komsomol membership, despite the advice of your fellow Communists, and knowing that Komsomol activism is the bulwark of every young soldier's collective? Plus, I am led to believe that you are an attendee rather than a prime activist in Communist party functions—a mistaken impression, I trust?"

Donskov allowed the edged questions to sink in, although he

had long ago readied his reply. He had always joined party organizations as a matter of course, and he possessed an enviable attendance record at the weekly Komsomol and now Communist party gatherings. But to be frank, although he accepted the broad tenets of Marxism-Leninism as the core of his country's beliefs, he found little of value in the repetitive theoretical arguments and silly boosterism of party meetings and staged public activities. These days, all that mattered to him was the army.

Donskov guessed that a hundred years earlier he would have been a committed Tsarist capitalist, and a thousand years earlier he might well have supported the loose raiders' tribute collection system that passed for a Kievan state. As a Russian professional soldier, he automatically accepted the prevailing societal ethos, just as his predecessors had done over the centuries. But having seen all too closely the tedious glories of Marxist-Leninist political work, the once fiery concern of his preteen Young Pioneer days had cooled considerably. His loyalty to the party reflected his commitment to Russia, not to some half-baked intellectual hypotheses. Naturally, he could not say such a thing officially, even though it typified the attitude of almost every professional soldier he knew. Just as nineteenth-century British officers professed Anglicanism whether they believed it or not, so modern Soviet Army officers mouthed Leninist canons as a matter of course.

"Comrade colonel," began Donskov, "I must apologize for any mistaken impressions created by the nature of my party activism. My extensive slate of attendances demonstrates my sincere convictions. I have allowed my Komsomol membership to lapse so that I may better develop as a mature Communist, in full devotion to the theoretical struggle to master the critical features of Marxism-Leninism as it relates to the contemporary material condition of the motherland in general and the army in particular. Such study and full understanding of Communist social-scientific literature is not an easy task, as you yourself know, comrade colonel. I would not have complete confidence in my moral-political indoctrination activities until I fully comprehend the many important nuances of Marxist-Leninist theory. The great Lenin stated that the party can expect work 'from each, according to his talents,' and he warned repeatedly against 'unfocused spontaneity.' I am striving to define a sound Leninist focus before leaping full tilt into extensive activist efforts. Currently, I continue to strive steadfastly toward all socialist competitive goals of my unit collective. I assure you that my talents are now and always in the service of the Communist party of the Soviet Union."

Well, there you go, you bilious asshole Nekrasov. Donskov retreated into the standard recommended military approach: shift into party-speak, emphasize your attendance marks, appear dutiful and stupid in the shadow of the genius of insightful party theoreticians, quote Lenin in or out of context as necessary, and end by singing the national anthem. It amounted to the Communist equivalent of donning sackcloth and ashes and reminding the confessor who fills the collection plate. Donskov knew immediately that Nekrasov was placated. He thought he noticed a tiny smirk on the face of Kavskiy, who probably had delivered a few similar speeches in his time. Chikrizov sat in silence, showing no emotion at all.

"Well, then, good, indeed—very good," said Nekrasov. "It is well known that new Communists' diligent theoretical work must precede their effective activism within the collective. Vladimir Ilyich Lenin reminds us to 'judge the party qualities and commitment of every member by specific deeds,' and I think we can all agree, comrades, yes we can, that Cadet Donskov's accomplishments to date promise magnificent future party-political exploits by this young Communist. Therefore, the party concurs with the recommendation of the deputy commandant for school activities. No further remarks at this time, comrade general."

Chikrizov made a note on a small white pad, and then looked all the way to his right. "Colonel Belov?" he said.

Belov shifted heavily on his wooden chair. "As the faculty's at-large representative"—and known Chekist, Donskov noted with the assurance of ignorance—"I normally ask a question designed to elicit the true character of each cadet who appears before this council. Generally, this is not a problem, given the limited intellect that all too often afflicts modern Soviet youth. In your case, Cadet Donskov, I find my task a bit more interesting. You have book knowledge;

you've memorized a fact here or there. So I can dispense with the usual juvenile conundrums that serve to trip up your less able comrades. Now here is a question worthy of these wonderful skills Colonel Kavskiy explained in such florid detail: Suppose your detachment is operating covertly in the rear of the American imperialists' sector in Germany. War has not yet broken out, and you are under strict orders not to provoke any incidents. You come upon an American Pershing rocket being erected for firing. You and your collective move into position for an attack, but a member of the KGB in proximity to your unit"–yes, thought Donskov, such as masquerading as a rifleman–"reminds you that you have no authority to destroy the imperialist rocket without permission from your headquarters. The imperialists have almost gotten their device ready, and you know that it will likely launch before your coded message is received at headquarters. Your decisions and actions, Cadet Donskov?"

Cadet stories about the examination board agreed that Belov always asked a question that somehow got around to an army/KGB conflict. This explained why everyone guessed him to be a security operative. The possibility that Belov was not a Chekist, that he merely liked to tweak the undercover men, never really occurred to Donskov or his friends. Donskov reasoned quickly to parry Belov's situational query.

The dilemma appeared difficult. Desantniks lived to destroy enemy nuclear devices, and standing orders mandated immediate attack of any opposing force nuclear-tipped rocket preparing for lift-off. These dictates, though, presumed a war in progress, not the confused condition described by Colonel Belov. Blowing up the imperialist rocket against orders and contrary to local KGB instructions definitely begged for trouble. But if he let it fly, might not General Chikrizov wonder what he really learned in four years of Air Assault schooling? All right, Belov, thought Donskov. We'll see who's really the cagey one. He started speaking even as the last pieces of his answer fell in place.

"My decision, comrade colonel, would be to follow my orders with full cognizance of the threatening immediate situation. I'd deploy my men for attack, and direct my Strela surface-to-air gunner and RPG gunner to engage as soon as the missile took off, but only once it cleared its trailer. If the imperialists chose not to launch, my element remains concealed and does not fire. Of course, I must submit a full report in accord with unit procedures."

Scholarly Colonel Belov looked crestfallen by the tall cadet's swift passage between Scylla and Charybdis. Donskov somewhat surprised himself at the rapid ingenuity of his solution. He was firing on all cylinders today. Belov shrugged his thin shoulders.

"Concur with previous recommendations. No further comments at this time, comrade general."

Chikrizov looked left toward Major Avidze: "Comrade major, anything from the Cadres Section?"

"Cadet Donskov's disciplinary file exhibits no irregularities beyond the most minor infractions of the cadet regulations," said the personnel officer with finality. Avidze flashed a sly smile at the cadet.

"Well then," General Major Chikrizov announced, "I believe that this collective body can recommend graduation, promotion to lieutenant, and assignment as requested. Well done, comrade Cadet Donskov. Welcome to the Air Assault Forces!"

With that, Chikrizov saluted smartly, thereby ending the pro forma inquiry. Donskov returned the salute immediately and stated forcefully, "I serve the Soviet Union!"

"We are glad you do, Cadet Donskov," concluded Chikrizov as Donskov marched out of the inquisitorial chamber. Another hurdle surmounted, thought the cadet.

"I serve the Soviet Union"– so went the preferred response to news of promotion, award, or any other favorable recognition. Donskov said it with plenty of conviction, but below the surface platitudes, he knew full well that he also served himself by his practiced sincerity and premeditated modesty. He thrived on deducing the motives of all around him in the massive human engine known as the Soviet Army. This quest for comprehension absorbed him completely, and lay beneath his powerful attraction to the military world, where many behavior avenues are strictly arranged and marked.

Detecting others' interests and needs only whetted Donskov's appetite to do something with his derived knowledge. To understand human nature and bend it to his will: that shone as his real goal, and consequently it became both his greatest strength and his greatest flaw. This capacity helped him to garner the praise of superiors without need for obsequiousness and to secure the willing obedience and heartfelt loyalty of peers and subordinates without resort to force. It looked like unselfish leadership to those around him, and perhaps the human spirit allowed for no more. The bright core of hungry ambition that drove Donskov surely propelled more than a few others who longed to make history rather than read it. But what would happen if Donskov's well-hidden personal tendencies ever clashed with those of the institution he proudly served? He chose not to think of such things.

Major Avidze did not have that luxury, although he, too, possessed a bit of the second sight necessary to discern the inner thoughts of others. His KGB commanders wondered at their subordinate's uncanny assessments of the Ryazan staff, faculty, and cadets, unaware that like Donskov, Avidze enjoyed analyzing the personal attributes of his many charges. But whereas the cadet longed to lead those he observed so carefully, Avidze settled happily for the rendering of passive judgments, and then reveled when his precise comments bore fruit in future events. He assessed; others decided.

Although Donskov never read the comments Avidze neatly penned into the special file, he especially would have been fascinated by them. All Soviet Army officers are tracked by such dossiers, but few carried words like these: "The commitment of this subject is unquestioned, yet I wonder. He is a solid performer in all respects, but his motivations seem completely opaque. He proves engagingly self-deprecating, and rarely says anything about himself to others. I can find no hooks to hang him on. He has no real family left, no known vices, and no evident passion except work. Something tells me, however, that this subject regularly sees what others do not–potentially a most dangerous man. May he always serve the Soviet Union."

Chapter Two

A Fine Fellow

Now watch this, Dmitriy. These lazy motor rifle bastards never get out of their vehicles anymore."

From their concealed command post, Capt. Boris Timofeyevich Korobchenko and his deputy commander, Senior Lieutenant Donskov, watched as a mounted patrol of three BMPs approached the wooden bridge. It was not easy to make out these menacing forms because the weak sun of a mid-April early morning barely illuminated the gloomy fir stands east of Lake Onega. Thick evergreens loomed over either side of the dirt trail. The whine of the BMPs' engines and squeaking of their tread connector pins reverberated up and down the narrow pathway. Dense, sound-deadening foliage to either side of the forest lane channelized the sound. Thanks to this ducting effect, vigilant desantniks heard their opponents coming long before the BMPs appeared.

Now the noise took shape as three low, flat-hulled armored fighting vehicles appeared around the small bend in the road. A stinking cloud of blue-gray diesel smoke hung above the advancing motor rifle platoon. The exhaust shrouded the dim figures of the vehicle commanders erect in their small turrets.

"Here we go," mumbled beefy Korobchenko. He leaned forward intently in his fighting position, his gaze fixed upon the causeway. Donskov squirmed up a bit to get a better view.

Just short of the sturdy plank bridge stood a small soldier

54

dressed in the red and white helmet, chest reflector, and white gloves of the Commandant's Branch, the military traffic police. The man held a black and white baton across his upper thighs. Obviously, he was blocking the bridge.

On the unpaved dirt road, the lead BMP creaked unevenly to a halt in the face of this unexpected obstacle. Metal grated as the first driver struggled with the balky manual transmission. Behind him, like perplexed baby ducks, the other two BMPs crowded together bumper to bumper, their motors throbbing in a ragged concerto. As Korobchenko predicted, no soldiers dismounted except the platoon commander, who crawled down from his spot in the lead BMP. The two following armored vehicle commanders stood idly in their little pillbox turrets. Not one of the three vehicles even bothered to turn their 73mm low-velocity cannons outward. So much for local security procedures in the 37th Guards Motor Rifle Division, thought Donskov.

It was easy to tell what was being said, even though the men in ambush heard only bits and pieces. The Commandant's Branch trooper firmly gestured to the bridge and then pointed back up the road, toward the direction from which the BMPs had come. The lieutenant seemed just as determined to proceed, and waved his map in the face of the obstinate military policeman. This went on for almost a minute. Meanwhile, the soldiers who were crammed into the 37th Guards BMPs likely slept. Maybe a few craned to look out their inadequate peepscopes. Nobody got out. The middle vehicle commander dropped down in his turret, probably to talk to the rifleman seated in the sealed rear troop compartment.

"Okay. Let's do it," whispered Korobchenko. He jabbed a finger into the shoulder of company radio operator Turskiy. The corporal raised a small brass horn to his lips and blew one long blast.

Three SVD sniper rifle blank shots sounded, followed immediately by three more. Simultaneously, the Commandant's Branch man at the bridge seized the shocked 37th Guards platoon commander and "executed" the unfortunate officer with a single pop from a Makarov pistol. Like phantoms, a platoon of white-clad paratroopers sprang up from the snowy forest floor only meters from the road and clambered quickly onto the stalled, unprotected BMPs. The rear armored vehicle raced its engine as if to drive away, but with an AKD 5.45mm assault rifle at his head, the driver thought better of it. A few wild, stray shots burped out from apertures on the BMPs, but the firing quickly died away.

Within seconds, the speedy air assault men shoved aside dazed drivers, dragged gunners from their turrets, and pried open the back troop doors, which opened outward like the doors on a kitchen cabinet. From the fetid interiors emerged the confused members of three rifle squads, hands held high as the efficient desantniks relieved them of their AKMS assault rifles and PKM machine guns.

"Good enough–to the road," said Korobchenko. The Ukrainian company commander led Donskov, Turskiy, and the rest of the 5th Company headquarters through the ten-meter stretch of old snow and deadfall that separated them from the scene of the ambush.

As soon as the commander and his associates stepped onto the half-thawed ruts of the forest trail, they were met by three men: desantnik platoon commander Filippov, a major in spotless overwhites who served as exercise inspector from the Leningrad Military District, and the highly agitated BMP lieutenant. The major spoke first.

"By my judgment, Korobchenko, you receive credit for capturing three BMPs intact, along with seventeen motor rifle soldiers. You have killed the platoon commander, the platoon sergeant, a squad leader, three gunners, and all three drivers. I assess your casualties as one rifleman killed due to unaimed counterfire from the BMPs."

"Understood, comrade major," agreed Korobchenko. His verdict rendered, the inspector stood aside slightly and added a few notes to his small green binder. The heavyset company captain turned to issue further orders to Gavril Alekseyevich Filippov and Donskov.

"Gavril, take the BMPs to the assembly area. Sergey's waiting there to scrub them for intelligence. Now you, Dmitriy, get ahold of Ilya and withdraw the base of fire and security elements. Sergeant major, take the prisoners–"

"Wait just one damn minute," shrieked the BMP officer, until now totally ignored. "Comrade major, do you mean to tell me that you are going to allow my platoon to be ruled destroyed due to this ridiculous subterfuge? I fully intend to report this outrageous breach of exercise regulations and customary military battle norms. The use of false uniforms is both unfair and illegal," the 37th Guards platoon commander concluded in a strangled, injured tone. The exercise grader looked up from his writings.

"Comrade lieutenant, the regulations for this exercise say nothing of the sort. Exercise NORTHERN LIGHTS is a free-play training maneuver. Your own lax security measures created this situation," explained the staff major coolly.

"But how can I explain all of this to my commander?" whined the frantic platoon commander. "These sons of bitches are taking my vehicles, my weapons, my codebooks . . . "

The major walked away as if the lieutenant did not exist. Korobchenko had already moved on to his duties, leaving only Donskov to confront the upset young motor rifle officer.

"You're dead, brother. And dead people don't have to explain anything," Donskov said with an empty smile. "By the way, I'll trouble you for that map."

A shrill whistle split the forest air. That's the signal— withdrawal. Donskov snatched the lieutenant's map without further comment. The other officer just stood there.

This poor guy's finished and he knows it, thought Donskov as he climbed aboard the BMP alongside Korobchenko. Too bad, but I don't have time to feel sorry for him. Already, the captain was busily studying a set of purloined radio codes. The three "borrowed" armored vehicles snorted, bucked, and turned around, churning brown clods from the soft shoulders of the logging path.

Behind them, the designated casualties stood in the trail, watching their armored carriers, weapons, and captured comrades dwindle into the amber morning haze. The discouraged band could only look forward to the embarrassment of pickup by an exercise control truck, then the inevitable repercussions. Lost in thought, their dejected officer absently looked off into the woods. Only one motor rifleman vented his frustration. Fists on hips, a purple-faced BMP sergeant bellowed, "Fucking desantniks! Assholes!"

Of course, none of the departing paratroopers heard him. The men of 5th Company, 234th Guards Air Assault Regiment, 76th Guards Air Assault Division, could have cared less. Like predators everywhere, all that mattered to them was the hunt.

Even in a gathering of hunters like the VDV, Capt. Boris Timofeyevich Korobchenko stood out. Thanks to months of tutelage under Korobchenko's demanding methods, Donskov and the rest of 5th Company believed that within a day they would take the 37th Guards Motor Rifle Division command post, their objective for Exercise NORTHERN LIGHTS 1981.

The 5th Company war game comprised one of nine similar evaluations, with each paratrooper company in the regiment taking its turn at the objective. Exercise norms required the desantniks to locate and destroy the enemy command center within seventy-two hours, a challenging task for a small parachute unit dumped into unfamiliar enemy territory in the midst of an alerted motorized force. Confronted with the daunting independent mission, the other eight companies made the usual vows of socialist competition, hedging their bets as always. The wary commanders did not wish to take any chances. The 3d Company, for example, pledged to find and eliminate the division headquarters in seventy hours. This was considered particularly daring by most of the regimental officers.

Korobchenko, of course, had no doubts about his unit's performance. He promised regimental commander Colonel Artmeyev that he would grab the 37th Guards' command post within twenty-four hours, although, he admitted, it might not take that long. Korobchenko's new battalion commander, the cautious Lieutenant Colonel Smirnitskiy, nearly choked when he heard of this claim. But Artmeyev said nothing; he already knew better.

Donskov too expected nothing but success. That typified the spirit infused by Korobchenko. The deputy commander rightly felt fortunate for the opportunity to serve with this crusty captain, so unlike the average run of officers in the Soviet Army. No, this burly old soldier would never attend a prestigious military academy or wear a general's shoulder boards. He knew only how to fight, a skill not always appreciated in the high command.

Donskov never forgot the night in June 1980 when he first met Korobchenko. The newly promoted senior lieutenant had just returned from a two-week leave, and that nasty scene with Valentina, with orders to report to 5th Company, 2d Battalion, as deputy commander. While happy about the promotion, Donskov was sorry to be leaving the 3d Battalion's 9th Company and genial, patient Captain Kotov. The unresolved blowup with his girlfriend hardly eased the transition.

He had no intention of signing in for duty that night; he was not expected until the next morning. But the soft, lingering twilight of summertime Pskov's white nights encouraged him to leave the junior officers' quarters for a stroll, although the hour was near midnight. Out of curiosity, he wandered into the 2d Battalion area, simply to be sure he knew where to go in the morning.

Donskov saw a light in the 5th Company commander's office. The big, graying man in there, stripped to his blue and white horizontally striped desantnik undershirt, had to be Korobchenko. So that was the famous Boris Timofeyevich! Donskov stopped on the deserted sidewalk and gazed absently at the bright window as he wondered what to expect.

He had been warned. The lieutenant reflected on Captain Kotov's thoughts about the Ukrainian: "He was in the ranks for eight years, Dmitriy. I know you've heard he's a Hero of the Soviet Union, but I tell you, he thinks like a crude peasant conscript. He's in command of his third company; he never has passed the exam for the military academy, so he'll never make it past major. He has a terrible drinking problem, and the only reason he hangs on is because he has known the division commander since the Czech incursion back in '68. Be careful. It may hurt your career to be associated with Korobchenko. Maybe you should see the battalion commander and ask for a change."

A thunderous shout blasted Donskov from his reverie. He focused on the discordant noise and saw his new commander leaning heavily out of his office window: "Hey! You! That's right, Senior Lieutenant Donskov! I'm talking to you! Leave's over, desantnik! Get your ass in here!"

Such a drill field exhortation produced an instinctive reaction. Donskov raced to the company office, slapped aside the screen door, and planted himself at the opening of Korobchenko's cubicle. How could a man he had never met identify him, at that distance and in poor lighting? Watch this one, he told himself. He's more than he appears.

There before him was a massive, muscular man in his late thirties, ten years the senior of every other company commander Donskov had ever known. Why, the man was older than the battalion commander! His face was lumpy and weatherbeaten, creased by days of squinting into the sun and across snowfields. A large, reddish nose with many prominent broken veins dominated his visage, offset by twinkling blue eyes that seemed many years younger than the rest of this man. Captain Korobchenko's torso belonged to a much taller man; seated, the commander appeared to be at least two meters tall. In fact, he was almost a head shorter than Donskov. The barest hint of a beer belly swelled at the captain's waist.

"Comrade captain, Senior Lieutenant D. I. Donskov reports for duty."

Korobchenko looked up from a small, dog-eared book, which he inverted and slapped down upon Donskov's entrance. Notes, scraps of message forms, and draft training schedules covered the battered little field desk. The captain returned the lieutenant's salute with a brisk motion of his huge, knobby red hand. "'All warfare is based on deception'–do you agree?"

Donskov paused a second. He anticipated all kinds of strange possibilities for this interview, but hardly expected a discussion on tactics. This guy has caught me off guard. When in doubt, reconnoiter. Donskov temporized.

"I admit that I don't know enough yet to agree or disagree, comrade captain," answered Donskov. True in both senses–he had not seen any real warfare, and he could not yet divine why his new captain would ask such an unusual opening question.

Korobchenko laughed heartily. "So! Fear not, you'll find out. Tell me, I know your school record was good. Do you recognize the source of the quotation?"

"Suvorov?" guessed Donskov.

"Excellent try, but the great Aleksandr Vasiliyevich Suvorov emphasized deception only indirectly, as a by-product of speed and rapid assimilation of reconnaissance. Does the name Sun Tzu mean anything to you?" asked Korobchenko.

This was a name that Donskov recognized, and he answered with certainty. "Yes, comrade captain. The classical Chinese martial theorist Sun Tzu wrote a treatise on the art of war more than 2,000 years ago. Modern Chinese revolutionary revisionists claim it inspired some of Mao Tse-tung's military-political theories. I am really not familiar with him beyond that."

Korobchenko chuckled again. "Very well. To be a good desant-nik officer, you must understand Sun Tzu. He's far more important to your battlefield performance than Marx or even Lenin–no, don't look at me like that, you'll soon know why it's true. So have a seat, Dmitriy, and let's get acquainted."

Donskov sat down on one of six 73mm ammunition boxes that served as furniture in Korobchenko's little office. The captain continued.

"Though all warfare is based on deception, too often our army spends too much effort fooling itself and almost none confusing the opposition. If we ever hope to cloud our enemies' minds, we soldiers must begin by *not* deceiving ourselves, by knowing who we really are.

"Therefore, I'll not deceive you. You've heard a lot about me, and all I can say is, I am what I am. I'm a good company commander, nothing more and nothing less, despite what others say. You should know that I asked the regimental commander for you because I think you see through the bullshit, but don't know what to do about it.

"If you can learn what to do, you might make a difference in this profession, not just make rank. Your record as a cadet and a platoon commander shows you to be competent, but so are many other officers. By being consistently mediocre, one can go pretty far in the army, but to what end? What the hell's the point of being in charge if you make no difference? Think how you've seen colonels cut each others' balls off to make general, and then try to remember all of the famous peacetime generals you know. Promotion without purpose is wasted effort. That's where you're headed now, Dmitriy, though you might well be derailed by your innate distrust of mindless loyalties to blundering institutions.

"My time is almost over; they'll retire me very soon. You've heard the stories. Yes, I like my booze and my girls. But I know my job, and I'm going to make sure you know every trick I've ever learned. You've heard of our international duty in Afghanistan? Well, get ready, Dmitriy. It's become a VDV war down there, and you'll be in it, sooner or later. You're going to be my last gift to the long-suffering soldiers of the great Soviet Army."

Taken aback, Donskov asked weakly, "Why me?"

"Because," said Korobchenko, "despite your smooth front, you always doubt yourself. Recognition of weakness is the beginning of strength; it bespeaks a respect for truth that must come before you learn the art of deception."

And with that enigmatic pronouncement, so typical of Korobchenko, began Donskov's apprenticeship to command. In Donskov, Korobchenko found a willing student, eager to learn how to motivate men. Like every conscript in the company, Donskov would grow to love Korobchenko, although the Ukrainian often cursed them and never compromised his exacting standards. The captain made them into the toughest desantniks in the VDV. At the same time, he molded Donskov into an able air assault company commander, always shaping him for the ultimate test: the south–deadly Afghanistan.

Korobchenko's experience certainly shaped his attitudes, and over time, Donskov uncovered his commander's past. Drafted in 1962 from what he called "the most piss-ant collective farm in the eastern Ukraine," young Korobchenko served his three years (the stint in those days) in the Air Assault Forces, strictly due to the whim of some local selection officials. He liked it so much that he signed up for more, much to the horror of his fellows. Thus, he became a senior noncommissioned officer in the usual Soviet way–he bothered to reenlist. Hardly any ever did.

By the summer of 1968, he was a company sergeant major in the 103d Guards Air Assault Division, and he participated in the Czechoslovakian operation. Korobchenko won the coveted gold star of the Hero of the Soviet Union for his performance in the only real fighting of that squalid invasion, the clash outside Prague's main radio transmitter. It took his commanders two years to convince their energetic noncom to accept promotion to junior lieutenant. "I hate officers; still do. I can't kiss ass," summarized Korobchenko. They promoted him anyway.

Korobchenko's performance during the 1970s reflected a strange oscillation between brilliance and blunders. In command, in the field, and at work in the battalion, Korobchenko could not be beat. A voracious reader of military history and student of tactics, the Ukrainian regularly bent rules to break records. "First know them, then stretch them," he asserted. Invariably his platoons and companies outmarched, outmaneuvered, and outshot every comparable unit at his station. Every lieutenant colonel wanted this fireball in his battalion, and every colonel desired him for his regiment.

But woe to the few superiors who tried to use him on a staff! Korobchenko proved to be the worst staff officer imaginable. Deprived of his troops, inserted into the realm of army politics, and given a soft schedule with access to vodka, the irascible old ranker made a mess of assignments, went "sick" all too often, and chased every skirt in sight, married or not. Once, when serving in the division's operations section, Korobchenko missed six straight days of work. Everybody assumed he was on secret assignment, and nobody dared question the situation because the general had specially chosen Korobchenko for his post. When the division chief of staff finally took action to locate the missing man, the Commandant's Branch troops surprised the old captain drunk in bed with a female signal conscript. Korobchenko found himself back in the regiment that afternoon.

The Ukrainian compounded his occasional liquor and sex escapades with a complete failure to qualify for entrance to a military academy. He took the test three times and registered abysmal scores.

The intervention of a group of VDV generals allowed him an unprecedented fourth attempt, but the results varied hardly at all. It had to be a mental block, since Korobchenko thoroughly understood the details of military art in both the theoretical and practical sense. Donskov never met another soldier so well versed in the literature of his craft, nor so able to employ that knowledge and transfer it to his men. But try as he might, Korobchenko, like the Germans at Verdun, could not pass.

Nevertheless, Korobchenko's bravery in Prague and superb training reputation made him a celebrity throughout the Air Assault Forces. His drinking, womanizing, and inability to translate his unquestioned grasp of tactics into a passing score on the academy examination only added to his notoriety. If someone needed a fighter, they thought of Boris Timofeyevich. In late 1979, when General Major Yevanov assembled his airborne task force for the Afghan invasion, he insisted that Korobchenko's company lead the effort to secure the critical Salang Tunnel. Wounded in the arm in a January skirmish, the disappointed captain returned to the USSR to convalesce. Upon recovery, he had been posted to Pskov's 76th Guards Air Assault Division, which is where Donskov found him that June night.

Korobchenko's innate charisma drew men to him regardless of his flaws. Unlike Donskov, who found himself weighing his actions to enhance his control over his men, the captain led effortlessly, as if by right of natural selection. Thanks to his time in the ranks, he completely comprehended the gripes and needs of the desantniks, and they knew it. His substantial reflection upon his profession, although sometimes hidden by his unrefined manners, allowed him to take full advantage of his long service.

Donskov saw how the company reflected the captain's will and thought as he thought–the product of shared hardships, well-chosen words, and their commander's unbounded moral courage. Korobchenko stood up for his company, right or wrong, an odd thing in an army groomed to blame others first. If the need for punishment came up, Korobchenko handled it without resort to higher headquarters. "We wash our own laundry, boys," he said. As a result, his subordinates knew that he would back them to the hilt. Even the political officer was utterly co-opted; the KGB Third Chief Directorate informers would have killed themselves rather than betray their commander. Korobchenko's trust in his men came back to him a hundredfold.

How did he do it? Senior officers protected him because this captain for life would never threaten their jobs, and his company regularly increased the luster of their units. Many peers loathed him, as his ample field skill routinely surpassed their efforts and made mockeries of the traditionally stage-managed socialist competitions. They attributed his triumphs to "connections," which would have made the rude Ukrainian farmer's son roar with laughter. But troopers, sergeants, and lieutenants just responded, learned, and marched on happily under Korobchenko's banner.

Aside from his veteran's knowledge and his inborn leadership, Korobchenko also bequeathed an approach to duty that served Donskov well from that time onward. This represented his rationalization and justification of his role as a Soviet soldier. As he put it: "You can't deceive yourself about why you're here, and you've got to be honest enough to see the objective truth, whatever the party or the chain of command says." Korobchenko called it his "warrior ethos."

Like a good Leninist, Korobchenko built his concepts upon the material conditions of modern warfare. Yet the peasant in him caused him to temper his cold logic with a sure allowance for human nature. Donskov knew intuitively that this hard-drinking captain saw some things that many of the so-called best and brightest never noticed.

"You know, Dmitriy," he explained late one night, "nobody will ever use atomic-tipped rockets in war. The searing blast, the frying heat and blazing light, and especially the horrific radiation – it's too damn ghastly, even for the imperialists, no matter how much money is involved. Since neither side can win, why use them? And if they do go mad and unleash these killer bombs, what good are a few desantniks more or less?"

Taken aback, Donskov quoted doctrine: "Ground forces are indispensable for the consolidation of atomic rocket strikes."

Korobchenko wagged his great head. "Oh," he snorted, "I've read Sokolovskiy and Sidorenko, but let's move beyond dry texts for a few moments. Do you have any idea what electromagnetic pulse would do to most of our targeting and signal devices? Ever seen a nuclear fire storm, fed by a tornado of radioactive winds as hot as a smelting furnace? Would you care to speculate on how our men would handle these horrific sights, scenes that few living men can even imagine in their most hellish nightmares? Who is to promise that multiple blasts might not alter our weather, or damage the atmosphere, or throw the earth off its axis? We can't say. Nobody's ever blown off thirty-thousand-odd thermonuclear charges. Yes, I've read the doctrinal literature. To me, it's all a lurid fantasy, if your tastes run toward human sacrifice. There wouldn't be enough left to take over, even if somebody survived to try it."

"Maybe we could fight without nuclear arms, or use only the small ones," offered Donskov. Until now, it had never occurred to the young officer to consider matters in this light. Korobchenko, on the other hand, seemed to believe that until you straightened out your attitude toward these big issues, the day-to-day things made little sense. Donskov knew that Korobchenko was not merely offering strategic opinions. He was putting 5th Company in perspective– Korobchenko's perspective, a warrior's perspective. All of the training had to be aimed at something, didn't it?

"There's too much risk, Dmitriy, of the little atomic devices leading to the big ones. Talk of war without these weapons of mass destruction is self-deception. Which side would tolerate a defeat without resort to every available thunderbolt? That's why we'll never fight the American imperialists or invade Western Europe. We'll liberate the West someday, but not with tanks and bombs."

Donskov listened, his face pensive.

"Maybe," Korobchenko granted, "either side will bump off an adviser or two or take a swipe at the odd wandering airplane, but the big war won't happen. Why risk the end of our civilization for nothing? Our party leadership has no death wish. After all, when you lead a country dedicated to atheism, what is there to look forward to?"

"But," began Donskov, "if a major war is an unlikely option–"

"Not an option at all," interrupted Korobchenko.

"Then we must resort to other means to prosecute the struggle for socialism."

"Exactly so!" barked Korobchenko. He paused, then continued in a low tone. "Think about what you've just said. Since there can be no great atomic rocket war, how can the international class struggle continue? The capitalists definitely hate us and wish us ill; we feel likewise. Deprived of the opportunities to strike directly at each other, we compete in the political, economic, and military struggle to dominate the underdeveloped countries of Asia, Africa, Latin America, and the Pacific. We must add them to our side in the correlation of forces. It is World War III, it is already underway, and we must win. If the capitalists enslave the Third World, they'll choke our revolution and finish us."

"Where do we come in?" wondered the lieutenant. "You seem to have ruled out a role for military forces."

Korobchenko shook his head vigorously. "No—only for the wrong *sorts* of military forces, and we have too damn many of them. Wouldn't you agree that the USSR still needs a capability to reach out at a moment's notice and protect its citizens, its interests, and its friends?"

"Of course, comrade captain."

"Well, consider it, Dmitriy. Can our vast, ponderous tank armies and combined arms forces do this? Of course not! They require a long mobilization, another Great Patriotic War. And when they arrive, they expect to fight imperialist tanks and shoot atomic rockets. That may do for the weak-kneed Czechs, but that's not the threat in the underdeveloped countries. Those societies are so far back on the socioeconomic scale that when you blast them into the Stone Age, it's an improvement! Explosives and tank treads cannot unearth and destroy guerrillas imbued with feudal Islamic death wishes, any more than one can use a bulldozer to kill a nest of snakes. The pressure just spreads them out, drives them deeper, and makes them mean. You should have seen our rocket-armed Wehrmacht in Afghanistan—pathetic! Wouldn't get off the roads or climb out of their tracks. Surefooted Pathan hill boys with ancient weapons picked them to pieces."

Donskov did not reply immediately. He had heard the horror stories.

"Apparently, we are the only real alternative," said Donskov.

"Yes, that's it. The VDV, the special forces, the naval infantry—they can reach out, and they are ready to fight in the enemy's rear. They look upon all battlefield objects as available to whichever side has the strength to take them. Desantniks work to poke out the enemy's eyes and tear out his innards. We destroy his command centers and supply depots. Paratroopers seek challenges and convert them to opportunities, just as I've taught you here in 5th Company. And we've got to be ready now–today. The VDV men are not at peace but at war, merely between operations, awaiting commitment to our international duty. Today, right now, some of our comrades are trying to clean up the botch made by our motor rifle comrades in Afghanistan. You'll join them before you know it. As for after Afghanistan, who knows?"

"So it's all on us then," stated Donskov with finality.

"Absolutely!" responded the captain. "You and I and all of our paratroops, we make the real difference. But there aren't many of us. Even in the Air Assault Forces, a tiny fraction of our army, there are damned few who will really be ready when the time comes. It's too easy to simulate training and please superiors; getting ready for combat is hard, dirty, ugly work. It makes shitty viewing for fat inspectors from the local military district."

Then Donskov asked the question that he always asked, at least inside his head. He already knew how he wanted it answered. "Can one man really make anything happen?"

"I have to think so," said Korobchenko. "Yes, I'm aware that Marx said an individual can no more shape the inevitable course of the historical class struggle than he can alter the ocean tides, but Lenin proved him wrong and showed that a dedicated man with the right ideas in the key place *can* change things, *can* make a difference. Lenin was outnumbered and had no more sophisticated technology than a pen, yet he toppled the world's largest empire and built the Soviet Union. Tanks and guns and helicopters, laser range finders and radars and cosmic rockets are all just means, and they will never make victory."

"Only men can do that," answered Donskov with quiet conviction.

Korobchenko nodded in agreement. A moment of silence followed. Then the captain spoke again.

"Remember the great Suvorov's dictum 'The bullet is a fool, but the bayonet is a fine fellow'?"

"I often heard it at bayonet training," recalled Donskov.

"Suvorov wasn't talking about bayonets. No, our greatest field commander meant to underscore the spirit of the troops behind the blades. What he meant, as is clear from his other writings, is that *men,* not technology or vast numbers, win wars. The determination, the cold courage to close with the enemy, rip his living guts out at tight quarters–that's the heart of the warrior ethos. Combined with the cunning minds of hunters, that spirit will win victories. And then let the enemies of this motherland beware!"

Korobchenko changed everything for his new deputy. Despite his impeccable credentials from the Ryazan Higher Command School, Donskov soon felt as if he had merely run through an academic and military obstacle course. He had hit all of the gates cleanly, but what had he done but finish? His platoon command in 9th Company looked equally pedestrian in retrospect.

Now with Korobchenko, Donskov discovered how little he actually knew. Before his tour with 5th Company, Donskov understood people, or thought he did. After, thanks to his veteran captain, he understood people *and* the army. Maybe, just maybe, he comprehended what war might be like, and that could prove important when the call to Afghanistan finally arrived. He hoped he perceived reality, because, as his captain taught him, truth must come before deception, and all warfare is based on deception.

"Now that we've grabbed the snake's tail," the captain explained, "all we have to do is creep up its spine and then smash its head."

That was how Korobchenko explained the tactical method that allowed him to predict swift success on Exercise NORTHERN LIGHTS. It differed sharply from the traditional techniques.

The rest of the 234th Guards Regiment's airborne companies chose their initial drop zones as near as possible to potential enemy command posts as determined by map reconnaissance. These other captains parachuted their soldiers into the area just after midnight. The men established an airhead. At dawn, they held their ground while fixed-wing transport planes brought in BMD armored fighting vehicles, little sawed-off versions of the BMPs seized by Korobchenko's men. After marrying men and machines, the companies fanned out and conducted mounted approach marches aimed at likely enemy headquarters sites.

Sometimes it worked. Often it did not. Everything depended upon the initial choice of drop zone and geographic objectives. Enemy motor rifle forces might raid the drop zone during the BMD deliveries, or catch the distinctive little airborne armored vehicles and chew them to bits in a hasty counterattack. After a few such sharp reverses, many senior commanders no longer believed that a company alone could conduct a successful raid on an opponent's divisional headquarters.

Korobchenko's method, rolling up the snake, proceeded differently. Rather than attempting to divine the possible command sites, the captain looked for something that almost always proved painfully obvious: the main supply route. Modern mechanized units like the 37th Guards Motor Rifle Division depended upon steady injections of fuel and spare parts. The trucks and tracks driving along that supply line constituted the tail of the snake, and that was where 5th Company would latch on.

His men also dropped after midnight. The Ukrainian disdained his BMDs, raising eyebrows among those of his superiors who did not know him. "There's a whole division's worth of stuff out there— we'll get what we need," argued Korobchenko. "We're here to surprise the enemy command post, not lay siege to it."

By dawn, 5th Company had established its ambush along the main supply route. The Commandant's Branch imposter ploy usually worked. It always stopped the traffic, and unlike an exploding mine or a physical obstacle, a military policeman engendered no special alarm. Sometimes Korobchenko used an "injured" man, or a dead animal, or even an abandoned weapon left in the road. It did not matter–they always stopped. By 0830, the three unlucky BMPs had fallen into the trap. Korobchenko preferred to grab fuel trucks or ammunition haulers, but he had to take what the road gave him. He chose to make do with the first catch rather than stretch his luck.

The BMP platoon gave 5th Company three important things. First, the platoon commander's stolen map depicted, with well-schooled thoroughness, the positions of his company and battalion command posts. This precisely accorded with Soviet Army doctrinal requirements to know the location of a commander two levels up. Second, the BMPs permitted rapid cross-country movement for the company, albeit not particularly comfortable. A few lifts were needed to move the whole unit to their next objective. The move went smoothly because of the third aspect of the seizure. The patrols of 37th Guards were looking for walking paratroopers or snub-nosed BMDs. Korobchenko's pirated tracks raised no particular interest as they rolled through the divisional sector. The radio codes and recognition signals taken with the BMPs eased passages of lines.

Thus by 1200, Korobchenko's company completed the second phase in rolling up the snake. After snipping wire communications, a platoon raid erased the battalion command post identified on the captured map. This melee cost 5th Company two more friendly "dead," but gained another BMP, a UAZ-469 jeep, two BTR-60PB wheeled armored personnel carriers, and a visiting T-72 tank. There were more prisoners and another platoon's worth of assessed enemy casualties. The inspector ruled that a third BTR, a second tank, and another jeep exploded during the assault.

Korobchenko took the vehicles to his next assembly area and left the company sergeant major to tie up and disperse the prisoners. As a final bit of obfuscation, he had Corporal Turskiy resplice the wire network and transmit a message to the regimental switchboard announcing that the command post would be moving and would tie back in after nightfall. By the time the regimental signalers discovered the ruse, their division headquarters would be long gone.

Once in the assembly area, with security out and alert, the officers collected around their battle-wise captain. The battalion commander's map had yielded the division command post site, as expected. Korobchenko also noted the location of the division Rear Services area, just off the main supply route. That would be helpful to set up the third stage of the plan. The captain drew his graphics on a rations box; he'd always said if you couldn't put the plan on a rations container, it was too damn complicated. In ten minutes of stark, clear sentences, he laid out the tactical scheme. The officers nodded. They'd done similar things many times before. Korobchenko turned to his deputy commander.

"The deception at 2000 paces the main attack. Dmitriy, this will be a big job for you. Take the BTRs and the jeep and invent some reason to get them into the divisional fuel dump. Your goal is to create absolute mayhem down there, enough to draw attention and maybe even commitment of the rear area tank units. A half hour later, I'll lead the other two platoons into the command post."

Donskov looked up from his notebook and map: "Can you be more specific, comrade captain?"

"Not this time, deputy. This time, you figure out the details. Surprise me as well as the 37th Guards. Comrades, time now is 1410. We move out at 1900. Remember, explanations, briefbacks, and rehearsals! Drill is the key."

Donskov knew exactly what Korobchenko was doing. After nine months, the captain wanted to see if his eaglet could fly. The deputy commander resolved to soar.

"What have we got here, comrade lieutenant?" asked the bored sentry. The skinny private huddled inside his greatcoat as winter made an unwelcome return on this black April night. In front of him, a motor rifle officer in a UAZ-469 waited to be waved through into the rough-hewn lane that held the fuel trucks. Behind the jeep waited a pair of boat-hulled BTR-60PBs, the rear one inert and linked to its live mate by a tow bar.

"Another numbnuts ran his BTR dry," said the officer. "The one in back needs a full tank."

"Okay, head in about a hundred meters. You'll see a chemical light on the left. That's the gasoline trailer. Sergeant Chivkhin's the man in charge," finished the soldier with a gesture up the dim path. Well, so far, so good, thought Donskov. Security back here is nonexistent. This cold wind has really helped.

When the little column got to the gasoline wagon, Donskov checked his watch: 1955. He got out of the jeep. His boots crunched on the crusty dirty and refrozen snow residue, as he searched in vain for the fuel man. There was no sign of Sergeant Chivkhin. A quick glance up and down the thin woodland road revealed a dozen glowing chemical light wands. Behind each, staggered to either side of the trail, loomed the shadowy bulks of the division's fuel trucks. No enemy troops could be seen.

Donskov guessed that Chivkhin probably hid out in the cab of his truck, and he would rouse him soon enough. But first, he wanted to deploy his men. With a quick pump of his arm, he attracted the attention of Filippov, standing in the tiny cupola of the first BTR. Donskov pointed at his watch and then circled his right arm. Filippov ducked down. Within seconds, desantniks in spectral overwhites slithered out of the two armored personnel carriers. One man slipped to the ground with a loud clatter, but the silent woods remained serene. Within minutes, Filippov's platoon had melted into the darkness under each of the great green fuel transports. The platoon commander remained on the ground, near his running vehicle, a hunting horn in his left hand. He looked to Donskov for the word, just as Donskov had so many times looked at Korobchenko.

The deputy commander's pulse raced, but he seemed perfectly calm to Filippov and the other desantniks near him. Only the quiet, detached form of a captain from the exercise inspectorate stood as a reminder that this was training, not war. Donskov checked his watch again: 1959. He walked loudly toward the truck cab. "Sergeant Chivkhin! Hey, Sergeant Chivkhin!"

The door cracked open a sliver: "What? Come back tomorrow, brother. It's too damn cold."

Perfect, Donskov said. He pointed to Filippov, who blew forcefully into his horn. Fuck you, Chivkhin, and all the other lazy Rear Services thieves wrapped in toasty blankets. I only wish these blank cartridges were real.

The trail rocked with a splatter of blanks and demolition simu-
lators, all carefully held away from the fuel tankers. No point in
creating a real explosion. Donskov observed the grader scribbling
furiously in his notebook. The desantniks had two minutes to blow
everything and remount.

Simultaneously with the explosions, three other events transpired.
First, the airborne men driving both BTRs, including the one "out of
gas," raced their engines and turned around. They had already undone
the tow bar that once connected them.

Second, Filippov's platoon sergeant fired a green parachute
flare high into the sky, well above the treetops. Along with a confirming radio blurb, the green light told Korobchenko that the deception
worked.

Finally, Donskov switched on the jeep's powerful R-107 radio,
tuned to the divisional frequency, and sent a panic-stricken account
of his own raid. He needed no acting to generate the right degree of
enthusiasm: "Stormcloud Base, Stormcloud Base, this is Stormcloud Rear. We are under attack by company-sized desantnik element. Fuel trucks lost. Casualties–"

Donskov yanked out the power cord to create an authentic-sound-
ing termination to his excited message. Oh well, I hope that plays
well in the big command center.

As he looked up from the radio, he saw his men already running
to remount their vehicles. Filippov's recall whistle shrilled in the
darkness, slicing through the gusting wind. "Let's go!" urged Donskov, waving and shouting.

From behind the supposed wreck of a diesel carrier, an opposition RPG gunner emerged and squeezed off a simulator. Two
paratroopers spun and ripped out bursts of blanks, but they reacted
too slowly.

"Three dead, your jeep and this BTR gone, lieutenant," commented the impassive exercise controller with a nod toward the lead
personnel carrier. Damn, thought Donskov. Now what?

A brace of four white parachute flares lit the trail suddenly. Not
mine, Donskov knew. Must get clear. Go now–go! "Pile onto the one
BTR, grab hold, and hang on!" he yelled. The men clawed onto the

sloped hull, flailing for straps, antennae, handrails, and their comrades' helping hands. Desantniks waiting to board knelt and fired at
indistinct muzzle flashes down the trail. Finally, the Rear Services
troops were shaking off their torpor.

By twos and threes, the airborne troops scrambled up, burdened by assault rifles, machine guns, demolitions bags, and RPG
tubes, all of which caught on protrusions and hung up the desperate
climbers. But at last the men were in or atop the quivering armored
vehicle. Donskov helped the inspector board, then pulled himself
across the slanting nose. The driver gunned the twin gasoline
motors. In the distance, Donskov heard the low grumble of tank
engines. The division's tank reserve was rising to the bait.

"Do we have everybody, even the dead guys?" asked Donskov.
He had no idea; please, let's hope Gavril had bothered to count.

Steady Lieutenant Gavril Filippov showed thumbs-up: "Twenty-
two with you and the grader."

"Let's go!" roared the deputy commander. And so Donskov
completed his first independent operation, flat on his stomach on
cold metal, gloved hand wrapped around a headlight stanchion,
holding on for dear life as the BTR jounced on the shredded, frozen
ruts and scraped him against the whipping boughs of overhanging
trees. Only an alert private's sure grasp on Donskov's left leg kept
him from going over on at least two occasions. But that's just the way
Korobchenko wanted it. The deception succeeded.

Assisted by the confusion, the rest of the 5th Company took the
divisional command post by 2045, a bit more than eighteen hours
into the mission. The next closest time in the regiment turned out to
be sixty-one hours. Half the units never even made it.

When Donskov finally linked up with Korobchenko, the older
soldier smiled and clapped his deputy on the shoulder. "That's the
way to ruffle up the chickens, deputy!" chortled the company commander. "Oh, that radio transmission really put a turd in their
punchbowl. Beautiful. Just lovely!"

"I serve the Soviet Union, comrade captain," Donskov replied
with a tired smile.

"Exactly so, Dmitriy. Exactly so."

❖❖❖

The NORTHERN LIGHTS maneuvers turned out to be Korob-chenko's last major undertaking as 5th Company commander. By June 1981, the veteran captain departed for "the south, to play with Allah's friends," as he put it. Although a bit too junior, Donskov assumed command. Thanks to the Ukrainian's thorough prepara-tion, the senior lieutenant continued to merit his conscripts' trust. The company prospered and remained the best in the regiment (and probably in the whole division). When asked to account for the con-sistent proficiency of his company, Donskov replied simply: "Korob-chenko."

While Donskov often remembered his teacher, he did not hear from him for more than two years. In the interim, 5th Company per-sisted in the standard Soviet Army routines of semiannual conscript accessions, unit weapons and tactical training and large-scale maneuvers, interspersed with inspections and ceremonies. Based upon his paratroopers' superb efforts, Donskov made captain rather sooner than normal. He enjoyed his command, but in his rare free hours, he found his attentions drifting toward something he knew only from stories—the south.

The real VDV worked there, and had done so since December 1979. What must it be like in the Afghan mountains? Will I measure up? Will I get a chance? He wondered if Korobchenko was okay, but always caught himself. Of course that airborne cutthroat would do fine! If Korobchenko couldn't dominate the Afghan battlefield, then who could?

Late one night in early October 1983, Donskov's lights burned a little later than usual. This brisk autumn evening, the new cap-tain's mind was not focused on the war in Afghanistan, but on the more mundane issue of Komsomol membership renewals for 5th Company. He wrote neat phrases on each soldier's papers, gradually building a tidy stack of completed forms on the corner of the bat-tered old field desk in the same tiny cell of an office where he had met Korobchenko—could it be?—more than three years ago.

"All warfare is based upon paperwork—so said Uncle Joe Stalin before he shot the general staff!" boomed a voice as familiar to Don-

skov, and as intimately associated with the VDV, as the firing snort
of his AKD autorifle. He looked up instantly. "Korobchenko!"

"Exactly so, Dmitriy Ivanovich," said the big man, even grayer
than before, his battered face showing a few more sun and wind
lines. He looked a bit thinner, and his light blue beret had turned
nearly white from prolonged exposure to the harsh Afghan daylight.

"I see you're a captain. Congratulations! A bit early, too. So now
we're equals."

"Never!" rejoined Donskov, who had sprung to his feet in glee
at seeing his old commander.

"Yes. From now on you must call me Boris Timofeyevich, and
we must drink to seal our new relationship, since I notice I missed
your promotion party."

Donskov dredged up his vodka bottle. He seldom touched it, but
Korobchenko made him glad he still kept it buried in his cluttered
desk drawer. "From the bottle, of course," Donskov said.

"Of course," retorted Korobchenko.

"To the VDV," offered Donskov, handing the cheap glass bottle
to the older man.

"To the men in the south," Korobchenko said, and then drank.
He stopped after two long gulps, and gave the bottle back to its
owner. Donskov raised the vodka, swallowed once, and set the bottle
on the desk.

"Damn, it's good to see you, comrade–uh, Boris Timofeyevich."

Korobchenko returned a wan smile. "Yes, but this is not just
a social call. Take a look at these," said Korobchenko. He handed
Donskov a thick manila envelope marked "EYES ONLY CADRES
SECTION AND INVOLVED PERSONNEL" in flaming red letters.

"Official orders," observed Donskov. "But I'm not due . . . "

Two pages of tightly spaced flimsy teletype sheets topped a wad
of ancillary instructions, travel directives, and itinerary information.
Donskov scanned them quickly, then looked up. "Temporary duty in
Cuba? I don't get it. Why me?"

"Because General Major Golitsyn told me that he wanted the
best young officer available for this conference with the Cuban airborne command," said Korobchenko.

"But com—Boris, I'm not suited for foreign advisory duties. What about the company? And more importantly, if I'm so good, why am I wasting two weeks on some junket to Havana instead of heading south to join the 103d Guards outside Kabul?"

Korobchenko laughed and snatched away the orders. "Don't jump to conclusions. The orders don't explain everything, so listen up, okay? Golitsyn's on his way to take over the 103d Guards, and this trip is to discuss counterinsurgency tactics with the Cuban paratroop leaders fresh from tangling with the Ethiopians and Angolans. You and I will be going with him to Havana, *and then on to Kabul.*"

The old soldier let the words sink in. Donskov realized that this truly marked the conclusion of his military novitiate. After a short Caribbean detour, he was going south.

Chapter Three

Colonel Tortolo's Wondrous Shoes

The sudden brightening of the sky marked the arrival of another flawless tropic dawn. Trouble came with it.

"There! Look! They're coming in to drop!"

Donskov strained his eyes to follow Korobchenko's outstretched arm toward the still-dark western horizon. He barely observed a few specks strung out just above the dark band that marked the Caribbean Sea. Having found his targets, he raised his binoculars and identified the fuzzy forms of seven turboprop transport planes.

"Okay–I see them," Donskov remarked. "I've only had time to move one gun so far, so we're still masked for almost anything below about 150 to 200 meters. Do you think they'll come in this low?"

"Don't know," said Korobchenko. "Some of our Spetsnaz units jump below 100 meters. If these are from the 82d Airborne, I don't think they're trained for that sort of thing."

Both men fell silent. Above and behind them, a Cuban officer issued orders to two intent Grenadian antiaircraft gunners, who spun elevation and traversing handwheels to align their sights on the approaching string of aircraft. The seated Grenadians flanked the base of their ZU-23 twin-barreled air defense weapon. Ready blocks of long-nosed 23mm rounds gleamed in the gray dawn as they rested on the feed trays, available for immediate use.

Five identical systems dotted the south-facing crest of the undistinguished ridge overlooking the sea and, on a narrow shelf of beach, the unfinished Point Salines airstrip that ran along this little sand spit on Grenada's southwest coast. Donskov had personally repositioned one of the deadly gun sets to allow fire down the long, long runway, but the other ones, including that behind the two paratroopers, reflected poor siting decisions. The guns were too high on the ridge line, thanks to a combination of Cuban stupidity and Grenadian sloth.

"Almost here–check your watch, Dmitriy. Assault's going in . . . now!"

Donskov wrote down the time in his pocket notebook: 0536 local.

From over the water, across the pounding surf, a four-engine transport pressed directly down the length of the east-west airstrip. The plane's metal skin showed no obvious national insignia, just a dull, mottled coat of black, gray, and very dark green. Two more just like it could be seen in trail, coming in a few hundred meters behind their leader. The American plane looked to be at most 150 meters above the tarmac.

"Some kind of C-130, and really low," shouted Korobchenko over the throbbing noise of the turboprops. As he said it, jumpers began to tumble out the doors on either side of the rear quarter of the U.S. transport. The Cubans and their Grenadian People's Revolutionary Army charges held fire briefly.

A searchlight flicked on, waved, and then steadied on the passing U.S. Air Force invader. Though hardly essential thanks to the steadily increasing daylight, the beam served nicely to focus the batteries. With that cue, the ZU-23s erupted in a pounding lattice of green tracers that seemed to engulf the American craft. The last few parachutists tumbled clear into the teeth of this vicious barrage, much of which passed above the plane. Then the big flying machine jerked away in a straining turn to the south, out to sea and to safety. Both following planes faltered and also turned away, well short of the drop zone.

About thirty drifting green canopies wafted down behind the departing aircraft, depositing U.S. jumpers in dispersed clusters here and there along the half-completed runway. The soldiers strug-

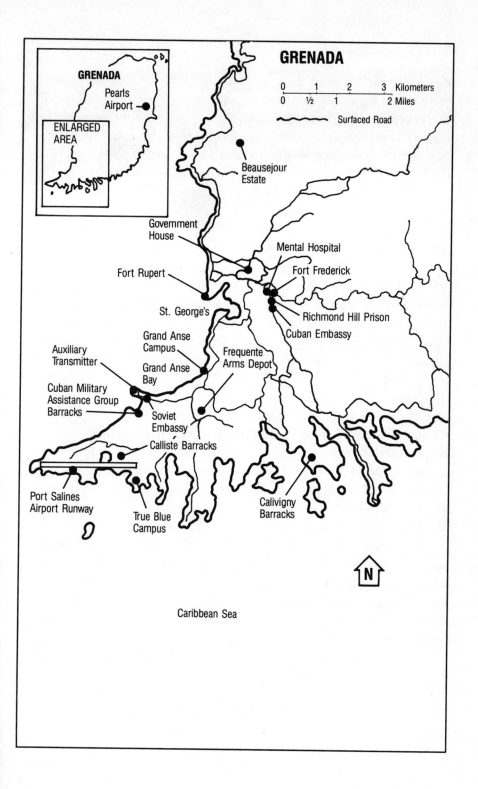

GRENADA

0   1   2   3   Kilometers
0   ½   1   2   Miles
Surfaced Road

GRENADA

Pearls
Airport

ENLARGED
AREA

Beausejour
Estate

Government
House

Mental Hospital

Fort Frederick

Fort Rupert

St. George's

Richmond Hill Prison

Cuban Embassy

Grand Anse
Campus

Frequente
Arms Depot

Auxiliary
Transmitter

Grand Anse
Bay

Cuban Military
Assistance Group
Barracks

Soviet
Embassy

Calliste Barracks

Port Salines
Airport Runway

True Blue
Campus

Calivigny
Barracks

N

Caribbean Sea

gled desperately out of their bulky chutes and sought cover among the barrels, logs, and construction equipment strewn down the strip to prevent a U.S. landing. The Americans carefully avoided the barbed wire and cables that snarled around the many obstacles. Above them, their transports dwindled away, out of the clutches of the hungry ZU-23s.

"They're turning off!" Donskov exclaimed. "The fire drove them away—the low gun especially."

Korobchenko shook his head: "No, they won't quit that easily. Stay down. They'll probably bring in air support."

For a few minutes, the thrumming of transport engines subsided. Down on the runway, Donskov saw a few green-uniformed Americans huddled behind barrels or prone beneath road graders and bulldozers. He heard the Grenadians cheering. Some Grenadian infantry low on the ridge traded random AK-47 shots with the Americans, who replied with M-16 rifles, sounds Donskov instantly recognized.

And then, without warning, the roar of engines returned, almost directly overhead. The desantnik saw tall black gouts of dirt spring up around the lowest gun position and, in less than a second, heard the heavy reports of impacting explosive rounds. He looked up to see another C-130 type, also darkly painted, its elephantine left side sparking as it disgorged 40mm shells into the pugnacious antiaircraft guns. When the dust settled, the ZU-23 spun slowly, its seats empty, its guns aimlessly vertical and mute.

Seconds later, unexpectedly, the ground rocked and spouted around Donskov. "Down, down, down" mouthed Korobchenko, whom the younger officer could not hear for the din. It didn't matter. Donskov automatically dropped on his belly, burrowed as flat as he could into the moist, tropical earth. Everything until now had seemed like an intriguing movie or some especially expensive training demonstration, a show for his benefit. I'm under fire, Donskov deduced in a brilliant grasp of the painfully obvious. His ears rang with ripping explosions.

Contorted face pressed into the grainy soil, Donskov wondered: Is that what war is like, to lie helpless and get shot at by men who can't see you? I'm not scared so much as anxious, frightened not of death, but of what may come next, what may be worse. If only I could do something besides hide. The shaking earth answered his musings with indifferent, impersonal heaves and spatters of dirt and charred vegetation.

Whizzing fragments tore through the air with each regular, rapid-fire crump of incoming shells. One, two, three, four . . . Donskov could not keep count, nor did he dare raise his head. His eyes closed, and his teeth ground together. He heard a sickening crack of metallic tearing, then the tinkling of small things breaking as the last 40mm projectile burst. Wet dirt (Donskov could only hope) rained on his back. A pause, then the murderous tattoo began again, more distant now, as the American gunship beat down yet a third gun site. Donskov's hearing faded in again, and he heard low moans. The poor gunners, he thought.

His skin felt clammy, and his stomach rolled like a wet log, but he knew what to do. Get busy, get over it. It's just like my first parachute jump back in DOSAAF—the worst thing in the world, but over soon enough, and survivable, and hence repeatable.

Good old Korobchenko was right there, and he displayed no special interest in the sudden pounding they'd suffered. Instead, the veteran devoted his attention to a quick survey of the antiaircraft gun behind them. His old commander regarded the scene much like a blood-drenched experienced surgeon about to explain a rather knotty bit of intestinal excision to a gaggle of wide-eyed interns. Korobchenko appeared clinical, detached, and faintly bored.

"This one's finished, Dmitriy," Korobchenko remarked almost casually with a wave toward the abandoned, holed ZU-23 behind them. The Ukrainian had risen to his knees like a curious prairie dog, and Donskov got up on his knees as well, still shaken from the 40mm aerial fusillade. Both men looked ridiculous in their dark trousers and short-sleeved white sports shirts, especially because clinging mud and green grass stains had ravaged their natty civilian garb. Mechanically brushing off his clothes, the junior captain forced himself to pay heed to the mess behind him.

He wished he had found something else to occupy his mind.

Donskov's first impression of the blasted gun was an ugly one. The smell of spent cordite and burned metal permeated the site. Spilled 23mm casings and live rounds lay all over the ground, along with one slumped Grenadian, oozing red from numerous holes and obviously dead. The ZU-23 mount leaned over crazily, a big strut broken and weaker sheet metal torn out. All of this had happened within a few short meters of the VDV duo's position. Donskov shuddered slightly—pretty close, and I doubt the Americans tried to be very careful. The dead man's eyes were open. He looked surprised.

Luckily there was no time to dwell on this sad scene, or to worry about a return pass from the U.S. warplane. Instead, the rhythmic, rolling drone of transport engines swelled much louder. The Americans were coming back. Again, the two captains settled down in their spots and resorted to binoculars in an attempt to see everything worth seeing.

This time, a loose column of six planes thundered down the long axis of the runway. The lead two sported the now-familiar dark camouflage, but the other four bore a more traditional tan and green blotching. On these Donskov could distinguish the outline of the U.S. insignia, confirming what he and Korobchenko already knew. In turn, each plane dropped their paratroopers in double streams, strung in perfect precision down the hardtop. The chutes blossomed briefly, just enough to slow these men before they landed on or around the embattled airstrip. Although some of the ZU-23s still engaged, their streams of fire waved uselessly high, well over the backs of the relentless American transports. Still very much on station, the wary U.S. gunship spat back its rapid-fire response, punching at each active antiaircraft battery in turn.

"Who are these guys?" asked Donskov. "They're crazy. At that height, their reserve parachutes could never open. What balls!"

The rising morning sun revealed a small battalion of determined Americans working their way off the airstrip. Aggressive knots of U.S. troops advanced from cover to cover, their way cleared by the intermittent hammering of their long black machine guns. Grenadian infantry, stiffened by Cuban advisers and engineer detachments, fell back in the face of the harsh, steady fire.

Within minutes, the Americans left the hardtop, skirted the half-built airport buildings, and reached the base of the low ridge that held the ZU-23s and the watching VDV pair. One plucky 82mm mortar offered the only consistent check to U.S. movement. A pattern of dirty little bursts flowered intermittently at the western end of the runway.

Korobchenko studied the developing firefight with his binoculars. "I don't think they're 82d Airborne."

"Then who?"

"Rangers, looks like. Sort of a USA version of our Spetsnaz. About half seem to be working their way toward the medical campus at the eastern end of the runway. I wonder if they think we're holding hostages down there?" offered Korobchenko.

"We're not."

"They don't know that. Wait . . . look, here's a second wave of jumpers."

Sure enough, even as the initial unit pushed off the narrow strip, five more C-130 aircraft appeared out of the now pale blue western sky. On the macadamized surface before and below the arriving transports, loose chips skittered and metal blockages sparked as unseen bullets smacked and ricocheted all over the airstrip. Seemingly oblivious to the heavy fire, a Cuban bulldozer and a steamroller scuttled about, shoving aside barriers, flattening stakes, and shredding barbed wire entanglements. Hot-wired by these damn Americans, Donskov noted. They're surely an industrious bunch – busy under fire. And then the second group was over Point Salines.

Bravely, if pointlessly, four ZU-23 sites opened fire, their green tracers arcing harmlessly over the American aircraft. The lumbering gunship again waded in, unloading spurts of deadly shots to suppress even these futile displays of resistance. Five more transports dropped their men unmolested and wheeled off, leaving behind a string of drifting pea-green canopies that quickly bore their owners to the ground. One man splashed into the Caribbean surf but quickly came ashore. As an air assault officer, Donskov could only be impressed by the speed and accuracy of the American descent onto the blocked, defended seaside drop zone.

Once more, the runway bustled with activity as men tore off their chutes and readied their weapons. After only the barest reorganization, the second element joined their predecessors in the struggle for the ridge. Donskov and Korobchenko had witnessed the spectacular panorama of a full-scale combat jump, but if they did not move soon, they would become part of the violent expansion of the American airhead. The imperialists showed no inclination to wait around. They were pressing hard all along the ridge line, their attack paced by the bang of hand grenades and the steady popping of machine guns.

It was time for the observers to pull out. Korobchenko stood erect and waved his AK-47, the one the Grenadians had given him the night before. "Let's get the hell out of here," he recommended.

Donskov jumped up immediately, shaking the dirt from his own venerable AK autorifle. "We've got to find Colonel Tortolo and make a report."

Korobchenko sneered. "Somehow I doubt we'll find that limp-dick anywhere near his command post. The imperialist gunship hosed the whole Cuban compound pretty well. But we might as well try."

With that, the two desantniks moved off across the crest of the hill. Above them, the U.S. Air Force gunship circled like a great hawk, anxious for prey.

It was supposed to be a vacation, a trip to exotic Cuba, a place Donskov had never expected to see. He and Korobchenko had come along with General Major Golitsyn as strap-hanging flunkies, and old Boris had assured his younger comrade that the hardest part of the trip would be fending off the dusky Cuban women. Had the Soviets merely attended the scheduled conference with their Cuban desantnik counterparts, Korobchenko's pleasant forecast might have proven correct.

But unexpected trouble intruded in the form of a bloody coup d'état on the nearby island of Grenada. Dissident hard-core Leninists, in league with the rapidly expanded army, deposed socialist strongman Maurice Bishop. In a subsequent street massacre, Bishop and his immediate followers died at the hands of the rebellious Grenadian military. The eruption threatened Cuban lives and interests and, to a lesser extent, those of the Soviet Union.

Grenada had joined the socialist camp back in 1979, and Castro's soldiers and advisers were heavily represented on the island. They were especially thick around the nearly finished Point Salines airport, designed specifically as a way station for Africa-bound Cuban troops. More than 700 Cubans found themselves right in the middle of a very dangerous situation. Castro heightened tensions by condemning the new Revolutionary Military Council, yet even so, he had no choice but to support his island allies. The Cubans were in too deep to pull out.

Things quickly deteriorated. Grenada's army commander, Gen. Hudson Austin, announced a shoot-on-sight curfew in an attempt to curb further factional bloodshed. Unfortunately, that measure promised mayhem to hundreds of American medical students trapped on the island. Immediately thereafter, Cuban and Soviet intelligence detected unmistakable signs of an impending airborne and amphibious intervention by the United States. Now Castro's people had a lot more to worry about than just random sniping. The Havana leader appealed to his Soviet friends for help in the face of his powerful northern neighbor. Given that the Soviet ambassador to Grenada had personally promoted and approved the coup that sparked U.S. concern, it really seemed like the least that Moscow could do for its oldest Cuban ally.

Donskov and Korobchenko got involved at this point, at the request of General Golitsyn. Soviet leader Andropov felt obliged to do something, although not too much, as Castro wisely elected not to attempt wholesale reinforcement of his deployed forces. The Cuban leader feared the wrath of the rapidly assembling American naval and air task forces. When the Soviets learned that Castro was sending in a chosen officer and a staff to direct the island's defense, Moscow grudgingly ordered Golitsyn to do something. The general talked to his entourage, Korobchenko volunteered ("It'll be fun, Dmitriy—you'll learn a lot."), and thus the Soviet Union offered a pair of air assault captains to supplement Cuba's largely symbolic effort.

The two provided some value beyond their presence. Being

paratroopers, Donskov and Korobchenko understood the likely tactics of an American airborne assault force. They also could claim some knowledge of the ZU-23s that provided the key to Grenada's air defenses, since those guns served the VDV for the antiaircraft role. Of course, neither captain had ever trained in air defense, but this was no time to be very choosy. Finally, and most importantly, both were available, anxious to go, and, of course, expendable. So Moscow could rest easy. Cuba had sent experts; the Soviet Union had sent experts. If the VDV men learned something interesting or helped bloody an imperialist nose or two, that certainly suited the USSR and its mighty army.

Thus on Monday afternoon, 24 October, both captains found themselves dressed in borrowed civilian clothes and seated aboard a stuffy, seedy Air Cubana Antonov-26 twin-engine transport, headed for Grenada. The officers possessed orders that eventually proved contradictory: report to and obey Soviet ambassador Colonel Sazhenev *and* do everything possible to advise and assist the Cuban commander, Colonel Tortolo.

Colonel Pedro Tortolo and a small staff shared the Antonov with the two desantniks. Outfitted in a neat short-sleeved civilian shirt, the big black man exuded a powerful gamy odor exacerbated by his profuse sweating. He looked nervous. Donskov sensed strongly that despite Tortolo's diplomas from the prestigious Frunze Academy and Voroshilov General Staff Academy, regardless of the colonel's previous service as chief of the Cuban military mission on Grenada, and even though he held the important duty of chief of staff for Cuba's Army of the Center, this man lacked the intestinal fortitude to do anything of use once he reached his destination. He's sweating fear; I hope our friend Sazhenev is in better shape, thought Donskov.

The Cuban colonel's fractured Russian made him hard to understand, but Korobchenko and Donskov listened carefully and absorbed some crucial data. Castro had ordered Tortolo to defend the island so as to make the Americans pay a high enough price to force negotiations. He authorized his officer to take direct command of all Cuban and Grenadian forces.

This amounted to a Cuban construction engineer battalion, a

single Grenadian regular infantry battalion, and five island militia battalions, equipped with a few BTR-60PB wheeled armored personnel carriers and an assortment of crew-served weapons. The militia had yet to be called up, and Tortolo had no idea how the forces had deployed to meet the imminent seaborne and airborne imperialist invaders. The colonel admitted that Grenadian training varied widely, and Tortolo expressed no special faith in his own engineer countrymen. "Construction troops they are – no sappers, no rifle troops," he said wearily.

The lineup of American forces remained vague but promised to be powerful, probably covered by flocks of jets from the lurking aircraft carrier USS *Independence.* Tortolo expected paratroopers, marines, and a variety of special raiding units, all backed by ample floating and flying firepower.

How could a few infantry units stop such an offensive? Tortolo correctly figured that if he made the initial landings costly at Salines and held the island capital at St. George's, he might persist long enough to bring on negotiations. He intended to concentrate his defensive attentions on those two areas. The colonel said he planned to put Cuban advisers in charge of these key positions. He implored the two paratroopers to devote their main efforts to antiaircraft batteries that ringed the two crucial locations.

"They shooting ZU-23, like VDV. Not many. Guard capital – St. George's. Guard airport at Salines. Kill Yankee planes. Kill many imperialists. You do this – I happy then."

The Soviet twosome nodded gravely. Donskov wished he remembered more about the rudiments of air defense gunnery, hardly an area of interest until now. He and Korobchenko lapsed into a tense silence for the rest of the flight.

Upon landing at the small Pearls Airport, the An-26 was met by battle-ready Grenadian soldiers and some uniformed Cuban advisers. The glum People's Revolutionary Army troops, loaded AK-47s at the ready, directed the arriving officers to an old Land Rover. This vehicle, preceded and followed by GAZ-69 gun jeeps, raced the fifteen kilometers to the Soviet Embassy, crossing the great green-swathed hills that made up the backbone of the island.

Donskov saw Grenada for the first time as a blur of brilliant green foliage run riot across the landscape, many collections of ramshackle tin-roofed wooden shacks, and ribbons of red mud trails feeding into the hardtop road that the little convoy followed. The heat and humidity proved the same as in Cuba, made significantly worse by the dread of the attack sure to come. Though they passed many settlements, none of Grenada's civil populace showed themselves, a sure sign of real trouble. Donskov felt the tension as an actual presence, hanging in the air like the moisture.

Upon reaching the walled Soviet Embassy compound, Tortolo and his two VDV associates dismounted from the Land Rover and went in. Donskov found it noteworthy that the Soviet Union's diplomatic mission had chosen to locate on a beachside hilltop between Point Salines and the Grenadian capital city. But this permitted full use of the well-sited InterSputnik transceiver and the nearby Radio Free Grenada auxiliary transmitter (a useful component of the militia call-up system). Also, the place allowed easy access to the Salines runway and the adjacent Calliste Barracks just north of the airport's low ridge line. When and if Cuban or even Soviet troops staged through Grenada, the embassy could easily control their activities. Donskov and Korobchenko only suspected these considerations, based on Golitsyn's hasty briefing and Tortolo's disjointed comments.

The two waited while Tortolo went into the ambassador's office. About ten minutes later, Tortolo emerged, sweating even more than usual. He smells like a molting bison, Donskov thought. A sinewy, short-haired man of indeterminate age waved the air assault duo into the inner sanctum.

The ambassador stood up and smiled broadly. "Captains Korobchenko and Donskov, I suppose?" asked tall, distinguished, white-haired Colonel Sazhenev of the GRU, alleged ambassador to the socialist state of Grenada and actual commander of the Soviet Union's Grenada Military Advisory Group, totaling almost forty officers. Heedless of the wilting temperature and moist air, Sazhenev wore a wonderful Italian-made light gray suit, a memento of service in the Mediterranean.

Korobchenko saluted and presented the two VDV captains'

orders. Sazhenev opened Korobchenko's folder deliberately, fished out and donned a small pair of black-rimmed reading glasses from his breast pocket, and sat down. He gestured for his two visitors to do likewise.

A few minutes passed in silence. Sazhenev finally looked up, gazing over the top of his glasses. "I have only one order: Do not get involved in the hostilities. The Center emphatically directs as much. You understand the delicate reasons why we must avoid direct confrontation with the United States troops."

Yes, thought Donskov. Nuclear weapons make us unwilling even to shadowbox. Korobchenko always said as much. Here, regardless of a lot of training exercises and written crap, was the real-life proof of the paralyzing effects of nuclear rocketry. By not getting involved, the Soviets could legitimately claim that they did nothing but act as innocent diplomats, and milk a sure U.S. victory for some useful propaganda. Sazhenev's attitude looked to be "let Castro eat this one."

"Current GRU estimates indicate that the imperialists might be here at any time, most likely tonight," continued Sazhenev. "Of course, these black baboons and our macho socialist brethren do not stand a chance. I've worked enough with them; they sicken me with all their posturing. The American imperialists will make short work of them. We know it, and behind their bluster, these apes outside know it too. Our participation can do nothing to alter the objective material factors of this struggle. The correlation of forces weighs completely against us. We have no tanks, no heavy artillery, and no Soviet Army units.

"As long as you are in this embassy, you are on Soviet soil and are safe. I am reasonably certain that even the most bloodthirsty Americans will not enter this compound. You must be here, and stay here, once the American attack begins."

Korobchenko stirred a bit. "Comrade colonel, what about Colonel Tortolo's needs?" asked the Ukrainian.

Sazhenev breathed deeply, in and out. His head dipped slightly. "You may and indeed must cooperate with him. Those are your orders from General Major Golitsyn, approved by Moscow. But you must listen to me, too. You can do whatever you might to aid Tortolo, but when the Americans come, you are to return to this embassy and leave the fighting to the locals, is that clear?"

Donskov thought it sounded obvious enough. But Korobchenko persisted. "Comrade colonel, it is possible that with the assistance of your advisers, we can create defensive positions sufficiently strong to cause heavy American casualties, perhaps even enough to force a cease-fire and negotiations. There are only so many ways onto this island, and the Cuban and Grenadian manpower available would permit much work if we start now. This is just a start. We can also commence organization of partisan cells in the hills to sustain resistance for some time. Colonel Tortolo's mission requires him to defend this island, and we can—"

Sazhenev's face darkened, but his voice remained calm. "Captain Korobchenko, perhaps you have not listened. We are not going to participate in this island's defense. I will not be part of an ignominious defeat for Soviet arms, and since we cannot save this situation, I choose not to join a lost cause. I repeat, we have no tanks, no rockets, no helicopters, no tactical aircraft, no heavy guns, and no reliable Soviet soldiers. All we have are a handful of GRU officers, a few KGB types, and this Third World rabble that passes for our faithful socialist comrades. You propose to throw this pittance against the mightiest capitalist forces, right here in their backyard? It's pointless. Of course, had you or your young protégé here ever attended a military academy, you would understand how to calculate correlations of forces."

Although stung by the barbed personal insult, Korobchenko did not back away. "Comrade colonel," he asked, "can we at least draw upon expertise from your unit? Do you have any trained air defenders, for example?"

Now Sazhenev's voice took an unpleasant edge, and his volume increased. "Captain Korobchenko, the composition of my group is not your concern. They are strictly under my orders, and as such are restricted to this site already. You would do well to follow their prudent example. I am certain you have provided, or can provide quickly, the needed expertise for Colonel Tortolo. It is your choice, and your responsibility, should you determine to wait until the imperialists arrive before you come back to this location. Neither I nor my men will come looking for you, and I warn you, you can expect the most dire consequences if you decide to exceed my guidance and become involved in the fighting. Now good day, comrades."

And with that Sazhenev's assistant entered and led away the two paratroopers. Korobchenko's face appeared unusually hard as Donskov eyed him. He's really pissed off. But his old commander said nothing until they crossed in front of the sentinel and left the walled structure. The Ukrainian seized Donskov's arm as soon as they got a hundred meters away, while still well short of Tortolo and the waiting Land Rover.

"Fucking old coot," hissed Korobchenko. "He doesn't give a shit what happens on this island, as long as he and his boys aren't involved. They're *already* involved, the cold bastards. Remember what Golitsyn said? Sazhenev and his cronies egged on the locals to start all of this crap. And now they're leaving these people to their own devices. So much for the Soviet Union's commitment to its friends. It's standard mealymouthed horseshit, I say."

"So what now?" Donskov asked.

"What else? We do our job, whistle the *1812 Overture* through our assholes, and hope we get back here before the damn imperialists. Dmitriy, we're on our own."

Donskov grinned broadly, blissfully ignorant of how serious that phrase could be. "Fine by me."

Captain Sergio Grandales-Nolasco spoke Russian fairly well, so he confidently greeted the two VDV captains as they broke through the thick underbrush on the north slope of the Salines airport ridge. Both Soviets showed enough dirt and sweat to indicate that they had been involved in the sporadic gun battle just over the rise.

Ahead of them lay the neat, low white buildings of the Calliste Barracks. A few tendrils of smoke marked structures punctured by the Americans' persistent flying gun platform.

"Comrades, what is your report?" asked the Cuban. From his right hand dangled a black radio handset, linked by looping wire to the parent R-150M set mounted on his GAZ-69 jeep. The Cuban captain had just driven into the Calliste facility, and the motor in his idling jeep putted behind him.

"Comrade Sergio, the imperialists put almost two battalions on the ground. Boris here thinks they're Rangers," said Donskov.

The Cuban inhaled sharply. "Interesting," he remarked. "Did we knock down any airplanes?"

Donskov glanced at Korobchenko briefly, who said nothing. He continued. "No. We had time to move only one gun before the enemy showed up."

"How about the Grenadian and Cuban ground troops? Have they held back the foes?" Grandales-Nolasco wondered.

"A little," offered Korobchenko. "A mortar crew did some good, but the Americans are damn tough–really hot to close in and fight. Have you anything extra to throw in?"

Grandales-Nolasco showed both rows of even white teeth. "Of course, comrade Boris. I have three BTRs with picked squads hidden in the warehouse back there. Maybe I let the Americans clear the runway, land their fat jet transports, relax their guard, then . . . smash!"

Both Soviets nodded approvingly. This man just might pull it off. Satisfied, Donskov changed the subject. "Any word from the capital? Have the imperialists put any of their marine naval infantry on the beaches up there?"

"No marines, but a big helicopter raid went in while I drove down here. I think . . . "

Almost as if on cue, the harsh fluttering of very fast helicopter blades filled the barracks area. Overhead, a disorganized flock of eight lean black-green helicopters bounced across the blue sky, their turbine engines racing at a much higher speed than any helicopters in the Soviet inventory. These unrelenting craft zipped across the sky without the usual "whop-whop" noise, so quickly did their rotors rip the air.

"Must be the new American UH-60s," Korobchenko yelled to his two mates.

A few of the UH-60s showed obvious rips and holes in their

otherwise rounded fuselages. All three soldiers dove into the red dirt when frustrated American door gunners sprayed Calliste with unaimed spurts from dangling machine guns. Little lines of dust kicked up in the wake of this careless shooting. As quickly as that, the speeding formation passed overhead, and the slashing rotor beat died away.

"I guess that was the raid," remarked Korobchenko as he stood up and whisked off the biggest pieces of dirt. Donskov and Grandales-Nolasco also gained their feet.

Just then a final U.S. helicopter bobbed over the far tree line, smoking from the cowling, dribbling misshapen little shards of metallic detritus, and wavering in its progress. Its motor missed and coughed, and the rotor blades spun unevenly as the chopper struggled to stay aloft. This one would not make it much farther. The three officers watched it rattle across the ridge line to a certain demise. Donskov cringed a bit, as did the Cuban, but in the absence of shooting, neither dropped to the ground. Old soldier Korobchenko stood like a rock, shading his eyes to get a better view of the stricken UH-60.

"So, that is one for the capital batteries, yes?" said the Cuban captain.

"Looks like it," mused Korobchenko.

"I ask you," Grandales-Nolasco said, "can you two comrades go to the capital and render a report back to me? I must take charge of the counterattack here at Calliste."

Korobchenko looked at his younger associate. Donskov was not sure. "We really need to speak to Colonel Tortolo," Donskov stated.

The Cuban's face clouded with disgust. Unlike Tortolo, this one's fair skin showed the Spanish strain of his people's heritage, and thereby better betrayed his emotions.

"You mean our Olympic star?" spat the Cuban. "Oh yes, he ran like a rabbit—yes he did, right for your embassy. I hope he can be ready for the 1984 games. Maybe he can recommend his wondrous shoes for sprinters everywhere. They sped him to safety like a flash. What a useless piece of shit!"

"I guessed that one," Korobchenko said, turning to his fellow captain. "So can we help comrade Sergio?"

Donskov knew that they should go back to the embassy. If Tortolo really hid out there, that was all the more reason to return to the Soviet facility in accord with Sazhenev's guidance. Just as surely, though, Donskov knew full well that he would follow Korobchenko, like always. Unable to say yes but unwilling to say no, Donskov simply stood mute.

Korobchenko took the initiative: "We're on our way."

"I am very appreciative. Here, why not take my GAZ-69?" The Cuban handed Korobchenko the keys and the R-105M handset.

"I'll stay here," Grandales-Nolasco noted. "Call me on the radio with your report. The frequency is tuned. I'll use the ground set in the headquarters building. Call me Dorado – speak Russian. And you will be . . . ?"

Donskov looked at Korobchenko.

"Nomad," said the Ukrainian. "We'll call us Nomad."

"Good. Thank-you. Now, I must find my subordinates and prepare a glorious counterstroke. Oh, won't those imperialists be surprised!"

And with that the lithe Cuban was off at double time. Korobchenko climbed into the driver's seat and motioned Donskov into the jeep.

"We should go back to the embassy," the younger officer said.

"Look, we're already late. Let's just swing through St. George's, a quick report, then straight back to Sazhenev. We can't leave this poor Cuban up shit creek!"

With that, Korobchenko pressed the gas pedal, and the jeep burped into motion. Donskov hoped Korobchenko knew what he was doing. He felt very uneasy.

I wish I really understood English, Donskov thought to himself as he stood among the People's Revolutionary Army gunners near Fort Frederick. Their excited black faces, wide eyes, and happy grins spoke volumes, however. These men had beaten back the American helicopter raid early that morning, and now they confidently, playfully waited for other challenges. A few Cuban officers encouraged the ZU-23 crews and helped them unload more ammunition from dirty East German IKA supply trucks.

Donskov and Korobchenko could take partial credit for these stout defenses. They had personally emplaced all six twin-gun sets the previous afternoon, taking advantage of the natural horseshoe of hills and ridges that hemmed in the Grenadian capital city of St. George's against the blue Caribbean. During the nineteenth century, the British had erected a chain of hill fortifications on this same high ground, designed to protect St. George's from naval attacks. Now the Grenadian gunners dominated that same harbor with a murderous crossfire, their batteries cleverly folded into the notches and fortresses that ringed the pretty little port city.

Donskov certainly had to grant the beauty of the scene unfolding before him. Nestled beneath its covering old hill redoubts and modern antiaircraft emplacements, the capital gleamed in the hot sun. Shining white, red-roofed buildings were clustered carelessly along the winding, narrow streets, most of which led down to the azure sea. A few rusting merchant ships, some neat sailboats, and a clutch of launches bobbed on the harbor swells.

On the steep green hillsides above the quiet, pristine little town, Donskov saw purposeful activity in every direction. Distant Fort Rupert, due west of Fort Frederick on a small peninsula jutting into the sleepy harbor, bustled with troops stacking ammunition. To the north, desultory firefight banged and smoldered around Government House, where imperialist SEAL naval commandos had rescued the imprisoned British Crown representative and his family, only to be pinned down by the Grenadian regular infantry companies charged with capital defense. Watchful antiaircraft sites opened up whenever American planes or helicopters approached their trapped special warfare team.

Just north of Fort Frederick lay old Fort Matthew, home to a ZU-23 system and a bunch of lighter machines guns as well. The Grenadian flag flew over the dilapidated bastion, which formed the center of the antiaircraft network. It also served as the island's insane asylum, or "Crazy House," as the locals called it. Donskov noted with some amusement that coal-black patients in long white nightshirts were crowded onto the battlements and waved merrily whenever the gunners opened fire. For them, the air-ground battles constituted a fireworks show. As Korobchenko remarked upon noticing these unusual neighbors, "All crazy people like war."

Fort Frederick itself served as the headquarters for the Grenadian battalion engaged down at Government House. Here, Donskov and Korobchenko had parked their GAZ-69 and tried to garner an accurate assessment of the situation from the Grenadian and Cuban headquarters officers stationed in the fortress. While Korobchenko searched for someone he could understand, Donskov walked out onto the breezy, sunny ridge top to watch the People's Revolutionary Army soldiers at work. He noticed that the Grenadians relied on telephone links to observers and their fellow antiaircraft sections. It was all business as the men readied for further action. Donskov had to admit, despite his gnawing concerns about Sazhenev's orders, that he hoped the Americans would try something so he would see this defensive array, *his* defensive scheme, do its duty.

South of Donskov at Fort Frederick were Richmond Hill Prison, the Venezuelan Embassy at Fort Adolphus, and Fort Lucas, the Cuban Embassy. The prison and Fort Lucas, aging British edifices, sported antiaircraft mounts and supporting lighter weapons. Indeed, the protectors of Richmond Hill claimed major credit for driving off the morning's helicopter assault on their facility. The capitalists in their UH-60s endeavored to seize the prison and free dangerous counterrevolutionary agitators. Thanks to sound gun deployment and aggressive shooting, the Americans did not take the installation. All of St. George's air defenses shared in the victory.

Korobchenko and Donskov could rightly take some pride in this achievement. When they had found the ZU-23s, the locals had merely lined them up on the city wharfs, as if for inspection rather than any real tactical work. Lacking formal air defense training, the two VDV men guessed and applied common sense, with the veteran Korobchenko taking the major role in positioning each of the half-dozen twin 23mm cannons. Donskov saw how well these weapons dominated both the seaward and landward approaches to St. George's. If only they had had enough time to make similar dispositions down at Salines. A quick glance well southward at the rising smoke, diving U.S. jets, and rattling gunfire around the airport reminded Donskov that time there had run out.

Just then Korobchenko grabbed his fellow paratrooper, breaking his train of thought. The older captain hopped on the jeep hood with slaps of his hands on the thin metal. "The Cuban major in there gave me a full report. These guys up here have done a hell of a job. They think they'll have those SEALs mopped up within the hour."

Good—we've done our duty then. Donskov hoped this would mean that they could leave and possibly deflect some of Sazhenev's wrath. He reached inside the jeep to find the handset and make the report to Grandales-Nolasco. "Do you want to call him, or shall I?" Donskov asked.

Korobchenko slid off the hood: "I'll do it."

It took a few minutes to raise the excited Cuban captain and pass along a detailed account of the conditions around St. George's. Grandales-Nolasco seemed pleased by the report, and signed off with a promise of "something big" cooking up down at Salines. Korobchenko replaced the radio handset and turned to Donskov. "Okay, let's get back down to the embassy."

Donskov climbed into the GAZ-69, and Korobchenko started the little truck and got ready to shift into reverse for the trip down from the hills to the Soviet beachfront compound. Donskov closed his eyes momentarily—what a day! Shot at, scared and–

"Comrade captains, come quick! Yankee marine helicopters!" shrieked a hatless Cuban soldier in tropical uniform. He pointed with a waving finger out over the bay.

Sure enough, a pair of slim silhouettes slipped languidly across the bright blue waves, picking their way through the moored watercraft toward embattled Government House. Korobchenko cut the motor and hopped out. "This could be interesting, Dmitriy."

Donskov, fascinated by the incoming slivers of death, forgot all about Sazhenev. He climbed swiftly from the jeep. Both Soviets ran toward the ZU-23 mount. Already the double gun turned to track the attackers.

"They're AH-1 Cobra attack helicopters, all right," said Korobchenko, squinting through his binoculars. "Marine Sea Cobras—two engines. This model's got a 20mm rotary cannon under the nose."

Donskov focused his own binoculars on each of the narrow choppers, rising now off the water as they homed in on the Grenadian troops beguiling the SEALs. None of the antiaircraft guns had yet opened fire. Just a few meters to his right, he heard the gunners' commands in unintelligible, lilting Caribbean English. The sharp clicks and snaps of 23mm rounds slamming into chambers cut through the steady drone of the Cobras' rotor blades.

"Lead ship's up," intoned Korobchenko, eyes still pressed against his binoculars as he followed the Americans. Donskov glanced to his right to see the gun commander with his ear to a telephone. Suddenly the Grenadian leader pointed to his men and shouted something.

The ZU-23 blasted off a short string of rounds, green tracers that reached out for the American aircraft. A web of similar fire fingered out across the red-topped white city, concentrated on the lead Cobra. The American helicopter staggered and dipped a bit as it absorbed hot fragments, then spun down and away, rebuffed by the fire.

The second Cobra charged in to cover its wounded mate. For some reason, this U.S. Marine flyer selected Fort Frederick as his most annoying tormentor, and turned its wicked 20mm cannon against the site. Donskov dropped to the ground for the third time that day as long slugs dug up the turf around him. At least I'm getting good at something, he thought.

The plucky ZU-23 crew traded shot for shot with the American helicopter, even as the roaring menace closed in on the stalwart battery. Donskov was lying so that he could see the big black men working their gun. They laughed and talked as they lowered the hot barrels to track their enemy. The crew seemed absolutely unaffected by the big rounds tearing strips out of the grassy slope.

But courage goes only so far. Donskov watched in horror as a trace of 20mm shots skipped up the lip of the ridge and into the gun mount. Both Grenadians opened their mouths, their screams absorbed in the cacophony of turbines, gunfire, and rotor wash. One man flipped backward in a shower of bright blood; the other slumped as if sleeping, his head sheared from the gory stalk of his neck. The gun stopped shooting. Blade noises and downwash flattened the grass, a speeding shadow briefly blackened the ground, and then the Marine chopper banked away, its mission accomplished.

This time Donskov was up along with Korobchenko.

"The gun's okay, Dmitriy. We've got to get this son of a bitch!"

"Exactly so!"

A Cuban officer lay still, oozing red into the dust. He'd be no help now. Donskov noticed a few Grenadian soldiers cowering at the abutments of nearby Fort Frederick. He waved them forward and yelled in Russian, "Come on, help us!" But the locals stayed put.

Korobchenko shoved aside the headless gunner and settled into the bloody seat. Donskov moved the other corpse, and the man's congealing blood smeared the captain's once-white shirt. Korobchenko insured that the heavy ammunition belt was still seated and ready. The distant whirring of helicopter blades gave an urgency to his work. Other guns pounded from around the bay, but this one had some paying back to do.

Donskov reached down and fed another fifty-round belt into the holding box on his side. He looked at Korobchenko, who nodded curtly and turned to his sights.

"Target–gunner identify!" barked Korobchenko, slipping automatically into BMD firing commands. Who knows what these air defenders say? Too bad, this will have to do.

Donskov looked into the elaborate gun sight. A maze of shattered metal made that useless. He ignored the sights, remembered his sturdy binoculars, and searched. There he is! The Sea Cobra flitted along the wave tops, again running toward Government House. You've given us a nice flank shot, asshole.

"Identified!"

"Tracking," Korobchenko improvised as he wheeled the gun to lead the oblivious imperialist chopper. Other guns shot well wide of the low-flying craft, which wove carefully through the anchored boats in St. George's harbor. Its slow speed and wide side allowed the sightless ZU-23 and its amateur crew to align all too easily.

"Ready to fire," answered Donskov, hoping he was.

"Fire!"

The guns pumped and rocked. Korobchenko twisted the lateral cranks, Donskov spun the elevation wheel, and within a second or two their twin stream of blazing green tracers ate into the right side of the Sea Cobra. The big blade slowed, the engines burped out jet-black soot, and the thing keeled over sickly to its right. After a graceless downward curve, the helicopter crunched into an open field near the docks and burst into flames.

"We got him!" whooped Donskov.

Korobchenko said nothing, but spun the carriage around. "Target—gunner identify!"

The other one. Oh shit. Donskov reloaded his gun even as he looked for the approaching Sea Cobra. The big box of heavy 23mm rounds slipped as he fumbled an oily belt up and into the chamber. His bloody, greasy, trembling fingers didn't help. The ammunition slipped to the dirt. Blade slaps reverberated, pressing him to action.

Clang, smack! Dust flew, and he saw a stitch of 20mm slugs working their way up the hill. The American was coming right at them, guns blazing. He couldn't hear Korobchenko clearly, but he knew what to do. Load! Somehow the slick 23mm rounds made it into the feed tray.

"Identified! Ready to fire!" he screamed.

"Fire!" bellowed Korobchenko.

And with that he grabbed the trigger handles instinctively and let her rip. Ever larger, the wrathful Cobra's turbine shrieked as it closed in. Dust and cordite caused Donskov to gag, but all he could think about was to put the green tracers on the black death approaching. Line up! Line up! The American killer roared, the mount shook as fragments spangled on its flimsy metal, and then the belt ran out and the gun fell dumb.

No more ammo! That's it!

"We got him, Dmitriy," remarked Korobchenko, wiping his brow.

Donskov, breathing like a runaway locomotive, bathed in grimy sweat, looked where Korobchenko pointed. Sure enough, the hapless U.S. Sea Cobra was sinking slowly into the harbor waters with a puff of hot steam.

So it ended, as simply as that. A twin-rotor American rescue helicopter wafted slowly over the bay, which still rang with a few stray shots. Even the firefight around Government House died away. Had the SEALs surrendered? Who could be sure?

In the lull, Donskov suddenly looked around him at the dead men, the cowering Grenadians, and the hundreds of pockmarks peppering the ridge line. Nicks, holes, and rents scored the surfaces of the battered ZU-23. Donskov shuddered. For a few heartbeats, his sweat ran cold.

One skinny Grenadian walked slowly toward the two desant-niks as they stood up from the smoking antiaircraft gun. "You big men—big men," he said in half-baked Russian, gesturing out to sea. The Soviets looked at each other. Korobchenko clapped the People's Revolutionary Army soldier on the back. "It's all yours, brother. We're late." The black man merely stared, not understanding the Ukrainian.

They left the Grenadian at the ZU-23 as they returned to their jeep. Both got in without a word. Korobchenko started the vehicle, and they were off.

"Big men! Big men!" they heard several of the Grenadians chanting before they rolled out of earshot.

Korobchenko joked as they at long last moved toward the Soviet Embassy. "Do you think," the Ukrainian remarked conversationally, "that I have a future in the Zenith Rocket Troops of air defense?"

Donskov made no answer. He hoped he still had any future at all. What an army! Here he sat, on the verge of being powdered for the heinous offense of doing his combat duty. For the first time in years, Donskov had a very strong urge to get utterly, despicably drunk.

"Where have you two been?" Sazhenev queried. His voice dripped venom and his tone cut the atmosphere in the hot, humid office. With the power off to his air-conditioner, the colonel's pallid gray suit had wilted and rumpled, but he wore it nevertheless.

"Detained by enemy action, comrade colonel," Korobchenko answered, his body at as rigid attention as if he guarded Lenin's tomb. Donskov also braced up, but said nothing.

"You are aware that the Center called for an accounting of my personnel, and that I was forced to report both of you as missing?" Sazhenev said, biting off each word.

"No, comrade colonel," Korobchenko replied neutrally.

"You two desantnik bastards went out to play war in direct violation of my orders. Considering that we are in combat, that is a court-martial offense meriting capital punishment!" the old colonel blared.

Considering we're in combat, why shouldn't we fight, Donskov wondered. I've gotten shot at and I've knocked down two imperialist helicopters. Your GRU buddies will interrogate me for a week straight after all I've seen. What have you done for the motherland today, Sazhenev? Of course, Donskov said nothing; he felt thankful for all those cadet days that taught him to look blank regardless of what he was really thinking.

"All right, get out of here," Sazhenev finished. "Report to my deputy for preliminary debriefing, and then stay the hell out of my way until we're evacuated. If you're both lucky, you might survive with only a few years in a penal battalion."

Both captains hustled out of the fetid office. As they turned down the dank hall to exit the building, the VDV men bowled into five jabbering Libyans wandering up the tiled passage.

"Great, just fucking great!" bawled Korobchenko. "We're hiding out with our Arab brothers! Well, why not? We belong with them!"

The big Ukrainian nearly brained one poor Libyan who was slow getting out of the way. Donskov said nothing. There was nothing to say.

It rained very hard that night. The power stayed off.

The second day of the Grenada campaign passed uneventfully in the Soviet compound. Without electrical power for air-conditioning, most of the solid chancery building was uninhabitable, and the constant American presence made communications from the island an exercise in futility, lest they be intercepted and their codes compromised. So the GRU men and their few KGB associates sat on folding chairs in the courtyard or slept in the shade. Sazhenev remained dressed in his business suit and spent the day seated regally on the stairs of the abandoned chancery. All of the Soviet soldier-diplomats wore civilian clothes and carried AK-47s borrowed from the Grenadians. A few soldiers stood guard on a rotating schedule, waiting for the inevitable American arrival.

It seemed like everybody came but the Americans. Along with the Libyans who arrived at the first sign of trouble, East Germans, North Koreans, and Bulgarians dribbled into the embassy to avoid the American onslaught. Some Grenadian officers and civil officials also sought refuge. All of these new arrivals brought bad news. Some stories were evidently wild rumors, but nothing sounded good.

The Soviet Embassy inmates learned that the 82d Airborne Division had landed at Salines and taken Calliste Barracks after a tough, grinding fight. Grandales-Nolasco's counterthrust failed with the loss of his entire force, including the bold captain. All the second day, U.S. Air Force transports were reported to be delivering U.S. paratroopers to reinforce the American assault elements at Salines.

Imperialist Marine companies had secured Pearls Airport and the northern part of the island. Other Marines, with a few tanks and armored carriers for support, had stormed ashore the night of the parachute assault and had taken St. George's the following morning. The embattled American SEALs somehow survived; the brave antiaircraft batteries on the hills did not. American aircraft carrier air strikes ravaged those air defenses. Grenadian resistance broke, and most of the Cubans surrendered.

All of these ill tidings became the subject of bitter conversations in the bypassed embassy. Tortolo and Sazhenev served as the butt of many grim jokes and vicious invective as the inactive soldiers blamed their superiors for their shameful situation.

Tortolo received much animosity intended for the Cubans in general. The Soviets ridiculed them for cracking under pressure, and all of the cooped-up men assured each other that they would not have given up so readily. This was unfair, as the Cuban engineers and the military assistance group had fought much more stoutly than their erstwhile leader. But with only Tortolo to judge, the Soviets assumed and asserted that Cuban cowardice had wrecked the island's defense.

Foolishly, Tortolo decided to meet insults with bombast. He refused to talk to Korobchenko and Donskov or anyone else of junior rank. Instead, he said loudly to all who might listen that he had followed Sazhenev's orders in making for the embassy, and then insisted that he had served only as an adviser, not the actual island commander. Donskov wondered what Grandales-Nolasco would think, but that Cuban captain thought nothing anymore. He had been roasted alive in his armored personnel carrier during his futile last-gasp attack on unloading U.S. Air Force airplanes.

If Tortolo attracted disdain, it was minor compared to the hatred generated by Sazhenev's steadfast refusal to assist with island defenses. Everyone knew that Sazhenev had spurred the coup d' état and then abandoned his Grenadian allies, and none of the Soviets felt good about hunkering down behind the shield of diplomatic immunity while the damned imperialists gleefully crushed their socialist brothers. Korobchenko and Donskov, still filthy with blood, grass, and the honest dirt of combat, found that many of their GRU and KGB comrades turned to them for eyewitness views of the fighting. Although Donskov stuck to straight narrative, Korobchenko insured that his audience understood that in his opinion, a bit more Soviet involvement could have tilted the balance. Sazhenev sat sublime and ignored the grumblings all around him in the small courtyard.

So it went all day and into the hot, stinking night. Helicopters, jets, and gunfire raged and ebbed all around them, but there sat the Soviets and their allies, trapped in their own embassy. Donskov wondered what would transpire when the Americans showed up.

The third day turned out to be the last day of suspense, although it began badly with the recognition that the compound's reserve fresh water supply had almost run dry. Sazhenev, increasingly remote from events, told one of his GRU deputies to get in touch with the Americans and request assistance "in accord with normal diplomatic courtesies." With U.S. soldiers dead from Russian-made weapons and ample evidence of Soviet complicity all over Grenada, Donskov wondered how the imperialists might answer this inquiry.

Two impetuous North Koreans did their bit to encourage a violent American reply. Like the other allies, these foreign soldiers were on Grenada as military advisers, and the Koreans impressed Donskov as particularly unwilling to sit still and wait for whatever came next. About midmorning, as Donskov lay in the shade rereading a year-old copy of *Military Herald,* he heard the burst of an AK-47, followed by another. He stood up just in time to see a pair of crew-cut, laughing little Koreans run through the front gate, their assault rifles smoking.

"What's up now?" Korobchenko growled, stirring from his sleep on the soft dirt.

"Those fucking Koreans just shot off a few rounds," Donskov observed. He watched a man he knew to be a KGB major, accompanied by another tall Chekist, an Estonian, run to apprehend and disarm the snickering Korean riflemen. Another KGB officer ran to the front gate and looked out. He stayed there.

This demanded investigation, even by VDV men in serious trouble with the local commander. Donskov stood up and walked to the gate. Korobchenko followed, curious. The two GRU sentinels on duty did not challenge the unshaven, dirty desantniks as they strolled out of the compound.

"Oh shit!" exclaimed Korobchenko. Donskov's heart sank.

Sprawled a few hundred meters away on the steep road that led down to the beachfront road to St. George's were the bodies of two American paratroopers. One was trying to sit up. All Donskov could focus on, for some reason, was that the capitalists wore Nazi Hitlerite-style coal scuttle helmets.

"Inside, all inside!" commanded the Estonian KGB officer. The Soviets abandoned the two Americans to their fate.

"We're in deep shit now," Korobchenko said, rubbing his stubbly chin.

Within an hour, around high noon, Korobchenko's prediction appeared to come true. Donskov had been pacing around in the shade, his AK-47 at the ready, longing to get outside and have a look. Korobchenko sat with his back to the embassy garage, his autorifle across his lap. They had heard trucks coming and going outside and speculated about what was going on. "The imperialists are surrounding us, Dmitriy," guessed Korobchenko gloomily.

The blast of a truck's air horn drew all eyes in the compound to the main gate. There, barely able to fit through, was a bright red Grenadian fire engine, led by a walking American soldier with a holstered pistol and a Nazi helmet. Another American with a loaded M-16 lay prone on the roof of the fire truck. Their greenish camouflage uniforms looked faded and dirty in the searing tropical sun, but their weapons appeared all too functional. Undoubtedly a whole company backed up this bold foray.

"They're coming into the embassy!" said a small Belorussian GRU captain, incredulous as the big black Grenadian driver eased his vehicle into the courtyard. On the chancery steps, Sazhenev stood up but said nothing. One of his underlings came forward, met the American, and did all the talking. The Soviet pointed to the water reservoir. The American nodded gravely.

Every AK-47 in the yard, including those of the desantniks, trained directly on the red-faced, determined U.S. paratrooper, who turned out to be a captain. The man appeared completely relaxed as he scanned the hostile sea of international Communist faces and their attendant rifle muzzles. Donskov admired the imperialist solider's aplomb. Korobchenko, for his part, wandered slowly toward the gate, determined to get a look outside at whatever spawned this brazen American undertaking.

It took about twenty minutes for the Grenadian fire pumper to fill the embassy's water tank. The American soldiers waited patiently, their eyes cold with the disdainful gaze of veterans who have already seen combat. Donskov knew that these men were too young for Vietnam. Perhaps they had served in the imperialist cadres in Central America. It would have shocked Donskov to discover that, like himself, the only combat these men had ever seen had been the last few days on Grenada. It might have surprised the desantnik even more to know that he showed exactly the same harsh visage.

Finally, the embarrassing interlude ended. The fire engine reversed gears and slowly pulled out, led by the unflappable 82d Airborne officer. More than eighty assault rifles relaxed once the American walked through the gate. The tension broken, a few men walked over to fill their canteens.

Donskov was about to do the same when Korobchenko reappeared and grabbed his left arm. He pulled the other captain into the corner formed by the garage and the compound's outer wall. "That guy was alone," he whispered harshly.

"What?" replied Donskov in disbelief.

"He was alone. I reconnoitered the immediate area. There was no backup. The brass-balled son of a bitch just rolled in and rolled out while Sazhenev and the rest of us shit our trousers."

Donskov shook his head. "We should have known better," he remarked. "That's nothing but dumb American luck."

"No, Dmitriy, *that* is the value of one man who knows the importance of deception. All warfare is based on deception."

Korobchenko sat down and stared off, gradually drifting into a world thousands of miles away. Donskov forgot about his canteen and his cracked lips and sat down beside his former commander. What next? Really, at this point, did it matter?

They left the island under heavy American guard a few days later. In the humiliating search that preceded their departure, the American airborne soldiers took the personal weapons of the GRU and KGB officers. They all left, rather fittingly, disarmed, dirty, and ashamed. The flight to Cuba turned out to be as silent as the grave.

"The Order of the Red Star? For what, comrade colonel?"

In his hot-weather uniform, cleaned and polished, Sazhenev stroked his chin. The light streamed into the air-conditioned office in downtown Havana.

"For personally destroying two imperialist attack helicopters, for designing and directing the defenses of St. George's, and for returning superb information on American tactics and organization, all at substantial risk to your life. Are you not aware that our Cuban comrade Fidel Castro has cited your superb military and political-motivational efforts in a private letter to our party leader, Yuri Vladimirovich Andropov?"

Scrubbed and once again properly dressed, his blue beret in his left hand, Donskov marveled. He had reported for what he assumed would be the presentation of court-martial charges. Korobchenko had gone earlier that day and returned in black despair, with his orders for Afghanistan canceled pending investigation for disobedience of a direct verbal order. And now, this. Something smelled very odd.

Sazhenev shifted ever so slightly in his fine leather-covered chair. "I'll need you to initial my draft report on the Grenada episode. Just a formality, you understand. Please, have a seat and look it over."

Donskov sensed trouble. Stay alert, desantnik. Oh, but it's hard to duck *these* rounds. "I will remain standing, comrade colonel."

"As you wish," sighed the colonel, handing Donskov a folder. "It's all rather dry, Donskov. You may not feel like reading it in detail."

Donskov said nothing. Instead, he opened the folder and began to read. Sazhenev swiveled his chair to look out the wide window, his long fingers touching to form a pensive pyramid as he waited for Donskov to read and initial the report.

The captain scanned the first few pages, a somewhat confused summary of the factional fighting before, during, and after the Grenadian coup. On about page four of the eight closely typed sheets, Donskov noted the heading "Military Events of the Imperialist Invasion." He began to read.

"The advisory group received instructions from Moscow on 22 October 1983 as follows: 'to assist energetically the Cuban/indigenous defense of the island without decisive engagement of large numbers of Soviet nationals in the fighting.' Of course, urged by the example of the commander/ambassador, the group worked diligently to prepare the moral-political fiber and military-technical basis of our socialist comrades under the threat of the treacherous imperialist attack. . . . "

Donskov's head swam. This scumbag had the same orders we did! *He* decided to hide in the embassy, and probably talked that weak sister Tortolo into doing likewise. Well, poor Tortolo was already en route to Angola as a private; Castro showed no mercy to cowards. Donskov knew the report would only get worse, but he read on.

"At the strong suggestion of the commander/ambassador, the VDV officers actively involved themselves in defensive preparations. KOROBCHENKO failed to prepare the Salines area for defense against parachute assault. DONSKOV, on the other hand, exerted a powerful and successful influence over air defensive subunits in the vital St. George's region. . . . The commander/ambassador personally took an active, right flanker role in the moral-political inspiration of the defenders of the Richmond Hill Prison. . . . DONSKOV then engaged the second imperialist helicopter, while KOROBCHENKO did nothing. . . . Thanks to KOROBCHENKO's hooliganism and irresponsibility, the Koreans shot both American soldiers in response to his direct orders. . . . Only the ambassador/commander's personal intervention convinced the strong American force to withdraw from the embassy and depart the sacred soil of the motherland. . . . "

The entire report went on in the same vein, an absolute fabrication. Donskov noted with horror that copies had already been dispatched to Moscow "for information." Apparently, enough other "witnesses" had already signed.

Sazhenev's motives were clear. His boys would not dare to blow the whistle on him, for he held their futures in his hands. How he bought off or hoodwinked the Chekists and political deputy, Donskov could only guess. In any event, only Korobchenko and Donskov might tell the truth behind Sazhenev's craven, disobedient performance. And apparently, the colonel decided to make the old captain the goat and Donskov the hero. All Donskov needed to do was deliver his initials, betray his most beloved fellow soldier, and pocket the reward. He didn't need to think at all.

"I cannot sign your report, comrade colonel."

Sazhenev spun around from his window and directed a particularly hard gaze at the VDV captain. The colonel's face indicated little surprise; he'd expected this.

"First, let me remind you that this report and your award recommendation are already a matter of record among the highest organs of the Center. Now, might I ask why you will not initial this report, Donskov?"

Donskov did not bat an eyelash. "It is grossly inaccurate, comrade colonel."

Sazhenev's face reddened and he roared like a volcano. "Grossly inaccurate, you say? You had better reconsider, young captain! I have statements and corroborating initials from my entire assistance group, including the KGB attachments and the political officer. I also have supporting comments from our Korean, German, Bulgarian, Cuban, and Grenadian allies."

"Then I suppose you will not need my initials, comrade colonel. I intend to apprise General Major Golitsyn of this entire conversation."

Sazhenev snorted ruefully. "You just do that, you pompous turd! I've reached out for you, and you've spurned my offer. Very well. The GRU has many eyes and hands, and a lot of them owe me favors. You'll see. You'll end up just like the broken-down drunk Korobchenko!"

Nothing could suit me more, Donskov told himself. But he resorted to the standard line. "I serve the Soviet Union, comrade colonel!"

"Get out of my sight," Sazhenev snarled.

Donskov saw Korobchenko briefly at the Havana transit point. The old desantnik shrugged and smiled weakly. "Ah, don't worry," he said. "Sazhenev's in big trouble, regardless of his fucking report. Two of the Chekists talked, I heard."

"I hope you're right. What about you?"

"Once this blows over, I'll retire. Mandatory. I'll be forty years old in four months. I've had enough of the crap," he said, not sounding too convincing.

Donskov changed to another issue. "You know the Red Star went through anyway," Donskov said. "I won't wear it."

"Do whatever you like. You earned it, Dmitriy. But you know

what I've always told you about awards–they're all just so much headquarters bullshit. Real soldiers don't need baubles to prove they've been there. They know."

Donskov nodded. He had already resolved never to wear any of his decorations again. The first step on the road to rebellion, he told himself. So be it. "I guess I won't see you until after Afghanistan," Donskov stated with finality.

"No," said Korobchenko. "I'll be out of the army by then."

"I just wish you were coming too. This Grenada thing is a hell of a way to part company."

"Consider the whole Grenada shit storm your last lesson before you go south. You know what it's like to shoot and get shot at in anger, and you've learned the most important lesson of all, one I couldn't teach you in training."

"What's that, Boris?" Donskov asked in a somber tone.

"Enemies come in all uniforms, including our own. But your mission remains the same."

"Kill them," said Donskov flatly.

"Exactly so."

About the same time that Donskov said good-bye to Korobchenko, General Major Golitsyn sat at his borrowed desk in the Soviet Embassy's military complex. His lengthy report on Grenada had just gone out with the courier. In accord with regulations, the general himself completed the routine destruction of his handwritten notes on the episode. The churning shredder sucked in the final batch of scraps and pages, dropping the resultant strips into the plastic bag marked "for burning only."

Finally, only one yellow corner of paper remained, with a sloppy ink scrawl. It read, "Donskov–Is he the one?"

Golitsyn held it up between his thumb and forefinger. He stared at it. "We'll see," he mumbled.

He slid the item into the shredder.

PART TWO

The Wood-Cutting Expedition

And so what is there for me in Russia?
It's all the same, you'll get shot here sooner or later.

from Leo Tolstoy, "The Wood-Cutting Expedition"

Chapter Four

On Afghanistan's Plains

The UAZ-469 jeep raced south along the deserted Kabul thoroughfare. Breaths of icy mountain winds swirled papers and brittle old snow against the little vehicle. The windshield wipers scraped across dry, cold glass as the driver tried to clear off the blowing particles.

Single-story brick buildings squatted along either side of the road, their whitewash faded to sickly gray. The street-front walls displayed garish red, white, and black propaganda posters as well as random sloppy spray-painted scrawls. Both the official decorations and the graffiti exhibited the scraggly, twisted curls that passed for the Pathan alphabet. Many houses and shops showed speckled gouges from bullets, scorches from glancing rock impacts, and even ragged holes torn by high explosives. Occasionally, the speeding jeep passed a pile of rubble or a blackened shell dusted with a layer of sooty snow. Most windows gaped black and empty, but a few showed weak orange lights on this overcast early afternoon, 9 January 1984. Not a soul walked this cold avenue.

"You're a day early, you know," offered the unshaven sergeant who piloted the UAZ-469. With his filthy old blue beret cocked on the back of his head, a burning cigarette dangling from his lips, and an oil-stained gray motor rifle overcoat, the driver looked more like a panhandler than a soldier.

The man's AKR automatic carbine, carelessly tossed between the front seats, sported a coat of rust that appeared months old. The neglected weapon fit in all too nicely with the overall disarray inside the cab. Crumpled papers, scraps of bent cardboard, empty ration containers, ripped bandages, tattered uniform fragments, and odd bits of personal field equipment littered the jeep's interior. The trash crunched and rustled beneath Donskov's boots.

"I caught the last flight out of Tashkent before the blizzard closed the airfield," said Donskov, his voice intentionally emotionless. The captain was taking it all in: dull-eyed Rear Services troops hanging around the Kabul airport, turbaned Afghans hawking bizarre trinkets outside the Soviet hangars, the shattered Kabul neighborhoods flashing by, this disheveled driver, and the general atmosphere of grayness, coldness, and demoralization. It did not look good. Welcome to the south, Dmitriy.

"Well, all I can say is six months to demob and fuck the wood chips," concluded the driver. "Wood chips" meant Afghans in the local soldier slang. It was one of the kinder terms. Donskov chose not to reply.

They drove on in silence for another half hour. A long column of BMPs clanked by, headed north, but the jeep did not slow its breakneck speed. Civilian buildings thinned out gradually, and Donskov saw Soviet Army tentage and motor pools scattered here and there among the sparse Afghan structures. The density of these temporary vehicle parks and logistics stockpiles increased with every kilometer that the road ran south from the crumbling center of sullen Kabul.

"Here we go—Desantnik Palace coming up," the sergeant announced. Ahead of them, on a rise almost 200 meters above the surrounding plateau, loomed the barbed wire, barracks, and blocky administrative structures of Kabul Southwest Camp, formerly known as Darulaman Palace. Once this installation served as the seat of the unlucky Hafizullah Amin, the Afghan leader killed in the initial Soviet takeover of December 1979. A combined detachment of Spetsnaz and Osnaz teams had assassinated him and his immediate

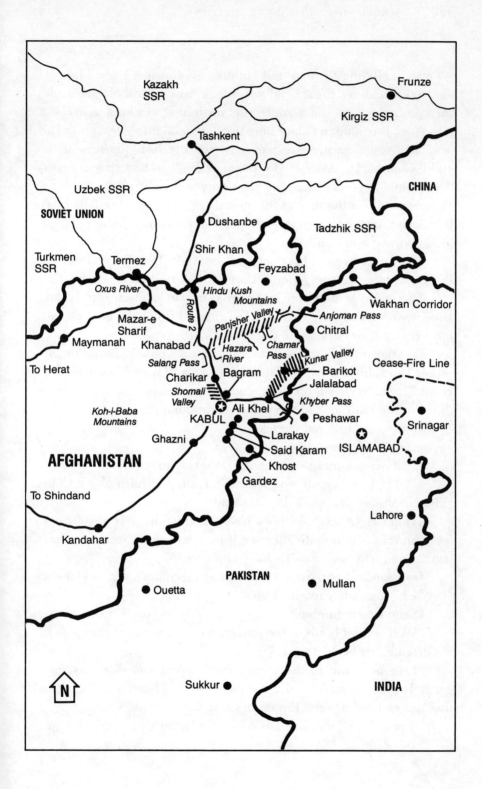

retinue, including women and children. Following a few hours of sharp skirmishing, the special forces took firm control of the Darula-man grounds. It proved a brief, cruel beginning to a long, cruel war.

Now, Darulaman Palace bore the unofficial title "Desantnik Palace," because its scarred expanse hosted the headquarters of the 103d Guards Air Assault Division. As his careless driver finally decelerated to greet the sentinels on duty at the entrance gate, Donskov noticed that the men at this portal appeared substantially more like Soviet Army paratroopers, properly shaven and outfitted in regulation winter overwhites.

The driver opened his door and shouted: "Leonid Feodorovich, I've got another future general. Care to look him over?"

The guard leaned over and peered in. He saluted smartly, and Donskov returned the greeting. "Don't mind Efremian, comrade captain. He's a little eccentric," the sentry said.

Donskov merely stared back, his eyes purposely devoid of anything. The soldier shrugged, backed away, and waved his arm. Sergeant Efremian closed his door, gunned the motor, and powered up the winding road toward the palace compound itself.

"Pull over," ordered Donskov.

Efremian ignored him.

"Pull over, comrade sergeant," Donskov hissed.

"What the—," sputtered the driver, feeling a sharp object in his side. He slowed and pulled to the side.

"That's right, asshole. It's a bayonet—the only part of your useless shit that wouldn't disintegrate if used in anger. Now, why don't you tell me why you're so fucking 'eccentric'?"

Donskov's eyes narrowed to slits as Efremian's eyes widened.

"Uh, comrade captain, I uh—"

"Seen much combat?"

"Well, I, that is we in the palace, we got mortared pretty badly about a month back. Tore a—"

"Ever been out in the mountains?" asked Donskov, his voice eerily conversational. He did not move his left hand and its implement, now hard against Efremian's heaving right side.

Efremian said nothing. His eyes rolled from side to side, looking for help that was nowhere to be found. There was only this wild man Donskov, insistent on an answer.

"Ever been out in the mountains, comrade sergeant?" Donskov queried again, pushing harder against the driver.

"No, comrade captain . . . "

"I didn't quite get that," Donskov retorted through his teeth.

"Not at all, comrade captain!"

Donskov moved his head close to Efremian, not relaxing the pressure on the sergeant's trembling torso.

"Then you'd better square away your headgear, find a fucking razor, dump this ragbag faggot motor rifle garbage sack of a coat, and rejoin the VDV, comrade sergeant. And the next time I see you around this division headquarters, you had better salute me with the greeting of the day. I don't give a shit if I'm a mile away. You haven't earned the *right* to eccentricity, comrade. I strongly advise you to give it up. It could be bad for your health."

Efremian gulped. "Exactly so, comrade captain." He immediately pulled his beret into its proper place.

"Now, please pull back on the road and take me to the adjutant's section," Donskov commanded with exaggerated cheerfulness. He relaxed the hard point against the sergeant's rib cage.

"Exactly so, comrade captain," said the man meekly.

They rolled through two more sentry posts without incident. The chastened driver pressed slowly through the maze of trucks, motorcycles, jeeps, and bustling foot soldiers that swarmed around the compound. It took some time to move through the busy barracks streets. Donskov made no further remarks. While gazing around, the captain noticed several other paratroopers who rivaled Efremian in their casual slovenliness. This was obviously a different sort of air assault unit than the 76th Guards of distant Pskov. Well, thanks to Korobchenko, I'm the same, Donskov thought. And I won't stand for this crap. What's wrong here?

Sergeant Efremian delivered his passenger directly to the two-story masonry building with a door marked "Fourth Section – Cadres Report Here." Without any comment, the tall captain unloaded his duffel bag and then bent to look through the UAZ- 469's door.

"Will that be all, comrade captain?" asked Sergeant Efremian, just as protocol required.

"Yes, comrade sergeant. Oh, and here's your bayonet back," said Donskov. He tossed a large metal spoon onto the seat, closed the jeep door, and slapped the hood.

Efremian drove away. A spoon! By nightfall, every soldier in the headquarters knew that some crazy man named Donskov had arrived. Quite a few also noticed that an unusually quiet Sergeant Efremian finally rediscovered his razor. The coincidence did not go unmarked.

The little basement office had no windows, and an armed guard waited outside its single closed door at all times. On the thick wood door, the neat words "Second Section" explained very little about the enclosure's contents.

Inside was a square room about the size of a walk-in closet. On each of the three doorless walls, a chipped, gouged field desk butted against the gray concrete blocks. Old gray metal folding chairs tucked under the desks. A new field telephone rested on each desk, along with boxes marked "In," "Hold," and "Ready." Racks of field manuals filled most of the remaining space around the floorboards of the cramped quarters. Above each desk, collages of carefully marked and pinned mapsheets covered almost every scrap of available vertical space between the small desks and the low ceiling. Immediately overhead, suspended so low that a tall man like Donskov would have to weave around them, six high-intensity incandescent bulbs lit the whole room in exquisite detail, a level of illumination suitable for surgery.

Surgery did occur here, because in this grim little cubicle, the reconnaissance cell of the 103d Guards Air Assault Division sliced and sutured incoming scraps of valuable information to feed the hungry maw of the operations section. Lieutenant Colonel Verskiy, the division's chief of reconnaissance, held sway from the center desk opposite the locked door. It was he who scraped his chair around and greeted Donskov early on the evening of his first day in Kabul. Just to the left of Verskiy, nervous Major Khavkov sat hunched over his desk, smoking furiously.

"Sit down, Donskov. Welcome to the 103d Guards. This is the reconnaissance section—I'm Verskiy. This is Major Khavkov."

As Donskov sat down in the third chair, the thin form grunted and kept scratching with a colored pencil, eyes glued to something spread across his desk. Blue smoke drifted over the major's desk.

"Khavkov's got the duty right now, 0800 to 2000 shift. So don't mind him. He's never very talkative, and we've been short a second duty officer for three weeks. Glad you made it down here a day early. We have plenty of work to do."

Donskov looked earnest and paid attention; it would have been stupid to do much more or less. Verskiy, a tall, thin man with coal-black eyes and a bald, shiny pink head, continued, fingering an unsharpened red pencil as he spoke. "Are all your personal matters in hand? Have you inprocessed?"

"No problems to speak of, comrade colonel. I haven't drawn my assault rifle yet."

"Right," answered Verskiy. "Ask for a Makarov pistol; you don't have time to mess with an AKD. You're not in a line company anymore."

Donskov nodded. Verskiy went on.

"You've an interesting record, Donskov. While you enjoyed that three weeks' leave, our new division commander has told us all about your exploits on Grenada. I've been looking forward to meeting you."

Donskov didn't know how to take this. The words "three weeks' leave" dripped with sarcasm, and Verskiy's tone indicated that he did not think much of the Grenada episode, either. Surely General Major Golitsyn's comments about Grenada only rankled these veterans of a "real" war. If Verskiy knew that most of the captain's twenty days' leave consisted of ill-tempered shouting matches with naive little Valentina he might not have been so smug.

As for Grenada, well, that seemed more and more like a distant dream, something from a childhood fairy tale. Only the sick, cold knot in the pit of his stomach, duller with each passing day, lingered to remind him when he conjured up images of being shot at for the motherland. With regard to his performance as a stand-in ZU-23 gunner, he recalled nothing special. It now smacked of some oddball range firing exercise: lots of noise, burned oil, cordite smoke, and targets destroyed. The dead men meant nothing to him, even the ones he had seen close up. They seemed like training accidents from another unit, certainly sad but not his responsibility. The bright green foliage, the stuttering imperialist Cobras, a bold American captain in the embassy yard, deceitful old Sazhenev—it all happened in another lifetime, didn't it? This tight room, gray and brown Kabul, now constituted reality.

"I'm glad to be here in the south, comrade lieutenant colonel," said Donskov quietly. Khavkov cleared his throat but said nothing. A monstrous cloud of stinking tobacco fumes punctuated the major's wordless interjection. Verskiy ignored it.

"Your position here is deputy chief of reconnaissance, on the 2000 to 0800 shift to be exact. You'll be working directly for me. This, obviously, is our working group's office. You're at your desk."

Donskov nodded, "Understood, comrade lieutenant colonel."

"You will find our tasks here particularly exhausting and challenging, perhaps too much so. Frankly, I'm deeply concerned about your ability to handle this posting, although General Major Golitsyn himself insisted that you serve in this staff section. I screened your records. You have no formal instruction in divisional staff work, or special training in reconnaissance and intelligence collection or analysis. You have not yet attended a military academy."

"I am on deferred orders pending completion of my tour here," Donskov stated. "I passed the entrance examination just prior to my temporary service in the Caribbean, for whatever that's worth."

"Yes, and I am aware of commendations from the highest directorates of the GRU for your afteraction reports on the Grenada incident. But you must trust me when I say this—this is my second tour here in the south—Afghanistan is different from anything you've ever done before. It's a hell of a place to learn the reconnaissance business."

"I'll do my best, comrade lieutenant colonel," answered Donskov.

Verskiy gave him a searching gaze and paused a second or two.

I'll bet you'd like to see me screw this up, Donskov thought. Nobody likes a general's fair-haired boy. Well, I never asked for such consideration. Why has Golitsyn put me in this section anyway? Donskov had a strange feeling that the division commander was making a statement by putting a junior-ranking line officer in the vital intelligence section. His two new comrades knew it, and he knew it. But why? That remained to be seen.

"Well then," Verskiy said, "let's begin your orientation. Today is 9 January. By the twelfth, you will need to be ready to take over your shift. Naturally, Major Khavkov will assist you as necessary. But you must plan on intensive study of these relevant documents, regulations, and updates"–he indicated a bulging case of fat, red-bound books–"in order to garner an appreciation of our situation here. The sooner you're ready to take over, the better. Khavkov has been doing most of it; he cannot keep up much longer with only three hours' sleep a night. Indeed, I'm standing a portion of your watches right now, in addition to commanding the divisional reconnaissance battalion."

Donskov's eyebrows raised at that.

"That's right, comrade captain. The old divisional reconnaissance company typical to airborne divisions just wasn't enough. Our area of responsibility ranges across the entire country of Afghanistan. We needed more coverage, so we formed a battalion."

"So I assume," Donskov asked, "that the little regimental pathfinder platoons have been similarly upgraded into companies?"

"Certainly not. You see, Donskov, this is what I meant when I said you're going to have trouble learning on the job. Modern warfare can only be supported by highly centralized intelligence collection and analysis efforts. Haven't you ever read Reznichenko's *Tactics?* I can quote it for you: 'This requires *a high level of control* of reconnaissance.' "

Donskov sat dumb, suitably embarrassed. Still, Korobchenko might have thought differently. Centralization always presumed that a remote commander knew best; plenty of training and the snapshot of Sazhenev on Grenada made Donskov think otherwise. Donskov elected to play this one carefully. Acting ignorant and diligent seemed like a workable approach. I've got to figure out why I've been sent here, Donskov thought.

"Sorry comrade lieutenant colonel."

Verskiy smiled. "That's okay, Donskov. You'll learn. Now, where was I? Oh, yes. Let me briefly outline our situation here." Verskiy explained the "internationalist mission" of the Limited Contingent of Soviet Forces–Afghanistan this way: "to defend Afghan socialism against counterrevolutionary bandits and hostile imperialist interventionists." It sounded intentionally reminiscent of the civil war and the struggle against the Allied expeditionary forces of 1918–20, although no superpower had stood alongside the embattled Russian Communists in their grim duels with marauding Whites. To Donskov, the stirring words seemed to camouflage more suitable analogies to the Soviet role: Nazi Germans in Yugoslavia, the French in Algeria, or the United States in Southeast Asia. These appeared to be unhealthy portents.

In concrete terms, this internationalist duty required 40th Army and its supporting Frontal Aviation and Rear Services to seek out and destroy the wily mujahidin, hopefully in concert with the Democratic Republic of Afghanistan's diffident armed forces. By 1984, the Soviet ground forces entailed three motor-rifle divisions and a collection of separate combined arms brigades, motorized regiments, and special action elements. The bulk of these outfits faced the craggy, embattled Pakistani border, and thus created a shield for the principal Afghan roads and cities through an array of stout fire bases and an irregular pattern of highly destructive sweeps. From its Kabul pivot, the 103d Guards Air Assault Division served as the Soviets' mobile reserve, a flashing sword that lashed out from behind the oft-tested shield of motor-rifle troops.

Verskiy's comments about the enemy turned out to be surprisingly short. He pointed to a two-inch thick binder on Donskov's desk, labeled "Bandit Factions." Verskiy waved his long fingers absently at the stuffed notebook.

"You'll hear a lot about the various factions here. Let's be blunt. These fuckers are just another breed of the same rag-headed, slit-eyed Tatars that Russians always fight, and always have fought. You remember the Basmachi insurgents of the 1920s and 1930s? These are their sons and grandsons. I won't bore you with the laborious details of the shifting patchwork of bandit thugs out there. It doesn't matter. We don't have to understand them. We just have to run their black asses to ground and exterminate them, along with their CIA and MI6 bankrollers. The ones on our side, by the way, aren't worth shit. And that's their best point."

This emotional attitude, however satisfying to frustrated Soviets, disturbed Donskov. His disquiet did not rise from any nobler stirrings of humanity, but because he feared preventable military reverses. Korobchenko's favorite, Sun Tzu, had always counseled one to know the enemy or expect defeat as often as victory. Verskiy simply dismissed his foes as subhuman highwaymen. It's not that easy, Donskov knew. But he just listened for now.

"Terrain here comes in two basic types. Rugged mountains, branching from the great Hindu Kush, spread to the east and center. Around this vast massif, deserts stretch to the north, west, and south. The whole war revolves around control of the mountain valleys and passes, and the only vegetation and forests of note can be found there. It's very cold in winter and very hot in summer. The rebels and more than four-fifths of their black-assed countrymen live like rats out in the rocks, where the crags and weather chew up our tracks and helicopters. It would take two million men to secure the mountain areas; we have to get by with fewer then 100,000. Oh, don't forget the help of our socialist Afghan brothers, who seem to be the only towel-headed bastards in the country who *don't* know their way through these damned mountains."

Donskov waited. Verskiy went on. "Our division is pretty much a standard VDV unit, with a few modifications. Our three regiments each orient in a certain direction: 393d to the west, 583d to the south, and 688th toward the east, the toughest area. We occasionally get attached air assault regiments flown in from the USSR, especially when we lose the usual percentage of demobilized conscripts in July and January. Naturally we've centralized our ZU-23 towed air defense cannons and ASU-85 armored assault guns for duty at fixed installations and convoy defense. You'll find that we've had to strip some men from our fighting battalions to defend our headquarters and supply dumps; the rebels are very active at times, even here in Kabul. Finally, we don't jump here, but we work a lot with helicopters: Mi-8s for troops, Mi-6s for our BMDs and guns, and Mi-24s–"

"The Gorbach?" asked Donskov. He had worked with early models of this big, heavily armed attack ship in Pskov with the 76th Guards.

"Yes, the Gorbach. The latest models fly cover on our raids – the guerrillas hate them. . . ."

Verskiy's words trailed off. The colonel looked vacantly over Donskov's head for a few seconds. *Have I triggered some unpleasant memory?* After an awkward pause, Verskiy resumed his speech.

"Now, as to our reconnaissance assets, we work with my provisional battalion of four companies. One line company supports each regimental area, but I assign their tasks. Centralization is the key. Our electronic reconnaissance company works for us throughout the divisional area – throughout the country, that is. The regimental pathfinder platoons also report to us, and line units have been known to provide some useful data. I disbanded the ridiculous Pathan and Tadzhik militia scouts we used to have. You can't trust them. Of course, we also tie in with 40th Army Spetsnaz, agents, our KGB cousins, and even cosmic capabilities as needed."

Donskov nodded.

"With regard to operations to date, 40th Army divides the internationalist effort into three phases. From December 1979 until December 1980, large-scale Soviet conventional operations, spearheaded by desantniks, saved Afghan socialism and scattered the bandits. The Limited Contingent reorganized–"

Thanks to Korobchenko's many stories, Donskov knew that this meant withdrawal of untrustworthy Muslim Central Asian reservists deployed on the original incursion. Come to think of it, Kabul looked all too similar to Termez, Karshi, Khorog, Kerki, and other small cities of the Kazakh, Turkmen, Uzbek, and Tadzhik SSRs. Was it any wonder that the Muslims of the USSR saw no quarrel with their coreligionists south of the Oxus River?

" . . . and commenced a period of small unit offensive sweeps and attempts to build up a reliable Afghan Army. While our combined arms columns grew increasingly powerful, the counter-revolutionary fringes invited in CIA, Chinese, and British mercenaries. Their treacherous assistance beat back many of our motor-rifle drives and rendered our buildup of the Afghan Army stillborn.

"Finally, starting last April, we retook threatened Herat with the help of extensive aerial fire strikes, and thereby moved into a third phase of the war. Our motor-rifle elements assumed control of convoys and fixed bases, and VDV, Spetsnaz, and certain classified special forces cooperated in precision raids, well-targeted mass bombardments, and carefully timed offensives designed to destroy the rebel command and supply architecture. This is what we should have done first, in my opinion. But at least we're on the right track now. So here we are."

Verskiy finished abruptly. Donskov had heard much of this from Korobchenko, although his Ukrainian comrade employed a slightly different taxonomy.

"In the first segment," Korobchenko had said, "we refought the Great Patriotic War while the bandits hid and stole weapons. In the second, we refought the American imperialist war in Vietnam. Our motor-rifle friends swept aimlessly about while our socialist brothers hid out. Meanwhile, the guerrillas consolidated their hold on the countryside. Now, in the third period, the VDV and special warfare units carry the weight for the Afghan Army cowards *and* the lazy motor riflemen. The rebels are ready, we're confused, and it's all degenerated into a mess of accusations, burning villages, and bloodletting that even our most sanguine high party organs would not dare label victory. We may be botching it, Dmitriy. And it's all on the backs of the desantniks now."

Until he knew better, Donskov determined to give more credence to Korobchenko than Verskiy. Donskov had the premonition that in some senses, both might be correct, or worse, neither.

The colonel stood up, his chair legs grating on the concrete as he did so. "Now, if you'll follow me, I'll show you around the headquarters complex. I'll be back shortly, Khavkov."

The man did not turn around. He kept scribbling away. "Learn fast Donskov," the major hissed. "Learn fast."

❖❖❖

The forward command post of the 688th Air Assault Regiment squatted in the scrubby low hummocks and folds south of Charikar, just off treacherous Route 2. This asphalt artery formed the main ground link to the Soviet Union, connecting Kabul with Shir Khan just south of the Soviet border, and intersecting with highways that led all the way to Dushanbe in the Tadzhik SSR. Soaring cliffs, crumbling pavement, unexpected rock slides, and screaming blizzards dogged its 425-kilometer length as it crossed the unforgiving western extension of the Hindu Kush. Numerous bridges, cutouts, and steep embankments required trucks to mind their speed and stay clear of treacherous shoulders. Chief among these choke points was the impressive, Soviet-built Salang Tunnel, more than a kilometer and a half in length. Soviet soldiers enjoyed precious little time to marvel at this or other wonders in the majestic mountains. For 40th Army troops, Route 2 amounted to an ambush waiting to happen. Rebels debouched from their Panjsher Valley base camps to block the key constrictions, often with disastrous results for unprepared Soviet Rear Services columns.

The 688th operated around the highway, securing a segment between Kabul and Charikar. This relatively routine duty allowed the regiment to assimilate its new men, the January batch of conscripts just released from their six-months' prebattle training in the Turkestan Military District, USSR. Despite the realism encouraged at the Ashkhabad indoctrination center, veteran VDV officers wisely insisted upon a further few weeks of in-country orientation, centered upon small unit actions. This additional shakedown period facilitated integration of the new men into their companies, with a concurrent improvement in unit performance. Equally important to soldier morale, the assimilation phase convinced the fledgling paratroopers that they really might survive their eighteen-month combat stint, regardless of the horror stories spread back in training camp. As part of the battlefield orientation process, the 688th's airborne companies mounted limited forays against the guerrillas active along this portion of troubled Route 2.

Certain fruits of these martial labors caused Donskov to pay a helicopter visit on a February midafternoon. The Mi-8 supply pilot, escorted by a pair of Mi-24 Gorbaches, expected to be on the ground about an hour. Seeking a chance to escape his lightless hole and talk to some line soldiers, Donskov jumped when Verskiy suggested the trip.

The colonel hungered for rather esoteric information, as usual. Preliminary reports indicated that the Islamic Society forces, supposedly maintaining a truce with the Soviet forces, were in fact engaged in armed patrols around Charikar in violation of the agreement. With the truce due for review in March, Verskiy recognized an opportunity to improve his standing by a choice selection of evidence designed to assist the 40th Army staff in its upcoming negotiations. He wanted to deliver a firsthand account of these incidents to his superiors. True, this had little to do with the 103d Guards' situation, but that wasn't the point. Currying favor with the 40th Army's mighty intelligence chief, frosty Colonel Shtern, constituted Verskiy's real goal. Then let General Golitsyn try to change things! Thus far, the new commander had made no real moves, but Donskov's daily presence must have made Verskiy wary. What better thing to do with an energetic young captain than send him out on a short mission that could only serve to benefit Verskiy.

Donskov didn't care about Verskiy's career. He had already seen enough in his first month to convince him of two things. First, Verskiy did not know what he was doing, as far as his actual duty, at least. With regard to personal aggrandizement, however, the man was a master. His insistence on direct control and approval of every reconnaissance mission, combined with his restrictions on independent analyses by Khavkov and Donskov, resulted in a steady flow of late intelligence. Verskiy worried every scrap of information to death, holding up these vital pieces for days past their useful life. Thus, units in the division found the enemy the hard way, by getting bushwhacked, or more precisely, "rockwhacked." Desantniks could be sure that after they suffered attack, Verskiy could explain with relative certainty what had just hit them. It seemed like a hell of a way to fight, this wandering around until one got shot at. But the briefing charts always looked crisp, and Verskiy never had to take chances.

Verskiy had nothing to fear from the enemy he so disdained. He certainly did not bother himself to command his provisional battalion in the field, although he departed his desk now and then to overfly his charges during daylight, at very high altitudes. Of course, the divisional reconnaissance battalion floundered without any real command, its companies wandering randomly through the subordinate regimental zones in pursuit of bizarre tidbits of data to liven up Verskiy's carefully staged presentations for 40th Army and the division commander. Meanwhile, the overmatched regimental pathfinder platoons scrambled to locate their wily foes, usually by the traditional method–getting shot up.

Second, with Verskiy unwilling to attempt the tough job of locating the enemy, and skittish Khavkov merely going along with the colonel's pointless busywork, Donskov felt duty bound to try his best to understand and forecast the opposition's activities. Once the winter weather broke, the division would probably begin a big offensive, and then the 103d Guards would receive a lot more than nicely packaged old news. I have to be ready, Donskov thought, both for the men and for myself. Maybe this is why Golitsyn put me here. Korobchenko called him a clever general.

So Verskiy wanted some juicy anecdotes about the Islamic Society's truce violations? Fine, Donskov figured. This powerful guerrilla group, based in the immense Panjsher Valley, bore further investigation. Donskov deduced that if he could understand this strong enemy faction, the activities of the rest of the bandits might make more sense. If the quest got him out to the field for a close-up look at the business end of the division's inept reconnaissance effort, so much the better.

Thus Donskov found himself, AKD in hand, seated in an unheated little brown tent tucked into a rocky slope. Despite Verskiy's suggestion, he'd taken a rifle, not a pistol. If anything happened, he wanted a weapon he knew how to use. In Korobchenko's words, a pistol was good only for suicide.

The small canvas shelter, erected to house transients at the regimental command post, had been commandeered by the 688th's reconnaissance chief, Capt. Kiril Pavlovich Losik, whose pathfinder platoon had made four contacts with Islamic Society fighters over the past week. Of medium height, and a bit older than Donskov, the paratrooper officer looked careworn. His overwhites featured several rips and had assumed a yellowish brown cast, accentuated by the golden winter afternoon sunlight streaming into the musty tent. Not far away, half a dozen D-30 122mm howitzers boomed together now and then, pounding distant targets. The thunderous cracks occasionally interrupted the two captains as they settled onto precarious camp stools for their discussion.

"I appreciate you taking the time out from your rest, Kiril Pavlovich. My chain of command is quite interested in certain details of your engagements with mujahidin of Rabanni's Islamic Society."

Losik said nothing. His gaunt face showed the roughening of the winter weather. Donskov proceeded, his pencil poised in his gloved hand. The sunshine was deceiving; the temperature still hovered around freezing.

"What were the bandits doing when you ran into them on the night of the tenth?"

"Do you mean the second engagement in the series?" intoned Losik.

"Yes."

"They looked to be sketching a built-up bend in the road where the embankments are particularly steep."

"What happened?"

"The night was clear–the moon hadn't come up yet. We saw them with our night vision devices at about 800 meters. Two were drawing or taking notes. Another paced along the road, obviously measuring. One other man seemed to be in charge. I didn't see any enemy security teams. All three of my BMDs occupied hull-down positions and maintained surveillance."

Donskov wrote carefully in his notebook. It still jolted him to think of a regimental pathfinder unit mounted in BMDs. Thin-skinned, wheeled BRDMs usually transported such troops, and they often went forth on foot. But here in the south, soldiers had discovered that their faithful BRDMs could neither climb the slopes nor survive much of the rebel arsenal. So recon desantniks resorted to the heavier armor, bigger guns, and ample traction of BMD fighting vehicles. Of course, what sort of reconnaissance could be done from armored fighting vehicles? The sort of reconnaissance suited to mechanized combat in Europe, thought Donskov. But he didn't follow up that disquieting issue.

"Then what?" prompted Donskov.

"After we watched for about ten minutes, I sent my 1st Squad forward in their BMD to develop the situation. The platoon minus took up firing positions to cover the 1st Squad."

Donskov wrote, "One Sqd draws fire." "Go on," he said.

"We didn't see the problem until we almost ran over it. The guerrilla security team was in a culvert—they popped off an RPG before we saw them. The BMD took a glancing hit, broke its right tread, and stopped in the road. All of us opened up on the enemy troops, and I brought forward the other two fighting vehicles. They got away, of course, but we killed two and picked up their sketchbook."

"Yes," Donskov said, "I saw it before we forwarded it to 40th Army for complete analysis."

"We dragged in the BMD the next morning," finished Losik. "The driver died—his femoral artery was ripped open and we couldn't stop the bleeding."

"Tough luck," Donskov commented. Losik looked back without any notable emotion. What can I expect? Donskov thought. To him, I'm another rear area staff puke. This guy could care less what I think. Donskov pressed on, uncomfortably aware of his status as a safe headquarters man stationed well out of harm's way. "How about the fourth engagement, the one in the village?"

"That happened in the snowstorm on the thirteenth."

"You mean the fourteenth?" Donskov suggested.

"Right," Losik said with a nod and wave of his hand. "It's been a rough week. Anyway, I had the men dismount when we hit the abandoned village overlooking the big bridge just the other side of Charikar. We were out on the ground when my platoon sergeant saw the ammunition crates."

"Were those the 82mm mortar boxes you sent our way?"

"Yes," Losik said. "Now I had a squad out forward on security while we checked the stockpile for booby traps. Our BMDs waited about 200 meters behind us, engines running. The ragheads hit us there first. I heard a huge explosion – an RPG hit a fuel cell. That did it for my command track. We couldn't find the source of the round due to the blowing snow. It was just luck that my outpost caught that sixteen-year-old running by and dropped him."

"The prisoner?"

"Right. We bandaged him up and shipped him your way."

"He definitely worked for the Islamic Society. He didn't know anything, but we got a nice map off him," Donskov stated. "Do you think the attack was deliberate?"

Losik's brow furrowed. He wagged his head. "Who knows? The snow and all made it hard to tell. We got so wrapped up trying to extract the hulk of the BMD and the four wounded that I couldn't mount a pursuit."

Donskov wrote steadily, taking down the gist of all of this. "What do you know about the Islamic Society?"

"They're damn good. That hard-core cutthroat Massoud trains them well up in the Panjsher. We've picked up a few Chinese-made weapons and other stuff that came from Egypt, but not a lot. They're well disciplined; they clear off their dead and their gear. Even though we've had a truce in effect since last March, we know they've been training and helping their rebel friends. I'm not surprised they're out here along the main road. They're up to something."

"What?"

Losik's eyes narrowed. "You tell me, Dmitriy Ivanovich. *You're* in the high command."

Donskov smiled weakly, a bit forced. "You think they're going to take out a convoy?"

"Maybe," Losik responded. "I can tell you this – that truce won't be renewed. All we did with that year off was give them time to sharpen their knives for a real nut-cutting. We've got to move first. If you give these black asses time, they'll build a trap for us the size of the whole Panjsher Valley."

Donskov wrote, "local cdr expects I.S. atk vs. Salang rd." He looked at the veteran officer across from him. "I have a few more general questions, if you don't mind."

"Go ahead," Losik said.

"Do you have any Pashto or Farsi speakers in your platoon?"

"Of course not. They're all *centralized* at division and higher, you know," Losik said sarcastically. Donskov knew this to be true.

"How about Pathan militia?"

"Useless. These are Farsi-speaking Tadzhik types up here around the Panjsher. Besides, your colonel prohibited the use of local scouts four months ago."

"I know," Donskov said. "Would Farsi-speaking militia be of some help if you could get them?"

"Absolutely! I'll take any help I can."

This was obviously a sore spot. Donskov changed the subject slightly. "What is the mandated strength of your unit?"

"Two officers, twenty-five men, three BRDMs, and three jeeps."

"And your actual strength?"

Losik snorted. "One officer, seventeen men, three BMDs—all tired, all overworked. Four of my people are new conscripts; I already lost one from the January batch. We're configured to identify landing sites, not look for main force enemy units. I simply don't have enough men to cover the regimental zone. Therefore, we have to work mounted too often. We have too much ground to cover. So we drive around and find the bandits by getting shot to pieces."

"Do you ever get any help from the 3d Recon Company from the division's battalion?"

Losik shook his head. "Far from it," he said, "Your boys zip through our areas without coordination. In the last seven months, I've gotten only one report from them of any use. They call in air strikes we don't need to flatten places that aren't important. When they're not doing that, they're blowing the shit out of every nearby hilltop with artillery. All the explosives have completely alienated the locals. They tell us nothing these days. Those divisional assholes are fire-strike happy. They never check with us before shooting, either. We've had some close calls. What's worse, they love to race around in their BMDs, and so they give away my outposts and ambushes. My radioman shot one of their track commanders by accident two months back–crazy bastard refused to identify himself when he cut through our jump-off area. They're useless."

"What if you had a whole company of your own, with linguists and local scouts?" Donskov asked.

"Well, of course that's the solution. But as long as your cheese-eating friend Verskiy is the divisional recon chief, it won't happen. He's still fighting the big one against NATO or some such shit. Besides, he needs credit for a successful battalion command, even if he has to fuck the line regiments to get it. Have you ever heard about his field command back in 1982?"

Donskov shook his head.

"His battalion got surrounded on a hilltop landing zone well up in the Panjsher. The bandits, in fact Massoud's Islamic Society, pressed him pretty hard. Only about half his BMDs were on the ground. The rest went down or aborted. The transport helicopters really got eaten alive. Ammo started to run short late in the afternoon, and our comrade Verskiy started to lose his grip. He called in an emergency suppression run by a flight of four Gorbaches. The Mi-24s were flown by rookie pilots fresh from some lazy German air base, and those new guys overreacted. They plastered the hilltop, all right. Massoud's forces got strafed, rocketed, and cooked alive by napalm canisters. Unfortunately, the Gorbach crews got a little sloppy and burned out a company and a half of VDV. Verskiy cracked completely. They found him sitting on the ground bawling like a toddler. The political deputy took over, reorganized the battalion, and held through the night. They got picked up in the morning."

Donskov whistled. So that's why the mere mention of attack helicopters made the colonel so nervous. "What happened to Verskiy?" Donskov asked.

"Oh, you didn't know? He received an Order of the Red Star for his allegedly bold decision to bring in the helicopter gunships. His brother's position in the Turkmen SSR's KGB and his wife's connections to the Leningrad party insured that he was a hero, not a failure. He even flew back home for a big awards review."

"And the political deputy?"

"Killed, of course," sighed Losik. "He got hit during the extraction. Verskiy didn't even put him in for a medal; the regimental commander had to see to that. But our boy still needs another battalion, just to square the record."

Donskov made no response, but his serious visage prompted Losik to say more.

"Yes, brother, I know what you're thinking. 'I'll permit no Verskiys once I get a field command,' you say. Dmitriy, the damnable Verskiys run this whole circus. They *like* it this way; it's good for their almighty careers. You can't reverse the weight of political-military odds that have piled up against us while we drove and shot and choppered around as if we were looking for Hitlerite panzers. Do your family a favor. Hide out on the staff. This shit isn't worth it."

Donskov could not believe his ears. Losik had been out here a year or so, but this degree of fatalism surprised the staff captain. "I'm not married, and my parents are dead," Donskov replied. "So it will be the field for me, as soon as I can go. The staff is no place for a fighter, I'm afraid."

Losik chortled ruefully. "Then do yourself a favor. Stay alive. This war is lost."

Donskov looked closely at the tired recon officer. "Don't you think the recent change in Moscow might help? Maybe Chernenko will send in enough men to win this thing?"

Losik shook his head. "Wise up, Dmitriy Ivanovich. It may interest you to know that dear old Chernenko spent a few years with the Border Guards in the early 1930s, chasing Ibrahim Beg and his Basmachi up around the Oxus River. He'll never give in to these black asses."

"Give in?" Donskov blurted. "I was referring to an increase in our strength, to finish this job."

Losik laughed slowly, a low, haunting laugh that almost faded into groans. "You've been reading too much of Verskiy's shit. Even with two million men, we won't beat these people. These bastards fight for a living, and they'd be fighting each other if they didn't have us to shoot. No, the best we can do is kill them all, and our beloved leadership haven't the stomachs for that anymore. In Stalin's day, when Chernenko marched against the Basmachi, we might have exterminated every fucking raghead here, or at least enough to cow the wretched remnant into submission. But that won't happen today. Instead we'll just putter along here, bleeding and dying, until the magic day when some old geezer up in the Kremlin finally declares victory and pulls the plug on this fiasco."

Donskov sat, mouth open, staring. He had heard a lot of loose talk from Korobchenko, but this, well, this bordered damn close to treason. Losik's bright eyes and animated mouth indicated that it was no act.

"Shocked, are you?" remarked Losik suddenly. "Well, don't be. You spend a few months out here losing your men to an unseen foe that multiplies like rats, so scum like Verskiy can write themselves up for decorations and promotions, and you'll see things my way. Nobody's ever subdued this rotten country. Why should we be any different? Tell me, have you ever heard of the nineteenth-century British imperialist writer Rudyard Kipling?"

"No," Donskov said. Foreign literature, particularly from obscure capitalist authors, was not his area of interest. He recalled some old Tolstoy story about artillerists chasing Tatars through the Caucasus Mountains, and he remembered a tone to the story that mirrored Losik's disillusion. Still, the details escaped him. Losik spoke again.

"This British fellow knew what we were up against out here. Even at the height of their imperialist-capitalist development, the British never held this rock heap. Kipling wrote: 'When you're wounded and left on Afghanistan's plains, and the women come out to cut up what remains, just roll to your rifle and blow out your brains, and go to your God like a soldier.' "

"God?" replied Donskov slowly. "I don't believe in God. Do you?"

"I don't know anymore. But," he said in low tones, pointing out the tent flap toward the barren hills, "*they* believe. Maybe that's why they'll outlast us. Marxist-Leninist social science is no substitute for faith."

Donskov stared into the other captain's burning eyes for a few heartbeats, then closed his notebook. The interview was over.

Chapter Five

The Lion of the Panjsher

Captain Donskov met Gen. Maj. Feodor Ivanovich Golitsyn as ordered, six kilometers south of the Darulaman headquarters encampment. There, from behind a nondescript, bare knoll, six RPU-14 140mm towed multiple rocket launchers squatted in an open field of dirty snow. As Donskov drove up, a roaring ripple of sixteen rockets flashed up and away from each piece in the battery, the massive conglomeration arcing toward the low brown hills nine kilometers away.

The driver halted the jeep on command, about fifty meters shy of a short, stocky white-haired man in a thick, short overcoat and the standard gray fur cap. The older man had his back to the jeep and his arms folded as he watched the rocket artillery crews bustle to reload their tubes.

Donskov got out of the jeep and strode briskly over to the division commander. The captain saluted and spoke. "Comrade general, Captain D. I. Donskov reports as ordered."

Golitsyn turned slowly and returned the younger man's salute. "Thank you for coming out here. I didn't feel we could talk in the office."

The shaved hairs on the back of Donskov's neck pricked up. He suspected that this meeting would answer a lot of his questions, and the remote location lent a disquieting, conspiratorial air to this conference.

"Your man Korobchenko always told me that you were his best

student," Golitsyn remarked casually. "Have you heard from him lately?"

"No, comrade general."

"You'll be happy to hear that Sazhenev dropped the charges against your old company commander. I'm not surprised; everyone who's studied the situation admits privately that Korobchenko performed well, even heroically, in a horribly bungled effort."

The general exhaled slowly before he went on. The white cloud of breath hung in front of Golitsyn's creased face and dimmed his shining blue eyes momentarily.

"Well, you know how the army is. Korobchenko's a great field soldier, but all his mischief finally caught up with him. You recall that he was at the mandatory retirement age for a captain. Based on the innuendos swirling around this Grenada thing, his request for an exceptional extension was unfavorably considered by the office of the chief of the VDV, General of the Army Sukhorukhov, an old desantnik who never had much love for Korobchenko. So Korobchenko's finished. He'll be on the street by the end of the month. At least he'll get his pension."

Donskov listened. Given the gist of their final conversation in Cuba, he was not surprised by the news about Korobchenko. I ought to write to him, he told himself without much conviction. He dreaded confirmation of the Ukrainian's certain retreat into the bottle after his retirement.

Still, Donskov knew that this news couldn't be the sole reason for this meeting. Concerned as he was about Korobchenko, the here and now took precedence over the past. Donskov had not been called to this unusual site to discuss a mutual acquaintance. There had to be more. There was, and it came quickly, as Golitsyn lowered his voice, almost to a whisper.

"You must know, Dmitriy Ivanovich, that your staff supervisor, Lieutenant Colonel Verskiy, is utterly inept. He's a selfish micromanager more interested in polishing his image than in providing quality assessments of our opponents' strength and dispositions. I judge him completely unfit for duties at this level."

Donskov's face stayed set, but inside, he relaxed immensely. So

Golitsyn knows. At least everything is not hopeless. But, where do I come in? Donskov already sensed that somehow he would have a role in Verskiy's eventual demise.

"I am aware of the problem, comrade general," Donskov responded.

"Good," Golitsyn said. "And are you also aware that your lieutenant colonel is a Chekist?"

Donskov blinked, surprised. "Not at all, comrade general. I had no idea."

Golitsyn shrugged slightly, tilting his head. He gestured with his gloved right hand as he spoke. "Don't worry, you'll get a feel for this sort of thing after you're in the army a bit longer. Old Korobchenko could spot them kilometers away. In this case, it wasn't too hard to figure out. Lieutenant Colonel Verskiy is not exactly subtle in throwing his weight around. His brother is a very powerful man in the KGB, really going places. Verskiy, naturally, fell in with the Third Chief Directorate some time during his GRU training. Our friends in state security love to keep their secret fingers on every pulse. I think Shtern, the intelligence chief up at 40th Army, suspects the connection. That's why he kisses your colonel's skinny ass despite Verskiy's inadequate coordination of our reconnaissance efforts. Of course, Verskiy's primary target is me, and as you have no doubt guessed by now, you are my counterspy, my guarantee against this weasel. Verskiy's got helpers, and I haven't found all of them. That's why I asked to see you out here. My office is not secure."

Donskov hung on the general's words. Behind the two paratroopers the whipping thunder of the multibarreled rocket launchers swelled and rolled again, peaking in great cracking waves of detonations before dying away as the volley finished.

"Dmitriy Ivanovich, the division can tolerate Chekists, but not incompetent Chekists, particularly as chief of our second section. He'll have to go before we get very far into Operation MARS."

Donskov returned a blank stare. "Operation MARS?"

"Yes. Oh, I'm sorry. You haven't been brought in yet—look at that, here I go violating my own security strictures! Well, being a general must be good for something. So pay attention. You would have been briefed sooner or later anyway. MARS entails another major offensive into the Panjsher Valley, the seventh since the arrival of the Limited Contingent. But this time we don't simply want to kill bandits. We're looking to tear out Massoud and his key subordinates, his supply system, and his intelligence net."

"But comrade general, what about the truce?" Donskov wondered.

Golitsyn shook his head. "It's over. MARS goes regardless of what Massoud decides during the upcoming negotiations. He has repeatedly refused to expand the agreement to include our Afghan Army comrades, and you yourself know that his men have been tangling with the 688th already. He's had a free ride long enough. If we want to break this character once and for all, I need solid data, not the warmed-over horseshit Verskiy dishes up. Without a decent reconnaissance performance, MARS will go awry, and many good desantniks will die. And because you're a hard worker as well as my inside man, that's where you come in."

Donskov stood, waiting. He felt a slight trembling on his skin. A light breeze blew, but Donskov knew that wasn't it. The electricity raced up his spine. His stomach tightened into an iron ball, almost the way it had under fire on Grenada.

"Next week, I'm sending you into the Panjsher," Golitsyn said quietly, "as our contribution to 40th Army's truce talks mission. You'll accompany the Soviet contingent into Massoud's rebel den, watching all the way, of course. The information you bring back should spur MARS to victory. It will lay the foundation for a focused operation rather than another frustrating stroll through the rocks. What you see inside the Islamic Society in the Panjsher may furnish the insights we need to hit the critical rebel nodes."

"I'll do my best, comrade general," Donskov said.

"When you return," Golitsyn continued, "report your impressions to Verskiy and, secretly, to me. He'll create a pointless stew out of what you tell him; most of the stuff will never get off his desk. That's his normal way, you know. When the division hits all of the kinds of resistance he neglected to mention, your actual report will give me a sound basis on which to remove Verskiy. It will prove the poor quality of his forecasting in a way that even the KGB cannot contest. I've already chosen a good man from the 393d to replace that Chekist worm. You need only bring me an accurate account of what you see. I'll do the rest."

"Exactly so, comrade general," Donskov agreed, his voice much surer than he really felt. Although he appreciated the general's confidence in him, he had to wonder if he could deliver the goods. I'm an air assault soldier, not a spy or a counterintelligence agent, Donskov reminded himself. Yet, the challenge enticed him, the way challenges always did. Golitsyn must have sensed this streak in Donskov when he picked him. Donskov recognized the general's method; he'd used it often enough himself.

"Naturally, I'll look after you," the general added. "Following a transition period in the Second Section, and once MARS ends, I'll send you down to a line unit where you belong."

Donskov nodded, but a slight wrinkle creased his brow.

"Second thoughts, Dmitriy Ivanovich?"

Donskov shook his head quickly. "Not at all, comrade general. But I was wondering, won't Verskiy suspect something if I go? After all, I think he knows that I'm your man."

"A good question. Don't worry. I've already taken care of that. Tomorrow, the division surgeon will conveniently place a medical restriction on your comrade Khavkov—he has high blood pressure, you know. I will then order Verskiy to send a Second Section man with the truce team into the Panjsher. He can't send poor Khavkov, and he won't dare send himself. So you can be certain that, in fact, Lieutenant Colonel Verskiy will gladly speed you on your way."

Donskov had to admit that the old man had concocted a neat little scheme.

Golitsyn issued some parting guidance. "Pay attention; be careful. And remember, we never had this conversation."

"Exactly so, comrade general," intoned the captain. Donskov had a funny feeling that he might have just sold his soul, if he had one, that is.

"What is this shit?" murmured Major Begraev, the big, jowly tanker from the Second Section of the 108th Motor Rifle Division headquarters. Inclining his head toward the mat, he indicated a platter about the size of a manhole cover, brimming with a mixture of quivering, shimmering, multicolored slop. Some of the orange gobs might have been carrots.

"It's *torshi*—a dish of pickled eggplant, carrots, beans, and peppers," whispered Uvarov, the Spetsnaz lieutenant colonel and the most experienced field soldier in the delegation. "Eat it and smile."

"It looks like the experimental swill we fed the hogs back on the state farm," Begraev muttered. But he ate, grinning like a drunk with a fresh liter of lemon vodka. Opposite, behind, and to all sides, the Afghans squatted and sat cross-legged alongside the wide woven mats and blankets. The rebels smiled and dug in with their right hands—the left being reserved for other needs.

Donskov ate heartily, gobbling up the torshi and the main course, the *kabli pilau*, or rice pilaf, as the British called it: a rich brown rice mixed with almonds, raisins, pistachio nuts, and shredded carrots, all cooked in sheep lard. Uvarov, who knew such things, remarked later that Afghans served kabli pilau only to guests they greatly respected. Regardless of how much they hate us, Donskov supposed.

Along with the pilau, the VDV captain also sampled side bowls of hot oval millet bread, pistachios, peach pits, and dried chick-peas. After the grueling climb up into this unremarkable mountain hollow, Donskov's hunger overcame his nervousness. He didn't even consider the possibility that the food could be poisoned until well into his meal. Then again, poison would have violated Islamic custom, and although unbelievers, the Soviets were Ahmed Shah Massoud's honored guests at this early afternoon feast.

Donskov sat on the far right of the rest of his collective. To his left were big Begraev and the veteran Uvarov, then fat Colonel Mesropov of 40th Army staff's second department, a happy and thoroughly unlikely blond Major Pavlenko of the KGB, and finally, curly-haired little Major Milstein, a rated Mi–24 flier and political deputy from the 262d Independent Tactical Reconnaissance Helicopter Squadron. Mesropov led the Soviet officers. Every one of them, naturally, represented a leg of the power triangle as well as the local facets of the vast Soviet intelligence empire. So much for honest brokers, thought Donskov. He assumed, pretty much correctly, that his Islamic Society hosts represented the bandit equivalents of the GRU and KGB.

"Ah, my esteemed guests, the tea is here," said the dark-eyed, hook-nosed Tadzhik chieftain seated directly across from Mesropov. He spoke Russian rather well, thanks to an education at the USSR-sponsored Kabul Polytechnic Institute. The infamous Massoud, self-styled "Lion of the Panjsher," remained seated as his two aides brought wicker trays, each with six small white cups. While one man wordlessly passed a cup to Massoud and his main lieutenants, the other simultaneously gave the miniature containers to the Soviet visitors.

"I apologize," Massoud said. "Normally, our womenfolk serve, but we must make do without them, even during a cease-fire. Now, esteemed guests, drink a cup of tea to mark your visit."

The Soviets, raised as Russians to drink tea but used to toasting with vodka, drained the strong green drink from their cups. Massoud and two Afghans sipped a bit. Two put their tiny ceramic tumblers down without drinking, and one scar-faced, bearded old fellow sucked in a bit and then turned to his left and spat loudly. Although Massoud's smile remained fixed, his deputies' actions could not be mistaken. The silent crowd of Afghan underlings watched tensely during the whole tea episode.

Donskov did not realize it, but Uvarov later told him that even the very act of offering a single cup of tea represented a vicious snub, and was an indicator of Massoud's distrust. Neighbors always received three drinks of tea, reflecting welcome, friendship, and hopes for return visits. Massoud welcomed the negotiators, but these were not friends, nor did he want to see them again.

"Please, eat!" Massoud enjoined. "Later we will talk. But now, we eat."

With that, the tension broke, and the gathering resumed its agitated assault on the half-filled platters and bowls. Donskov grabbed another handful of pilau from a fresh batch. Though it looked the same, this rice was heavily seasoned. Donskov's tongue burned as he recognized the hot chutney sauce running through his dirty fingers. It made him wish for more tea, but he did not ask. I'll get to my canteen when this ends, he figured. In the meantime, he avoided the spicy pilau plate. Instead, he ate the bland bread, scooped at the torshi, and, as carefully as he could, examined the opposition.

They looked like apes imitating men, these Panjsher guerrillas, as they alternately picked and shoveled chunks of food off the trays. They chattered away in their strange Dari dialect of Farsi, a language Donskov had barely begun to understand. Long brown fingers, jet-black hair, dark faces, high cheekbones, that faint Tatar folding around their greedy eyes – their appearance marked these men as aliens and enemies. It was a visceral thing. Donskov knew in the marrow of his Great Russian bones that he was breaking bread with the wrong kind of people, the evil others who dared contend with the relentless Slavs for control of Asia.

The Panjsher men looked like fighters, ready to challenge even the great Soviet Army. Their drab clothes camouflaged them well, since the garments mimicked the prevalent browns and grays of the winter hillside. Most wore cast-off or stolen pieces of dark green or khaki Afghan or Soviet Army uniforms, interspersed with locally made vests and blanket-style robes. Many possessed high Soviet boots. Every man sported a head cover, ranging from a pillaged Soviet helmet through Afghan Army forage models and boxy Soviet fur varieties down to tied rag turbans and a very popular kind of locally made flat wool cap, almost like a floppy version of a Soviet sailor's dress headgear. Bandoliers, snatches of scrounged fighting harnesses, and an occasional set of binoculars distinguished many mujahidin.

Weapons were everywhere in the small hillside cutout. Donskov observed RPG launchers stacked carelessly against rockwork, along with racks of their deadly antitank rounds. In the distance, a potent DShK heavy 12.7mm machine gun draped with linked bullets stood on its tripod, unmanned but obviously sited for antiaircraft work. A box of grenades lay open and unattended near the tea samovar. It's like eating in an armory, Donskov observed.

Each Afghan cradled a personal weapon, even as he ate. Some

held well-oiled RPK and PKM light machine guns. The desantnik noticed AKs of every nature: old 47s, more modern AKMs, folding stock AKMSs, brand-new AK-74s, folding-stock AKDs like his own, and runty AKR carbines. A few men even carried elderly Lee-Enfield Mark IIIs, excellent sniping rifles. Beadwork, lovely paintings, bright green and red cloth wrappings, and waving tassels personalized these firearms. "Every Afghan has his God and his gun" went the saying in Kabul.

It all made Donskov glad that he had been allowed to keep his AKD, although his life was forfeit if he used it as anything more than a lap ornament. His thighs ached from the ascent to this meeting, and every so often, his more logical faculties reminded him that he and five men he barely knew were stuck deep in hostile territory, without a map, a radio, or any idea of their location. My life depends on the good nature of these brigands, the same bloodthirsty monsters who would just as soon poke a hot cleaning rod through my ears. Donskov nibbled almonds, nodded amiably at the curious banditry, and marveled at his own brash stupidity.

If one wanted to assess the rebels in the Panjsher, the previous three days had been a real education. Verskiy had badgered him to the last, insisting that he bring back certain ridiculous snippets of information "even on pain of death." Donskov merely nodded and left for the southeastern suburbs of Kabul, 40th Army headquarters at brooding Bala Hisar Fortress. The midday helicopter jaunt up to the agreed linkup point, a flattened hamlet, proved to be the only easy part of the entire undertaking.

No sooner had the helicopter clattered away than more than three dozen armed guerrillas materialized from the wrecked Panjsher village. Although both sides wore white arm bands, neither disarmed. The Soviets were, however, vastly outnumbered and therefore forced to submit to a virtual strip search. Recording systems, cameras, electronic beacons, maps, pens, pencils, notebooks, binoculars, watches – all went into a dark green bag, never to be seen again. Boots, belts, and weapons all were searched for listening and homing devices; the KGB major and political officer lost several apiece. The Afghans were not thieves, simply security conscious. "We give what you need, Russian," leered an onion-breathed old ridge runner as he filched Donskov's prized binoculars, a graduation gift from his brother. They had survived Grenada, and now they would serve a Soviet enemy.

Once the Soviet team had given up their record-keeping materials, the Islamic Society escorts and their charges set off on a rather circuitous route. Expeditious movement was not important; the goal seemed to be deception and confusion. The march up through the maze of mountain passes served this purpose admirably. The guerrillas pushed along well into the first night, halting only at sunset for prayer.

This had been interesting. The first time, the group stopped at a rather flat place on the slope. Donskov had been concentrating on avoiding the particularly loose gravel when he heard a loud cry, quite different from the steady grunts and sighs that had served as a background to the climb. The captain looked up to see and hear a strapping young man in a black turban bellowing "Allah o akbar, Allah o akbar, Allah o akbar," followed by similar gibberish. Every Afghan ceased moving as if shot, turned to the southwest, and prostrated himself. At intervals, by commands from the prayer leader, the bandits commenced a communal sequence of scrapes and bows mixed with chanted responses. Nobody bothered to watch the unbelievers, who stood dumbfounded in the midst of this display. The Soviet men said nothing; they dared not.

With prayers over, the formation had picked up and resumed its march as if nothing odd had transpired. The men finally stopped in a cave an hour before midnight. Again, the Muslims prayed. The bandits and Soviets broke open their packs and ate some cold rations in stony silence in the dark. No sharing occurred. Then almost everyone rolled out their blankets and collapsed. By previous agreement, each Soviet stood an hour watch to insure that one remained awake all night. "Just in case," as Mesropov said. The mujahidin also rotated about four sentries. It was best that neither enemy tested the other's good will too much.

The second day in the mountains had started with worship, and then breakfast. Donskov noticed that everyone ate Soviet rations, six meals issued in Kabul, the other thirty-eight assuredly stolen on Route 2. This day proved overcast and chilly, and a few snow flurries blew through as the group weaved over the narrow, twisting valley paths. Mesropov huffed and puffed, and Uvarov and Donskov ended up trading off the colonel's pack for much of the afternoon. Even the captain's own trained VDV legs felt this march over uneven, ever-upward ground, but the sight of old men and thirteen-year-olds padding calmly along beside him kept him going. Donskov grew to appreciate the prayer halts at noon, midafternoon, and dusk. Again, the men made camp just prior to midnight. Night devotions, rations, and a guard stint rounded out the exhausting day. With no sun all day and no stars this night, Donskov could not tell where they were going. Probably in circles, he guessed. He had kept count of his paces, but to what end?

The third day, after another religious interlude and more Soviet rations, the group had marched up again, winding through cold, snow-choked meadows and over logs across icy mountain streams. Telltale smoke cresting a ridge just before noon prayer told Donskov that they had reached Massoud at last. He gladly removed his pack and waited while the now-united band of guerrillas conducted their midday ritual. Only then had everyone sat down to share Massoud's food.

Three things struck him about the trip to the conference site. First, the guerrillas moved through the rocks effortlessly, like sure-footed goats. Their physical conditioning was awesome, a by-product of a primitive style of life spent wandering the steep Panjsher heights. None of them broke into a sweat, breathed hard, or even adjusted their haversacks, except after bending in prayer. Perhaps they were showing off, but Donskov's muscles told him otherwise. A century of industrial life, even the oft-maligned Russian and Soviet brand of industrialization, had taken a toll on the modern socialist man. The BMDs and helicopters were no substitutes for strong legs. To chase the mujahidin, one must march like them. Donskov himself, a trained paratrooper under thirty years of age, was not ready. How much less so the motor riflemen, the tankers, the gunners, and the soft Rear Services people? A look at his comrades showed him as much. Only hard-bitten Uvarov, the seasoned special forces man, looked unfazed by the walk up here.

Donskov's second observation was that the discriminating initial search and complex route showed a solid understanding of counterintelligence, and, by inference, battlefield tactics. Donskov knew that his instructors back at Ryazan, and especially Korobchenko, would applaud these illiterates' thorough attention to security. True, the longer movement gave Donskov a better look at the enemy, but he also had no idea of his position or any way to record spot impressions. Whoever developed these procedures knows his business, Donskov told himself. These bandits will not be easy to find and destroy, despite a lot of loose talk he had heard back in Darulaman. They have little education or technology, but their native cunning goes a long way to affect the correlation of forces in their favor.

Finally, the Afghans' evident devotion to Islam impressed Donskov. Losik had warned him about this. I must learn more, he resolved. These simple hill folk really have faith. We don't truly believe in communism compared to their fervor. Their powerful faith binds them together, just as communism is intended to cement all types of socialist collectives. But Marxism-Leninism is pretty thin modern gruel compared to this rock-solid medieval philosophy. Communism barely holds the Soviet Union together; Islam apparently crosses tribal, ethnic, and even linguistic lines. It is the one thing all mujahidin have in common.

Yet, Donskov reasoned, perhaps their belief also bred weaknesses. Two sprang to mind. In the tactical arena, Islam must serve as a pattern that regularized the otherwise mystifying Afghan activities. Certainly the mujahidin understood and capitalized upon Soviet doctrinal stereotypes. Did Islam furnish a similar systemization of Afghan life, liable to Soviet exploitation? Once the local varieties of Islam were understood, attacks could be timed to hit during the worship periods, or during religious holidays. Islamic "commissars," if such people existed, required particular attention.

Afghan Islam's second potential weakness applied more at the operational level. Donskov's study of history told him that any philosophy, whether Islam or communism, must have its splitters, Trot-skyites, opportunists, and Peking deviationists. Might these parallel the Farsi/Pashto linguistic cleavages or the ever-present struggle between Afghanistan's many minorities and the dominant Pathan majority? Could we turn them against each other instead of against us? He had heard that the KGB was experimenting with this approach.

Donskov pondered the possibilities. That crafty Chinese troublemaker Mao Tse-tung might have distorted Marxism-Leninism, but he obviously knew something about guerrilla warfare. He wrote, quite accurately, that insurgents are fish, swimming in the sea of the people. Thus far, the Soviets had alternated between ineffectual fishing and some arbitrary attempts to drain the water. What if, instead, we could get some fish to eat the others? Maybe I'm on to something that could help desantniks, not just Chekists, Donskov hoped. It certainly bore further investigation.

"So, now we talk, my esteemed guests," announced Massoud. Swiftly, selected Afghans cleared off the mats. A few lumps of spilled food remained behind on the off-white woven rectangles and brown army blankets. These were not rolled up, but remained to separate the antagonists.

"Allow me to introduce my comrades, Ahmed Shad Massoud," began Colonel Mesropov. "They represent our various forces with an interest in this truce. Major Begraev of the motor rifle troops, Captain Donskov of the air assault forces, Major Pavlenko of the Kabul advisory element, Lieutenant Colonel Uvarov of the Rear Services, and Major Milstein of the troops of transport aviation. We appreciate your kind hospitality."

Massoud smiled broadly, unaware of or purposely ignoring the bald lies. He gestured toward his five closest associates.

"Respected Colonel Mesropov, I also make the following intro-ductions. You have already met Asif, one of the leaders of my Central Forces, who took charge of your journey to this site. Also, here is Ayyub, a village representative. This is Balkhi, one of our Islamic teachers—a mullah, we say. Doctor Abdul Hay is my deputy. Lastly, our great friend, Allah be praised, from the Islamic party, Saleh Kakar."

The last looked a bit different, with a white turban rather than the flat wool caps or military leftovers favored by Massoud's men. Four large men with similar head wrappings and gaily painted AKMS rifles loomed behind him, obviously bodyguards. From Kakar's confused face, it was evident he did not understand Russian and probably not Farsi, either. He's a Pathan, Donskov guessed, though there was little physical difference between these men and Massoud's Tadzhik bunch. Here was factionalism, Donskov thought. But what to do about it?

Donskov also took note of Massoud's reference to "Central Forces." That suggested other types or locations of forces, and the concept of Central Forces implied a reserve role of some sort, perhaps even elite status. Maybe these are the Islamic Society's version of the 103d Guards Air Assault Division, Donskov concluded. Of course, he had to allow for Massoud's deceptive abilities. The Soviets had covered much of their true nature; wouldn't a smart rebel do likewise?

"So then," Mesropov stated, "when can we expect a widening of this excellent truce to include the defensive forces of the lawful Democratic Republic of Afghanistan?"

Massoud looked down briefly and stroked the tuft of beard on his chin. He looks sort of like Lenin from this angle, Donskov observed. The Panjsher leader looked up, straight at the 40th Army colonel.

"You know that we can make no peace with those devils in Kabul," Massoud said. "They have turned on their faith and their kin. Your ruling Communist party promotes national self-determination. Why do you interfere in internal Afghan matters?"

Mesropov tried a different tack. "Let us leave aside your country's civil quarrels for the moment. Can we agree that the current truce between the Soviet Army and the Islamic Society and its allies should persist?"

Massoud smiled. "We could agree to that, but I and my associates are not convinced of Soviet sincerity. You talk of continuing a cease-fire, yet you break it regularly. Your bomber planes and Gorbach helicopters indiscriminately attack peaceful villages–"

"They only return fire in self-defense," Mesropov offered.

Massoud snorted, then his grin returned. Donskov was beginning to understand that Massoud's smile did not represent pleasure, but rather the baring of teeth common to most hunting mammals engaged in a confrontation.

"I suppose," Massoud asked calmly, "that you know nothing of the great fire strike in the Anjoman Pass last November? A nomad band of four hundred or so died. That includes more than a hundred children."

Mesropov stared back impassively. Massoud went on.

"Perhaps you know something about the aerial minelaying last August north of Peshgor, in the sheep pastures. Thousands of your damned PFM-1 butterflies dropped into the grass. We lost many tens of guiltless boys and girls out there."

Mesropov just sat there, silent.

"Should I go on? Might we discuss your desantnik murderers' activities along Route 2, to include the rocketing of three settlements just last month? Or would you rather talk about the Osnaz man we caught in October, the one dressed in Afghan Army attire and claiming to be a defector? He almost wriggled his way into my presence, no doubt to kill me, but he made the mistake of wearing some wonderful East German hiking socks. He couldn't explain how an Afghan had such a nice pair of foreign footwear. He whined like a woman, also, when we shot him. Too bad. Your KGB assassins should be more careful. Should I say more, about the perfidious agents, the indiscriminate rocket strikes, the horrific helicopter strafing, the barbaric chemical clouds, and the illegal napalm? Or have I made my point about how you Russians keep your truce?"

"Really, Massoud, this is somewhat tiresome," Mesropov growled. A few Afghans who understood Russian shifted noticeably, fingering their AKs. Oh shit, thought Donskov, this is no time to stand on principle. But Mesropov went on.

"We also have charges of ambushes conducted by your men, to include an attack on a group of visiting Soviet Foreign Ministry wives in Kabul. Sixteen unfortunate women died in this terrorist action. Islamic Society rocket barrages destroyed a children's hospital in

Charikar in December. Your people destroyed an unarmed pipeline
survey truck near Route 2 as recently as the fourteenth of February–"

"Not to be contrary, my esteemed colonel, but do you not mean
a 103d Guards armored infantry fighting vehicle engaged in theft of
innocent civilians' personal property?"

Mesropov did not bat an eyelash. "Certainly not. I might add,
though, that the volunteer drivers uncovered a stockpile of 82mm
mortar rounds while going about their peaceful duties, just prior to
your treacherous, unprovoked attack."

Donskov could barely keep up with the swarm of lies and half-
truths spewed by both men. He knew the facts in many of the incidents, yet both men so twisted reality that little more than empty
shells of events remained behind, to be filled as necessary with
propaganda, in which all of one's own activities were lawful and ami-
able, and every vile enemy blow fell directly on defenseless women
and children.

Massoud held up his right hand. "Enough, enough. Let us grant
that you could be more stringent in adhering to the details of the
agreement."

"Not us, but you and your men," rejoined Mesropov, not giving
a millimeter.

Massoud sighed. "Whatever," he said. "Allah knows the truth,
and He alone wills as He must."

Both men sat quietly, facing each other. A few Afghans
whispered in their lilting Farsi. The Soviets sat like lumps of cement,
unmoving, following the example of their hefty colonel. This went on
for about five minutes, until the Soviet negotiator broke the impasse.

"The Limited Contingent of Soviet forces," Mesropov stated
casually, "would rather consider a six-month extension of the current cease-fire if the Islamic Society will renounce all support from
the United States of America's Central Intelligence Agency and the
United Kingdom of Great Britain's MI6. A public statement thereof
from your illicit Pakistani hideout in Peshawar, clearly identifying
the unlawful role of the imperialist secret intelligence services,
would be deemed sufficient proof of your good intentions."

Massoud drew a deep breath and exhaled it through clenched

teeth. His mouth smiled, but his eyes did not. "We in the Panjsher fight our own fight. I and my associates know nothing of this American CIA or British MI6. But we know much of Russian GRU Spetsnaz and KGB Osnaz, who have *not* stayed out of the Panjsher during this past year. I cannot make any promises at this time. I must consult with my political superiors, my fellow mujahidin, and my allies, like my great friend, Allah be praised, the honored Saleh Kakar." He inclined his head toward the visiting rebel leader.

"Then the Limited Contingent will await an announcement from your Peshawar organization," summarized Mesropov.

"If Allah wills it," Massoud finished. He stood up. "This conference is over. Asif will take you back down to meet your helicopter. He will provide you with a radio when that becomes necessary."

The Soviets stood up, tired legs burning with cramps from the hard march and unyielding rock seats. Donskov reached back for his rucksack.

"Allah o akbar! Allah o akbar! Allah o akbar!" came the call, familiar now, echoed by several mullahs among the hundred or so scroungy rebels gathered around the parley mats. The short ritual of midafternoon devotion followed. Only when it ended did the Soviet delegation depart.

It took two more days to work back to the valley floor, back down to the crumbling wreckage of the agreed village, the same one they had left five days earlier. Two Afghans with a chunky old R-105M were there to meet them. Milstein dialed in the frequency, tied in to the retransmission stations, and called in the extraction Mi-8 from Bagram air base.

The six Soviets and their platoon of Afghan escorts stood or sat in the silence during the hour or so before the helicopter arrived. Some of the rebels smoked, and exhausted old Colonel Mesropov rested on a flat boulder. At last, the steady thrumming of rotor wash reverberated up the valley, and everyone turned to the southwest. Milstein shaded his eyes.

"There he is!" the aviator yelled. Sure enough, the weak late afternoon sun sparkled on the Mi-8's buglike nose Plexiglas as the dull brown craft skipped toward them. Donskov was never so happy to see a helicopter in his life, although later events would make this entire trip to Massoud seem like a midsummer evening walk along the Volga River. The Soviets adjusted their packs and waited to leave this grim valley.

The helicopter settled into the flattened, yellowed thatch of last season's grass. Donskov and his comrades bent over and strode toward the open side door and the helmeted crew chief waving them aboard. A step up, a quick check, and the chopper lurched skyward unmolested. It flared out and swung around, toward the setting sun, toward Bagram and safety.

Donskov stole a look behind as the Mi-8 came about. Far below, every *mujahid* lay face down – prayer at dusk, of course. The helicopter sped away.

The captain arrived back in the staff office about 2100. "Comrade lieutenant colonel, Captain D. I. Donskov reports back to duty with the section," he said with a salute.

Verskiy scraped about in his flimsy chair, returned the greeting hastily, and leapt to his feet. "Not a moment too soon, Donskov. Assume your shift. There's much to do."

Donskov returned a vacant expression.

"Didn't you hear?" Verskiy exploded. "While you were busy sucking down rebel booze, that treacherous snake's henchmen destroyed a fuel convoy near the Salang Tunnel. I'll expect a full report on your experiences by morning. I need everything. There's a big push coming in less than a month. Khavkov, fill him in. I'm overdue for a meeting."

And with that, Verskiy tore out of the room, slamming the door behind him. Major Khavkov, his ever-present cigarette in his mouth, looked over his shoulder at the captain. He picked up his metal chair and spun it around to face his associate. "Sit down, Donskov, and I'll explain the upcoming show. It's called Operation MARS. . . . "

Dmitriy planted himself and listened, his face reflecting interest and even surprise as Khavkov told him things he already knew. Donskov heard only bits and pieces of the rambling speech. Instead, his mind drifted over his brief excursion into bandit country. How would he write it all down? He did not know yet, but he could be sure that his colonel's fate, a general's fate, many soldiers' fates, and not least his own fate all hung on those as-yet unwritten words.

Chapter Six

The Valley of the Shadow of Death

It's all gone wrong, all wrong," stated General Major Golitsyn, hands on hips as he faced the big easel that held the map of the Panjsher Valley. His dirty green and tan blotched camouflage suit reeked of cordite and spilled diesel fuel, pungent odors that hung in the dank air under the low wooden beams of the forward command post bunker. A wide, discolored brown patch spotted the general's left sleeve, a dried souvenir from the bloody demise of Golitsyn's radio operator. The general had removed his blue beret, but he still wore his dusty old fighting harness, to include his loaded Makarov pistol.

To his left, the 103d Guards Division's chief of staff, the impeccable Colonel Fominskiy, stood silently, his camouflage uniform still bright from lack of hard use. At Fominskiy's left elbow, bright-eyed Lieutenant Colonel Seleznev, Verskiy's successor as chief of reconnaissance, listened to the division commander. The officious Verskiy's swift, surgical replacement had proven the only success thus far in the badly miscarried Operation MARS.

Captain Donskov waited behind the chief of staff and the recon chief, his notebook open. He had intended to brief Golitsyn on some recent radio intercepts from the electronic reconnaissance company. Instead, he too faced the situation map and paid attention to the general.

"The bandits are calling the tune, not us," Golitsyn sighed. "They have done so since back in March, when they ambushed that fuel convoy near the Salang Tunnel. The pursuit and reprisal cost us the 393d, and we had to borrow that ruffian mob from Bagram to fill their role. Those scum—we would have been better off to fight short."

The general was referring to the notorious 375th Independent Guards Air Assault Regiment, the rump of the badly ravaged 105th Guards Air Assault Division, disbanded in 1980 following numerous battlefield reverses and a near-mutiny in an artillery outfit. All of the 103d Guards soldiers looked down on their discredited brother regiment, which had a bad reputation for atrocities against the Afghans. But thanks to the disruption caused by the unexpected Islamic Society attack on vulnerable Route 2, the suspect 375th had temporarily joined the 103d Guards. As expected, the 375th proved slow, undisciplined, and excessively trigger-happy around the already skittish Afghan civilians.

"So then, comrades, what has our far-flung collective accomplished?" asked Golitsyn, still addressing the marked battle map rather than his small audience of staff officers. "We've put 20,000 Soviet troops into this cursed Panjsher—our division minus the 393d, the rotten dogs of that bastard 375th, a crop of those road-bound slugs from the 108th Motor Rifle Division, the fancy rotor boys from the 56th Air Assault Brigade, the Spetsnaz, the KGB, Frontal Aviation with their fierce Gorbaches, Long Range Aviation's big blind Tu-16 bombers, the ration-sorters and time-servers of the lazy Rear Services, and all the rest of the fat, crawling things that drift along behind the fighters. And that's not to mention our superb socialist allies, the mighty forces of the Democratic Republic of Afghanistan, all 6,000 of those brave fellows, give or take the hundreds of deserters who left before MARS started. Oh yes, everyone made it into the big valley; everyone, that is, except the fucking rebel black asses, who probably laughed themselves sick watching our big red machine crunch up their valley, then scooted up and out to wait for their chances."

Fominskiy shifted his boots a bit nervously, with a sidelong glance at Seleznev. Donskov imagined what they were thinking—the old man has lost his edge. He's talking like a bitter conscript on the eve of demobilization rather than the commander of the USSR's premier airborne formation. Donskov recognized the tone, if not the words; Losik had spoken in the same harsh manner. Golitsyn continued after a short pause, his eyes still fixed on the neatly marked mapsheets.

"We've been in the Panjsher now since 21 April. Today is 4 May, isn't it?"

"Yes, comrade general," replied Fominskiy crisply, only too happy to deal with a concrete fact rather than this disturbing diatribe.

"Thirteen days of driving and flying and shooting and damn little walking, mostly by day. The Afghans own the darkness, and use it as they see fit. We're searching and pawing through their shit heaps, like detectives on the hunt for clues, and finding damn little. The locals stare holes in us by day and shoot holes in us by night, or whenever else it suits them. MARS is wearing our men down, while the black asses wait us out, holding on for the night, circling like greedy wolves, ready to catch us that one time our campfire burns low. . . . "

The general trailed off, his head lowered. The three paratroop officers waited for more; it came. Golitsyn looked up with a start and talked again, his voice rattling like an RPK-74 machine gun.

"And what have we done to speed the victory of Afghan socialism?" Golitsyn asked rhetorically. "First we used our armada of Tu-16 bombers to carpet the choke points with high explosives and incendiaries, which made small stones from boulders, heated the wreckage, and announced our coming like a fanfare. Our helicopter-borne detachments grabbed some random high ground here and there, making it easier for the watchful bandits to pick their routes around us. And then, having struck by fire and supposedly sealed our traps, we searched the valley bottom settlements, and of course found almost nothing—no warriors, no equipment. So we began scrambling up the slopes, our BMDs crabbing among the rocks. And when we found a few tiny caches of arms and ammunition, we blasted dozens of the mountainside villages—pardon me, 'counter-revolutionary logistics depots'—into dust. Thanks to mines, bombs, and shells, our comrades at 40th Army tell me we have generated almost 50,000 refugees, all enraged at us and eager to help the mujahidin. Naturally, we didn't nab Massoud or his ringleaders. The biggest catch we landed was the wife of a district economic chief. I should have known better; I knew the nature of our foes"–the commander averted the barest hint of a glance at Donskov–"but 40th Army and our brotherly Afghan comrades convinced me to follow the usual battle norms. So there it is."

Another wordless interlude broke the gush of speech. In the background, Donskov could hear the chatter of the night's radio traffic and the steady pecking of the First Section's old typewriter as the operations men plugged out the day's combat journal. The muffled noises of artillery grumbled down into the bunker.

"And how many guerrillas have we killed?" Golitsyn snapped, looking directly at his recon chief.

"Four hundred and twelve as of 2000 today," Seleznev answered after checking his notepad.

"How many weapons taken, comrade lieutenant colonel?" Golitsyn asked.

"Fifty-one, comrade general."

Golitsyn shook his head slowly, uttering a choking sneer of a laugh. "Yes, another glorious victory. Tell me, chief, how many desantniks have we lost to buy daytime control of a few patchy kilometers of the Panjsher?"

Fominskiy cleared his throat: "Sixty-six killed, seventeen missing, twenty-one died of wounds, two hundred and eight wounded, and fifty-seven nonhostile injuries as of 2000 today."

"And do those statistics include Sergeant Vasiliy Andreyevich Ulitsov, my communications specialist, killed this afternoon while we visited the 583d command post?" Golitsyn shot back.

Fominskiy hesitated momentarily. He checked his small fold-out pad again, as if hoping to conjure Ulitsov's name. "Uh, comrade general, I do not maintain a by-name roster. The Fourth Section has –"

Golitsyn raised his right hand. "Enough," he said. "I'm tired."

The trio of other officers could vouch for that. The lines in Golitsyn's face looked as deep as new spring furrows, and his sparkling blue eyes had faded to the color of dirty April ice. He looks like he's carrying all of us on the back, Donskov observed. Why in hell would anyone want to be a general? Yet almost all Soviet officers yearned mightily to be generals. Maybe they would not be so anxious if they could see this exhausted, dispirited, disheveled old man.

"Is there anything pressing," Golitsyn said, "anything that won't wait four hours or so while I roll out my blankets?"

Fominskiy answered immediately. "No, comrade general, normal combat routine." He did not seem aware of the grim irony of that phrase.

Golitsyn nodded. Donskov started to open his mouth, but Seleznev was watching, and gave a curt shake of his head. Not now, Donskov. Forget it. But the general had not become a general by missing cues, even when tired.

"Something of interest, comrade captain?" Golitsyn wondered.

"It's just that, well, comrade general, the divisional staff procedures require that the commander review all radio intercepts of tactical value within eight hours of collection," Donskov explained.

"Who promulgated those procedures?" Golitsyn asked evenly, knowing the answer quite well.

"You did, comrade general," responded Donskov.

"So I take responsibility for ignoring my own orders. You give it to the chief. I've already seen enough today. Insure that I'm woken in four hours, chief," finished Golitsyn. With that, the commander turned and departed, leaving the three officers behind.

"What's eating him?" Seleznev asked in a hushed voice. "You'd think he'd never been on an operation before. Didn't he command a regiment here back in 1980?"

"Certainly," Fominskiy retorted. "I think it's this Ulitsov matter. I heard that a sniper snapped the sergeant's neck while the general was checking his map. Nobody ever saw the mujahid who fired the shot; troops in the area didn't hear anything. Ulitsov bled to death in the command chopper."

"I've always heard that it's bad for generals to see the consequences of their decisions," offered Seleznev.

"Obviously it's bad for this one," Fominskiy said. "Maybe some rest will help. . . . Well then, Captain Donskov, how about coming over to my work area and filling me in on the latest radio eavesdropping?"

"Exactly so, comrade colonel," Donskov said.

The whole time he spent briefing Colonel Fominskiy, all he could think about was Golitsyn's haunted face.

"Donskov."

He stirred, pulling the covers off his head, staring into the unblinking yellow bulb of the bunker's light. He sat up, rubbing his forehead. Cadaverous Khavkov was kneeling near the captain's rude pallet. As usual, the major drew on a smoldering cigarette, chugging out wisps of bluish smoke.

"Yes, comrade major?" Donskov automatically checked his watch. Only 1037. He had almost an hour and a half left to sleep, unless they were moving the bunker, or an emergency had arisen. "What is it?" Donskov asked in a hoarse voice. "I still have some of my rest period left, you know."

"Forget your sleep," said Khavkov. "Get up and get dressed—roll up your shit. The chief of reconnaissance wants to see you immediately."

"What's up?"

Khavkov smiled faintly. "You'll see."

The major glided away, and Donskov rose to his feet, scratching his crotch absently. Damn lice, he thought. The captain's curiosity increased as he swiftly pulled on his clothes. Have I screwed something up? He wracked his brain but could generate no serious possibilities. It took him only a minute to pack up his blankets and his ground cloth. Around him, the inert bodies of other sleeping soldiers sprawled as if dead. He stepped nimbly over their forms and out of the warm sleeping bunker into the brisk midmorning sunshine.

A bright sun warmed him a bit, although he could see his breath. Donskov splashed some water at the washup point just outside. He shaved in minutes, swabbed off his teeth with a single swipe of his toothbrush, and then packed up his few toilet articles. It always felt better to clean up; it served as an anchor of personal routine amid the roiling, unexpected waves of activity provided on a daily basis, courtesy of the great Soviet Army.

Within ten minutes of Donskov rising, he stood before Lieu-

tenant Colonel Seleznev, the recently appointed chief of reconnaissance and the Second Section of the 103d Guards. Seleznev bent
over a map table, scribbling numbers on a small piece of paper.

"Comrade lieutenant colonel, Captain D. I. Donskov reports as
ordered."

The lieutenant colonel stood up, returned Donskov's salute, and
chuckled. "Relax, Dmitriy Ivanovich. No need to be so formal; you're
not in trouble. Far from it, in fact. Didn't Khavkov tell you?"

"Not at all, comrade lieutenant colonel."

"Be assured I don't just go around waking up hard-working staff
men for no reason. No indeed, Captain Donskov. It is my pleasure to
inform you that, at the earliest possible time but without fail before
1200 today, you are detached from the Second Section"–he paused
dramatically, a smile creeping onto his face–"and assigned to command 3d Company, Provisional Reconnaissance Battalion. Congratulations, Dmitriy!" Seleznev gripped the captain's hand and
pumped hard.

A field command! Great! But, Donskov caught himself, why
now? Why in the middle of Operation MARS? Something odd was
up.

"I serve the Soviet Union, comrade lieutenant colonel." Ah yes,
the standard answer. It definitely beat thinking, didn't it?

"Exactly so, comrade captain," Seleznev replied. "I wish I'd had
more time to work with you. You've got a real talent for the intelligence task. You know, the general thinks very highly of you. He says
that you'll be the best recon man in the division, precisely because
you think like a line desantnik, not a GRU spy. So he says."

Donskov simply stood there. He accepted the praise as awkwardly as usual. Fortunately, Seleznev had more to say, so no
response was needed.

"I should warn you, you're stepping into a tough spot. Golitsyn's
breaking up the provisional battalion. You're going to the 688th, as
a regimental recon company, with you as the regimental recon chief."

"Where's Captain Losik?" Donskov asked.

Seleznev looked away, then spoke.

"Nobody's heard from Losik's platoon for five days. They're

missing and presumed lost. Colonel Leonov requires a recon unit. Golitsyn and I were going to break up Verskiy's silly battalion anyway after MARS. This is a regimental war at best, and the colonels need the eyes and ears more than those of us up here at division. But Leonov's stuck with an especially tough mission tonight, and he needs a recon company now, so—"

"So the reorganization is effective today, and I'm to implement it," Donskov surmised.

"Right. You're the man; we all know it. It won't be easy. But you've heard the saying: If you fear the wolves, stay out of the forest."

"I'll do my best, comrade lieutenant colonel," Donskov replied.

"Of course, Dmitriy Ivanovich. I'll be looking for great things from the new 688th Recon. Good luck," concluded Seleznev.

"Thank you, comrade lieutenant colonel," said Donskov. He left immediately, heading out into the forest of stone, out among the wolves.

"We can't do it, comrade captain. We're not trained for it."

Senior Lieutenant Molodets sounded adamant, and the expressions on the faces of four of the other five officers showed that they agreed with the political deputy's summation. Only the short, muscular 1st Platoon commander, Savitskiy, displayed any evidence of dismay over Molodets's pronouncement.

Rain drummed steadily on the tarpaulin stretched behind the command BMD. The sunny morning had given way to a dreary, chilly late afternoon, all too closely mirroring Donskov's sinking spirits as he acquainted himself with his new company. Few men moved along the irregular perimeter of Fire Base Emerald, home of the 2d Battalion, 688th Guards Air Assault Regiment, site of two batteries of 122mm howitzers, and temporary stopping place for the newly designated regimental reconnaissance company and its equally new commander.

There was damn little time for amenities, what with the pressure of the 1930 departure time. The captain's rapid transfer from the divisional staff had come about not by careful calculation but because of an unexplained accident in the 688th zone of action, near the Chamar Pass.

A big Tu-16 bomber had gone down around dawn, breaking into four major clots of wreckage surrounded by an irregular carpet of shining metallic shreds. The six-man crew did not survive the disintegration. Unfortunately, much of their bomber's cockpit structure, replete with the latest secure-voice communications modules and an advanced radar-jamming pod, withstood the impact all too well. Frantic Long Range Aviation commanders beseeched 40th Army to secure the wreckage before it passed into the hands of the curious Afghans and their presumed CIA and MI6 associates.

The army headquarters consulted their situation maps and passed the urgent mission to an eleven-man Spetsnaz element that controlled air strikes in the Chamar Pass. Of course, these hard soldiers moved on foot, and they could not hope to remove the heavy electronic components without help. The special forces reached the shattered cockpit chunk by 0900, and immediately fell into a long-range sniping duel with a shadowing group of Islamic Society rebels. An attempt to bring in an Mi-8 helicopter failed due to heavy ground fire, including SA-7 Strela heat-seeker missiles. A string of strong air strikes pummeled the growing band of mujahidin that hemmed in the Spetsnaz and their treasures.

Faced with an accident that had now mushroomed into a crisis, 40th Army turned to its nearest available line unit, the 103d Guards. Division commander Golitsyn alerted the 688th Regiment, whose 2d Battalion's Fire Base Emerald lay only eight kilometers from the Tu-16's valuable carcass. Six of Col. Ivan Sergeyevich Leonov's nine airborne companies were dispersed on village and cave searches, and two of these had met substantial resistance. The other three companies guarded their battalion fire bases and were not available for service.

Normally, the regimental recon unit would have been employed. But reliable old Losik had been swallowed up by the heartless Panjsher, and thus Leonov had demanded a piece of the provisional reconnaissance battalion. Anxious to accomplish the task and already committed to dissolution of the unlamented Verskiy's cumbersome divisional recon force, Golitsyn had detached the erstwhile 3d Recon Company to Leonov. Donskov was inserted as insurance, an officer expected to make things happen. Only the general and the captain understood that this surprise assignment fulfilled part of an earlier bargain. Golitsyn alone knew that the posting constituted part three of a character test begun months before in the Caribbean.

It had taken only a few hours for Donskov to fly out to his new regiment. A soldier from the 688th's headquarters met him as he ran off the helipad, and the man motioned Donskov into the nearby command post bunker. Almost everyone looked up when he came in.

Tall, distinguished Colonel Leonov strode forward. After an exchange of salutes, the colonel drew his new recon chief over to the situation map. "Glad you're here, Dmitriy Ivanovich. We don't have much time."

With that brief introductory remark, the regimental commander launched into an explanation of the mission at hand. Leonov spoke for about five minutes in his usual measured, pleasant tones. He sounded absolutely relaxed, as if describing last week's soccer match rather than outlining a critical combat tasking. He finished by saying, "You've got to get up to the crash site tonight or we'll lose the Spetsnaz men *and* the Tu-16 materials. The bandits are already all around them. I know that this is no way to assume command of a new company, but I couldn't truly trust the old commander, and my man Losik is gone, probably forever. So you're it."

It had taken about another half hour to receive inbriefings from the remainder of the regimental staff. Donskov took careful notes, but he really heard very little. All he could see was a very tough mission, a unit of unknown quality, and hardly any time.

Welcome to Operation MARS, Donskov! Here's a forward detachment job that you might enjoy. Grab hold of your surly new company and push eight kilometers up an unexplored narrow side valley, at night to boot. Link up with a threatened special forces team you've never met, and then defend the crash site until the 2d Battalion can come forward at dawn to relieve you and protect the helicopter extraction of the classified items. Don't mind the foul weather or the stalking Tatar bandits determined to cut off your balls.

It occurred to Donskov, somewhere in the back of his mind, that this sort of haphazard introduction to battle was how novice wartime company commanders got killed. Grenada offered poor preparation for this, and the visit to Massoud had only deepened Donskov's awareness of the opposition's cunning and determination. Surely, if he took a slug in the head, some post-mission analyst would write as his epitaph: "Another smug staff hotshot killed by wily guerrillas."

And now, with the weather gone to hell and the merciless clock ticking down, Donskov was finding out about his command. Having presented the mission, he faced his political deputy, three platoon commanders, artillery observer, and air controller. When Donskov simply stared at their hostile faces, pasty-faced Molodets repeated his assertion.

"Really, comrade captain, I don't believe you know what you're saying. Moving dismounted at night through these mountains is a Spetsnaz duty. But for the likes of us, it's simply suicidal! It's just not done."

Donskov responded, parrying the political officer with a question of his own. "What do you propose?"

Molodets smiled a half-smile, showing a row of even, yellowing teeth. "Captain Pliyev, your predecessor, drilled us extensively to function as a mounted forward detachment. I recommend we make the approach march in our BMDs. It increases available firepower, provides armored protection for our paratroopers, and allows for rapid maneuver in the event of an ambush. That's how we're trained and equipped, comrade captain."

Donskov gazed down at his marked mapsheet, spread on the damp dirt between him and his officers. Sulking Captain Pliyev, a man described by Colonel Leonov as "a sycophantic little shit," was gone, but regardless of what Donskov thought, he was saddled with Pliyev's methods because there was not time enough to make any changes. The captain put his head to his chin, then spoke, not bothering to look up.

"Opinions, comrades? Mounted or dismounted? Third Platoon?"

Big, slow-talking Ivolukhin replied instantly: "Mounted."

"Second?"

Hairy, dark-eyed Karpov nodded his head: "Mounted, comrade captain."

"First?"

Jug-eared, broad-shouldered little Savitskiy furrowed his wide brow. "I'd like to try a dismounted effort. This rain would cover our movement nicely. But I must confess that my men are not physically ready to march across the ridges to the objective. I must agree with the other two platoon commanders. Go mounted."

Donskov waited. The rain splattered on the taut canvas. Nobody else spoke for a minute.

"God of war? Nothing from you?"

Senior Lieutenant Menzhinskiy twitched noticeably, obviously not anticipating this query. He never said much in orders groups; instead, he had listened to Pliyev and plotted fires as he saw fit. Pliyev had never cared about his artillerists' ideas. The former commander merely used to point at the map and order Menzhinskiy to conjure up fire strikes. Now this Donskov wanted a tactical opinion.

"Well, comrade captain, I . . . uh, I really am not versed in these maneuver unit matters. Fire Base Emerald can support either a mounted or dismounted approach march."

The captain did not raise his eyes. "Mounted or dismounted, comrade gunner? I know the range characteristics of our batteries. You've served four months out here. Draw on your experience. Mounted or dismounted?"

Menzhinskiy's voice wavered very slightly as he chose his words. "Comrade captain, I must recommend a mounted march. I, uh, have never been on a dismounted movement."

Great, thought Donskov. Exactly what I suspected. But he kept his composure.

The aviation officer spoke up next, without prompting. "I recommend mounted, too. That's the way we always do it," offered Senior Lieutenant Suslov. "And I want to add that we may well need our BMD cannons. With this rotten weather, most of the air regiments are grounded. The 688th Regiment can call on a limited number of all-weather sorties, and they've been given over to the Spetsnaz at the crash location. We won't have any night bombardment or chopper help until we link up, I'm afraid. Unless we really get into the shit, I mean."

Donskov jerked his head up from the map as Suslov completed his comments. "Well, then, the collective has little choice. So it will be a mounted move. I think you all realize that this is the wrong way to fight Afghan bandits."

He saw Karpov and Ivolukhin exchange knowing smirks. He'll find out, they no doubt told themselves and, by grimaces, each other.

"Assuming we get through this one—and that will take more luck than I prefer to count upon—you can all plan on an extensive retraining period when we return. Captain Pliyev had his methods. I have mine. But for now, we'll follow the familiar script."

Donskov paused, then glanced toward Molodets. Strings of pale blond hair clung to the political deputy's forehead. Let's get the ball rolling, Donskov thought. What have we got to work with? The fact that the political officer was the only deputy in the field boded ill. But Donskov was dismayed by how bad things turned out to be in his company.

"What's our strength, deputy?"

"Eight BMDs, forty-nine officers and men," Molodets said softly.

Donskov asked the inevitable next question. "Our strength is listed at regiment as seventy-four men and ten BMDs. Where is the balance of our forces?"

"Well, comrade captain, two BMDs are down for mine damage, one each from the 2d and 3d platoons. They're back at Bagram, along with twenty-five troops. The company rear area is there. Our deputy commander, Senior Lieutenant Balashov, and Company Sergeant Major Kabanovskiy are at Bagram to coordinate support functions. Captain Pliyev preferred a sound, well-organized rear area."

"What are twenty-five troops doing at Bagram?" Donskov asked, trying to keep his voice under control.

Molodets plucked a small notebook from his camouflage suit. He opened it and read: "Two lightly wounded and recovering, four accompanying BMDs under repairs, sixteen on sick list, plus the sergeant major, the deputy commander, and their radio operator."

"That sick list seems awfully large," Donskov remarked with a bit more disgust than he wanted to show.

"Well," Molodets said, "Captain Pliyev tried to take special pains with soldiers about to be demobilized, if you know what I mean."

Donskov understood immediately. Pliyev had held back troops due for July departure, a favor to "build morale," of course. Battle requirements and the morale of those men left to shoulder additional loads obviously did not affect Pliyev's reasoning. All right, I've heard enough, Donskov decided. Let's end these painful preliminaries.

"Understood, comrade senior lieutenant," Donskov responded neutrally. He checked his watch. "Time now is 1647. Operation order here at 1720. That will be all."

The officers stood up, shouldering their AKR carbines as they rustled out from under the canvas. The rain had not abated. Donskov was left alone with his map and the crackling remote radio set tied to his BMD by a thin black wire. He opened his notebook and began to study the map when he heard a thin, reedy laugh just in front of his tracked command vehicle. The captain's ears tuned in. It sounded like Molodets and Ivolukhin.

"Another staff hero here to win the war," Molodets's tinny tone was unmistakable.

"Fuck him. He'll soon change his tune," Ivolukhin replied.

"Or die," said Molodets.

"Either way, it won't last."

Sloppy footsteps of boots on wet, oozing dirt followed the exchange. The two officers had gone.

Donskov wanted to race outside and reprimand them, but he held back. There would be time for that later. For now, he turned to the knottier problems of accomplishing a difficult mission and keeping his ill-trained charges alive, all the while hamstrung by decisions he had not made. It was a good thing he had so much to do, or the desire to hurt someone for all of this laxity might have consumed him. Somehow, Donskov both realized and feared that Massoud's ragged warriors would do the hurting for him.

Cold rain dribbled off his helmet and down his neck. The radio hummed in his ears, all that he could hear over the rumbling V-6 diesel engine roaring in back of him as he turned in the turret hatch. He could see almost nothing in the black, wet night, except another squat BMD pitching along just behind him and the dark flanks of the rocky, shrub-encrusted walls of the gully that the recon company traversed. Donskov trusted that the other six armored fighting vehicles were still back there. Nobody had broken radio silence, so he had to assume that they trundled along behind him.

Donskov's map study told him that if he stuck to this twisting ascending crevasse, he would emerge just shy of the shelf of rock that held the Spetsnaz and their important jet parts. Supposedly, the speed gained by driving right up this obvious approach outweighed the dangers of giving the steep, high ground to the mujahidin. Of course, in normal Afghanistan recon work, getting ambushed meant locating the elusive enemy, so such baiting tactics made sense. In this case, it begged for an undesirable rebel response.

The rain made a bad job worse. It stung the eyes and degraded the starlight scopes, infrared vision systems, and thermal imaging devices. The air controller, artillery observer, and political deputy were sitting on the open cargo hatch, with their legs dangling into the troop bay behind the turret. They craned their wet heads here and there as they tried to see through the drenching night. Below the slick, dull green metal deck, Donskov's radio operator and bodyguard nestled in dry discomfort, crammed into the two seats on either side of his turret. The BMD driver, Corporal Padorin, sat forward of the turret. Donskov resolved to do something about this private army of retainers bequeathed by Pliyev. But for now, they filled their usual roles.

The captain clung to the wet, slippery lip of his turret hatch, bouncing from side to side as Padorin chewed his way over the wet rocks. Streaming water trickled into his ear canals and dripped from his nose, which was also running with mucus. When he wiped his nose on his soaked sleeve, all he did was trade warm snot for cold rainwater. He was absolutely miserable.

Maybe if we can't see them, they can't see us, Donskov hoped. But they can hear us, and all we can hear are our engines. There's another "benefit" of using BMDs. Padorin came on over the intercom with the odometer reading: "Two kilometers." So far, so good.

The radio, which shared the headset with the BMD's intercom, stuttered to life. "Eagle Base, this is Javelin Leader. Over."

The Spetsnaz commander was calling the 688th. Donskov monitored the frequency but remained shrouded by radio silence.

"This is Eagle Base. Over."

"This is Javelin Leader. Situation report: as before. Over."

"Confirmed. Out."

So they were still up there. Hold on, we're coming. Donskov estimated he'd be in their vicinity before midnight. He checked the pouch inside the turret rim. Two green flares waited there, for use as recognition signals during the linkup. I wonder if the rebels . . .

Without warning, the track jolted hard and rocked to the right. It stopped. "Comrade captain, there's a big hole or something up here. I need a ground guide to take a look."

"Wait a minute," Donskov answered. Here was a good chance to check the column. Donskov turned around and snagged Molodets. He put his mouth directly up to the political deputy's ear: "You take my headset. I'm getting out for a minute to check an obstacle."

Molodets nodded and reached for the radio rig.

Donskov then pulled at the shoulder of Suslov, the flier. Again he hollered right into the man's ear in order to overcome the noise of the idling diesel engine. "Hey, red falcon, get down and run the column. Make sure we're all here, and make sure each track puts some desantniks out for local security."

The air force officer looked horrified, as if to say that he did not do such things.

Well, flyboy, thought Donskov, you can't get us any sorties in this rain, so make yourself useful. He leaned over to the flier again. "Let's go, Suslov!"

The aviator clambered up and out of the cargo opening, his little AKR smacking on the wet metal as he jumped down into the gravel.

Donskov had one other thing to do. He ducked into the tiny turret and saw the wide eyes of his radio operator, Junior Sergeant Goshov, barely visible in the telltale luminescence of the radio dials. "Come up top and man the turret. I'm getting off for a few minutes."

"Exactly so, comrade captain."

Donskov went up and out, and Goshov stood up in the turret.

The commander walked forward. Padorin's helmeted head poked out of the hull just under the BMD's 73mm gun barrel. Donskov tapped him on the head as he stepped forward.

Whoa! What the . . .

Donskov's foot slipped and he threw up his arms and went skidding a few meters over sharp rocks into a crater of some sort. His AKD fell loose, connected only by the "dummy cord" he had thankfully used. When he stopped sliding, he immediately reeled in his autorifle like a metal fish. The sure grip of his weapon helped him orient his rain-dulled senses. He sat there on the wet boulders and checked. Nothing broken. The water fell in sheets, and he heard the BMD engine throbbing through the darkness. He flicked on his red-filtered penlight for a look around.

Yes, I'm definitely in a bomb crater. Some lucky pilot put one of his babies right in here. Luckily, it had happened some time ago, and stones and brush had filled in the once-pronounced depression, smoothing its edges. Donskov guessed that the BMDs could handle it. He rose to his feet and carefully traversed the few uneven meters back up the incline to his armored vehicle.

Back in front of his BMD, he tapped Padorin again, who raced the engine in response. Then Donskov moved to the track's side, put a foot onto the still tread, and boosted himself up to the deck. Suslov was back. "All okay, comrade captain. Security was out. I told them we had a drop-off ahead, and to mount up when they saw us move."

"Good work," said the captain, clapping Suslov on the shoulder. The aviation lieutenant had done the right things. Well, maybe it wasn't hopeless. Donskov displaced Goshov and retrieved his headset from Molodets. "Anything up?"

Molodets shook his head. Donskov plugged back in. "Okay, Padorin, now take it slow."

At the very end of the column, 3d Platoon's second track stayed in place. Its driver had fallen asleep and the 3d Platoon sergeant had closed his hatch to stay dry as soon as Senior Lieutenant Suslov had come and gone. The sergeant assumed he would hear the other BMDs revving their engines when they left. Instead, mesmerized by the steady rhythm of their own diesel, unwarned by the dazed trio up in the cargo hatch, the squad in this armored vehicle lost touch with their fellows.

The rain washed over in torrents, chilly and thick. It reminded Donskov of standing in a huge cold shower. He could barely make out the luminous dial of his watch: 2135. Padorin had just marked five kilometers. Considering that a man could walk at least four kilometers an hour on level ground and two even along the spur trails of these awful mountains, the BMDs were not making much speed compared to a theoretical dismounted effort. If we make this trip without a disaster, I vow I'll never go on another such jaunt. Hopefully, the rain will save us from the rightful consequences of our own laziness.

"Sparrow Leader, Sparrow Three Leader. Message. Over."

Donskov stood up and instinctively pushed the earpiece onto his wet head. Why was Ivolukhin breaking radio silence?

"This is Sparrow Leader. Send it. Over."

"Sparrow Leader, Sparrow Three is missing its Sparrow Three Two element. Over."

Donskov's mouth dropped open, an act rewarded by a few droplets of icy rain on his tongue. What was the 3d Platoon commander doing? That incompetent clown! But Donskov reacted with coolness. What good would anger do at this point?

"Understood, Sparrow Three Leader. When did you last see the Three Two element? Over."

The radio hissed in silence, then Ivolukhin's deliberate speech pattern came through. "Sparrow Leader, I last saw him at the halt. Over."

The halt! That was more than an hour ago. Donskov slammed his hand on the turret ring in wordless frustration. Meanwhile, Padorin chugged onward, each meter pulling the company farther away from its lost sheep.

"Sparrow Three Leader, this is Sparrow Leader. Try three calls to raise him on his net. He should be monitoring. If not, there's nothing we can do for him now. Sparrow Leader. Out."

Donskov endured the next few minutes in pained silence. Ivolu-khin called once. No answer. He delayed a minute or so, then called again. Nothing came back. After a few minutes, a third attempt also failed. Donskov made no call to Ivolukhin. His stray BMD was on its own now.

"Six kilometers," remarked Padorin nonchalantly. The engine rumbled and the rain poured.

At seven kilometers, Donskov contacted Javelin Leader, as arranged. "Javelin Leader, this is Sparrow Leader. Yellow. Over."

"This is Javelin. Understand yellow. Out."

The code word meant that they were within a kilometer, on the agreed route. Javelin was supposed to notify Donskov if the rebels were active. Donskov took the lack of any such information to mean that the way was clear up to the shelf. Once within 500 meters, the recon commander would fire his two green flares to facilitate posi-tive recognition at the linkup.

The horrible, streaming, pelting rain had done the desantniks a good turn. Now there remained only the actual joining up and then the establishment of an all-round defense until daybreak, when the helicopters could fly in. The rain was forecasted to end around sunrise.

Only the case of the wandering 3d Platoon track marred the wet but otherwise benign approach march. That squad would probably show up at daybreak, Donskov figured, sheepishly awaiting their reprimand, just like on exercises. He leaned back against the biting rear edge of the turret aperture, remembering an incident back in his own platoon commander days, when that irascible Sergeant Oronodze . . .

A scintillating blue flash severed his reverie. The track halted with a horrid forward lurch, flinging Donskov clear of the turret. His intercom wire broke in two as he rolled off the tilted wet deck, his AKD slithering behind him on its faithful cord. His helmet fell over his eyes as he hit the harsh rocks alongside his stricken BMD. The awful smell of burning diesel filled his nostrils. And when he shoved his helmet up he could see his BMD quite clearly, thanks to the yel-low light of its blazing fuel cells.

Two more BMDs were also burning. The bandits had caught the column on a curve, so Donskov could see only four of his tracks. Only the fourth one was not on fire, and its 73mm cannon was aimed upward, lobbing low velocity shells at unseen enemies. The cannon could not elevate much past thirty degrees, so most of these rounds pounded uselessly into the hillside.

Paratroopers were climbing off the burning wrecks, shouting, shooting wildly into the dark, steep walls that pressed down on the narrow trail. Unable to see enemy troops at all, shaking with combined fear and rage, Donskov got to his knees.

It looked about as bad as it could be. Fiery BMD wrecks lit the narrow gorge and highlighted the panicky desantniks. The flickering diesel fires showed Donskov plenty about his own men and nothing about the enemy. Molodets slumped lifeless atop the burning BMD, his arm torn off, his head crushed. Padorin was out of the track, without any weapon, his vehicle helmet trailing a vestigial intercom cord to match Donskov's useless, torn headset line. Suslov lay in the trailside gravel next to Donskov, breathing hard. We're trapped. I'm going to be killed—we all are. Donskov felt powerless. What now?

Senior Lieutenant Menzhinskiy knew. Busy Menzhinskiy, beautiful artilleryman Menzhinskiy, lay in the rain talking on his backpack R-114D radio, reading his map by the scorching firelight as casually as if reading a newspaper. The gunner was calling his comrades back at Emerald, and already Donskov could hear the friendly sigh of incoming 122mm shells, followed by the happy crumps of Soviet explosives dusting the hateful hilltops.

An RPG round whooshed by to impact on the third BMD back, which was already smoldering. Confused air assault men clustered in the trail beside their burning vehicles. Only a few returned fire. Most simply lay there, waiting for somebody to tell them what to do. Unless somebody took charge, they all might die down in this crack in the rocks. The artillery alone wouldn't be enough.

The god of war was doing his job. That was the idea. Do your duty, Donskov. Remember Grenada. Get working; you're the commander. Well, comrade, take command! The airborne men around him looked at the captain, wondering, worried, wet and lost.

Donskov shook his head, clearing his mind. I have to get control of these people. He ditched his useless headset and, with his ears uncovered, heard clearly for the first time the steady popping of gunfire. "Menzhinskiy, get on Eagle's frequency and give him a situation report. Padorin, help him. Suslov, you come with me." The steadiness and timbre of his voice amazed Donskov. He sounded calm and firm, as if on an exercise. If only I felt as certain as I sound, thought the captain.

The aviator and Donskov crouched and ran back down the halted, staggered column. As he left his BMD, Donskov could have sworn he heard a baby crying, not just the usual infant bawls, but the steady, shrieking wail of a sick child. He shook his head, flinging raindrops like a drenched dog, but the sound persisted. Oh well, maybe your mind plays tricks on you at a time like this. He had too much to do to indulge his curiosity now.

"We've got to get clear of these vehicles, Suslov. The trail's too tight to move the good ones; we've got to dump them all. Diesel won't explode, but the ammunition will." The flier nodded as he ran with his stubby AKR tucked under his right arm.

What was that snick, snick noise? Donskov knew, but he couldn't place it. A stone shattered near his right boot, pumping chips into the leather. He felt it and looked down. The wet toe looked like a pincushion. Snick, snick. Snick. Then he remembered. The snapping marked the passage of speeding bullets. Those bandits are shooting at us! Of course, Donskov, said his innermost voice. What did you expect? No time to worry–keep moving.

"Suslov, you bring forward 1st Platoon and the headquarters. Get the wounded, the dead, and the codebooks. Move the troops two hundred meters in front of my track, secure a halt site, and wait. I'll get the men from the other three tracks around the corner. Expect us in two groups. Code word 'sparrow.' We have to get away from these BMDs before they blow."

The two men split up, and Donskov moved as quickly as he could, weaving to and fro over the slippery gravel bottom of the gully. Boxy little Savitskiy was among his paratroopers, firing away and howling like a demon. A few wide-eyed men looked up as Donskov passed, and he pointed up to the rocks. "Return fire, men! Don't just lie there." He wished he could tell them what to shoot at. Thanks to the three brightly lit BMDs, the rebels had no such trouble choosing their targets.

Six loud, thumping explosions announced a second artillery volley, and Donskov heard rocks skittering down the hillsides after the shells hit. Keep it coming, Menzhinskiy! He rounded the corner to find 2d Platoon and the half of 3d Platoon that had not gotten lost.

One track of three burned. Unlike Savitskiy's men, some of whom were at least trying to fight, these soldiers lay dumbfounded in the rocks and shrubs, not even facing the enemy on the heights. Donskov noticed no effective opposing firing back here.

"Where's Karpov?"

"Dead. Drilled right in the face," said a prostrate form. It was Ivolukhin, who had obviously been shot, too. Nobody moved. Could they all be wounded? I can't move this many.

"Where are the platoon sergeants for 2d and 3d Platoon?" Donskov had no sooner yelled his question than he realized that Ivolukhin's platoon sergeant was with the missing track, somewhere back behind the battered column.

Senior Sergeant Levkhin raised his hand. "Second Platoon sergeant here."

"On your feet, platoon sergeant. Are you okay?"

"Yes, comrade captain." Levkhin climbed to his feet.

"All right. Take charge of your platoon and this portion of 3d Platoon. There's still enemy resistance around the corner. You take two of your squads. Get Lieutenant Ivolukhin's codebook, and have that piece of 3d Platoon carry the wounded. I'll cover your ass end with your third squad. Move it."

It took Levkhin about two minutes to sort out his men. There were three wounded, including Ivolukhin. Karpov and the driver from the burning track were dead.

"The dead, too?" asked Levkhin as the soaked 3d Platoon squad divided its burdens. Back here, out of the rebel firing line, Donskov again became aware of the steady rain.

"Yes, absolutely! I'll carry Karpov myself," Donskov said. Best to set the example on this. As a staff recon officer, Donskov had read enough grisly accounts of mutilated corpses. Not in my company, he had long ago resolved. He hefted up Karpov's sagging form, after grabbing the bloody, ripped codebook.

"Here's your squad," Levkhin said. "Sergeant Trofimenko is their leader."

Donskov grabbed Trofimenko. "Check your men. Tell them the enemy is on the left side of the gully, around the corner, about a hundred meters up in those rocks." He pointed up the steep cliff face. Trofimenko followed his hand. It was a hunch, but Donskov felt pretty sure about it. Another set of welcome howitzer rounds whizzed in and exploded. Excellent.

Senior Sergeant Levkhin reported back. "Ready to move."

"Good. Spread out, and move quickly past all of the BMDs. Get about 200 meters out front—look out for the rest of the company. When challenged, reply with 'sparrow.' We'll be two minutes behind you."

Levkhin's files headed off, weapons at the ready. A few small arms rounds already had begun to cook off in the BMD flaming near Sergeant Trofimenko's anxious men.

Donskov glued his eyes to his watch. The rain was still falling, hissing lightly on the burning armored vehicles. Two minutes passed. "Let's go!"

The men marched up the twisting, uneven gorge. They could not run; Donskov was laboring hard under the burden of Karpov, slung fireman-style across his back. They turned the corner, to see the three scorching, golden pyres. No other desantniks could be seen. Rebel gunfire had died away.

"Sergeant Trofimenko, hold up. Give me your RPK-74 man and his assistant. We'll cover you."

Donskov put down Karpov and directed the machine gunner to a misshapen, slimy boulder. Those damned bandits are not gone yet, Donskov assured himself. I'd better be careful. Overhead, yet another wave of 122mm shells crashed into the ridge top.

"Okay, go!"

Trofimenko and his men moved swiftly, working their way

around the burning BMDs. That ammo will blow any minute, thought Donskov. The four men walked awkwardly, their upper bodies dipping as they tried to stay down and move forward simultaneously.

There! He saw a muzzle flash up on the rocks. Those bastard rebels never quit. Donskov pulled his assault rifle to his shoulder. "Fire at the spot marked by my tracers."

Crack, crack went the captain's AKD, zipping two green sparks rather close to the source of enemy fire. The RPK man opened up, ripping off two long bursts. There were no more muzzle flashes.

"That got them or at least scared them," Donskov told the two conscripts.

The gunner grinned. "They got us tonight, but we'll pay them back," he growled.

"Exactly so, comrade!" exclaimed Donskov. "Let's go."

He picked up the sodden Karpov, and the three paratroopers staggered and slipped around the crackling bonfires. It took about ten minutes to get totally clear and out of sight of the armored deathtraps. The deep, harsh booms of exploding 73mm rounds sounded in the distance as the three finally linked up with their fellow recon men.

"Sparrow, sparrow, sparrow," whispered Donskov hoarsely. A paratrooper loomed up and waved the commander into the small circle of alert soldiers.

Suslov and Savitskiy met him. Donskov let poor Karpov thud to the ground atop a stunted tangle of brush. The rain streamed down on Donskov's surprisingly dry lips. He opened his mouth and sucked in a few chill drops.

"You and your party make forty-seven. Senior Sergeant Levkhin's holding the south half of our circle; my platoon's got the north," reported Savitskiy as if on field maneuvers near Pskov.

"Menzhinskiy raised the Spetsnaz. They're expecting us on foot. Eagle says forget about the BMDs. He's got a line company coming in at dawn to retrieve the ones that still work and pull off the derelicts. We can move out from this security position at your order."

Despite all the travails of this evil night, Donskov felt as light as a feather. It was the excitement, of course, the adrenaline, the battle frenzy, the thrill of almost getting killed and, so far, surviving. He wanted to hug homely little Savitskiy, and worried Suslov, and especially the god of war's favorite son, Menzhinskiy, not to mention Senior Sergeant Levkhin and that anonymous RPK-74 machine gunner itching for vengeance. These magnificent ball-busting desantniks! There's something here in this unit to build on, regardless of the damage done by Pliyev and now the Afghans. He smiled and at the same time felt tears welling up in his eyes. Fortunately, in the rain and dark, his subordinates noticed neither reaction.

"Our losses are five dead, eleven wounded, and two missing," Suslov finished.

Donskov asked, "Who's missing?"

Suslov lowered his voice. "Did you hear something odd when we first left your track?"

"Now that you mention it, yes. It sounded like a little baby screeching."

Suslov snorted and shuddered. "No, it was Goshov and that other guy, burning to death. We couldn't get them out . . . the heat . . . "

Donskov felt a dropping sensation in his gut. At least there wouldn't be anything left for the Afghans. Small comfort, that, to men roasted alive. He looked around in the stygian gloom, already exhausted and facing a hard climb up to the Spetsnaz position. The exhilaration of combat faded quickly as he smelled his own singed clothes and imagined the gruesome concept of burning to death.

"Let's go," said Donskov. "Follow me." The column of tired, bloody, fire-blackened men, bowed by the wounded and dead, slogged slowly up the gully. The rain fell as hard as ever.

Like all things good or bad, Operation MARS ended. The 688th returned to stout Fire Base Bagration, in its usual security zone along troubled Route 2, north of Kabul.

"Listen to this," said Savitskiy early one morning as the shrunken recon company command group boiled water for morning tea. The gnomelike platoon commander was reading from the Afghanistan edition of *Red Star*, the Soviet Army's official newspaper.

"'Among those subunits that distinguished themselves on internationalist duty was the reconnaissance detachment of the 688th Guards Red Banner Air Assault Regiment. They advanced against heavy bandit resistance and arrived ready for battle at a key location, where they saved a beleaguered comrade unit. It proved another noteworthy blow against the counterrevolutionary parasites. Element leader Captain D. I. Doskoviy'"–

"That's you, I guess," Suslov interjected.

–"'told his men, "The working peoples of our motherland and the world salute your bravery in performance of our socialist duty."'"

"I never said any such thing," Donskov said. "Where do they get this bullshit?"

"Admit it, comrade captain," Savitskiy continued. "The Spetsnaz held their position, the Long Range Aviation regiment retrieved its goodies, and all because we tied down the guerrillas by our bold approach march. Why, even our lost BMD made it back to Emerald unscathed. It all worked out."

Donskov laughed derisively. "And we lost four BMDs and eighteen men–a rather steep price for our supposedly brilliant victory. Did you ever hear of Pyrrhus of Epirus, Igor?"

The lieutenant shook his round head.

"Back in classical times," Donskov explained, "Pyrrhus made war against the Roman legions. He won possession of the field of Heraclea after a terrible battle, but he lost a third of his army. His generals lavished praise on their king, but Pyrrhus recognized that a triumph won at such cost hardly constituted a success. 'One more such victory and I am lost,' said the king. Pyrrhus speaks for me in this case."

The men drank their tea without further conversation.

Chapter Seven

Under the Wolf's Sun

An interesting report, Dmitriy Ivanovich," said Colonel Leonov. He held the two-page handwritten summary of his recon company's escapade in the Tu-16 incident. The colonel absently ran his long fingers over his bald head, then spoke again. "So you're not satisfied with your famous mission. That speaks well of your candor. As the great Lenin once said, What is to be done?"

"I think the answer is obvious, comrade colonel," Donskov answered. "The bandits always know our moves; we at best can react to theirs. To have a chance in these mountains, we must break that cycle, right here at regimental level. Perhaps 40th Army or divisional headquarters knows exactly what the Afghans are doing, but their news always arrives too late, and therefore has no real value. Our tested GRU system isn't working. I don't know why–it's just not. Perhaps we're looking for what's not there."

"You know, this is my second tour down south," Leonov mused. "It's always seemed strange that an intelligence structure that penetrated the Nazi high command during the Great Patriotic War cannot figure out what a few mud-kicking peasants are doing. I've forever heard how our system is so superior to the disjointed American configuration, where the intelligence analysts have no command authority at all over their hodgepodge of cavalry, electronic warfare units, chemical detectors, aerial scouts, and artillery radars. American military intelligence staffers have to beg for data from their collecting units. Our GRU officers both collect and analyze, yet somehow they haven't been fast enough to keep up with a tribal society stumbling along in the feudal stage of material development."

"I agree that this strange counterrevolutionary situation has confounded us," countered Donskov. "But as you said, we still retain the Soviet Army advantage of unified collection and analysis capabilities. Up till now, you haven't had the recon strength to get your own data in a timely fashion. So you relied on a higher headquarters, who act at their own speed and for their own convenience. The addition of a full company to your organization changes this condition. In order to give the regiment the intelligence we need to destroy these Afghan rebels, we must plan to procure it ourselves. As your chief of reconnaissance, I think I know some ways to do that, but I need a free hand."

Leonov's smooth brow wrinkled. His eyes remained locked on Donskov. "I accept your argument. I'll support your alterations. You realize, however, that there are limits: moral-political factors, material-technical resources, available cadres, and our battle norms and algorithms."

Donskov understood exactly what the colonel was saying in that peculiar but perfectly evident double-talk. In sum, Leonov had reminded his new recon commander not to expect relief from party or KGB surveillance, not to hope for new or exotic equipment, not to count on special personnel allocations, and not to wander too far beyond the standard tactical procedures of the Soviet Army.

I can live with most of that, thought Donskov, although I'll have to stretch the edges. Leonov is telling me that any excesses will be on my head. Fine. If I don't make necessary changes, the guerrillas may see to me anyway. One fumbling excursion up the Panjsher is enough. Korobchenko always said that nobody argues with results. He taught me how to get results. Now, it's time to put that tutelage into practice.

"I just want to find the bandits, comrade colonel. I accept full responsibility for any changes to established methods, in accord with our one-man command tradition."

"Naturally," the colonel replied. "But don't misunderstand me,

Dmitriy Ivanovich. I'm not trying to dump all of this on your head. Far from it. I stand behind you all the way. It's just that I have seen other energetic young officers try to wrestle with the complexities of the Afghan conflict. Sometimes I think that there are men in our army, in our country, who'd rather not solve any problems here in the south. It would necessitate admission that other more serious problems exist, and we are not a people attuned to honesty when it conflicts with predetermined goals. Nervous types get upset when someone makes bold changes. They take it as criticism of the general line. What I'm saying, not too well, I'm afraid, is that I sense that you intend to turn things upside down. Just remember, when you tip up the cabinet, sometimes items fall out that you'd rather never have found."

Donskov sat quietly on the camp stool. Outside the small tent, through the bright triangle of the entrance, he saw a dirty jeep bounce away toward the main road. He made no verbal response to Colonel Leonov's comments.

Leonov took that as evidence of understanding and moved on. "Now, what can I do to assist you?" asked the regimental commander. "Do you want a special selection of the June crop of conscripts and cadres?"

Donskov shook his head. "I can work with whatever I'm sent. I ask only two things. First, I would like to get the men who arrive earliest, the group that shows up on 1 June. That will allow for a maximum amount of training. Second, I want two particular officers."

"Name them."

"Senior Lieutenant Yegorov from the Regimental Mortar Battery and Senior Lieutenant Zharkowskiy from the Regimental Transport Company."

The colonel stared at Donskov a few seconds. "Unusual choices," he said. "Zharkowskiy I somewhat understand; you need a political deputy now that you've lost Molodets. But Zharkowskiy's always sick, I hear. He has no combat experience to speak of. And Yegorov makes no sense at all. He's overqualified to lead a platoon."

"I want him for deputy commander, comrade colonel."

Leonov shifted a bit on his ammunition crate seat. "What's

wrong with Balashov? I'll admit I met him only once, but I am told that your predecessor, Captain Pliyev, gave him a glowing efficiency report. Pliyev told me he had the best deputy in the division."

"He certainly had the safest, comrade colonel. Balashov never went to the field on operations. He's a standing joke in the company. I don't want him. And for the record, I intend to replace that fat, thieving excuse for a sergeant major as well."

"What's wrong with Kabanovskiy?" asked Colonel Leonov.

"He's also glued to the base camp. There's no intelligence to be gathered in the rear. I don't need sock sorters and paper stampers. I need combat leaders. I've already got Kabanovskiy's replacement—Senior Sergeant Rozhenko, from my 1st Platoon."

"Isn't he a conscript?"

"He's a fighter, comrade colonel. His platoon commander, Lieutenant Savitskiy, says he's the smartest, toughest soldier in the company. I want to promote him, but in the meantime, he'll be my acting company sergeant major."

Leonov laughed weakly, his eyes crinkling. "Well, well. You've obviously done some good recon already, although I find your selections strange. Consider it all approved. You'll have Zharkowskiy tomorrow. Yegorov and Balashov will swap positions, so he'll be over to you within the week. As for old Kabanovskiy, I'll call division and see if they can stash him somewhere."

"Thank you, comrade colonel," said Donskov.

"Don't thank me, Dmitriy Ivanovich. Get your people organized and find me some black asses. You do whatever is necessary. But remember, you must be ready for action by 1 July, just like the rest of the regiment."

"The recon company will be ready," Donskov said.

Senior Sergeant Yuriy Andreyevich Rozhenko was a young, red-haired man with pale blue eyes and the wide shoulders of a collective farmer. He reported to Donskov within two hours after the captain returned from the regimental command post. The two men exchanged salutes in the half-light of the bunker, and Donskov motioned the non-commissioned officer to a wooden ammunition box.

"Have a seat, comrade sergeant."

Rozhenko planted himself immediately.

"How much time till your demob?" asked Donskov.

"One hundred eighty-four days, comrade captain."

"That's enough. I have a proposition for you. How would you like to be the sergeant major for Recon Company?"

Rozhenko's open Ukrainian features crinkled a bit. His eyes narrowed. "I am not a career soldier, nor do I intend to be. I just want to do my duty and go home," he said.

"That's one of the reasons I want you," stated Donskov. "The life-time soldiers lack a sense of urgency about this war. They don't give a shit how long it lasts, because they've got nothing better to do. I have no intention of repeating our little joyride up in the Panjsher. Do you?"

Rozhenko smiled slightly. "Not at all, comrade captain."

"Good then," said Donskov. "I must admit that I am particularly impressed with your combat record. Lieutenant Savitskiy says you taught him almost everything he has learned here in the south. It may also interest you to know that yours is the one name every private has mentioned when I ask who is the best fighter in the company."

Rozhenko reddened a little at that. Donskov went on.

"Still, I found it a bit odd that when I checked your personnel file, I saw no recommendations for awards beyond the usual campaign participation credits."

Rozhenko responded immediately: "Captain Pliyev did not submit conscripts for awards. When he finally chose to send my name in, after a big fight near Jalalabad, I refused to play along. I convinced my comrades not to bother writing all the stupid witness statements. It's all just bullshit, comrade captain. Did you know that Captain Pliyev wrote up that lazy bastard Kabanovskiy for a Red Star and the son of a bitch has never left the rear area?"

"I'm not surprised," Donskov said. "But I'm also not Pliyev. Kabanovskiy is already back in Kabul doing what he's best at— nothing. This is a war, not a job. We're not just fulfilling our socialist competition quotas down here. Personally, I'm more than satisfied with your performance. Will you be my sergeant major?"

"Yes, I'll do it. But I don't expect it to stand. The cadres pukes at division will never approve it. They protect their own," Rozhenko replied gloomily.

"Fuck them. You put on the rank, I'll sort out the paperwork. What are a few rubles a month more or less when you can't spend them anyway? Now, Sergeant Major, I have two tasks for you, to be accomplished by 1 June when our new people arrive."

Rozhenko dredged a dog-eared notebook out of his uniform pocket. He pulled a pencil stub from another frayed pocket and waited. Once Donskov saw that he was ready, he spoke again.

"First, I want you and your sergeants to conduct a thorough inspection of all weapons and radios, to include range firing and field tests. Insure that they are all serviceable. Of course, get our veterans squared away—fighting harnesses, uniforms, boots, rucksacks, blankets, the works. And insure that every man currently on our roster has a blue beret."

Rozhenko looked at his commander quizzically at the mention of the berets, but wrote it down nevertheless.

"What about the BMDs?" Rozhenko asked. "Our four replacements are ready for pickup at Darulaman, and our two inoperative tracks have been repaired and are waiting at the Bagram shops."

"Forget about the vehicles for now. Concentrate on weapons, radios, and individual gear. Get it straight—use casualty surplus as necessary."

"Exactly so, comrade captain," Rozhenko said.

"Your second task is more important. I want *you* to pick our sergeants for all nine squads and all three platoons. You know who the real paratroopers are."

This caused Rozhenko to stir a bit on his box. Donskov thought it would; it represented a major departure from the usual method. Normally, Soviet Army sergeants were merely conscripts chosen at induction for a special noncommissioned officers' course. By regulation, wartime commanders could promote and demote, presumably to replace losses. Donskov elected to delegate that authority to someone who knew the men better, so as to prevent losses.

"Do I have authority," Rozhenko asked, "to pick senior privates and corporals to replace the so-called trained sergeants we have been sent?"

"Exactly so!" Donskov said emphatically. "That's precisely what I want. *You* decide over the next six days. Have your chosen men put on their new rank; tell the limp-dicks to take off their shoulder boards. Tell me when you're finished."

"You can expect things to be turned upside down, comrade captain."

"I hope so, comrade sergeant major. I hope so."

Senior Lt. Andrey Viktorovich Zharkowskiy's smallish bony body, thin dark face, and probing black eyes gave him the appearance of a nervous man. Yet this image deceived, for Zharkowskiy turned out to be one of the calmest men Donskov had ever met. He came to Recon Company a day after Donskov asked for him, as promised by Colonel Leonov. He saluted, the captain returned it, and Donskov indicated the 73mm ammunition container. Zharkowskiy sat down, and, to Donskov's surprise, started talking.

"When the order came down, I told the clerk to quit playing jokes. I have no recon skills or experience. So I'm curious: Why would you want me as a political deputy?"

Donskov laughed. "Because you have some special skills and the right sort of personality. Indeed, you're exactly the one I asked for. You're the only political deputy I even considered."

"Don't count on too many lectures and a neat Lenin Room, or do we have Lenin bunkers up here in the combat units? No matter. Cheerleading bores me. Now as to the theoretical struggle to bring socialism to these benighted Afghans, well, I note a marked discrepancy between party goals and practical possibilities. About all I've learned in the last four months is how to remove shot-out truck tires in an ambush."

"How is that?"

"Drive the fuckers right off the rim!" responded Zharkowskiy. "Now with technical knowledge like that, imagine what I can do for Recon Company."

"Andrey Viktorovich," said Donskov, "I have done just that. That's why I sent for you. I understand that you are from Tashkent, and I'm told you speak both Farsi and Pashto—"

"Exactly so! That's why our farsighted Cadres Section assigned me to the Regimental Transport Company, so I could provide Marxist-Leninist agitation among our impressed local labor types. Ever tried explaining the material basis of the class struggle to a man whose proudest possession is a cracked teacup? It really falls a little short."

This one was surely a free spirit, all right. Donskov picked up his thread of commentary where Zharkowskiy had cut it. "As a linguist, I'll want you to organize and train a scout section for our company. More importantly, I will rely on you as the recon man of the recon men, so to speak. I know you're a persuasive and perceptive soldier. Persuade the Afghans, and perceive the enemy. And permeate this company with the knowledge you gain. You'll be our eyes."

Zharkowskiy smiled. "Now that's something to my liking. It beats the hell out of lectures on imperialist encroachment or the evils of Chinese revisionism—"

"It's critically important," Donskov interjected.

"Exactly so, comrade captain. You know, this reminds me of why I became a political deputy in the first place. I read all those wonderful, romantic novels of the civil war, and always the hero was the tough Red commissar, the fellow who understood that fighting had a real political component, both inside and *outside* his unit. That is why we beat the Whites and their capitalist interventionist allies, isn't it? They just wanted to fight; we realized that it was a fight for the people. Four years in the Novosibirsk Higher Military School and four years in the VDV have convinced me otherwise. Political deputies are card checkers and droning bores. And now, here in this stone-strewn slag heap of Afghanistan, we find ourselves in another civil war, and our political officers have no role beyond chanting sterile slogans prescribed by central organs so far away that they might as well be on the moon. So I just helped get the trucks in and out. Until now, that is."

"Here's your chance to be a commissar," Donskov said.

"Ah yes, a commissar. The word has a quaint, brave ring to it, don't you think? I'd prefer to try to win the hearts and minds of the locals and turn them into loyal Reds, but I think we're about five years too late and five levels of command too low to do anything about that situation. So I'll be happy to talk some of these pathetic people into locating and killing their neighbors. It was the major outdoor pastime here before the Limited Contingent showed up."

"Excellent." Donskov leaned forward. "Now as to our company's mandatory party-political work—"

"Not a problem. I'll deliver my weekly lessons. But you know, sometimes the missives from the Main Political Administration get lost in the mail. Perhaps I might choose to improvise. I could foresee fine political discussion on such topics as local Tadzhik rebel organizational methods, village infrastructures, Islamic customs and traditions, and the integration of local agriculture into the bandit logistics network. The late Vladimir Ilyich Lenin would approve, because he always told his followers that the revolution could only be advanced by those with 'a thorough knowledge of the mood prevailing among all opposition strata.' So I think you can see how I'll educate my young Communist paratroopers."

"Perfect. I think we see eye to eye on your priorities," Donskov agreed. "But we have to be careful not to blow off too much of the mandatory stuff. There are the Third Chief Directorate men—"

"Still can't find the Chekists? I always told my truckers that a Soviet soldier who cannot spot a Chekist in his own squad will never spot a guerrilla ambush in the dark rockwork. I'll give you the names of all your Chekists in three days. Just let me hold a few routine Communist information sessions. Once we've found the snitches, we'll co-opt them."

"That easily?"

"Come now, any conscript willing to inform for the KGB is not a cosmic physicist. Stool pigeons tend to be manipulable. If the Chekists can play with them, we can double them back and do as we please. Besides, we're only trying to win the war. It's not as if we're plotting a revolution. Are we?"

Donskov found himself smiling uncontrollably. Zharkowskiy made it all sound so simple. "No revolution, Andrey. But a lot of changes, with you and your role being one of the biggest."

"How long do I have to organize my intelligence, counterintelligence, and native scout projects?" asked Zharkowskiy.

"We begin a dedicated train-up on 1 June, when the new conscripts arrive. You'll play a big part in that, of course. But your scouts need not be combat-qualified until 1 July."

"I can get it done," assured Zharkowskiy. "By the way, just out of curiosity, did anyone tell you about my supposedly sickly constitution?"

"Now that you mention it, Colonel Leonov said something like that."

Zharkowskiy smirked. "Typical. You see, I used to go out on convoys and postpone my indoctrination periods. When Lieutenant Colonel Kharskiy up at regiment checked on me, my commander used to say that I was sick. I guess I was, to be off riding dangerous truck runs when I could have been in a deep dugout gassing about our benevolent socialist paradise. In any event, Kharskiy wrote on my last efficiency report that 'due to unfortunate illnesses,' I 'demonstrated only moderate progress in the struggle to inculcate party culture' in my truck drivers. If the scumbag ever would have come down and checked, he'd have known where I was. Anyway, I guess I'm not much of a political officer."

"I think you'll do well as our commissar."

"Well, at least I'll do something," finished Zharkowskiy.

Donskov recognized Senior Lt. Kliment Ivanovich Yegorov as soon as he came into the low-roofed bunker. Yegorov had graduated from Ryazan a year behind Donskov, and the captain recalled this handsome, sturdy blond officer as an equally solid young cadet. Yegorov reported, and Donskov offered him the usual 73mm box as a seat.

"Thank you, comrade captain."

Yegorov instantly produced a small notebook and a pencil. He had always been a hard worker back at Ryazan.

"I'm very glad you're here," Donskov said. "We have two days before our conscripts get here, and much to do. Did you know Balashov at all?"

Yegorov shrugged: "Not really. He has a poor reputation in the regiment. I can tell you that the Mortar Battery was not looking forward to getting him."

"Indeed," Donskov said. "He established a new low standard for deputies. Basically, he shirked. That wasn't bad enough. I actually saw a write-up for a valor award in his file, for 'extraordinary performance of duty.' And this for a prima donna who never left the chain of fire bases! How that jerk-off made it through the reserve officers' course, I'll never know. He'd have been run out of Ryazan."

"Senior Sergeant Tobulkhin would have seen to that," Yegorov remarked.

"Yes," Donskov mused. "Our dear old Tatar Yoke. . . . Well, enough of that. You're no Balashov, Kliment Ivanovich. This company hasn't had a decent deputy for almost a year. But now it does."

"I'm ready to do my best, comrade captain."

"You know the usual duties of the deputy, I assume?" queried Donskov.

"Second in command, supervision of logistics, and control of the unit headquarters," answered Yegorov readily.

"The first is the most important. You should be aware that the company is on the verge of a month of retraining for its reconnaissance tasks."

"I should warn you, I have no formal GRU schooling," Yegorov noted.

"Understood. Neither do I, and that will probably work to our advantage. The trained guys, like Balashov and my predecessor, Captain Pliyev, think that you recon by driving around and drawing fire. That may do against NATO imperialists, but out here, it's pointless and often fatal. So we'll retrain this company to find the enemy hidden in the rocks instead of the mechanized opposition we're trained to locate."

"What's your plan, comrade captain?"

"I'll give you the details during an orders group tomorrow night, but in general, I intend to develop a company skilled in night dismounted tactics. I want us to be able to operate as squads, platoons, or a company, working with native scouts, to find these damned rebels. Once we find them, the regiment can do the rest. Right now, they find us."

"What sort of training have you designed?" asked Yegorov, writing furiously on his pad.

"A program of marches, patrols, and ambushes should do the trick. I plan to train the officers and platoon sergeants this week while the new men inprocess. Each of us should be able to accompany, coach, and evaluate squads out on their exercises. We commence on 1 June with our daily schedule of squad movements, linkups, surveillance techniques, weapons firing, and deception measures. Every man in this company will be able to read a map, talk on a radio, and move in the mountains. We'll shift gradually to a night program by midmonth."

Yegorov's face showed concern. "Where are you going to do this? It will require a big, secure area."

"Not at all, Kliment Ivanovich. We'll train right outside the wire, in the Shomali Valley, along Route 2."

"That's awfully challenging. The division lost two assault guns out there just yesterday."

"We don't have time to hold their hands. We'll do our best to avoid putting anyone in real jeopardy until they know their tasks. But it seems to me that the lowest private conscript will pay attention to drills when he realizes that we will lead him that night into bandit country. So that's what you can look forward to as deputy."

"What about logistics and the headquarters?"

"With regard to logistics, we'll carry, cache, or airlift for our needs."

"How about the BMDs?" Yegorov wondered.

"I've gotten the okay to turn them in. We lost the ten drivers when I gave up the BMDs, but so what? Maybe they'll be helpful for regimental convoys," Donskov confided.

Yegorov looked shocked. "Don't be so amazed, Kliment. They're steel cocoons, rolling bunkers. They're for the bogus World War III that won't ever come. We're in the real World War III, and we don't need them. The guerrillas don't use armored vehicles because the cursed things dull the senses and trumpet their own arrivals. We may hitch rides now and then with trucks or tracks or choppers, but like our adversaries, we'll usually walk."

This made Yegorov uneasy. "I'm almost afraid to ask about the headquarters."

"Seven men. You, our political deputy, the aviator, the gunner, the sergeant major, the aidman, and a radioman. No bodyguards, air defense gunners, mechanics, runners, drivers, supply clerks, administrators, or orderlies."

"This should prove interesting, comrade captain," Yegorov said with a curt dip of his head. "It sounds more like a Spetsnaz company than a line VDV unit."

"Except we're going to make an average crop of supposed recon specialists into real recon desantniks, not handpick them like the Spetsnaz. Other than you and the political deputy, everyone else represents the luck of the draw—properly rearranged and soon to be properly trained, of course."

"I know that we're short some officers. What have you done about the two new platoon commanders?"

"I actually planned to work with whatever we get," Donskov offered.

"I know a lieutenant up at division cadres. Let me go up and poke around. I think I know what we want."

"Battlefield commissions or Ryazan men, if possible."

"I'll bring back some hungry young wolves, comrade captain."

"That's it. Wolves." Donskov looked directly at his new deputy. "This is a war for wolves, all right."

"The company is formed, comrade captain."

Company Sergeant Major Rozhenko saluted Captain Donskov. Behind him, at attention, stood the seven officers and fifty-eight men of Reconnaissance Company, 688th Guards Air Assault Regiment, organized into three platoons of an officer and nineteen men and a headquarters of four officers and three conscripts. Every soldier had his weapon, and all wore fighting harnesses. Heavy rucksacks, thirty unforgiving kilograms on the average, rested in neat lines at the paratroopers' feet.

Almost half of the men wore bright new camouflage suits and unscratched gray helmets: They had just arrived. They mixed in with the faded, rawboned veterans of six- and twelve-months' service. All of the older men wore their VDV berets, as ordered by Donskov. Two of the platoon commanders wore the crisp new uniforms and issued helmets.

In Afghanistan, such parade ground formations could only be seen in the relative safety of the larger Soviet installations, like the 688th Regiment's well-defended Fire Base Bagration. After all the scrupulous close-order drill back at Ryazan, Donskov normally avoided these holdovers from the time of Peter the Great. But today, in the bright June sun, Donskov made an exception. Formations do serve certain purposes, after all.

"Take your post, comrade sergeant major."

Rozhenko faced about and moved to his post. Donskov took one step forward.

"Stand easy."

With an audible shuffle, the men relaxed their bodies. Donskov felt their collective gaze shift to him. New men wondered who he was; old men knew, or thought they did. As he scanned the collage of faces, he saw some attentive and some bored, a few friendly and many not, and a sprinkling of Asian visages among the majority of broad Slavic types. Donskov imagined that the immortal Suvorov had seen many a similar gathering as he walked among his beloved soldiers before he led them on their epic march across the snowy Alps, back in 1799, in service to a Russia quite different yet all too unchanged. The oration before battle was a hackneyed scene in every war novel, good or bad. And here I am, a pale imitation of the fearless Suvorov, playing my part.

It really is just acting, Donskov knew. I have to convince them to think like me. And that, after all, was why he had joined the army so long ago, to make others want to do things that he directed. Or, as Korobchenko once put it, to tell them to go to hell and make them enjoy the trip. Now these paratroopers were hostage to his ideas, as yet untested in this Afghan crucible. He might well have doubted himself more, but he did not have time for the luxury of introspection. That was the beauty of the army; there was never enough time to worry, only to do. His blue beret squared on his closely shaved head, Donskov addressed his men.

"Desantniks! I welcome our new comrades. Reconnaissance Company trusts you have what it takes. The older men have seen much combat . . . "

(Here Donskov exaggerated. As a chunk of the unlamented Provisional Reconnaissance Battalion, the company had avoided most heavy action for almost a year. Its scrapes resulted from accidents, not intent. That's going to change, Donskov promised himself.)

" . . . and they're going to work with you to insure you learn your duties. We have about one month to prepare. I tell you that we will prepare through combat. Every one of you here will be in action by tonight."

(Of course, the first week's patrols would be stage-managed to try to insure benign routes, but the mujahidin could be unpredictable.)

"Once you have met the test of enemy fire, you can turn in these silly turtle-shell helmets and don the blue berets you've earned as jumpers, as VDV, and now as recon wolves!"

(Rozhenko had reminded him the night before that this contradicted 40th Army uniform policy. "They've made their policy; let them enforce it," said Donskov. The captain wanted a distinctive look. Thus, berets became the standard company headgear, to be earned by service under fire.)

"In the next month, this company will learn to rule the rocks. To rule the rocks we must march. There are no BMDs in this company. We will learn to cross these mountains and valleys like the bandits – on foot and unafraid. To rule the rocks we all must think. It's not enough to follow orders. A recon desantnik must read the map, talk on the radio, and take charge when necessary, day or night, rain or shine, hurt or whole. Finally, to rule the rocks we must hunt. Seek out the rebels in their lairs. Right now they find us. Soon, we will find them, and they will learn to fear us."

The men were utterly silent now, their ears open, their eyes glued to him. Combat tonight, no BMDs, marching, hurt or whole, and "we"–the key points hit home. Officers didn't usually talk like this. Donskov swept his gaze across them.

"We can trust only ourselves, brothers. Nobody else dares to do our duties for us. The Afghan bandits are vicious and relentless, but you are Soviet desantniks, hard men indeed. We must, all of us, get harder still, brother wolves. And we will."

Donskov stopped right there. "Company!"

"Platoon!" echoed the lieutenants.

"Ah-ten . . . shun!"

Heels crashed together, sending up small billows of yellow dust. "Sergeant major!"

Rozhenko strode forward and halted before Donskov.

"Take charge of the company and prepare for training," commanded the captain.

"Exactly so, comrade captain!" said Rozhenko. Both men saluted. Donskov marched off a dozen meters, followed by his officers. The sergeants took charge as the company saddled up for their upcoming trek.

Five hundred meters away, a battery of six D-30 howitzers cracked loudly, sending six 122mm shells out into the low hills. The six tubes lowered in rough unison after the loud discharge. Ten minutes after this unintended salute, Recon Company set off on its first foot march.

"Security out! Take five!" bawled hulking Lt. Pyotr Vasiliyevich Knyazin, the new 3d Platoon commander. The lead squad deployed two men out front; the center squad put two men on either flank. The rear squad dropped a pair back. Meanwhile, the rest of the sweating paratroopers slumped to either side of the narrow trail, dotting the rutted roadside about every three meters.

The platoon was moving through the remnants of a prewar peach orchard, along the lower slopes of the mountains forming the western side of the Shomali basin. Many of the men rested their heavy packs against the thin, unpruned trees. The noon sun blistered their skin, as it had for six days straight since that first march out from Fire Base Bagration.

Sergeant Ponomarev, newly promoted from senior private, had completed twelve of his eighteen months in Afghanistan. He pushed his blue beret back on his head and slurped loudly on his canteen. "This stupid fucker is trying to kill us, brothers!" he announced to Private Dalmatov, his newly arrived RPG-74 machine gunner. Dalmatov only gasped under his shiny helmet, dazed and confused, his legs throbbing.

Veteran Corporal Sviridov, who carried an AKD rifle with a BG-15 grenade launcher, had enough energy to answer his squad leader. "Why are we on foot, Ponomarev? Where are our BMDs?"

The squad sergeant shook his head. "Beats the shit out of me. What's the point of living in an advanced socialist country if we can't use battle technology?"

The corporal wiped his face with a moistened rag. "A few more days of this crap and we'll all be dead."

"Exactly so, brother," finished Ponomarev. "On no, here he comes. . . . "

The company commander strode up the trail, sweating lightly but obviously energetic. A full pack, including an R-114D radio, decorated the tall officer's back. His AKD hung loosely in his big right hand. Donskov could not help but hear the grousing, yet his demeanor betrayed nothing but determination. If they've got enough strength to complain, they're not tired yet, thought the commander.

"Spread these people out, comrade lieutenant! Five meters' dispersion," ordered Donskov, his face burned red under his blue beret.

Knyazin, who had just sat down himself, was slow getting up. The platoon sergeant, Senior Sergeant Milyukov, did not budge, but sat against a stump, his beret off, his eyes closed.

Donskov's eyes narrowed. "Too fucking slow. On your feet, Third! On your feet!"

The break had lasted only two minutes. Now it was over. It would be one hour, and six more kilometers, before another break.

"All right, saddle up," commanded Lieutenant Knyazin, finally on his feet. His sweat-lined face showed pure rage. The platoon struggled up, propelled by groans and swearing. Donskov stood like a basalt rock pillar, his lip curled in contempt. It was all a show. The captain longed to sit down and relax, but this was no time for weakness.

"Security in!" hollered Knyazin. Within thirty seconds, the platoon was on its way. Adjusting his pack straps as he stepped off, Ponomarev muttered, "Somebody ought to kill that crazy asshole."

"Really?"

Ponomarev looked to his left to see Sergeant Major Rozhenko padding along. The big redhead had materialized like a genie at his side. "Tired, comrade sergeant?"

"Not at all, comrade sergeant major," Ponomarev grunted.

Rozhenko nodded. "I didn't think so."

Donskov swung by the two conscript sergeants, stepping out toward the front of the platoon. "Pick up the pace, Lieutenant Knyazin!" he yelled.

"Asshole," breathed Ponomarev. But he kept going, cursing with every step. Company Sergeant Major Rozhenko just smiled.

With small stones hard against his flat stomach, Donskov shifted his numb legs a fraction, barely rustling the scattered gravel. He lifted his night vision goggles. Inky blackness, barely relieved by the moonlight, flooded in to replace the green, glowing imagery provided by the PNV-57 night observation device. The officer rubbed his eyes as he readjusted to the dimness. He checked his watch: 0112.

Thin shreds of clouds drifted across the half moon, hard, bright, and high in the black sky. Russian peasants often called the lunar orb the wolf's sun, and in the more remote forests in winter still took care to be safe indoors when the hungry packs barked and howled. But on this summer night, Donskov's wolves had not yet found their prey in the scrubby Afghan rockwork.

It took almost a minute for Donskov's eyes to adapt to the darkness. He gradually made out the indistinct, lumpy forms around him. To his right, lying prone in the stunted brush, an intent Sergeant Ponomarev also tweaked the focus rings on his own passive observation viewer, an irregular black tube locked atop the squad leader's SVD Dragunov sniper rifle. The squad's watchful RPG gunner flanked Donskov on the other side, almost invisible in the entwined foliage.

Beyond the thicket, the pebble-strewn hillside sloped down 200 meters to a dirt perimeter road wide enough for a heavy truck. This dusty sixteen-kilometer trace circumscribed the neat, rectangular fields of the Route 2 Friedrich Engels Experimental Agronomy Station. Two kilometers to the east, the trail tied into troubled Route 2.

Just the other side of the boundary path, across a nicely cut drainage ditch, a one-story whitewashed concrete-block equipment shelter stood among orderly rows of thick green wheat hybrids, black in the fitful moonlight. The knee-high shoots rippled in the light evening breeze. Almost two kilometers away to the north of the surveillance site, in the exact center of the manicured crops, stood the floodlit concrete mushrooms that marked the station offices. Although the lights still blazed inside the tall electrified fence, Donskov knew that nobody stayed there anymore at night. This was bandit country.

The captain and Ponomarev's 2d Squad, 3d Platoon, had spent two hours looking at slowly undulating grain and an untouched little building. A pair of men, one carrying the squad's RPK-74 machine gun, secured the right flank about 200 meters on the right; a second twosome hid in the gnarled mulberry bushes 200 meters to the left. But the compound that Soviet soldiers had long ago nicknamed "the Wheat Farm" remained completely inactive. Well, at least we've gotten some more night training out of all this, Donskov figured.

Learning to find and fight the mujahidin on foot proved to be every bit as difficult as Donskov had expected. After nearly three weeks of hard marching, tough land navigation by day and night, communications drills with and without radios, extensive weapons firing, and challenging patrols among the heights and depths of the broad, contested Shomali Valley, the men of Recon Company began to demonstrate confidence in their developing abilities. Following a daylight shakedown period, Donskov shifted his men gradually into night work. For a week now, forays went only after sunset.

Despite an initial period of aches and pains as the men acclimated to Donskov's hard methods, the real cost of training proved mercifully low. So far, three men had suffered wounds, two from mines and the other from a sniper. None had died, despite four substantial skirmishes. One squad tangled twice with a particularly hardheaded group of mujahidin minelayers right on Route 2.

Along with the three battle casualties, about ten men fell sick or injured in the unforgiving scrub and rocks. While all eventually came back, their loss demonstrated the challenging nature of reconnaissance in Afghanistan. Many mistakes were made. A lot of hours were wasted. But as the hours and days accumulated, so did a few tantalizing pieces of the puzzle. Donskov's men not only became familiar with their foes, they also developed techniques that insured an ever-increasing flow of vital battlefield intelligence. In short, the recon paratroopers gave up many traditional Soviet Army preconceptions and relearned their duties as the regiment's eyes and ears in the real world of Afghanistan, a harsh, dangerous, reeducation in the face of rebel gun muzzles.

Almost from the first tentative efforts, Donskov's wolf cubs located interesting threads of local resistance, clues easily missed when traveling by BMD or helicopter. Zharkowskiy and his coalescing group of ten or so Tadzhik and Pathan scouts worked the local villages, painting a dim but intriguing picture of the fragmented opposition and their capabilities. Donskov could hardly claim to understand the complicated situation in the Shomali, but already he was beginning to discern a few critical patterns, people, and places. And not unlike Korobchenko's old methods for finding enemy command posts, certain contacts and observations led to others.

The enemy in the Shomali Valley began to mutate from a collection of fleeting, faceless shadows into a struggling patchwork of real people, with strengths to be avoided and definite weaknesses to be exploited. By mid-June, if directed to recommend objectives for a conventional operation, Donskov could be sure to place his regiment on a few definite targets rather than dump them at random in deference to some divisional staff officer's guesses.

Motivated by their observations and Zharkowskiy's hunches, Donskov's paratroopers methodically felt their way around the Shomali. Recon Company squads learned to identify the different rebel contingents by language, clothing, weaponry, and methods of fieldcraft. For example, Donskov's men discovered that the pugnacious road-mining teams usually represented the long arm of Massoud's Tadzhik Islamic Society, a group that specialized in attempts to cut the vital Route 2. Whereas most bandits ran from battle, Massoud's trained fighters preferred to shoot it out, as Donskov's desantniks had found in their two scrapes.

Careful postmission debriefings motivated most subsequent efforts. In one case, careful paratroopers found a pouch of documents tossed into a wooden bucket suspended over an old well. Once translated, these papers led to a hut used for political organization work, resulting in a windfall of other records, including cell rosters for Massoud's neighborhood supporters. These people bore watching, and both Soviet KGB agents and their loyal Afghan KhAD counterparts eagerly jumped at the opportunities unearthed.

In another case, residual ammunition and papers allowed Zharkowskiy to track down a weapons cache that belonged to Sibghatullah Mujaddidi's small but active National Liberation Front, a band of Pathans normally based in the Kunar Valley along the Pakistani border. The arms stockpile represented the end of a shadowy trail stretching all the way into the refugee camps just inside Pakistan. If only we could follow this lead, Donskov thought. But that sort of tricky long-range scouting still lay in the company's future. Division recon chief Lieutenant Colonel Seleznev alerted 40th Army's Spetsnaz directorate to pick up this string.

As impressed as he was with Zharkowskiy's growing proficiency as a one-man intelligence processing section, Donskov found special comfort in his company's willingness to recognize useful clues and pursue them to the finish. A diligent squad, alerted by abandoned cellophane wrappers, cardboard sleeves, and a discarded battery pack, just missed nabbing an adventurous British television crew. Gleeful desantniks did bring back numerous documents and videotapes proving covert British military assistance, and, more importantly for the 688th, full-color images of certain publicity-conscious local Afghan leaders.

A similar persistence had brought Donskov and his 3d Platoon to the Wheat Farm. A week before, strictly by accident, a road watch squad along Route 2 happened to be facing west, hoping to see a bit of nocturnal demolition work. Instead, the men spotted the distant, indistinct yellow tongues of rocket launches along the periphery of the otherwise deserted agronomy installation. The whine and crash of three projectiles about a kilometer north on the highway, near a concrete-slab bridge spanning a deep crevasse, offered a harsh punctuation to the sighting.

Immediately sensing that this unexpected situation demanded investigation, yet too distant to reach the firing positions quickly and unwilling to desert his road surveillance task, the clever squad leader split the difference. After finishing his original observation duties, he altered his return route to skirt the Wheat Farm. A search along the perimeter road disclosed a twisted piece of metal—a broken folding fin from a Soviet-manufactured 122mm Grad rocket. While the squad could not find the exact launch site, the stabilizer shard encouraged Donskov to recommend observation of the Wheat Farm complex on a nightly basis. Colonel Leonov concurred, and division headquarters expressed interest, especially after confirming reports of serious damage to the Route 2 bridge.

The recon captain had not intended to do the job himself. Donskov envisioned use of the division artillery's BMD-SON counterbattery radars, relatively new technological marvels reputed to be capable of tracking enemy rounds back to their source. But radar men of the 271st Guards Air Assault Artillery Regiment gave Donskov a nasty surprise when they admitted that their sets' computer software restricted their utility in locating rockets. It seemed that the BMD-SONs could trace only items that decelerated along their upward trajectory, like mortar and cannon shells. Powered rockets, which sped up as they rose, confused the Soviet counterbattery radars' calculation systems. Rockets, said one artillery major, are best located by sound and flash ranging, crater analysis, and, no surprise to Donskov, aggressive foot patrolling. The artillerists promised to stake out the Wheat Farm with their survey teams, although these gods of war protested that it would be some time before they could do so. In the meantime—well, Donskov understood.

Thus Recon Company inherited the Wheat Farm along with its other training and fighting areas. It served Donskov's purposes as well as anything else, of course. Careful surveillance and searches by other squads on subsequent nights disclosed actual firing debris, to include used igniter wires, pieces of homemade launching troughs, and even an intact firing generator and its distinctive "clacker" palm switch. These rocket scraps turned up near one of the Wheat Farm's half-dozen outbuildings. The small structure itself was filled only with seed and hand tools, and there were no false floors, walls, or ceilings.

It took the thoughtful Yegorov, the former mortar man, to discern a likely scenario. He proposed that the rebels fired from near the tiny building because it represented a fixed point, and hence a known distance, to the target bridge. Yegorov suspected that one or two of the Wheat Farm's day workers had managed to pace off the relevant distances. Armed with this range data, prospective shooters could perform any firing calculations at their leisure in their hideouts. During the actual firing, the Afghans had merely to set up, point their weapon in the correct direction, establish the necessary angle of elevation, and let fly.

Another barrage occurred three nights after the first, catching a squad of five desantniks as they worked their way into their chosen observation post. Guerrillas popped four Grad rounds into the south end of the newly repaired Route 2 bridge. The recon squad gave chase, but the Afghans were moving too fast and had too much of a head start. An intense sweep of the Wheat Farm's border trail turned up more telltale wires. Once more, they lay in the dust right near a whitewashed toolshed.

The confirmed use of 122mm Grad rockets raised Zharkowskiy's level of interest. The political deputy's intelligence work allowed him to hypothesize about their origins. Massoud's Islamic Society and most of the other mujahidin factions preferred mortars to the heavy rockets. When these bandits chose rocketry, they usually employed the much simpler, somewhat lighter 107mm rocket, typically of Chinese manufacture. Grad models came directly from Soviet stockpiles, and the political deputy opined that this reflected the hand of the predominantly Pathan National Islamic Front, a group almost wholly comprised of deserters from the Democratic Republic of Afghanistan's shaky army. Soviet advisers had taught them how to fire 122mm rockets, and while their allegiance proved tenuous, their memory of the training seemed all too exact. Apparently, these guerrillas also retained their connections with the Afghan military, or at least its ammunition depots. Zharkowskiy longed to pin down one of these characters. It could lead to many interesting things.

Donskov could not guarantee a firing incident the night his 3d Platoon staked out the agricultural facility, but the timing looked good. It had been three nights since the last rocket shots, and a detachment of highway engineers had just repaired the bridge that attracted the rocketeers' attention. Besides, the company was working on squad-to-platoon linkups, so the mission suited Donskov's training schedule.

Thus, Recon Company's 3d Platoon outposted the three sides that did not front Route 2, with a squad watching each leg of the perimeter road. So far, there had been no activity. Both previous rocket firings had occurred right after midnight, but the desantniks already knew that regularity was not an Afghan trait, nor should it have been. A predictable guerrilla is soon a dead one. Maybe, though, these bandits would give this project one more try. Donskov hoped so.

Unwilling to count only on the vagaries of the Afghan rebels' schedule, Donskov baited his trap with a lure reminiscent of Korobchenko. The captain wanted to insure a target worthy of any rebel's attention. Thanks to Zharkowskiy's connections to his old unit, Recon borrowed one of the Regimental Transport Company's GAZ-66B four-wheeled cargo trucks. Donskov arranged for it to "fall out" of a regularly scheduled ammunition convoy running south from Fire Base Bagration toward Kabul.

Stacked high with empty crates, the truck leaned drunkenly along the approach to the cement-slab bridge that formed the standard target for the National Islamic Front harassers. Its hood opened, a tire off, and its two-man crew bustling about in obvious consternation, the truck provided a perfect target. A few listless motor riflemen in camouflage battle dress and issue helmets guarded the broken-down vehicle.

Clad in the shapeless overalls of Soviet Army truckers, Senior Lieutenant Yegorov and Corporal Padorin delivered award-winning performances as they cavorted around the GAZ-66B. Equally fine efforts came from the six recon soldiers playing the part of the bored sentries. Donskov had positioned another squad from 1st Platoon in the bushy hummocks on the nearby ravine slope. These hidden troops protected the deception effort, just in case the guerrillas tried another means of attack besides rockets. The desantniks had covered all their bets, all right.

Yet, as Donskov replaced his night-vision goggles and swept across the silent, dark field of wheat hybrids, he was beginning to believe that it had all been a waste. Although he could not see them, he pictured his deputy commander and radioman continuing their charade down along the roadway. Indeed, all elements were in place, except of course the mujahidin. It did not bother Donskov that the mission turned up nothing; that was the story of recon work. You learned as much from what wasn't there as from what showed up.

It did annoy him, however, to think that he had committed five of nine precious dismounted squads chasing a single scrap of information, no matter how intriguing. This is my error; I'll have to be more careful about this, he chided himself. Zharkowskiy is working hard, but he's not infallible. As for himself, Donskov felt the only-too-familiar feeling of another dry hole.

A hard pressure on his right elbow caused Donskov to look sharply in that direction. Even in the indistinct greenish soup of the night sights, Donskov recognized Sergeant Ponomarev lying right beside him, his camouflage-painted face turned up from the shining green eyepiece of his SVD sniperscope. The squad leader held up his right hand, and Donskov saw the thin wire trailing from the noncom's wrist – the pull string linking the sergeant to his flank security. Now the fisherman had a bite.

"Four tugs, right," whispered Ponomarev, in a voice so faint that it might have been a thought. But it was real – Donskov knew it. He nodded in reply. Two hundred meters to the east, the right security men had detected four intruders coming down the trail. Might this be our rocket boys? Donskov's body tingled as he waited.

Yes, now I hear them, their small, swishing sounds carried on the weak night winds. He heard the steady shuffling of boots on dirt. He wanted to say it sounded like the measured trudging of men under a burden, but that was wishful thinking. He strained to see more clearly through the passive viewing goggles, but the scene remained maddeningly soft, slightly blurred, and all too regular. The little white structure stood serene; the field and road remained undisturbed.

Donskov's right hand tightened on his AKD's pistol grip, his index finger slipped into the trigger ring. His left hand slid smoothly down the handgrips, and he raised his forearm, bringing the welcome heft of the barrel up toward a standard firing position. I can't fire this sucker with these goggles on, but I can't see well enough without them. I'm a reconnaissance officer, Donskov reminded himself. Seeing is more important than shooting. Besides, Ponomarev has the SVD.

In accord with the platoon commander's mission orders, the crack-shooting squad sergeant would take out the Afghans before they fired any rockets. After all, there was no point in sacrificing Yegorov and Padorin. Dead rebel rocket men would explain a lot; a wounded or whole prisoner, if nabbed, might reveal even more. So Donskov watched, secure that Lieutenant Knyazin's patrol plan accounted for all the likely contingencies.

And then, looking like translucent wraiths through Donskov's night vision goggles, the four Afghans came into view. One, wearing a Soviet bush hat, a uniform tunic, and baggy native trousers, was a bit ahead of the rest. He carried a bipod launch tube across his shoulders like a shepherd carrying a lamb. An AK-47 hung from its sling, suspended diagonally across the Afghan's back. The firearm clicked notably against the dark metal launcher.

Behind the leader came three others, all huffing under their almost-fifty-kilogram burdens. Along with their own slung Kalashnikovs, the rocket bearers carried the heavy projectiles crosswise atop their shoulders, with arms flung across nose and tail for stability. The balanced rockets made the threesome look like an old icon of the legendary Jesus Christ and the two thieves at their crucifixion, thereby conjuring an image from Donskov's childhood of a visit to a dingy Voronezh church, a scene so remote and bizarre that he wondered if it had really happened or if he had dreamed it. Was he dreaming now?

He glanced to his right. Ponomarev's steady gaze through his sniper rifle's night sight and audibly quick breathing told him otherwise.

The captain felt anticipation but no physical fear. He perceived no direct personal danger. If anything worried him it was the possibility that the snare might not work. Nevertheless, the usual precombat rush of adrenaline, familiar now from Grenada and the Panjsher ambush, surged through Donskov. Before parachute jumps, before big live-fire exercises, under pressure back in school at Ryazan, he had sometimes detected distant echoes of the same strong emotional upwelling. Now he knew what these sensations were, and perhaps understood one reason why he had undergone such training. And so, although the night was warm, he lay there trembling ever so slightly. His teeth chattered a bit, and he longed for bodily activity, any activity, to curb his anxieties. Good thing the men can't see me, Donskov thought. But he knew that they were undoubtedly just as keyed up.

The four guerrillas slowed in their progress down the trail as they approached the little white building. Within a few meters of the shed, the launch-tube man held up his hand, and the procession halted. The burdened men shifted their heavy loads but said nothing. The lead bandit sniffed the air, like a big dog. Satisfied, he pulled the launcher up over his head and plopped it heavily onto the trail. Motioning to the first rocket holder, the guerrilla adjusted the bipod legs on the firing device, sliding it around to set up the chosen trajectory. While the second rebel prepared his projectile for loading, the other two men slid their rockets down to the dust and moved over to watch. None of the four mujahidin touched their AKs, nor did they assume any sort of local security position. They think they're alone, Donskov decided. Excellent.

A sharp metallic click, as loud as a rifle shot, reverberated in the almost-still night air. What the hell could that be? Then Donskov knew. It was the safety on the SVD. Ponomarev had waited until now to switch to the fire setting. The captain's stomach inverted; he tasted bile and felt the clammy start of a cold sweat. The stupid bastard – how could anyone be so careless!

The Afghans heard it too; how could they have missed that clear, crisp snap of new metal on new metal? The leader stood up from his crouched working stance and turned to stare directly at Donskov's underbrush position. He motioned harshly to his men. One began to unsling his AK-47. The leader reached back to do likewise as the four bandits separated, moving faster.

Do something – it's falling apart! Ponomarev did not shoot. Donskov could not shoot to kill, as he was unable to sight through his goggles. He reached over and rapped the sergeant's back. "Fire!" he hissed.

Crack! No click, this one; Ponomarev's SVD Dragunov had definitely fired. A whiff of expended gunpowder stung the captain's nose. The bright muzzle flash blanked out Donskov's goggles for a second, but when the green-hued view resumed, he saw all four Afghans down. They can't all be dead. The rippling reports of AK-47s told him that the rebels were still very much alive.

From the right, a sudden string of tracers picked at the prone Afghans. The tracers seemed as bright as fireflies in the night goggles. A stuttering, popping noise sounded from Donskov's right. The RPK-74 machine gun was being heard from. Sergeant Ponomarev shot another round. This time, once the flash bloom dulled back to fuzzy green, Donskov saw an enemy fighter writhing in evident pain. The RPK-74 tore along the trail again. Donskov saw dust puff up and watched tracers spin away in crazy ricochets. Some seemed to strike the four enemy troops. Yet an AK-47 still replied in short bursts. Ponomarev shot once more.

A little sun erupted on the trail, finally causing Donskov to pull off the night viewer. The grating blast of a 40mm round from a BG-15 rifle-mounted grenade launcher confirmed Donskov's guess as to the source. Three more of the deadly eggs detonated in quick succession. Even with his unaccustomed eyes, Donskov could see the four immobile hostiles silhouetted by the silver-electric grenade flashes. The RPK-74 snorted out another dozen rounds. No AK-47 firing came back. Another BG-15 grenade exploded, and then the machine gun kicked in again, a particularly long, wicked tear that raised geysers of dirt and thudded into the inert bodies sprawled in the pathway. The captain found his signal flare and fired it up at a slight angle. A brilliant ruby spark ignited almost overhead. Cease fire, search the kill zone. The shooting stopped instantly, as if Donskov had flipped a toggle switch.

The commander was up on his feet immediately, following Ponomarev and the RPG gunner down the gradual slope, down to the dead bandits. The two pairs of security men continued to guard the flanks.

Donskov's legs felt heavy and cramped by the hours of inactivity, and his eyesight was only about half what it should have been. The blocky R-114D radio bounced against his spinal column. Yet the captain's excitement overcame these minor discomforts as he raced to see what his trap had caught.

One needed no passive night sights to see the results of the engagement. The machine gun bursts, sniper bullets, and 40mm grenades had shredded the lead Afghan almost beyond recognition. Dark ooze, which Donskov knew to be red blood, smeared the torn remnants of the man's torso. Another man had lost a whole leg, cut as cleanly as if by a cleaver; in this case, cleft by 5.45mm machine gun fire. Other little holes flowered on his old Afghan Army field jacket. The third corpse still looked like a man, albeit a man with a bloody pencil hole above his staring right eye–the SVD Dragunov's grim work. But where was the fourth one?

Ponomarev hastily searched the three bodies, snatching up their battered weapons and rifling their pockets like an experienced thief, which he had been back on the Vladivostok wharves. He found a few blood-soaked items and stuffed them rapidly into his cargo pockets.

Donskov examined the unfired rockets and the launcher, quickly disconnecting the priming wires to prevent an accident.

Although nicked by grenade fragments and a few stray bullets, the three thick projectiles looked quite serviceable. Their ammunition lot numbers might reveal their original storage sites and, hoped Donskov, indicate who took them. He surely did not relish dragging the damn things back. But, after all, we still have choppers on call for a dawn extraction, and—

"This one's alive!" squealed little Private Latyshev, the RPG man. The short desantnik was at the lip of the drainage ditch, holding the left arm of a slack-jawed, rangy, taller youngster. Latyshev had his Makarov 9mm pistol squarely against the Afghan's drooping head. The bandit's dangling right arm showed a huge discolored splotch and looked broken.

"Good work, Latyshev," said Sergeant Ponomarev. "Comrade captain?"

"No orders. Good job, comrade sergeant. Let me help with this gear."

It took a long time to clear out the treasure trove, and in the end, most of Lieutenant Knyazin's 3d Platoon got involved with the removal of the rocketry and corpses. The Mi-6 heavy-lift helicopter that came out just before daybreak carted away the wolves and their spoils, including the deception force and their 3,600-kilogram truck. It was dangerous, exhausting work, and Donskov felt lucky that they had gotten away without meeting more guerrillas.

The commander's radio message to the political deputy almost atoned for the trouble of hauling out all of the detritus and loot. Zharkowskiy's reaction was nothing short of ecstatic. After weeks of patrolling, he was about to meet his first live Afghan rebel.

"Well, was he interesting?"

Zharkowskiy smiled broadly. "Certainly."

Donskov positioned himself on a water can opposite his political officer. Afternoon sunlight streamed in through the apertures, burnishing the hanging dust inside the Recon Company command post bunker, softening the hard edges of hanging weaponry and radios, and painting everything brown, orange, yellow, and gold. Even Zharkowskiy's dark features brightened in this golden haze.

"Was he a deserter? Was he from the National Islamic Front?"

"No to both questions," the political deputy answered. "His name is Saddiq Wajid, age seventeen, a Tadzhik from the Panjsher."

"One of Massoud's men?"

"Exactly so. Unfortunately, he's a real small fry. He and his associates were nothing special; even the leader was appointed only because he had fired a few Grads while in the loyal Afghan Army. But young Wajid did give me two valuable pieces of information."

Donskov hunched forward on his perch, waiting. Zharkowskiy lowered his voice.

"First, those rockets probably came from our 108th Motor Rifle Division main base at Khair Khana, just north of Kabul. The lot numbers are still being cross-checked, but Wajid's recollections of how he came by the Grads coincides with reports of a February raid on the 108th's ammo dump."

Donskov whistled. This was not good news.

"Second, we were lucky that 3d Platoon grabbed a literate bandit. Wajid was kind enough to provide a fairly elaborate map and organizational blueprint for the lower Panjsher, around the Afghan fire bases outside Rokka," said the deputy commander. He unrolled a neatly inked sketch and a few loose-leaf notebook sheets covered with Farsi scrawl. "Beyond those two revelations, he couldn't tell us much," Zharkowskiy added.

Donskov considered his deputy's report. Colonel Leonov had told him that once this training period ended, the regiment could expect another excursion into the Panjsher Valley, probably by mid-August. This Wajid's map gave the 688th a foot into a few interesting doors.

"What did you do with him?" asked Donskov. "Did you ship him off to division?"

Zharkowskiy shrugged. "They didn't want him, or his dead friends, either. The Second Section sent a courier down here to fetch the documentation, copies of Wajid's interrogation, and the original for the logistics overlay that I just showed you. Oh, and they took all of the captured weapons and ammunition, as usual."

Aside from the intelligence value gained by tracing these serial-numbered items, Donskov knew from his own brief stint in the 103d Guards headquarters that enemy arms served as prime bartering materials for bored rear area personnel. Division always took the weapons.

"So what did you do with him?" persisted Donskov.

"The same thing I did with the corpses, comrade captain," said the senior lieutenant quietly.

Donskov looked closely at his political officer. The captain knew immediately that something ugly had happened. "What do you mean by that, Andrey?" asked Donskov calmly, fearing for what he was about to hear.

"I put them all back out where they belonged," said Zharkowskiy, his ebony eyes glittering. "I had my man Abdullah and his Pathans bundle up the bodies with communications wire; you know how they love their Tadzhik cousins! Then I cajoled our rotary-wing falcons into giving me a lift in an Mi-8. We flew the bandits up to the bridge they almost knocked out. There, my Pathans and I tied them onto a post along the northern approach. We put a big sign on them, in Farsi and Pashto: 'Bandits liquidated courtesy of the VDV Wolves. Long live Socialist Afghanistan!' Kind of dramatic, don't you think?"

Donskov rubbed his jawbone. I don't know whether to be horrified or humored, he thought. "So you killed Wajid, then?" he queried.

"Of course not, comrade captain. I tied him to the corpses, so he can tell his friends about us. The only time he wasn't blindfolded was right here in this bunker, so he won't be able to give them much of tactical value."

He stopped speaking, but Donskov knew that Zharkowskiy wasn't finished yet.

"Go on, Andrey."

The political deputy sighed. The words came slowly but clearly. "Wajid was a rather hard case. He answered my questions with spitting and curses. So . . . "

Donskov looked right into Zharkowskiy's dark eyes. "So you tortured him?"

"Do you know how easy it is to make a man talk once you put an eye out? A hot screwdriver, a flick of the wrist . . . " He gestured quickly, reliving the scene for his commander's benefit. The lieutenant rotated his wrist as if spinning a doorknob. "And then Wajid told us whatever we wanted to know. He serves us still."

Donskov raised his eyebrows. Zharkowskiy spoke, his tone measured. "Comrade captain, the time for kindness with these Tatars passed years ago, if there ever was a time for compassion. Our bombers and guns have wiped away any chance to win them to socialism by reason. So only terror remains. Wajid is our vanguard, a warning to Massoud and his vipers that the Russians are coming for him, not with a sloppy bludgeon that may miss, but with a stiletto aimed right for him. As for the general populace, we don't need their love, just their fear and obedience. Maimed young men, doomed to live out their miserable lives in pain, make our case far better than dead martyrs."

"I understand," said Donskov. And he did.

Chapter Eight

The Means of Production

Its dull brown hull glowing in the last rays of sunset, the helicopter bounced along only a dozen meters above the shrub-dotted, razor-backed ridge. Rotor blades beat out a harsh tattoo as the craft crested the boulder-strewn height and then dropped like a stone into the shadowy ravine beyond. The veteran pilots swung the laboring machine from side to side, hugging the scrubby rockwork and throwing up dirt and sticks in the process. Despite the gathering gloom and the boiling cloud of swirling dust, the fliers pressed on just above the rugged terrain. Soviet aviators did not live to become veterans by flying higher in this cursed, contested Panjsher Valley.

The lurching descent caused the chopper's passengers to feel as though gravity were pulling out the pits of their stomachs. The desantniks aboard, familiar with these unpleasant sensations yet hardly reconciled to the experience, clutched their weapons tighter. The men exchanged nervous grins and knowing glances, the whites of their worried eyes evident in the pitching, dim cabin. Nobody wanted to think about what came after the jarring aerial approach, but all knew how these trips ended. The image of a dusk firefight for a tiny landing zone hung on the fringes of their consciousness, growing ever more insistent as the ride continued, much like the slow but inexorable mushrooming of summer thunderheads over the parched steppes of southern Russia.

Donskov always dreaded the undulating, jerky motion of

helicopter flight. In training back in Pskov, his stomach had often grown queasy as he watched the ground rise and fall beneath the clattering, twisting aircraft. True, the helicopter promised precision delivery of intact units, far preferable to the dumping of parachutists into the screaming, muddling windblast that always made for confusion on the drop zone. Getting sorted out after a jump could take hours. Heliborne efforts avoided all that. Instead, Donskov figured, you had to accept a slow, gut-wrenching flight in a vulnerable vehicle that, minus its rotor, had all of the aerodynamic qualities of a potato.

So Donskov was not much of a helicopter advocate. Parachuting from fixed-wing transport airplanes was no easier, however, and not just because of the usual drop zone reorganization follies. Although the planes droned along in stately, steady level flight for most of the way, the final run to the drop zone often rivaled any helicopter travel for uneven, unpredictable up, down, and sideways jolting. Donskov recalled many jumps in which a half inch of oozing, stinking vomit sloshed across the floor plates as the paratroopers waited to exit their bucking transport. And, like the American planes on Grenada, the big aircraft were extremely exposed during the actual drop. In truth, the captain preferred to go by foot or land vehicle, not by air. This constituted a rather heretical position for a VDV man, even one with a weak stomach.

Now, his carefully plotted map spread open, a headset clamped over his blue beret, Donskov leaned forward between the two helmeted pilots and guided them toward the chosen landing zone. As a commander, he had no time for the luxury of nausea. He was only vaguely aware of his headquarters squad packed into the compartment behind him. The craft had dipped into the canyon, below the light of the dying sun, and only telltale red interior lights and the phosphorescent instrument panels lit the helicopter's cabin. Donskov found it necessary to flick on his penlight in order to read his map.

A gleaming ribbon bisected the darkening valley floor. There, that's the Hazara River. Donskov told the pilots to bear right, southeast along the meandering waterway. The chopper tilted hard over, its rotors sweeping perilously close to the tangled trees of an overgrown fruit orchard. When his aircraft heeled over, Donskov instinctively looked through the small side window and saw the faint outline of the accompanying helicopter with the squad from 2d Platoon aboard. After a quick pop-up to make the turn, the pair dropped into the rocks, straightened up, and resumed their tortuous course.

The two Mi-24 Gorbach gunships hailed from the 262d Independent Tactical Reconnaissance Helicopter Squadron, one of the few units trained and equipped to fly at night. Stoutly armored, equipped with a four-barreled 12.7mm Gatling gun in a chin turret and rocket pods on stub wings, and powered by two Isotov TV3-117 turboshaft engines, the large Gorbach models had originally been designed to serve the KGB Border Guards along the troubled Chinese frontier. The KGB wanted a flying, fighting squad carrier to move men and firepower quickly into action on the world's longest disputed boundary, so the big Mi-24s retained a passenger capacity, unlike most Western attack helicopters. Soviet heliborne forces usually employed the purpose-built Mi-8 troop transports for major assaults, allowing the escorting Gorbach firing platforms to carry extra ammunition in their cargo spaces. Gorbaches also went hunting on their own, usually in pairs, on sweeps of bandit-held areas. Donskov heard that the Spetsnaz and Osnaz routinely used these sweeps to drop recon and snatch teams. He liked the idea, and from the time Yegorov had told him about it two weeks ago, squads from the 688th Reconnaissance Company had begun to hitch rides on Mi-24 dusk patrols.

"Coming up on the landing zone," intoned the command pilot. The captain craned his head to peer through the Plexiglas canopy. A kilometer south of the squiggling river, the small, flat, matted field looked just like the aerial reconnaissance photographs. As requested, Savitskiy's squad had placed tiny canned candles at each corner, their faint lights visible only from overhead.

Donskov palmed the headset microphone switch. "This is it; exactly so," he answered. He looked over his shoulder, catching Sergeant Major Rozhenko's eye. Donskov gestured, his right thumb down. Rozhenko nodded and nudged the men in swift sequence. It was time.

The twilight had already become night as the two Gorbaches

slowed, nearing their destination. Both pulled up slightly, kicking up dust, grass, and leaves as they settled to hover over the selected flat spot.

"That's good. Watch out for the markers."

"Got it," grunted the bug-faced pilot, his night-goggled head bent in concentration as he nursed the large helicopter almost to the ground. His taciturn partner had his head almost out of the window, scanning the ground.

"Go!" ordered the pilot.

With that, the Mi-24 crew chief and Sergeant Major Rozhenko threw open the doors. The desantniks stumbled out, stooped by their rucksacks, weapons in hand.

"We're out!" yelled Donskov, tearing off his headset with a quick yank. He tossed it onto the canvas seat and followed his men out of the quivering craft. Two steps, three, and out the door, almost slipping, falling the last meter or so into the brambles.

The twin turbines roared overhead, pressing down on Donskov as he regained his footing. Crouched beneath the whirling blades, he headed out ten meters and dropped into the soft, dark grass, his feet toward the Gorbach. Automatically, he shouldered his AKD, brushing aside the annoying but essential dummy cord. You'd have to be a dummy *not* to tie things to you, Donskov knew. Everything not attached had a tendency to get lost at night, especially once the adrenaline started pumping. Any item left in the Gorbach would be lost, gone forever, or at least until, and if, the chopper returned.

He heard the beating blades accelerate. The grass flattened and grit particles whizzed through the air as the Mi-24 bobbed unsteadily out of its hover and surged skyward, slowly at first, then gathering velocity. Its nearby partner followed within a second. Ten seconds later, both Gorbaches were nothing but throbbing echoes, black spots dwindling against the darkening sky.

Grass rustled, and Donskov stood up to find two small groups assembling at opposite ends of the overgrown meadow. Two men stepped carefully around the leaning wooden posts and stone urns, treading lightly on the irregular mounded rectangles of newly turned earth. The headquarters element and 1st Squad, 2d Platoon, cleared the landing zone in record time, heading in opposite directions. Soviet soldiers, even confirmed Marxist-Leninist materialists, had no love for grave sites.

It had been Zharkowskiy's idea. He had found out by accident, while recruiting and testing prospective Tadzhik scouts, that the locals refused to transit or even skirt graveyards at night. The men told the political deputy that no Afghan dared enter a burial area after sunset, for fear of the djinns and ghosts who lived there. "If they won't go there, it's precisely where we want to be," deduced Zharkowskiy.

This graveyard, on the edge of a village burned out and abandoned during the May fighting, lay far from any known habitation. A few relatives, refugees now, still visited during the day. They had even added a few more unfortunates to the field. But at night they fled, unwilling to meet the demons.

Real flesh and blood demons are here now, mused Donskov as he led his men out from the landing zone. We're wearing blue berets and carrying AKDs, and we're looking for you, Panjsheri bandits. Or haven't you heard of Wajid? He's met the wolves. But don't worry, Tadzhiks; there will be others besides Wajid. Of that Donskov could be certain.

"Wolfpack net, Wolfpack Leader, report. Over."

Donskov released the transmission switch on his R-114D radio, waiting. Across the eighty square kilometers of the Hazara River valley, a side channel of the much bigger Panjsher corridor, six squads of the 688th Reconnaissance Company, plus the political deputy's scouts, worked through a lengthy list of likely guerrilla hideout, cache, and headquarters locations. The desantniks were trying to confirm clues unearthed back in the Shomali. The map that had been coerced from poor Wajid formed the base document, embellished with additional fragments, including the first fruits of Zharkowskiy's newly prepared Tadzhik group.

Five squads, plus the political deputy's men, were already on the ground when Donskov landed. It had taken almost a week to send them in. Most of these men had flown up to the Afghan Army fort at Rokka and walked from there, tagging onto scheduled patrols and then staying out. One squad, plus Zharkowskiy's Tadzhiks, had slipped out of the back of a lengthy Afghan Ministry of Agriculture truck convoy distributing fertilizer throughout the lower Panjsher. The three squads of Knyazin's 3d Platoon would infiltrate over the next two nights, accompanied by Senior Lieutenant Yegorov. Decentralized movements like this were time-consuming and required careful navigation by the squad sergeants. But thanks to the strenuous Shomali training period, the recon troops could handle the challenge.

"Wolfpack Leader, Gray One. Negative report. Over."

"Gray One, confirmed. Out," replied the company commander. The units on the Wolfpack net, designated by the appropriate lupine colors Gray (1st Platoon), White (2d), and Black (3d), were supposed to answer in series. It worked in training. We'll see about out here, Donskov thought.

"Wolfpack Leader, Gray Leader; am with Gray Two. Message. Over."

"Send it," answered Donskov. Corporal Padorin, lugging a second R-114D that was tuned into the 688th command frequency, sat next to his commander in the wide semicircle of the dark, crumbling culvert. The conscript waited to copy Gray Leader's message. Outside the culvert, in a loose ring, forward air controller Suslov, gunner Menzhinskiy, aidman Zhivanetsyn, and Sergeant Major Rozhenko provided security.

"Wolfpack Leader, Gray Leader. Three groups. Six zero eight. Seven three two. Zero zero four. Three groups. Over."

Donskov turned to Padorin. "Got it?" The corporal nodded. Once all stations had made their reports, he would decode this message, plus any others.

"Gray Leader and Gray Two, confirmed. Out."

"Wolfpack Leader, Gray Three. Negative report. Over."

"Gray Three, confirmed. Out."

A negative report did not necessarily mean that nothing had been found. What it meant was that nothing *extraordinary* had been discovered; the routine data would be collected at prearranged face-to-face linkups. Donskov received similar negative reports from the White elements of 2d Platoon, to include White One, which had arrived alongside Donskov's headquarters squad. Black was not on the net, nor would they be until they began to arrive in the area the next evening.

"Wolfpack Leader, Wolfpack Three. Negative report. Over."

It was Zharkowskiy. His husky voice betrayed no special concern, although by plan, he was likely right in the midst of a complex of presumed rebel encampments and known hostile villages.

"Wolfpack Three, confirmed. Out."

So there was not a nibble, despite seven lines dunked into the Hazara. Well, it had taken awhile to find things in the Shomali, too, and now my men are much more fully trained, Donskov rationalized. On the other hand, the first few spots revealed through Wajid's interrogation had proven to be of little interest. It's almost as if the bastards know we're here. And why shouldn't they? After all, this was the Panjsher, the heart of Massoud's domain. Most of the guerrilla groups merely cut through the Shomali. Massoud and his Islamic Society warriors *lived* in the Panjsher.

"Comrade captain, I've broken Lieutenant Savitskiy's message," Padorin whispered.

"Go ahead."

"'One wounded in action mines'—that's it."

"Mines. Shit. Ours or theirs?" asked Donskov. Padorin said nothing, merely lifting his shoulders. How could he know?

"Well, we'll get the story in the morning. We're headed to see Lieutenant Savitskiy right now."

Donskov stood up and motioned for his headquarters men to follow. They had at least a four-hour march up the long, steep slope to Checkpoint 45, where they'd rendezvous with 1st Platoon. The valley seemed so empty. But Donskov knew better.

"It might be a meeting of Nabi Bakhtari's district headquarters, no less."

Zharkowskiy spoke with certainty, his body leaning forward from his seated position. Behind him, curly-haired, sharp-faced

Ibrahim, leader of the Tadzhik scouts, squatted up against the flat stone slab that marked the cave entrance. The Afghan's AKD featured a bright red and green tassel on the folding metal stock. Sergeant Major Rozhenko sat next to Donskov. The four men surrounded Zharkowskiy's map, which was spread flat on the sandy cave floor. Here and there on the crinkling, smudged sheet, a few cryptic blue marks, far too few, marked almost three hot, draining weeks of work.

"I know who Bakhtari is, but I didn't think we'd placed his position in the Islamic Society yet. What's his job?" asked Donskov.

Zharkowskiy pulled out a dog-eared field notepad. He picked through it, surveying a page briefly. "Bakhtari's in the top ten, the Politburo, if you will. Massoud's Islamic Society has about 3,000 armed men in the Panjsher, plus at least 20,000 civilians acting as auxiliaries. We're all aware that this bandit group fields three types of forces: Massoud's own picked Central Forces battalion, seven mobile companies, and about forty static local platoons. I'm fairly certain Bakhtari commands the mobile company based here in the Hazara branch of the Panjsher. He also acts as the district commander. His military council would likely include a political agitator, a Muslim mullah or two, a tax collector, and maybe some village representatives. We don't know for sure. Now this village in question"–the political officer tapped the map–"Checkpoint 18, Aq Khater, has a population of 100 by my estimate. About two dozen or so are squatters, run out of smaller hamlets by our air strikes back in the springtime. There couldn't be more than ten fighters in the town. I've counted eleven permanent structures, three sheds, and two tents. Just to refresh your memory, Wajid marked this small settlement as a big ammunition dump, although he didn't connect it with Bakhtari."

"Up till now," cautioned Donskov, "Wajid's map has been only about half right, and only on the most rudimentary stuff like small ammo caches or well-used trail junctions."

Zharkowskiy listened and nodded slightly. "Yes, I'll agree that the Wajid interrogation hasn't completely panned out yet. After all, he was only a mujahid, not a chieftain. But I'm basing this suggestion on much more than Wajid's word. After all, that was a month ago."

Donskov did not reply. He averted his gaze back to the map and waited.

"A series of developments have convinced me that there will be a meeting of the Hazara district military council two nights from now," continued Zharkowskiy. "We've found five of these handbills in the trash heaps outside Khawak and Shahr-i-Saqqao."

Donskov regarded the scrawled curves and spots on the torn yellow papers. The markings were as inexplicable as always.

"These broadsheets are titled 'The Struggle against the Godless Devils,' " explained Zharkowskiy. "The rest of the verbiage promises big news for all believers on the fifth day of the month of Asad–28 July by our calendar. That's three days from now, or two nights, to be proper. I think it means that orders will be coming, following this meeting. Why do I figure that, you ask?" Zharkowskiy turned rapidly to another page in his book. "Last week, during a patrol of the ridge overlooking the Panjsher-Hazara River confluence, our White Two desantniks surprised a mining team and picked up a drawing titled 'meeting place,' and listing the date '5 Asad.' The diagram is rough, but it corresponds nicely with Aq Khater."

The political deputy added the paper to the five crumpled announcements. Donskov recognized it, and he instantly recalled the sharp little encounter that had delivered this item. A remote Muslim security element killed one of his men during the firefight. Unlucky Private Breshkarev died messily from an old Enfield slug, leaking clots of brain into aidman Zhivanetsyn's lap as they waited for a helicopter that came too late. That constituted the going price for a vague, dirty sketch here in the Panjsher.

"Village rumors, picked up by my scouts and also Black One more than six kilometers away, suggest a meeting in the next few days," Zharkowskiy stated. He purposely slowed the cadence of his speech and lowered his voice. "Finally, we've been watching Aq Khater for four nights. We had some luck. An old herdsman that Ibrahim caught last night told us all about Bakhtari, who just happens to be his nephew."

Donskov did not pursue the talking uncle issue. Ibrahim's wicked smile and Zharkowskiy's intense demeanor explained plenty.

"Where does this put us, Andrey?"

"It seems to me, comrade captain," intoned the political officer, "that we can learn a lot by observation of this possible meeting at Aq Khater. We must prepare, both to watch who comes in and pursue who goes out. They'll take us to the more critical points in this valley if we are ready to trail them. This may be the break we've been waiting for. We're down to a little more than a week before extraction, and what do we have to show for our efforts?"

"Two dead, five wounded, and only some low-quality shit— mortar rounds here, rebel trails there," said Donskov glumly. "We haven't found much. These bandits seem to smell us coming and pull away before we can find them. All we see are sleeping villagers, goats, sheep, and rocks. We know they're here. We've taken the damage to prove that. But where are they?"

"This is the best lead we've had so far," Zharkowskiy reminded his commander. Donskov paused, thinking it over. *This will take more than just the Tadzhik scouts. I'll have to bring in backup, alter the patrol patterns. But it could be done.*

Redheaded Rozhenko spoke up, breaking Donskov's concentration. "I have something to say here, comrades."

"Certainly," the recon commander said.

"There may be no meeting there," warned the company sergeant major. "Worse, it may be some kind of ambush. I wouldn't put it past that yapping wood chip Wajid or this old-timer you folks slapped around. Didn't you find it curious that you just *happened* to pick up Bakhtari's uncle, out chasing goats at midnight, right in front of your observation posts? These bandits are incredibly treacherous, you know. I recommend caution. This smells funny."

Zharkowskiy shrugged. "True enough. But if we don't follow up on this, we'll never know. And we may never get such a good grip on this Hazara district leadership, and maybe even its mobile company. If we follow these people, even a few of them, it could lead a long way. Come on now, can we afford to pass up a chance to pull ourselves right in toward Massoud? What if, somehow, we got to him? The entire Panjsher counterrevolution might crumble. Right?"

Donskov weighed the recommendation. Catching Massoud was

a pipedream; two Osnaz teams, Afghan KhAD agents, and at least one Spetsnaz company worked full time trying to do that. How could a regimental recon unit succeed where all of these elite experts had failed? Not that it mattered. If the 688th could destroy a sizable chunk of Massoud's forces, catching the slippery Tadzhik leader might become unnecessary. Tearing open the Hazara structure, after all, was why Donskov had brought the company out here. Zharkowskiy's exaggeration aside, Donskov had to admit that his deputy was correct. It was a chance to latch onto a target worthy of his parent regiment's attention.

"We'll set up and have a look," Donskov announced. He turned toward Rozhenko. "But I'm going to arrange a pretty hefty surveillance and pursuit effort, with two full-strength platoons and preplotted supporting fires. Just in case."

"The scouts will maintain observation on Aq Khater until you get the show ready," said Zharkowskiy.

"Rendezvous for orders tomorrow morning, 0500, at Checkpoint 24," Donskov concluded.

"I serve the Soviet Union," responded Zharkowskiy. Swarthy Ibrahim simply leered, baring all of his great white teeth.

Another night out with the boys and the bandits, thought Donskov. He adjusted his night vision goggles, scanning slowly back and forth across sleeping Aq Khater. Nothing moved; no lights showed. But not every inhabitant was sleeping.

The meeting had been underway an hour, inside a nondescript, windowless square hut near the center of the cluster. Now, with the prey on scene, all the desantnik commander could do was wait.

The 2d Platoon waited around him, here to the east. The 3d Platoon guarded the village's northern approaches, and the Tadzhik scouts screened the south end. The high, uneven cliff made enemy movement to the west highly unlikely; none of the nine arrivals had entered town that way, of course. All three units stood ready to dispatch chase squads. Once the rebel leaders dispersed, they would be followed to their lairs and thereby expose part of the guerrilla infrastructure, all neatly recorded as potential objectives for the future endeavors of the 688th Guards. This night, patience appeared certain to bring rewards.

Waiting and watching had become regular pastimes for Donskov. It had been less than two months since he had begun his weird nocturnal life, yet already it felt unpleasantly normal, this stalking of men. It should have been nothing but frustration. Reconnaissance offered the tension of the hunt without the satisfaction of the catch. Recon work compared to actual combat as voyeurism related to real sex – all looking and no doing. It was strange business, although the all-too-typical frictions and mistakes that engendered firefights were hardly welcome interludes in the general drudgery of gathering information.

Yet I do like it, Donskov reflected. I relish the challenge of operating alone deep in the enemy's home territory, piecing together his deepest secrets, and delivering solid targets to the clumsy but powerful line units. Why? Because I can do as I please, my way, Donskov knew. Out here, far outside the fire bases and way past the jump-off lines, there were no party flunkies, or Chekists, or niggling nervous army chains of command. There were only us and them, guns and wits, life and death. It became simultaneously the most complex and yet the simplest situation possible, a dialectic that might have even amused Marx himself. Solve your problems and live; fuck up, and pass into the great beyond.

"Hey, what are they doing?" Rozhenko rasped in a grating whisper. Donskov turned toward his company sergeant major's voice and followed the man's outstretched arm. Sure enough, from the south, two of Zharkowskiy's Tadzhik scouts were crawling slowly, wriggling like snakes, into the town. Donskov grabbed at his hand mike.

"Wolfpack Three, Wolfpack Leader. What's going on? Over."

A pause, static rushing, and then Zharkowskiy's voice came through. " . . . away with the camera. I couldn't stop them. Over."

"Wolfpack Three, say again –"

The detonation of a mine broke off Donskov's transmission. The white-hot flash overtaxed the PNV-57 passive night viewing device, and Donskov pulled it off immediately. The echo of the explosion bounced off the rockwork and reverberated, giving way to moaning as the scout writhed helpless in the mine field. His partner was an immobile pile of rags.

The village, including the meeting hut, remained as dead as a tomb. Nobody came out. The mujahidin had to hear the blast, didn't they? Why no reaction? Donskov's pulse began to race. This felt bad, very bad.

The vicious eruption of a DShK heavy machine gun to his right rear made survival Donskov's immediate goal. Just to his right, a corporal's prone form twitched and rolled, his RPG launcher bouncing away, chased by big 12.7mm bullets. Donskov clawed the gravelly earth as a belt of the powerful machine gun rounds cracked down the length of the trapped recon platoon's position. He felt bits of stone pelting his uniform as the rounds stitched back and forth.

Lieutenant Beregovoy, the 2d Platoon commander, bellowed, "Ambush! Ambush!"

But everyone knew that. Donskov needed help from 3d Platoon. He longed to slide the radio microphone to his lips, now pressed against the musty, coarse brown loam. He trembled, nearly paralyzed, afraid to move. If I stand up, I'm dead, his mind told him. The warm darkness, the wild, strobing muzzle flashes, and the unexpected bushwhacking all coalesced to pin him to the ground—inert, useless, unthinking, with flared nostrils and wincing with anticipation as the bullets beat around him. He served no purpose other than his own. He felt like a target. And he was.

The machine gun hammered down the line again. Green tracers whipped overhead, some from the town. Donskov could hear sobbing, and no AKDs or RPK-74s at all. Where are my other two elements? How can I get control of this mess? How can I get control of myself? Oh, how grand it would be to bound upward, full of energy and anger, and turn on the bandit ambushers. He tried to nerve himself to push up. He'd done it in Grenada, and in the BMD march through the rainstorm, but this time his legs and arms could not be convinced. Whining ricochets and sprinkling dirt kept him down in the rocks.

He wished he had brought Yegorov here. Kliment Ivanovich would know what to do. Zharkowskiy had his hands full with the

Tadzhiks. Those stupid fuckers, they had caused all of this. Intentionally? No—be reasonable, Dmitriy. Two of them are down, too. The DShK fired again, a long chattering rattle, striking home with sick, wet sounds and the cracks of supersonic metal bolts breaking large bones. Lighter, discordant Kalashnikov shooting came out of the village, probing for Russian flesh with hot, insistent firing. Hidden AK snipers loosed a round, or pulled off a brace of two or three, all marked by intermittent, jumping green tracers that smacked and whirled among the hard, low rocks behind which the desantniks cowered.

"No guns! No guns! I can't raise them," Menzhinskiy's disembodied voice drifted in. There would be no help from the god of war tonight. An air strike was out of the question, at least in time to do any good. Nobody else will do it. It's me or death, calculated Donskov. He raised his head a fraction, an effort that strained him as greatly as would lifting a tank.

The DShK opened up again, its regular pounding drowning out the AK-47s. Only the paratroopers' good cover and concealment, and the bandits' obvious lack of night sights, prevented a massacre. He's behind us on the right, I think, with AKs there and some in the town to create a cross fire. Oh, they've cooked our asses. If only 3d Platoon could maneuver against him. If they're free. If they can see what's happened.

Another stutter of machine gun bullets raced along the desantnik perimeter. A shriek, a Russian curse, and more sloppy impacts. Donskov barely made out a form slithering through the position. I've got to do something or we're going to die down here, Donskov told himself. When he finishes firing . . .

But Lieutenant Beregovoy, the most average-looking blackhaired, green-eyed Muscovite in the world, was already up. "Come on, comrades! Let's take these bastards! Up! Up!"

The desantniks began to jump to their feet. The rebel machine gunner must have been changing a belt, or had a stoppage, or was merely waiting for a nice set of erect targets, because he didn't fire. Donskov reared up to his knees, snagged his dangling radio microphone by habit, and pressed the transmit bar.

He did not get a word out before the DShK began another burst. Its location was obvious, betrayed by the ugly spray of yellow muzzle flashes about fifty meters away, up a few meters on the slope. That's him! He's close. A grenadier lowered his AKD and pumped a BG-15 40mm grenade directly at the brightly sparking DShK. The potent little round splashed a millisecond's worth of silver illumination as it discharged into a thousand hot fragments. The enemy firers hesitated.

Beregovoy did not.

"Go, go, go!" chanted the lieutenant, driving his legs and waving his arms as he began to run toward the machine gun. Beregovoy fired his AKD from the hip. A group of men sprang up behind him, spread out in echelon to either side, like pilot fish trailing a shark. Tactics, battle drills, and formations deteriorated into this— desperate men scrambling to kill their tormenters before they themselves died. Donskov, his blood roaring in his ears, followed too. Raging with excitement, faced by this clearcut danger, he forgot any sort of radio message.

Get the gun. Get the gun! The captain fired his autorifle and shouted something guttural. The dozen or so airborne soldiers began to close on the DShK.

The long black barrel looked as big as a tank cannon when it barked again, bowling down two blue berets. One desantnik threw a grenade, which popped harmlessly behind a boulder, lighting the impromptu attack like a newsman's flashbulb. The instant of white glare showed at least four turbaned heads near the DShK.

The side guerrillas were firing too, their AKs jumping and snarling on full automatic, and therefore wildly inaccurate. Wandering, random tracers still emanated from the town behind, but now as the paratroopers closed on the machine gun site, these shots threatened the bandits themselves. But one bullet, machine gun, AK-47, or maybe even a stray AKD, tagged Beregovoy, who went down as if poleaxed, dropping his rifle, choking out blood and chunks of bone from his shattered lower jaw. The Soviets wavered, staring at their officer.

"Follow me!" roared Donskov, leaping forward. It was instinctive, not rational, as Donskov found himself wholly possessed by the immediacy of the task. The paratroopers stiffened and surged on. One tumbled, tripping on the rocks. A small voice far beyond questioned Donskov: Are you out of your mind? But he didn't listen. He was an animal, not a man, with one need: Get the gun. The gun, damn it! Danger, fear, and logic meant nothing. All that mattered was grabbing that gun and finishing its operators.

Wanting to be pulled along, needing direction like cattle behind a horseman, or more like wolves behind their gray-furred leader, the men followed eagerly. They funneled toward the enemy position. A low, horrid "urrah," spawned on a thousand Russian battlegrounds over a millennium, thundered from their parched throats. The VDV riflemen fired from their hips as they advanced.

A sharp snap, a ripping metallic screech, and the DShK quit firing, a half belt dangling unused on the broken weapon. We're almost on you, you devils! One rebel slumped over. The other three panicked.

They began to run, but there would be none of that. It was dark, and they were almost ten meters away and moving as fast as they could over the broken ground, running down toward the village.

Donskov swung his AKD to his shoulder, squinting as if on the rifle range back in Pskov. He aligned on one weaving, flailing hostile soldier. The twisting figure filled the sights. Donskov kept the AKD's snout on target, and his head drummed out the old commands: offhand, slow fire, ten rounds, commence. Pop! Miss. Pop! Hit, on the left arm. The man held it and kept going. Pop! Miss. Pop! Miss. Pop! Hit, and a solid one. The guerrilla's head flew apart like a dropped rotten melon, and his legs staggered on a step, two, then he spun and pitched forward, utterly dead. Donskov dropped his barrel slightly to search for the other two. Too late. His men had accounted for them already, at close range. One Soviet emphasized his bullets by a bayonet coup de grace, howling with exhilaration.

Breathing hard, sweating, and a bit disoriented, Donskov automatically fell back on old habits. Attack complete; rally and reorganize. He shouted: "Platoon sergeant!"

"Right here," Senior Sergeant Levkhin replied from his left rear. The little Tatar, eyes bright in the gloom, was panting like a tired dog.

"Get them together. Establish security. Account for casualties."

"We've got the lieutenant already, comrade captain," gasped the sergeant.

"Right. Good," said Donskov. The desantniks around him stood, weapons just lowering, wary and tense, alive with an almost tangible electricity. So this was real war—not just hiding or getting shot at, but closing with the scumbags and finishing them off. Despite the black of an Afghan midnight, Donskov saw everything with crystalline clarity: the sweating men, the crumpled, bleeding Afghan bandits, the chipped rocks, the smoking rifle muzzles.

"Radio reports from Black Leader and Wolfpack Three," said Corporal Padorin, walking up slowly through the jumbled, rock-strewn stretch of slope that lay between the bandit DShK post and the former 2d Platoon perimeter. "Haven't you been monitoring, comrade captain?"

Like a man woken suddenly from a vivid dream, the commander shook his head to clear it. He remembered his 3d Platoon, the scouts, the village, and the mission. What about all that? He twirled around, fumbling for his own radio handset.

Things had definitely changed. Four of the hamlet's squalid huts were on fire, blazing merrily in the night. A long file of robed people stood silhouetted against the conflagration. What the hell had happened? The crack of AKDs sounded from the hamlet, and with dawning horror, his torrent of adrenaline dwindling into cold drops of perspiration, Donskov realized what was going on. He began to run.

Eight bodies, neatly punctured and neatly arranged, lay where they had fallen, face down in the dirt path that separated six of Aq Khater's hovels from the rest of the ramshackle shelters. Three of the corpses were women, and one was a little girl, aged under ten. All wore flowing off-white robes, probably sleeping gowns, now stained by regular patterns of crimson rosettes.

The remaining eighty-one Tadzhik villagers stood to the left of the eight bodies. The people formed a long, ragged rank, their backs to the quartet of flaming clay brick family dwellings. In front of them, at defined intervals, hard-faced young paratroopers of 3d Platoon stood with legs spread and assault rifles trained. A Tadzhik scout and big Lieutenant Knyazin faced the old man at the end of the line, nearest the dead villagers. Both soldiers had their rifles pointed at the frail, white-bearded elder.

"What is going on, Pyotr Vasiliyevich?" asked Donskov quietly, sidling up behind the massive platoon commander.

Knyazin turned half about, his eyes wide with fear, like a teenager caught smoking behind the barn. The stocky little scout did not react at all, nor did the threatened Afghan. A child cried near the far end of the line, but other than that, the locals made no gesture to acknowledge the commander's arrival.

"Comrade captain, I . . . uh, that is, I'm waiting for orders."

"Indeed. From whom?" queried Donskov, his voice as cutting as ice-cold steel.

Knyazin jerked his head toward an intact hut just past a crackling pyre. "From the deputy commander for political affairs."

Donskov could see two Tadzhik irregulars on guard outside the black rectangle that marked the primitive building's entrance. Small artifacts were flying out of the door at odd intervals, and Donskov thought he detected the wavering beam of a penlight inside.

What are you up to, Zharkowskiy? Donskov wanted to know, yet there were these slain Afghans, high-strung desantniks with loaded weapons, and a very guilty platoon commander right here, demanding immediate attention. Zharkowskiy could wait a bit. The captain returned to the issue at hand.

"Did you shoot these people, Lieutenant Knyazin?"

The platoon commander, his face smeared with sweat and dirt, nodded slightly. "Yes. The two toughs here," he said, indicating two stiff male bodies, "ran out with AKs—they hit a machine gunner, Dalmatov. Sergeant Ponomarev got one, but the other went into that first house."

"And?"

"The sergeant and Corporal Sviridov cleaned it out. It was dark inside, and they weren't careful. They nailed this woman and the fat man here." Knyazin nudged the scuffed toe of his right boot toward two still bodies. "The squad got a little overexcited and torched the place. One of our men dumped a white phosphorous grenade into the neighbors' shack. Whoosh! It went up. *That* brought the Afghan villagers into the street. Senior Sergeant Milyukov and I gained control; we stopped the wild shit right there. Two huts were already aflame. The political officer arrived at this point, bringing his men in from the opposite end of town. He assumed command. Four natives were dead, including those two without weapons. A search began, looking for the black-ass leadership cadres. We couldn't find them. Nobody talked. We'd been ambushed, and there'd been Ponomarev's little fire show already." He inclined his head toward the first roaring inferno of a house. "So . . . "

"So?" prompted Donskov.

"So, on the political deputy's orders, to put pressure on the father, I killed the girl and her mother," finished Knyazin, his voice quavering just a hair. "He didn't talk, but when we dropped two more, bang, bang, then a lot of wood chips started jabbering."

Donskov looked away, staring into the hot golden fire. A roofing beam collapsed, trailing a string of smoldering ceiling matting into the heart of the blaze and landing with a muffled thump and a shower of orange sparks. What next, commander? A mission compromised by ambuscade, black and bloody confusion, and now eight orderly cadavers, all within minutes, and to what end? Donskov had to talk to Zharkowskiy immediately.

"Lieutenant Knyazin, hold these villagers under close guard, but no more shootings. Understand?"

The officer nodded. "Exactly so, comrade captain," replied Knyazin nervously. He paused, then asked, already knowing the answer, "Did I do something wrong?"

"I hope not," Donskov muttered. Then he shifted on his feet and stepped off toward the building that contained Zharkowskiy.

It took only a few dozen seconds to cross in front of the vacant-eyed Afghans and their taciturn sentries. The burning clay and wood structures belched tall flames and cast long, lurid shadows. Donskov reached the door of the hut just as his thin, dark political officer emerged. He was speaking in Farsi, to Ibrahim at his side, gesticulating with animation, and evidently preoccupied. As a result, he nearly blundered into his company commander. Ibrahim hurried away, toward Knyazin.

"What's the situation here, senior lieutenant?" requested Donskov with that peculiar, forced modulation that usually preceded an eruption. The very form of address, by rank rather than name, told Zharkowskiy that regardless of his interest in ongoing efforts, he had better devote a minute or two to his captain.

"Search in progress, comrade captain. The ambush caused us to revert to an alternate plan. We obviously can't follow anybody home, so we're trying to unearth the nine visiting mujahidin leaders, their local host, and their papers. Then we go from there. I believe they're hiding out in one of these miserable dung heaps, in a camouflaged underground bunker, to be precise. It took only a few minutes to narrow the possibilities once I ordered a little encouragement to speed the questioning process."

He said it so matter-of-factly, as he always did. Donskov was about to ask for more of an explanation when a camouflage-clad Tadzhik scout, along with a horribly grinning Ibrahim, popped out of a dark hut. The scout yanked on a rope. Ten men, a few showing bruises and all dragging their feet, shuffled out into the dusty street, propelled by the AKD of another recon auxiliary.

"Bandits here – bandits in floor!" announced Ibrahim proudly in his pidgin Russian. He pointed to the bound men as if displaying a string of especially fat fish. Here were the subjects of this evening's festivities, garbed in the usual strange collage of cast-off khaki uniforms, native rags, and Soviet boots. They looked small, weak, and totally harmless. It seemed hard to believe that these frightened men were the wily Bakhtari and his hardened battle cadres, but they were.

Two more Tadzhik irregulars came out of the same hut that had just disgorged the rebel prisoners. The scouts carried four bags of what had to be documents. It looked like a significant haul.

Zharkowskiy smiled, his pleasure quite plain in the leaping firelight. He clapped his hands once, rubbing the palms together. "Search completed, comrade captain. We can evacuate these prisoners and documents by helicopter, along with our wounded. It didn't work out quite right, but it's close enough. In fact, it may be better. These characters may tell us more than we could have learned from our intended trailing effort. And the interrogations might reveal the entire Islamic Society network."

Donskov just stood there, listening, wondering. Another triumph for 688th Recon, right? He puzzled over how every bloody reverse seemed somehow to right itself into a success. Donskov feared that perhaps he was beginning to grasp the real meaning of small unit combat—a series of gory little slugfests that left both adversaries reeling. The side able to get up first and totter away could claim victory, and then rationalize the whole thing into clever phrases and neat lines and arrows.

"Of course," Zharkowskiy said breezily, "we'll have to clean this up." He swept his arm along the silent row of Afghans—bent old men, liquid-eyed women, snub-nosed children.

Donskov pressed him, although he already knew what hid behind the euphemisms. "What do you mean, 'clean this up'?"

Zharkowskiy dropped his voice a few notches, leaning closer. "Well, surely you realize that we can't leave eighty-one live witnesses behind to tell the tale of our impromptu raid on Aq Khater. We're carting off the district high command, but Massoud can't know that. Therefore, we need to clean up."

"Shoot the civilians?"

"Naturally. And bomb and burn out the village. That's essential. We must cover up this episode, so the Islamic Society can't figure out what happened to their missing friends until it's too late. Maybe they'll just think it was a random air strike," remarked Zharkowskiy conversationally. He sounded as calm and detached as if on the training grounds outside Ryazan.

Donskov did not reply. His face said enough, its lines etched deeper by the brightness of the hot yellow flames.

Zharkowskiy recognized the doubt and spoke again. "Now, comrade captain, you know I'm right."

"Yes, exactly so," sighed Donskov. "Objectively, you're correct. Still . . . "

Zharkowskiy's black eyes grew thin with derision. "They're savages, fucking Mongol half-breeds. I ought to know, I was raised among them. Remember, any chance for a political solution was blasted away five years ago. We're soldiers; we didn't choose that. But like it or not, it's us against them. They ambushed us, after all. This place is lousy with ammo caches; there aren't any innocents here, comrade captain."

Donskov gazed past his political officer, regarding the stoic Afghan faces arrayed opposite him. Try as he might, he could engender no hatred. But neither could he generate pity. These dark-skinned, rag-swaddled beings were alien creatures. How could their eventual fate affect him?

Donskov contemplated the direction that this night had taken. He knew it had to end in a massacre. The weight of history, the unforgettable horrors of the Tatar Yoke, impelled Russians to distrust those with slanted eyes, swarthy complexions, and Muslim customs, in reflexive response to a thousand grisly medieval slaughters perpetrated by Mongol-Turkic overlords. Now the tide of time had turned to favor the Slavs, and woe to the degenerate residue of the once all-powerful khans. Donskov accepted it subconsciously, just as the tsars' lieutenants and Stalin's border commandants understood. Aq Khater was merely the last 500 years of Russian border fighting writ small, but no less final.

Consciously, Donskov wanted to be outraged. Soldiers were honorable men, or should be, and slaying defenseless civilians hardly squared with that ideal. Perhaps I'm concerned because I think I *should* be, he thought. But I don't feel anything beyond a gnawing unease. When I saw the dead civilians, I was more worried that my men had done something undisciplined than that they had killed Afghans. After all, what's the difference between an unfortunate citizen and a bandit auxiliary? Either way, they're dead, never to aid another rebel, or even think about it. If only *I* didn't have to think about it.

"Logically, I know you're right, Andrey," said Donskov. "But this seems a hell of a way to gather battle information."

Zharkowskiy eyed his commander intently. "It's the only way. Our duty is to bring in data, and the struggle for combat information has yet to be socialized."

"Meaning?"

"If you want to know things out here, it's a dog-eat-dog capitalist market. We pay the market rate for every bit of knowledge, whether in sore feet, frayed nerves, broken bones, or bleeding wounds. Sometimes for the really choice items, we have to pay very dearly. You see, our prized commodity is information, and among these black-hearted Muslims, hard terror is often the means of production. Nothing comes easily."

Nothing—that's what this may all be worth. If the regiment is too slow, or the Afghans too clever, this may be for nothing. Intelligence is as fragile as gossamer, and all of our tricks can't change that. When it comes down to it, we're no different than any other recon outfit. We kill to know who else to kill. And they kill us in the meantime. And for what? To bring socialism to the dead?

No, to keep the war going. That's all I'm doing here. I'm not solving anything. I'm just pouring blood, maybe a bit less or a bit more skillfully than most, but it all dumps into the same sordid stream, greasing our long, dark slide to nowhere.

He caught himself, his tired mind lurching. What the hell am I thinking? The marching, the ambush, and now this. The shit must be getting to me. I know better—it's us or them. Zharkowskiy understands what he's doing. It was going to happen anyway. I don't want to show my doubts. But despite these intentions, the words spilled out. "I'm afraid we'll pay for this one for a long time."

Zharkowskiy shrugged. "We've already paid, with our own blood, Russian blood. We can take our winnings and move on, or let these scum survive and throw our fates to the night winds. Regiment is counting on us to come through."

The political deputy finished his sentence and stopped. Both men stared at each other, as if hoping that scrutiny would allow each to see what wasn't there. A few seconds ticked by.

"Do it," said Donskov firmly. And with that, he sealed the hamlet's fate. The captain intentionally avoided making eye contact with the string of patient villagers, waiting in ignorance for the result of a decision they would discover much too late.

"My scouts and I will take care of the arrangements," assured Zharkowskiy. "Give me an hour, then have Suslov call in the falcons to pulverize this place."

Ninety minutes afterward, as they climbed far up and away from Aq Khater, the desantniks sensed the far-off rumbling of a major bombardment, followed by the sharper reports of secondary explosions. Days later, Donskov heard from a mujahidin deserter that the fires had burned for three days at Aq Khater. But there was no Aq Khater anymore.

Chapter Nine

The Road to Ali Khel

Colonel Leonov turned to his chief of staff, Lieutenant Colonel Rotmistrov. "Impressive work, eh Pavel Grigorevich?"

The burr-headed blond young chief agreed: "Exactly so, comrade colonel. If only half of this is accurate, it would still represent a quantum leap in our reconnaissance effort."

"I'm hoping it is all accurate, comrade lieutenant colonel," said Captain Donskov lightly. "Naturally, it's changing even as we speak. Recon Company will continue to produce updates until the line companies enter the Panjsher on the initial sequence of raids. I've got a platoon out right now, and I'm prepared to rotate the other two through the observation posts for the next week or so, until Operation THUNDER begins. Has division determined a start date?"

"They have," responded Leonov without any particular conviction.

At this, Rotmistrov looked nervously to the regimental commander. Even in the relatively dim light of the regimental command post bunker, Donskov noticed the fleeting glance. What was up? Donskov wanted to ask, but the impassive expression on the chief of staff's face told him that the colonel would explain. After a few uncomfortable seconds, Leonov fixed his eyes on Donskov. The colonel spoke, each word distinct.

"The 688th won't be going on THUNDER, Dmitriy Ivanovich. We're pulling back down to Fire Base Bagration, to act as 40th Army reserve. The 393d will go in our place, with the 593d as a second echelon."

The colonel paused. Rotmistrov stared absently at Donskov's wonderfully detailed enemy situation map. The chief of staff already knew.

"But why, comrade colonel?" Donskov asked.

"Army's worried about our casualty rate. The 3d Battalion took quite a bloody nose in that tangle two weeks ago at Landing Zone Vyazma, and we lost a good chunk of our last ammunition convoy from Bagram. Combined with the beating we took back during MARS—well, you can see the argument, can't you?"

Donskov said nothing. His face looked as unemotional as ever, but disappointment clouded his normally bright brown eyes.

"Division's Second Section is using all of your data, Dmitriy Ivanovich. So the last five weeks have not been in vain," Rotmistrov interjected hopefully.

That's small comfort to tired men who've spent more than a month tracking down Massoud's minions in their rocky lairs, Donskov reminded himself. What of my two paratroopers who died in that damn scrap in the hamlet north of Rokka? How about the four dead that night in Aq Khater? What of the eleven wounded airborne men lifted out of the Panjsher, their blood soaking the makeshift poncho stretchers? What for? We've brought the 688th Massoud's fucking head on a platter, or at least close, and now . . .

"How soon can you turn over your patrol routes to 393d Recon Company?" inquired the chief of staff in a pointedly official tone of voice. There would be no complaining in this headquarters, at least not out in the open.

Donskov sighed ever so slightly. Back to the damn Shomali! Shit! "Forty-eight hours, comrade lieutenant colonel," he said softly.

Leonov cleared his throat. "That's good, Dmitriy Ivanovich. Take another forty-eight hours to rest and refit at Bagration. As of 0001 on 12 August, your outfit is attached to the 217th Guards Air Assault Regiment from the 104th Division."

Donskov's wide eyes mirrored his absolute surprise at this news.

Rotmistrov chimed in. "Right now, they're flying in from Kirovabad in the Caucasus to Kabul International. They're using their pathfinder platoon strictly to organize the airflow. General Major Golitsyn insisted that the 217th have the best available intelligence capability. So you'll be working as their recon chief."

"The 217th is coming in for a very important task. Your mission will be to relieve Ali Khel," stated Colonel Leonov.

The gravity of this last sentence registered immediately on Donskov. Every Soviet soldier in the Limited Contingent knew about the embattled border fortresses at Ali Khel, Khost, and Barikot. In theory, these reinforced positions interdicted mujahidin supplies from neighboring Pakistan. In practice, the fixed valley posts became beleaguered hellholes, defended by battered Afghan Army units and their jaded Soviet advisers. The garrisons lived from helicopter and paradrop resupply. They barely held on under an irregular succession of violent guerrilla barrages, nightly infiltration attempts, and even occasional full-tilt infantry assaults. Of the three, Ali Khel was under the heaviest pressure. The captain guessed that the situation there must have deteriorated badly to call for such an extraordinary Soviet measure as the insertion of a fresh VDV regiment from the motherland reserves.

This promises to be a hell of job, Donskov reckoned ruefully, especially if the timetable is too short. Recon Company will have to guide an effort to break through a well-established rebel cordon to save this encircled Afghan Army fire base, well south and east of anywhere Donskov and his wolves had ever been. I don't know anything about that area, let alone about these 217th Guards people. Why me, and why my tired men? Donskov would have been happy to let this cup pass, but he knew that he had no such option.

The captain simply wanted to get out of the regimental headquarters bunker. It seemed like the ceiling was pushing down on him, and the air felt too thick to breathe. The colonel and chief of staff appeared to be frozen in place, small, distant, and insignificant as Donskov absorbed the new information. After the previous weeks' painstaking surveillance work and the discouraging cancellation of the regiment's Panjsher push, compounded by his personal exhaustion and now the news of this wild Ali Khel thing, was it any wonder that Donskov began to feel his composure slipping? He felt the strain of inchoate, raging frustration building up.

But he was a trained Soviet officer, a Ryazan graduate, and his logical faculties still held sway over his emotions. His intellect told him not to blame Leonov for this. Orders were orders, however strange or unwelcome. It's better to get to work on the problem. Yes, work: It's a numbing tonic for any disappointment, no matter how sharp. Marx would approve.

The two senior officers noticed nothing during the several seconds it took Donskov to assimilate his change of mission. Their recon chief merely appeared contemplative. Perhaps they noticed a cloud crossing the sun of Donskov's visage, but the passage was very swift. The captain looked up.

"Do you have liaison directives, comrade colonel?" he asked simply.

The colonel turned to his chief of staff. "Pavel Grigorevich?"

"Colonel Kurolesov, the regimental commander, and his chief of staff will be flying in to this location at 0900 tomorrow, just to meet you," remarked Rotmistrov.

"This whole mission is a real vote of confidence, Dmitriy. The general chose you especially for this task. If you have no further questions, you're released. Good work on the Panjsher project," concluded the colonel.

"I serve the Soviet Union," Donskov replied. He exited, already lost in concentration.

"That's everything I could get on the Khalis Faction of the Islamic party, comrade captain," said Zharkowskiy. "I'll know more tomorrow."

"It's a start," offered Donskov hopefully.

Zharkowskiy, Yegorov, Sergeant Major Rozhenko, and Captain Donskov sat on the bunker floor, the clean, new Paktia mapsheet spread between them. Corporal Padorin stood guard at the bunker entrance as the command group worked, with firm orders to keep interlopers well outside.

The gunner, the air controller, and Savitskiy were still en route back from the Panjsher, having handed over their patrol sites to the 393d recon desantniks. Donskov knew he would have to hold another orders group with all of the platoon commanders and the two fire support officers, but he hated to waste time while he waited for his company to reassemble. So he had started work with what he had.

Already, the political deputy's preliminary findings had begun to give this unknown Khalis Faction a few faces and places. Yegorov, who had the neatest handwriting, had begun to plot tentative enemy sightings. In crudest form, the situation in the Paktia region looked much more conventional than Massoud's vast, shadowy guerrilla network. The other soldiers watched Yegorov work; they sat mesmerized, undoubtedly thinking of the drastic change of scene to come.

"Here's another thing, along the lines of general situational awareness," Zharkowskiy piped up. "I've got some inside commentary on our new regimental commander, Colonel Kurolesov."

The men turned toward the political deputy. Once he was certain he had their attention, he continued, very quietly. "A classmate of mine from Novosibirsk is in the 217th. He's served under Colonel Kurolesov for seven months." Zharkowskiy paused, selecting his words carefully. "He had already made it to Kabul, and I ran into him while I was poking around up at the divisional political section— showing my face, a little agitprop update, you know? When I told him we'd be working with the 217th, he suggested we find a way out of this mission. He said we'd be sorry to serve under this commander. His precise words were: 'Kurolesov is a manipulative careerist weasel who would betray his mother for a general's gold-braided shoulder boards.' "

"He didn't seem that bad when we met him yesterday," said Yegorov. "In fact, he was quite impressive."

Zharkowskiy frowned. "So was that fascist madman Hitler, Kliment, at least on first meeting. Or so I've read. I strongly recommend caution in dealing with this one, comrade captain. He's not Colonel Leonov."

"I guess not," answered Donskov, reluctant to criticize Zharkowskiy's judgment. The commander, too, had been favorably influenced by his first discussion with Colonel Kurolesov. But Zharkowskiy rarely erred, so Donskov did not discount the information.

"I'll keep that warning in mind, Andrey, and I'd urge the rest of you to do likewise. But until it's proven, let's give this colonel the benefit of the doubt. Now," said the recon captain, "about the Khalis Faction's units . . . "

The small, chubby chief of staff touched the planning map with his pointer one last time. "Just a reminder. All units are to occupy their jump-off area positions no later than 1200 on 21 August. I will entertain your questions following the commander's orders."

With that, the colorless Lieutenant Colonel Gamarnik moved aside. Trim Col. Vasiliy Nikolayevich Kurolesov stood up briskly, exuding confidence. Fresh-faced, almost boyish, with scintillating blue eyes and a friendly shock of neatly combed dark hair, the commander of the 217th Guards Air Assault Regiment dominated the small bunker. His subordinate commanders and staff officers, including Donskov, could not help but focus on this energetic, youthful man.

"My dear comrades," he began in a honeyed voice. "I think we can all thank Lieutenant Colonel Gamarnik for a masterful plan, one certain to fulfill our important internationalist duty at Ali Khel. I would like to stress three points of special importance as you begin to conduct detailed planning, rehearsals, commanders' reconnaissance, and troop movements."

He paused for effect. "First, party political work will be absolutely critical. I expect all Communists and Komsomol members to exert maximum agitation efforts. Explain the sound ideological background of our regiment's important deployment into Afghanistan, and spare nothing in inculcating the burning necessity of saving our fraternal Afghan socialist brothers from the grip of these bloodthirsty CIA marauders. A full-scale, all-out struggle to enlighten the collective must become a point of honor for all party members and candidate members. Commanders and political deputies should devote their entire energies to this vital political task.

"Second, with regard to the tactical realm, speed must key our attack. My careful objective analysis of previous military operations here in Afghanistan indicates an excess of caution. For some reason, most of the commanders down here have forgotten their doctrinal schooling. They creep and sneak as if tanks and infantry fighting vehicles did not exist. Let's not forget that our enemies are merely lightly armed primitives, not the Hitlerite panzer divisions. These wood chips cannot stand up to a massive armored thrust! Smash them with fire strikes, find the gaps, rush through, and keep driving, all the way to Ali Khel!

"Finally, I expect complete, detailed reports and prompt, enthusiastic obedience to my orders. Let there be no deviations from the approved decision algorithms and designated battle drills. Loyal, wholehearted execution of my orders is every officer's primary duty. Indeed, loyalty is the best trait for any good subordinate. I'll do the thinking; you carry out my desires. And let's flush these rebel shits once and for all, okay?"

The regular staff and commanders laughed loudly, much too loudly to be genuine. Kurolesov beamed and even chuckled at his own weak joke. Donskov and Zharkowskiy, who were not laughing, exchanged worried glances.

"Well?" whispered the deputy.

"Your friend might have been right."

The ensuing question-and-answer session with Lieutenant Colonel Gamarnik lasted only a few minutes. After a three-hour briefing, there were not many questions left to be asked. Gamarnik dismissed the group with a distracted wave of his hand, then turned to concentrate on the attached tank battalion commander from the 70th Motor Rifle Brigade, who had some serious concerns.

Donskov and Zharkowskiy stood up from their camp stools, gathered their maps and notes, and prepared to leave. Donskov was pulling his blue beret from under his belt when a neat orderly tapped him on the shoulder.

"Are you the attached recon company commander?" asked the corporal.

"I am."

"The regimental commander wants to see you and your deputy in his cubicle, comrade captain."

"Okay," said Donskov, with a sideward gesture to his bemused political officer.

"Follow me, comrades."

Colonel Kurolesov stood up and grabbed Donskov's hand as soon as the orderly pulled the canvas curtain aside from the small warren of an office tucked into a flank of the wide regimental command bunker. The colonel's new field desk was covered with papers, including several folded maps.

"Thank you so much for your wonderful briefing, Dmitriy Ivanovich. I was extremely pleased with your preliminary hostile forces survey, not to mention your insightful contributions to our battle plan. And this must be your deputy commander?"

"For political affairs, comrade colonel," corrected Zharkowskiy. Kurolesov relinquished his grip on Donskov's right hand and effortlessly snagged that of the senior lieutenant.

He's a smooth character, Donskov observed. What a politician! This guy should run for government office. Donskov would discover later that, in fact, Kurolesov was a delegate in the legislature of the Azerbaydzhan SSR. It did not surprise the captain.

"My pleasure," responded Kurolesov. "It's always wonderful to be reminded of our party's wise and useful role in military affairs, thanks to the diligent Main Political Administration. I trust you've prepared a stimulating series of discussion outlines for the use of your unit propagandists and party activists. Recon troopers especially must strive for the highest degree of ideological commitment as they ready themselves for the missions beyond the main body of advancing soldiery."

The fulsome exhortation caught even the normally sardonic Zharkowskiy by surprise. "Exactly so, comrade colonel," he replied by rote. Zharkowskiy looked extremely uncomfortable, as if closeted with a pit viper. In a sense, he was.

No doubt the colonel would have been shocked to discover that formal Marxist-Leninist instruction had fallen a bit behind in the 688th Reconnaissance Company; it had been virtually eliminated, to

be precise. The good colonel might have been even more distressed
to discover that this political deputy was in fact the recon officer of
the recon unit, and had devoted most of his time to gathering intelligence of esoteric and ugly types, not to mention commanding local
Afghan auxiliaries. Zharkowskiy, of course, elected to keep his new
regimental commander blissfully ignorant.

"Excellent," said Kurolesov. "You're probably wondering,
Dmitriy Ivanovich, why I asked to see you. It's fine that you've
brought your political deputy, because he can insure that the decisions we discuss here can be properly explained to your men. There
are two things I need to clarify with regard to your subunit battle
plan. I expect your enthusiastic and loyal compliance."

"Naturally, comrade colonel," Donskov said, a bit uneasily. This
colonel surely had a fixation on loyalty. That set off alarm bells.
Officers who deserved loyalty never discussed the issue. The con-
verse, unfortunately, held all too true. With this unwelcome prospect
in mind, the captain dutifully yanked out his notebook, flipped it
open, and positioned his pencil.

Kurolesov's blue eyes twinkled. He spoke crisply, with chop-
ping hand gestures. "First, with regard to your personal role. My
evaluation of the situation has forced me to a decision that may seem
unpalatable to you. But it is necessary, and it deserves your absolute
support. Despite our previous agreement, and in alteration of my
original intentions, I have elected to retain Major Zhimovin as my
chief of reconnaissance. He is GRU trained, a military academy
graduate, and well versed in interactions with this regimental staff.
He will exercise supervision over your recon efforts."

Donskov objected immediately. The words poured out: "Comrade colonel, this is not the best way to operate. Recon assets must
respond to one commander–"

"And so they shall," interrupted the colonel, his voice smooth as
silk. "You'll command your men, the eyes of our regiment. With my
pathfinder platoon already gainfully employed elsewhere, your company must do its full duty. Major Zhimovin will coordinate your
unit's actions in support of my decisions."

"Has he been in the south, comrade colonel?" asked Donskov.

"Is that relevant?" the colonel shot back. "It seems to me that it is not, given how little you all have learned down here. I consider him untainted. Like myself, he's served proudly in the western military districts, backing up the groups of Soviet forces facing the real threat, the saber rattlers of NATO. For your information, Dmitriy Ivanovich, Major Zhimovin is superbly qualified for his role. He performed with distinction in the 107th Guards Air Assault Division in Lithuania, graduated with honors from the Reconnaissance Faculty of the prestigious Frunze Military Academy, and holds an Order of Service to the Motherland, 3d Class, among other distinctions. You, my friend, would do well to place more trust in the decisions of your superiors and confine your energies to execution of orders."

He flashed a winning smile. But Donskov, used to speaking his mind with Leonov, trained to give his opinion by Korobchenko, did not let it go that easily.

"I'll agree that the major is qualified," said Donskov tactfully. "But one should not overlook the value of experience. I've been a regimental recon chief in combat for more than two months."

"I fully concur," said Kurolesov. "That's why I want to let you do your job, unfettered by tedious requirements to deal with routine staff necessities. Do you deny that you are usually forward with your outfit?"

"Radios and rendezvous procedures have allowed me to function in the 688th, quite well, I'm told," retorted Donskov.

"And I'm sure that it will work out here. Cooperate with Major Zhimovin as ordered," said Kurolesov, biting off the words through his rows of white teeth. The colonel forced another smile.

"Exactly so, comrade general," said Donskov quietly, beaten down. The phrase hung in the air for a few seconds, unchallenged. Then Kurolesov charged in to fill the void.

"Well then," said the colonel, "with that minor matter disposed of, let me discuss a slight change of the battle plan. You intended to deploy into the zone of advance tomorrow night?"

"It will take three nights to get fully into the Gardez–Ali Khel corridor," explained Donskov, relieved to be dealing with the nuts and bolts of combat preparations rather than Kurolesov's quirky command structure. "I estimate that we'll be on station by 16 August, at least as far in as Larakay. Six days is not a lot of time, but I think we can get a grasp of the basic situation by 0500 on 22 August, when Operation RED HAMMER kicks off."

Kurolesov clapped Donskov on the shoulder, and stared into the captain's eyes with boundless sincerity. "Dmitriy Ivanovich, this would all be fine if the relief of Ali Khel was to be a typical, plodding mission by the Limited Contingent. But that's not the way we worked in the western military districts. We had to worry about imperialist NATO tank divisions, and in our many realistic high-intensity maneuvers, we learned to move swiftly. That's why I'm here, I believe, to infuse the Limited Contingent with a little regard for mass and velocity. Thus, I don't intend to walk in at leisure and turn the valley into a virgin land reclamation project. We won't need to know the soil composition, native religious practices, or traditional beverage preferences. I want to smash through and be done with it!"

He halted, looking to Donskov for a response. All his speech produced was a confused: "Comrade colonel?"

"Don't you see it, my friend? Isn't it obvious?"

Donskov looked back, completely lost. Zharkowskiy appeared not only lost, but nervous, a very rare state for him.

"Surprise, comrade captain, surprise! How can we shock and overwhelm these black-assed ridge runners if your methodical patrolling effort gives away the whole mission? I cannot permit even the remote possibility of that. No, there will be no troop reconnaissance in the zone of advance. It's too risky. We already know enough. Concentrate on conducting your heliborne forward detachment tasks. That's why I asked for a company trained in tactical helicopter raids, day and night. I assure you, you will have plenty to do along our line of march."

Incredible, thought Donskov. This crazy son of a bitch has completely hamstrung our company's method of fighting. We're fucked, and I cannot do a thing about it. The glowing colonel saw no need to continue the rather one-sided discussion. He pumped Zharkowskiy's right hand, then Donskov's.

"Thank you in advance for your help. Operation RED HAM-

MER will establish new norms for combined arms battles. Perhaps you both will read about it some day in military academy texts. Remember, comrades—speed. Driving, ruthless speed will carry the day. And please, see Major Zhimovin if you have any questions or recommendations, comrades."

Kurolesov swung open the green canvas curtain and motioned them out with a graceful sweep of his arm.

The two officers walked out into the bunker proper. Radios crackled, clerks walked back and forth, and the nondescript chief of staff was still explaining some fine points to the tank commander.

"We're headed for a lot of trouble," mumbled Donskov.

"Not headed, comrade captain. We're in the shit already. And sinking."

Operation RED HAMMER commenced on schedule at 0500 on 22 August 1984 with a massive program of near simultaneous aerial bombardments along the sixty-six-kilometer gravel road between Gardez and Ali Khel. Great silver Tu-16s, flying so high that their contrails barely scratched the blue dome of the Afghan skies, came from Long Range Aviation bases in the USSR. They dumped hundreds of metric tons of high explosives and incendiaries along the convoluted ridges that defined the long, exposed approach to Ali Khel. One string of bombs caught a Khalis Faction platoon at prayer; another detonated an ammunition dump in the caves outside the encircled Afghan garrison at Said Karam. Most of the ordnance just rearranged the rocks.

Under the soaring Tu-16s, sturdy Su-25 ground attack jets spun and dove like birds of prey, slinging 500-kilogram bombs into villages identified as "suspicious" by Lieutenant Colonel Gamarnik and his regimental staff. Follow-on aircraft released RBK-250 cluster munitions, each such container spewing sixty lethal bomblets that struck with the force of sixty 82mm mortar shells. Alternative loads included scorching napalm, the unquenchable creeping horror of white phosphorus, and a novel type of munition called fuel air explosives. This new class of weapons created a fine suspended mist of volatile liquid and then set it off in a thunderclap, smashing brick buildings flat, rupturing internal organs in humans, and setting the wretched leftovers aflame. Finally, after battering chosen targets, the Su-25s wheeled about and ripped off 30mm strafing bursts, clearing their magazines and finishing their grim work. Unlike the Tu-16s, these did a lot of damage to hamlets all along the road to Ali Khel. Hundreds of civilians, dozens of houses, and a few slow-moving guerrillas fell to the wave of Su-25 jets.

Artillery in Gardez, Said Karam, and Ali Khel pounded out a ten-minute opening barrage on more than a hundred preplanned locations, plastering these sites with rockets and shells of various types. Guided by forward observers overhead, this fire did a great deal of tactically significant damage throughout the valley. Villages that escaped the roving Su-25s or the far-off Tu-16s did not avoid at least some attention from the well-stocked batteries supporting RED HAMMER. In fact, Kurolesov's fire preparation schedule did not discriminate. Every settlement along the route that appeared on the current maps felt the sting of the Soviet god of war.

Their initial program completed, the gunners shut down, waiting for calls from the advancing echelons of the 217th Guards Air Assault Regiment (Reinforced). As the dust from the air strikes and cannonades settled, in came flocks of Mi-8 helicopter transports and escorting Mi-24 gunships. Blazing away with cannons and 57mm rockets, these low-flying warbirds jostled their way onto the crests overlooking both sides of the roadway. There, they off-loaded clots of 104th Guards paratroopers, with 1st Battalion on the northern ridges and 2d Battalion inserted to the south. Airborne companies secured positions on each slope, guarding the flanks of the driving armored column. A couple of platoons of tired, dirty Afghan soldiers from the grandiosely named 38th Commando Brigade provided a veneer of socialist solidarity.

Down the center barreled the 70th Independent Tank Battalion, on loan from 70th Motor Rifle Brigade. Right behind, choking on the stinking diesel exhaust, raced the BMD-mounted men of Kurolesov's 3d Battalion. A borrowed regimental artillery group of 122mm self-propelled 2S1 howitzers rolled along to deliver immediate fires. Engineers, equipped to breach mine fields and obstacles, also accompanied this assault echelon. Finally, just ahead of the trundling Rear Services cavalcade came Kurolesov's pathetic excuse for second echelon, the dispirited, truck-borne conscripts of the Afghan Army's grossly understrength 67th Brigade, 12th Infantry Division. What this rump outfit could contribute was anybody's guess. The entire steel armada rumbled along under a flitting air cover of circling jets, weaving Gorbach helicopters, and hanging yellow dust.

Twenty-one kilometers today, twenty-seven tomorrow, eighteen on the final run—that was all it would take, by Kurolesov's estimate. He set the objectives accordingly; link up with the Afghan militia outpost at Said Karam by nightfall, meet the attached 688th Reconnaissance Company at Larakay the next afternoon, and then punch into Ali Khel on the following day, to shake hands with the long-surrounded Afghan 36th Regiment. It would be over and done before the Khalis Faction could react.

Surprise appeared to be complete. The reinforced regiment moved forward against only the most feeble, disorganized resistance. Vigilant aerial observers roamed the zone of advance all the way to Ali Khel. These helicopter scouts found only two small armed groups, even though the upper valley crawled with moving people, a disorderly human torrent of ragtag refugee bands fleeing out of the path of the onrushing Soviet juggernaut. Flashing Su-25 attack jets and galloping Gorbach chopper gunships dogged the panicky civilian herds with pitiless strafing runs, tearing screaming strips out of the amorphous, faltering crowds. It was right in accord with the plan.

When the virtually unscathed 70th Tanks reached Said Karam shortly before nightfall, Kurolesov bubbled over with glee. He transmitted an encouraging message to all units, concluding with this flourish: "Our firepower and speed of advance have restored mobility to the Limited Contingent. Heedless of everything this hellish land could throw against us, we have wrought a miracle."

Forty-eight kilometers beyond the jump-off line, twenty-seven kilometers ahead of their nearest VDV comrades, in a desolate moonscape outside the shattered town of Larakay, Donskov and his wolves heard the message. They spread out, hunkered down, and waited for the miracle to continue. Like all good materialists, Donskov did not really believe in miracles.

The Khalis Faction men, of course, believed. And as the warm night shrouded the valley and hid the final escape of the last frightened flocks of women and children, the lean, veteran Afghan rebels set about making some miracles of their own.

"Exactly so, Wolfpack Leader. At least twenty, four with rocket launchers, three with machine guns. Over."

Donskov marked the sighting and rechecked his map. "Gray Leader, say again hostile direction of movement. Over."

"Southwest, along the outside crest. Over," answered Lieutenant Savitskiy.

Donskov replied, "Confirmed. Out." Then he consulted his map again, considering this identification of a fifth separate Khalis Faction element moving southwest, laden with heavy weapons. The company had not seen a refugee for hours. In fact, the gush of people trudging out of the valley had abated completely, to be replaced by armed, purposeful trickles headed right for the approaching Soviets. Only the Afghan fighters were left, and those bandits were wriggling into positions for a series of ambushes between Said Karam and Larakay.

The recon desantniks' deployment on the high ground allowed them to detect all of this movement. This very placement, however, violated (or at best grossly stretched) Kurolesov's explicit orders. Donskov wagged his head in dismay. Never had the vast gulf between war on paper and war on the ground seemed so immediate.

The exquisitely designed 217th Guards battle plan inserted Donskov's company just north of the tumbledown remnants of Larakay, once a town of a thousand souls, now a scarred trash heap populated by ghosts, dogs, and rats. Larakay itself possessed no intrinsic value; only its location made it important, at least to Colonel Kurolesov. This was because shattered Larakay was built around a road junction, the tie-in point of a twenty-odd kilometer route from Pakistan. This east-west gravel highway followed the bottom of a canyon piercing the eastern ridges that defined the main valley, and thereby constituted the only noteworthy high-speed avenue of approach into the Gardez-to-Ali Khel corridor. Kurolesov worried that a mobile enemy force could hit him through this side door, and this probably made perfect sense in the European mechanized combat that the colonel understood so well. Here in the south, it was a misplaced concern.

Nevertheless, the regimental combat scheme assigned Donskov's recon unit a two-part mission: as a forward detachment, to secure the road junction at Larakay, and, once there, to provide an early warning screen along the eastbound spur trail. Kurolesov's grumpy chief of staff, Gamarnik, cautioned Donskov: "Stay out of the hills; those belong to the line battalions. You just keep an eye on that flank entrance and hold the trail junction till the combined arms column arrives. Then we'll bounce you ahead to Ali Khel."

Donskov took one look at the map, consulted the exceedingly optimistic RED HAMMER timetable, and disposed his company as he saw fit across seven kilometers of broken terrain. Seeing as much as possible, as usual, keyed Donskov's deployment. A reconnaissance element must sense its surroundings, or it becomes nothing more than a weak line unit. Donskov preached it often enough, and specific orders from regiment or not, he did not forego his conviction. As the captain hoped, some of the moving Afghan bandits rewarded Donskov's precautions.

It was a loose net indeed, but good enough to get the job done. Sound camouflage techniques, schooled in the Shomali and Panjsher, provided a degree of protection from mujahidin attack, despite the dispersion. The Grays of the 1st Platoon drew the difficult Pakistani side roadway and its overarching cliffs. Reliable, practical Savitskiy strung a squad on each crest and one in the low ground between. Lieutenant Knyazin's 3d Platoon Blacks outposted the northwestern heights with one squad, then set up the other two squads on the lower slope, one north and one south of Larakay. Both flank platoons chose sites that allowed them to see over the tops of their respective chains of high ground; this permitted Savitskiy's report of rebels on the outside crest.

In the valley proper, around Larakay, Donskov employed his

rebuilt 2d Platoon and his hastily reconstituted Pathan scout contingent. The 2d Platoon outposted the southern face of the thin, permeable company perimeter and waited for the appearance of the Soviet armor. Zharkowskiy's rusty Pathans, still under that broken-nosed, big old graybeard Abdullah, patrolled the northern face of the circle. Both units required serious retraining. But there had been no time. So Donskov kept them near at hand and positioned his headquarters in between these two units.

In 2d Platoon, several replacements filled the holes torn open back in the bloody Panjsher. Chief among the recent arrivals was cheerful Lt. Oleg Danilovich Popov, a weight-lifting enthusiast, who replaced the stricken Beregovoy. The new lieutenant had undergone only a few days of rudimentary training before plunging into this mess. Donskov used to promise himself that he would never do such a thing to a novice officer, and here he had already done it. Luckily, strapping Popov, a former conscript with Afghan convoy service in the motor rifles, seemed up to the pressures. This mission has bent too many of my rules, mused Donskov.

As for Zharkowskiy's dozen auxiliaries, the shift to Paktia province necessitated reversion to Pathan rather than Tadzhik scouts. Not all of the Pathans who had served in the Shomali shakedown were willing or available to go on this excursion into unfamiliar Paktia province. Five new, almost untrained Pathan men joined the detachment in their stead. Worse than the personnel turnover, the conventional, short-notice forward detachment mission, especially under Kurolesov's strictures with regard to premission intelligence collection, obviated the scouts' major role—the patient, long-term gathering of political and military data from the locals. Zharkowskiy, although definitely uneasy about the entire escapade, still vouched for his team's performance: "They'll do fine; these people are born soldiers, remember?"

Donskov did remember, and that was exactly the issue as he contemplated his map at 0337 on 23 August. Those bandits infiltrating south will be in place by the time the Soviets close on Larakay, he calculated. Donskov expected that the Khalis Faction mujahidin would lace the valley floor with mines, set lethal ambushes on the few obvious hilltop landing zones, and burrow resolute RPG tank killer teams along both sides of the highway. The thing might seem disorganized by Soviet standards, and it would bear no resemblance to the American imperialist antiarmor kill zone that Kurolesov apparently anticipated. Instead, the unsuspecting 217th Guards faced the usual Afghan version of the death of a thousand cuts – dropping a tank here, a helicopter there, and pairs and threes of unfortunate desantniks everywhere. If the Khalis guerrillas got very lucky, or Kurolesov turned out to be especially stupid, an isolated Soviet detachment, maybe even a company, could be wiped out. Donskov vowed that his recon company would not serve as such a sacrifice.

"They're moving by us, aren't they?" It was Yegorov, squatting there in the darkness. He, too, had been monitoring the latest reports.

"Yes, Kliment, they are."

"You've got to call regiment immediately," said Yegorov.

Donskov rubbed his chin, toying with his mapsheet. "I know. But I'm convinced they won't listen. If I were Kurolesov's recon chief–"

"You'd be up with us and not sitting on your ass back in the command post," chimed in Rozhenko, who had also come over when he saw the commander and deputy in conversation. "But you're not the regimental recon chief. Major Zhimovin is."

"I don't look forward to sparring with him. He's a creature of the colonel. He'll reject any bad news out of hand, even if it's true."

"Still, comrade captain," remarked Yegorov, "it's our duty to keep them informed. Regimental headquarters can disregard your report, but they must hear it."

"I'd send it right to the commander, comrade captain," suggested Rozhenko.

"Exactly so," replied Donskov. He nudged dozing Padorin. "Give me the handset, comrade corporal."

Padorin sat up instantly and passed over the handset. "Regiment is Hero," said the corporal mechanically. Kurolesov's very call sign, its smug presumption, made Donskov's skin crawl. If we get out of this one . . .

"Hero Leader, this is Wolfpack Leader. Message. Over," enunciated Donskov. Here we go. While he waited for his words to skip through the retransmission lattice, the diverse files of the Khalis Faction rebels moved steadily along the ridges. For now they marched, but within hours they would begin coming together like the fingers of a hand, a great hand determined to close on the throat of Operation RED HAMMER.

"Here he comes," announced Sergeant Major Rozhenko, crouching and pointing at a black dot wavering along the pearly western horizon. Donskov tossed a smoke grenade onto the level spot just off the side of the highway proper.

"Firefly, this is Wolfpack Leader. Identify the smoke," ordered the recon commander.

A rush of static, the muffled sound of rotor noise, and then the voice of Firefly, the pilot, came through loud and clear: "Wolfpack Leader, identify yellow. Over."

"Exactly so, Firefly. Clear to land. Over."

The little, beetle-shaped Mi-2M loomed larger now, silhouetted against the dawn as the flier pulled up to hover. Dust and pebbles flew as the helicopter neared touchdown, its twin Isotov GTD-350 turbines whining, its long, straight tail dragging low. With a jerk, the fat-bellied brown craft leveled up and popped its plump black side tires and nose carriage onto the dirt. An RPK-74 machine gun poked from each side, dangling through the portals left by the missing Plexiglas windows just aft of the cockpit. The watchful gunners swiveled their weapons, which made Donskov a little nervous. The blades kept whirling, and dust and debris continued to blow everywhere. Daylight landings in contested areas made good aviators very apprehensive, and this one evidently was taking no chances. If anything dangerous occurred, he'd be in the air in split seconds.

The cockpit door snapped open, and out came Colonel Kurolesov, clad in a spotless camouflage uniform, a gleaming new helmet, and wonderfully polished boots. A holstered Makarov pistol represented the commander's only concession to the ongoing war. As he drew close to Donskov, the captain realized that his commander smelled as dapper as he looked, courtesy of fine soap and probably some cologne.

Donskov, Yegorov, Popov, Rozhenko, and Padorin constituted a motley reception committee by comparison. Their camouflage suits were dingy and patched, and their shaven faces had already grown dirty from the churning dust. The five appeared scuffed and scruffy, definitely worse for the wear, burdened with the canteens and ammunition of their fighting harnesses, and armed with long, clean, lethal AKD assault rifles. All but Popov wore their rakish blue berets, faded almost to white by sun and rain. The freshly assigned officer, as with all replacements, wore his steel helmet, and would do so until he came under fire and survived. So went the law of Donskov's wolf pack.

The colonel walked over to the paratroopers. He smiled broadly and shouted to be heard above the Mi-2M's thrumming engines. "Comrade captain, a wonderful morning for battle, don't you think?"

It wasn't exactly Donskov's thought, but he replied instinctively, "Exactly so, comrade colonel."

Kurolesov came up within a few inches of the recon commander. "As soon as I received your message, I knew I had to meet with you face to face," said Kurolesov, radiating good humor.

"Exactly so, comrade colonel. As to the Khalis bandits—"

The regimental commander cut Donskov off abruptly, hissing through his grin. "Don't you ever pay attention? I just want to talk with *you*. Get rid of these fucking conscripts."

Donskov was completely taken aback, like a swimmer who encounters a cold current a few feet down in a warm lake. He responded with his unvarnished reaction. "These are key men of my military headquarters collective. I—"

"Get rid of them," ordered Kurolesov with unmistakable menace.

Donskov waved them away. The sergeant major and Yegorov instantly grasped the situation and led the others away quickly. This was not a social call.

As soon as the four paratroopers were out of earshot, Kurolesov dropped any pretense of joviality. "Absolutely typical! You're so busy grandstanding for the lumpen proletariat that you forget your responsibilities to your superior officers. I suppose if you ran an asylum, you'd consult the inmates."

Kurolesov spat out the last word. The captain stood, loose-jointed, silent, and awaiting more. This would obviously be a one-way conversation.

The senior officer paused, drawing a tiny circular jar from his pocket, unscrewing the flat lid, and dipping his right index finger into the contents. Nimbly, swiftly, he smeared the balm on his lips, pursed them, replaced the lid on the container, and then returned the item to his pocket. He went on, his speech slower but no less angry.

"Lieutenant Colonel Gamarnik directed you to stay off the high ground. As my chief of staff, he speaks with full command authority. Yet you, for whatever bizarre reasons, assume you know better, and you've put men up on the heights in full contradiction of those orders. You've hazarded your forward detachment mission and your men. I did not want a nebulous screen. I want Larakay *held* and the Larakay trail into Pakistan *outposted*. Is that clear enough, or must I find an officer more capable of following cogent orders? You're lucky that you're in an attached capacity, or I'd relieve you on the spot. But any further disloyalty or disobedience and I guarantee you not only relief but also formal charges."

Donskov fully intended to take his rebuke in silence, but he could not do it. Doesn't the colonel realize what those contact reports mean? I have to give it one more try, one last attempt to get through to this guy. Too many troops, including me, will pay the price if I can't convince him to worry about those guerrillas. My troop setup isn't the real issue; that can be altered. But Kurolesov must understand the threatening guerrilla buildup.

Donskov proceeded cautiously but stayed aligned on his objective. This colonel is the enemy now; figure him out. What makes Kurolesov tick? I know how to influence people; where is this one's hot button? Donskov spoke up, stalling and thinking, alert for any clue. "Exactly so, comrade colonel. I apologize for my error of deployment, and will correct it."

The colonel listened carefully, his head close to Donskov's to overcome the rotor downwash. When Donskov finished, Kurolesov's grin slowly reappeared. His cold blue eyes softened, as if Donskov had never exceeded his authority and occupied the forbidden ridges. Satisfied that he'd gotten his way, or close enough, the colonel again donned his friendly mask. That's it, Donskov decided suddenly. It all clicked into place.

Now I've got it. He's not just a doctrinaire, self-serving asshole. Those kind simply bluster, fire people, and make big waves, whatever it takes to remake the world to their benefit. I mistook Kurolesov for a smoother version of the standard careerist son of a bitch. But I was wrong. Kurolesov is a more complex breed of cat. The swings between being so sugary sweet and then talking fire and brimstone should have been the tip-off. And now, when he certainly flew out here intending to rip me to shreds, he backs down as soon as I assure him I'll follow his orders.

This regimental commander can't follow through on his threats, Donskov realized. He wants to be *liked,* certainly by superiors, but also by his subordinates, in the manner of some tinhorn bourgeois political dealer anxious to please his party bosses and his local voters. In short, Kurolesov demanded obedience, but not at the cost of unit harmony.

Every officer understood that dichotomy, but the crucial test of character was not the ability to go along with the routine, but to know when to buck it, to know when *not* to be liked, indeed, when to be hated, by both overlords and lower ranks. Lenin understood that, as did Peter the Great, Suvorov, Zhukov, and Korobchenko.

Kurolesov wanted too much to be liked by everyone. The possible tactical implications of this tendency could not be good, unless one considered indecision a virtue. Faced with a conflict between his perceived mission and reality, or between a hardheaded superior and an equally adamant subordinate, Kurolesov would compromise at best and evade at worst. Hence, he could neither fire Major Zhimovin nor steal Donskov's company, so he split the difference and kept both men in an uneasy tandem role. Unwilling to face the unsuitability of European tactics against this Muslim insurgency, Kurolesov had retreated into his copy of Reznichenko's *Tactics* and spouted doctrine like dogma. No wonder the colonel tried so hard to fill his headquarters with clones who thought as he did, and clung to doctrine like a drowning man pawing for flotsam. Such methods reduced the chance for disputes and, hence, decisions.

This dovetailed nicely with Kurolesov's vast ambition. A decision unmade is a decision uncriticized. Routines and systems, well emplaced and allowed to run unchecked thanks to loyal, like-minded subordinates, might not produce spectacular successes. But they guaranteed the kind of steady, marginal progress that could be properly packaged and well explained. Over time, it brought notice by the army and party. Anything that threatened that grudging style of barely winning had to be controlled, diverted, or converted.

My company and I are threats, and that's why he came out here like this. We're endangering the approved structure. News of approaching bandits didn't fit Kurolesov's scheme, so he discounted it. Indeed, if he could penetrate the colonel's skull, Donskov would not have been surprised to see that his superior somehow blamed the Khalis rebels' movement on Donskov's supposed maldeployment. If the plan failed, the Kurolesovs of the world always fixed responsibility on the executors, on those who strayed outside the lines. Hadn't Stalin found plenty of "wreckers" in his time?

But winning a war required risks, and risks necessitated bold decisions, with the possibility of defeat and the probability of offending many above and below in the pecking order. Kurolesov's type wasn't up for that. The best he could do was plug away and not lose. Donskov filed that idea in a back slot of his mind. Given the prevalence of Kurolesovs in the post-1945 Soviet military, this could well explain a lot of things about our doomed southern war, reckoned the recon captain.

It took a few seconds to whip through all of that, to size up his adversary. Donskov found the colonel already speaking when he tuned back in.

"... that's more like it, Dmitriy Ivanovich. RED HAMMER is proceeding wonderfully, and I see no reason for it to go awry now. Consider this conversation forgotten, just a bit of coordination. Any other problems I should be aware of?"

Donskov hesitated, then went ahead, testing. He predicted the responses and was not disappointed. "Comrade colonel, we *did* see those bandits heading down the ridges, toward you. They were heavily armed, with RPGs–"

Kurolesov raised his right palm and shook his head. "Refugees, simply more poor refugees hightailing it out of our way. You know how the night can play tricks on your eyes, and I'll bet your boys were so spread out that they got edgy and overreacted. You've got to trust us up at regiment, Dmitriy Ivanovich. Major Zhimovin knows what he's doing. His electronic and aerial surveillance have been exhaustive, well into the enemy's tactical depth. Our intelligence shows that the wood chips are gone. Ali Khel hasn't taken a single shell for more than eighteen hours. RED HAMMER has scared the bandits away, as well it should. I understand your concern, but I think once you get your conscripts in a tight circle down here around Larakay, they'll settle down and that will be the end of this unnecessary overreaction."

Overreaction! This stupid brass hat will rue the day he trusted in gadgets to find the mujahidin. Trained men who've walked the Afghan hills don't often fall victim to night jitters. But Donskov knew enough now about his commander, and he had his orders. The colonel's mindset actually made his guidance applicable–right for the wrong reasons, so to speak. If regimental headquarters is ignoring the Khalis Faction's maneuver, the tanks and BMDs won't get here soon or intact. We've already seen the flow of enemy forces, so pulling in tight made sense.

Donskov faced a tough withdrawal and defensive consolidation, and his camouflage couldn't be helped by this painfully evident helicopter puttering away in broad daylight right in the center of his extended company position. So he just nodded his head. Get out of here, colonel. I have work to do.

"One last thing, comrade captain," confided Kurolesov in a fatherly tone.

Donskov waited, anxious to end the discussion. His face, though, betrayed nothing but respectful interest.

"Get your men in helmets. These berets are out of place in combat."

Dare I explain this? No, Donskov concluded. He let it ride.

"Exactly so, comrade colonel," said Donskov, exactly promising nothing. He had no helmets out here anyway, except on the replacements, and Donskov knew they were itching to ditch theirs.

"And let's have no more overreaction, okay?"

Kurolesov spread a particularly toothy smile, shook Donskov's hand, and sprang away like a human rabbit, bounding for the rattling helicopter. It started lifting upward even before the colonel closed the flimsy door.

The bulbous Mi-2M raced its motors and drifted unsteadily, slowly levitating. With a lurch, it accelerated forward. After about a hundred meters, gathering speed, the craft swung about and raced away, its slapping blade noises echoing from the stark valley ramparts.

No sooner had the helicopter gained altitude than a sick whistle slit the air, followed by a smashing detonation. Donskov had automatically dropped flat, covering his head with his arms. Dirt pelted his back, and experience comforted him with the recognition that the speeding steel fragments had missed him.

The last notes of the chopper rotors faded away as the captain clambered to his knees. Donskov saw a knotted tower of dirty smoke twirling skyward about fifty meters away, emanating from a shallow, brown-streaked scoop in the baked hardpan. *So the fun is starting already, eh?*

Senior Lieutenant Yegorov loomed near and crouched down by his commander. He had been running toward Donskov when the helicopter lifted off, no doubt intending to find out what the colonel said. The unexpected explosion caused the deputy commander to hit the dirt, and when he got to Donskov, his curiosity about Kurolesov was preempted by the surprise projectile.

"What the hell was that? A rocket?" Yegorov asked Donskov.

"Overreaction, I think," said Donskov, standing up. "Come on, Kliment. We've got a lot to do."

By the next morning, the situation around Larakay had degenerated markedly, and that was no overreaction. In fact, Donskov could truthfully say that he found himself in the most desperate straits of his brief combat career. Given the overall turn of fortunes, the plight of Donskov's wolves appeared rather minor, except to them. Even though the experienced 688th men had forecast the major reverses, their grim condition outweighed any sterile pleasure in being correct.

Operation RED HAMMER had run completely off the rails. By midday on 24 August, when the first T-62E tanks should have been rumbling triumphantly into Ali Khel, the entire task force was still locked in battle well short of Larakay, which was supposed to fall on 23 August. The Khalis Faction, their homes blasted, their families hurt, had decided otherwise.

The 217th Guards' advance lost momentum late on 23 August. On the flanking high ground, both dismounted battalions had gotten bogged down more than ten kilometers short of Larakay, unable to bound forward due to aggressive rebel contact. Chopper extraction attempts failed miserably. About a dozen helicopters, Mi-8s and Mi-24s, broke apart on the various embattled hilltop landing zones, victims of small arms, DShK heavy machine guns, RPGs, and even a few Strela missiles. Another Gorbach crashed after nightfall, striking an outcropping while trying to pick up casualties. The shrunken, encircled companies held their rocky precipices all night, supplied by a few boxes of ammunition kicked out of speeding, boldly flown helicopters. Soviet artillery and multiple rocket launchers banged away in support, and uneven strings of parachute flares hung above both valley walls all night long.

One isolated 2d Battalion unit attracted a great deal of bandit attention. Persistent rebels on the southeastern ridge line surrounded 4th Company and launched two infantry assaults overnight. The desantnik defenders took a toll, but the tough Pathans also made their impact. Only fourteen men remained unwounded, and ammunition and water were running out.

The central ground effort nearly made it, but the 70th Independent Tank Battalion stalled in a massive mine field six kilometers short of Larakay, right at dusk. Toiling engineers tumbled off their vehicles, victims of crack-shooting snipers. An attempt to ravage the mines with Mi-24 deliveries of fuel air explosives achieved only partial success, at the cost of a downed helicopter and two tanks broiled by a short bomb. Once full darkness descended, bandit RPG gunners plucked and tore at the fringes of the halted armored column. Dismounted VDV men and fleeting guerrillas played cat and mouse among the hardy scrub, rocks, and stopped vehicles, all illuminated by swaying artillery flares and crackling armored wreckage. More than a few Soviet paratroopers fell to their nervous comrades' weapons.

This was not all of it. Bad as the situation had become, the real damage was being done in the vulnerable rear. The road back to Gardez was littered with smoking truck carcasses and even a few tank and BMD wrecks. Clever Khalis Faction teams, only too happy to avoid the combat forces, worked over the regimental supply lines. Without artillery or air power to spare for his supply trains, Kurolesov watched his logistics start to dry up even as he poured all resources into beating frantically at the spidery but unbreakable bandit web that snarled his forward progress.

Nobody wanted to see things start moving more than Dmitriy Ivanovich Donskov. In Larakay's crumbling ruins, Operation RED HAMMER's most distant forward detachment, the seventy-four Soviets and Pathans of 688th Reconnaissance Company, held on by mere fingernails. Ammunition, water, and medical supplies dwindled by the hour.

Ever since Kurolesov's chopper had flitted away, the Khalis guerrillas turned more and more firepower against the compressed oval position around Larakay. Getting the company down to the valley floor proved tough, especially in daylight. Savitskiy made a fighting disengagement from the cliffs along the open Pakistan road; he lost two dead and four wounded in the effort. Knyazin made it down without loss, then promptly attracted a mortar barrage that killed three men and wounded eight.

Those mortar rounds blurred into many others. The first lone rocket had been followed by a hundred more as of noon on 24 August, not to mention uncounted 82mm mortar bombs. With only hand weapons, and unwilling to expend all of his ordnance, Donskov and his men dug in along the rim of crumbling Larakay. Recon men, used to moving fast by night and hiding deep by day, found themselves in a totally unfamiliar setting: a static defense, much of it under a blazing hot sun. The men learned quickly. They flipped hard earth and chipped at foundations with their tiny folding shovels. Thanks to incoming munitions, the paratroopers spent many hours face down, grinding their teeth while hot metal chips whirred through the air and skipped off the battered brickwork.

The Afghans did not rely solely on explosives. Enemy sniping also kept heads down. At night, one could see a muzzle burst now and then. By day, even the sharp-eyed recon men saw nothing. But two fell, injured by Lee-Enfield bullets. The desantniks, apparently, were not so invisible to guerrillas in the surrounding stoneworks.

Donskov had often wondered what a daylight battle in Afghanistan would look like. Now he knew only too well: crouching, crawling men tormented by unseen gunners, hidden riflemen, lethal puffs of ripping shell casings, merciless sunlight, baking dust jumping at ricochets, all against a hazy tan landscape dotted by dull green balls of stunted bushes. The fantasy of seeing the foe was exposed as a cruel hoax. The only real difference involved the blood, which flowed bright red in the sunshine, not gleaming black as it did under the silver moon.

The tough Khalis folks created lots of opportunities to see blood, too many. Medical Sergeant Zhivanetsyn nearly exhausted his rucksack of consumables within a few hours. A helpful Gorbach dropped a resupply container unhelpfully 200 meters outside the lines. Sergeant Major Rozhenko earned a moral victory by greasing three bandits who attempted to retrieve the valuable bundle. Sooner or later, Donskov feared, casualties might necessitate a foray to recover the battered cargo pack. Aerial medical evacuation had become a hollow joke.

Air, artillery, and rocket support also never came. This did not surprise Donskov. The book clearly dictated that all firepower support the main effort, and Donskov's unit did not occupy that role. Without tanks, mortars, or much more than a few hoarded RPG rockets, the recon keenly felt the lack of assistance.

Now and then, Senior Lieutenant Menzhinskiy raised the Afghan Army M-46 130mm battery up at Ali Khel, but the disorderly loyal Afghans proved unable to adjust the rounds onto any of the targets requested, even though the pieces easily ranged out to Lara-kay. Donskov allowed his gunner to call in one battery sheaf anyway, just for morale purposes. A ragged, mistimed sextet of dirt spouts sprang up randomly and uselessly at a distance, the company jeered, and Donskov told Menzhinskiy to forget about help from the Afghans.

"Comrade captain?"

It was Rozhenko, lying on his belly, his head near Donskov and Padorin's scrawny, bricked-up foxhole. The captain leaned back.

"Go ahead."

"Noon report. Effective strength: thirty-nine Soviets, ten Pathan scouts. Seven dead, eighteen wounded – two seriously. Zhivanetsyn says they'll die this afternoon without evacuation. One RPK-74 broken – a bad bolt, I think. Consumables: ammunition down to sixty rounds per man, about two hundred per RPK, plenty of BG-15 grenades. About two hand fragmentation grenades per man. Water's a problem: We're down to less than a half canteen per man. We will be out by sunset."

Padorin dozed in the hole, a fat fly walking slowly across his sunburned forehead. Just tasting, eh? You'll likely get the real thing in a day or so. Donskov sighed loudly.

"What do you think, Rozhenko?"

"They'll try us tonight. Lieutenant Knyazin says he's pretty sure he's seen the shine of several sets of binoculars up his way. Probably a command recon of our lines."

"Well," said Donskov calmly, "that is the logical way to come in. Savitskiy's got all those nice open shots down the Pakistan highway. But Knyazin's 3d Platoon butts against the lower slope. They could work right out of the rocks."

"Any word from Hero?"

Donskov closed his eyes and shook his head. Both men could hear the steady ebb and flow of fighting to the south. I haven't slept in more than two days, Donskov observed silently. No wonder everything sounds tinny. He treated himself to a half swallow of water, then replaced his canteen, his hands working on autopilot.

"I think you have to call him, comrade captain. We need artillery or air to make it through tonight. Either that or extraction."

"Agreed. I'll try to reason with the bastard." He turned up the volume and grabbed the hand mike.

The fourth rocket landed much too close, and Donskov's ears rang. He tasted blood in his mouth. Damn, bit my lip. He sucked it for moisture. The captain absently looked at his watch, smudging dust off the cracked crystal: 1437. He was too tired to realize that it had been 1437 for almost two hours.

"Will you look at that!" Yegorov pointed up. Donskov, Padorin, Suslov, Menzhinskiy, and Rozhenko reflexively turned their faces to the sky, like five dirty sunflowers. Even if they had not, only a dead man (and there were now nine resting in the perimeter) would have missed the roaring of the armada of Mi-8s and Mi-24s chattering overhead. There must be more than twenty, a battalion's lift at least.

The bobbing, shaking flotilla attracted a veritable fireworks display of fat green tracers, white Strela trails, and even a few RPG shots. One Mi-8 faltered a bit, smoking, but pressed gamely onward. Spinning Gorbaches curved down to loose 57mm rockets and conduct strafing runs. With enough ammunition, dug-in rebels could deny a fixed landing zone, but knocking down all these moving targets would not happen. Heading up the valley, the relentless choppers flowed across the tired, hungry, thirsty knot of recon men.

"He's going to make his deadline," shouted Yegorov. "That's all it is. The colonel promised to reach Ali Khel by 24 August; this will do the trick."

"He could have done *that* three days ago," retorted Menzhinskiy. "The son of a bitch. What about us?"

Four camouflaged Su-17s came in low, following the ungainly helicopters, spreading death down the lower slopes of the northwest massif. They flew in two pairs. The leaders dropped first, skidding long, narrow containers into the boulders. Napalm blossomed in hot yellow pillows, then the first two jets pulled up, streaking right over Knyazin's end of the company position.

"That's pretty damn close," observed Senior Lieutenant Suslov, fiddling with the knobs on his ground-to-air radio set. "I wonder who's controlling that strike."

The second pair roared in. A Strela fired, its squiggling white smoke trace reaching for the trailing jet. The leader pulled up but jinked left instead of right, a fatal guess as he nicked an overhanging boulder and exploded in a bright white flash that birthed a dirty orange flaming chunk of plane. The wreckage gyrated downward, careening off the cliffs. Black, oily smoke rushed upward.

"Shit! Watch the . . . " said Donskov, unheard in the blast and shrieking jet engine turbines. The next few seconds happened very, very fast, yet the commander perceived every segment of the grim sequence with utter clarity and total impotence.

The other jet pilot also turned hard and climbed, inadvertently unloading a 500-kilogram high-explosive bomb as he struggled to get clear of the deadly valley, the seeking Strela, and the tumbling fiery garbage of his comrade. The black ovoid arced up gracefully, perfectly evident to the horror-struck desantnik command group. It topped out, tipped down, and plunged, gathering speed, turning into a black blur, sucking into the ground, the ground occupied by 3d Platoon, men who couldn't move, or fight back, or do anything but scream and scream and . . .

The thing erupted, a sharp, throaty crack and a substantial yellow flash, and that was that. Forgetting the danger from Afghan shells, Donskov was up and running, shedding exhaustion. Sergeant Zhivanetsyn got there first, then Donskov, then Rozhenko, Yegorov, and the rest. Zharkowskiy and an unfamiliar Pathan ran over.

The crater wasn't large, only about two or three meters across and a half meter deep. A bomb stabilizing fin lay near the center, smoking just a little. The rocks and light brown dirt looked scorched, and a fine set of dust and pebble rays spread out from the hellish dimple, just as one would expect with a lunar crater.

Around it, blown apart, knocked out of their boots, lay at least a dozen torsos, some with legs or arms appended, others trailing them on gory, tangled strings of gristle. Bent rifles, a replacement's turtle-like helmet, a blood-matted beret, and a torn map lay around the site. They were all dead, small face bones broken flat by the concussion. Big Knyazin had been having a conference with some of his men.

Nobody said anything for a few minutes. Senior Sergeant

Milyukov came up from his position. He crossed himself, a gesture that Donskov noticed. A fat lot of good your God did these people!

"Senior Sergeant Milyukov, get a report," said Donskov quietly.

"Exactly so," he replied in a cracked, weak voice.

"The rest of you, back to your positions. Except the medical orderly."

The men turned and walked back slowly, in a dreamy gait. Padorin stayed, as did Zharkowskiy. Zhivanetsyn moved from body to body, confirming the obvious. Donskov heard a distant rifle shot.

"Hero wants you, comrade captain," said Padorin. He handed his commander the microphone.

"This is Wolfpack Leader. Over," stated Donskov, distracted. The sound of rotor wash came over the net, followed by Kurolesov's cheery tones.

"My mistake, Wolfpack Leader. Forgot you were up there. Sorry. Out." And he dropped off the net for an instant, only to come back seconds later, calling the senior Soviet adviser at Ali Khel to announce his imminent salvation.

On the ground, near the smoking 500-kilogram bomb crater, Donskov dropped the radio handset. "He's sorry. Fucking great. Sorry."

Zharkowskiy stood there. "What did you expect?"

The captain rolled his eyes, and slowly tossed his AKD from one hand to the other. "Nothing. I expected nothing."

"And you've got it," Zharkowskiy said, searching his commander's face.

"Andrey, this is no way to make war. What is to be done?"

The senior lieutenant smiled in his evil, knowing way. "Finally," he said, "a question made for a political deputy. Vladimir Ilyich Lenin himself gave the answer, so applicable to us, too, as is all Lenin's wisdom. Right?"

Donskov looked back.

"You told me yourself that we've fought this war in three stages: conventional, search and destroy, and now a third period, a half-assed counterinsurgency that rides on the backs of the poor VDV. Now, remember your Komsomol training? According to Lenin's great 1902 pamphlet, *What is to be done?*"

The old catechism swam out of his brain readily. "Put an end to the third period," said Donskov.

"Exactly so. Put an end to the fucking third period of this fucking war. Lenin knew."

The ground column linked up two hours later. The elated 40th Army commander recommended Colonel Kurolesov for the Order of Kutuzov. He received this honor in due course, along with his promotion to general major.

PART THREE
The Third Rome

All Christian empires are fallen, and in their stead stands alone the empire of our ruler, in accordance with the prophetical books. Two Romes have fallen, but the Third stands, and a fourth there will not be.

from a letter by Pilotheus, monk of Pskov, circa 1500

Chapter Ten

The Brotherhood of the South

Colonel Leonov looked out through the venetian blinds, watching the sparse afternoon traffic on October Revolution Street, three stories below. A big ZIL limousine purred away from the curb, probably carrying some high-rolling party secretary. Across the street, three tawny-skinned men dumped trash cans into a dull gray Ural salvage truck. The architecture and cars appeared unmistakably Russian in design, but even here, right in front of the Southern Theater headquarters building, the sprinkling of people on the sidewalks told Leonov that he was still in Asia–Tashkent, to be exact. The regimental commander ran his thumb around his starched collar and languidly drummed his fingers on the neatly painted window frame.

Captain Donskov, equally uncomfortable in his winter dress uniform, stood with feet apart and arms crossed. Just over seventy-two hours before, he, his men, and the guerrilla Ismail had been extracted from a snowy pickup zone on the Pakistani border. His toes and fingers still tingled and felt thick from exposure to the biting mountain cold. The Recon Company waited for him back in Afghanistan. He wished he was back there, where he belonged. He surely felt out of place here.

The captain confronted a beautifully framed map of Afghanistan mounted at eye level on the dark wood paneling of the wall. The legend proclaimed "Major Units, Limited Contingent of Soviet Forces in Afghanistan, as of December 1984." Donskov's eye swept across the glass-covered paper and he ticked off the neatly printed unit markers: the 108th Motor Rifle Division north of Kabul, the 375th Guards Air Assault Regiment at Bagram, the 262d Independent Tactical Reconnaissance Helicopter Squadron at Kabul International Airport, and the command post of his own 103d Guards Air Assault Division at Darulaman Palace, southwest of the Afghan capital. Those he recognized quite well.

But others, indeed the majority of the four divisions, fifteen-odd aviation outfits, and a half dozen or so separate ground regiments represented on the map, were far less familiar to him. What was going on with this 5th Guards Motor Rifle Division at desolate, sandy Shindand to the west? So the 70th Motor Rifle Brigade usually worked near unfriendly Kandahar in the south; that's news to me. And what of these motor rifle and KGB Border Guards units based on Soviet soil just across the Oxus? What did they contribute? The mighty force array impressed the recon captain, even though he understood precisely what those distinctive, fleshless notations truly reflected.

I wonder if our highest leadership receives briefings from such a map? At this scale, the vast Panjsher Valley ran about ten centimeters, the Kunar stretched less than half that, the Shomali became a thumb blot, Ali Khel resolved down to a speck, and Aq Khater, as in reality now, did not exist at all. The Afghan resistance forces were not depicted. To see the war this way, Soviet victory must be foreordained. Maybe it was, if only at this level. One would need a much wider mapsheet, soaked in Afghan and Russian blood, to show the war the desantniks knew.

The big door opened behind the two visiting officers.

"Comrades, the general will see you now," intoned the tall, brown-haired staff major. He motioned them into the inner office.

Leonov marched in briskly, followed by Donskov. Both men halted before the general's desk, faced left simultaneously, and saluted. Leonov reported loudly. "Comrade general, Colonel I. S. Leonov and Captain D. I. Donskov report as ordered."

General of the Army Yuriy Pavlovich Maksimov returned the salute with strict formality. He remained seated at his massive desk.

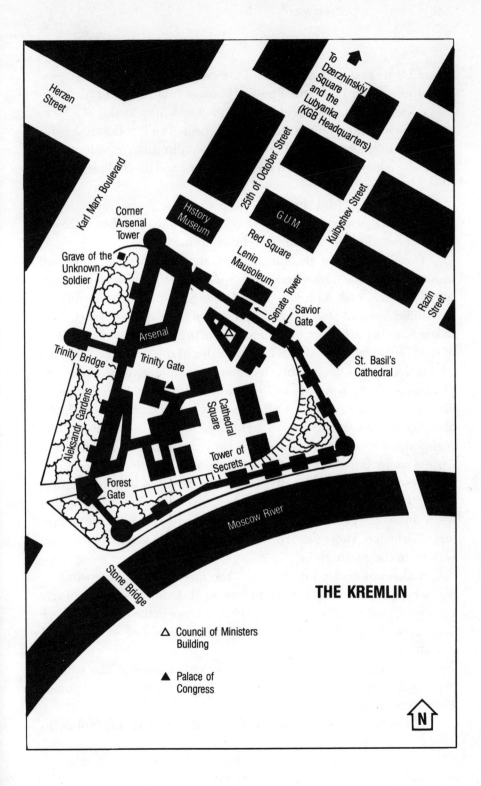

THE KREMLIN

△ Council of Ministers
Building

▲ Palace of
Congress

A handsome man, the general had piercing, dark brown eyes, receding, iron-colored hair, and a powerful torso that filled out his faultless dress uniform. Donskov noticed the Gold Star Medal of a Hero of the Soviet Union on the older man's chest. The fact that it was for service to the state rather than valor did not diminish its value. Only the really big names achieved the distinction, and this fellow was one of the biggest.

"Stand easy," Maksimov said in a surprisingly mellow voice. A growl or bark from this old soldier would not have shocked Donskov in the least. Both VDV officers relaxed a little.

Donskov noticed the furnishings and trappings of power all around him on the dark wood walls, well above the thick maroon carpet. Citations and diplomas crowded together: Frunze Academy, Voroshilov General Staff Academy, Deputy of the Supreme Soviet, Candidate Member of the Central Committee of the Communist Party, Hero of the Soviet Union, Order of Lenin, Order of the Red Star, Order of Aleksandr Nevsky, and numerous other state and foreign awards. Several traced all the way back to 1942, when Maksimov joined the wartime Red Army as a gunner. Unit memorabilia and framed photographs also covered the wall space, to include gaudy plaques from artillery regiments, rocket brigades, and the Turkestan Military District, and a great many posed group shots of batteries, battalions, regiments, brigades, and countless staffs. Donskov could not help but notice, squarely behind Maksimov's chair, a sequence of three stark, intriguing black-and-white glossy photos of the general with Brezhnev, Andropov, and Chernenko. These were the rewards of forty-two years of successful service to the motherland.

Maksimov cleared his throat. "You are both probably wondering why I summoned you from the operational area, seemingly bypassing your division and army commanders in the process. There is no need to equivocate. I desired to deliver these orders myself. So pay attention."

The general held his tongue for a few moments. The colonel and captain tensed. What have we done? they wondered as one man. Then Maksimov spoke again.

"Frankly, your regiment's performance has been exemplary in

every respect. I have recommended the 688th for a second Order of the Red Banner. My contacts in the General Staff tell me that it will be approved."

"Thank you, comrade general," answered Leonov. "The men will appreciate the recognition."

"They'll appreciate even more the terrific ceremony planned for Red Square in Moscow on Soviet Army and Navy Day, 23 February," responded Maksimov. Both VDV officers looked confused. Were they hearing correctly?

"Yes, comrades, your regiment is being withdrawn to home soil, if only temporarily. You will swap out with the 236th Guards at Tula, who will deploy south to replace you. Congratulations on your distinguished performance of some very tough internationalist socialist duty."

The general rose from his comfortable swivel chair and lunged across the wide desk. He solemnly, slowly shook Donskov's right hand, then Leonov's.

Donskov noticed an unexpected tingle on his palm, and he sensed the presence of a tiny, creased slip of paper. A shiver zipped along the knobs of his spine. What is this about? Since when do full generals pass cryptic notes to captains?

"That will be all," finished Maksimov, his face betraying nothing unusual. Trembling slightly, Donskov wedged the clandestine message between his fingers, so that he could salute, depart, and reach a place safe enough to figure out what was going on.

Beside him, Leonov snapped to attention. Donskov, too, stiffened. Both officers saluted, faced right, and swiftly walked out.

They did not talk at all in the antechamber. It took only minutes to don their dark gray overcoats with the light blue airborne trim. The pair then gathered their peaked "SS" visor caps, hated by paratroopers and patriots alike as strange concessions to Hitlerite uniform fashion. It took only a few minutes to walk down three flights of wide marble stairs, through the street-front security station, and out into Tashkent.

"I'll stand you a drink, Dmitriy," said the colonel conversationally as the pair cleared the building.

"That sounds good, comrade colonel."

"The officers' club is over on Engels Street. Follow me," said Leonov.

Donskov waited until they were well down the street, a block away from the headquarters, before he opened the folded scrap of paper. It said in a scrawl: "Southern Theater helipad, 2330 tonight."

Wordlessly, he held up his palm, displaying the note to Colonel Leonov. The regimental commander nodded so slightly that only his recon chief could detect it. He said nothing.

What does Leonov know? Donskov burned with curiosity and more than a little fear. As always, all he could do was wait.

Brilliant mercury vapor lights illuminated the two Mi-2M light helicopters and the Mi-8 transport parked in front of the immense aluminum hangar on the outskirts of the Tashkent airfield. Inside the open hangar doors, bustling mechanics fiddled with another Mi-8, its engine access panels open to allow for surgery. A cart-mounted auxiliary power unit, a little jet engine in its own right, blared away near the ill helicopter, providing electricity, compressed air, and a lot of noise, so much so that none of the intent aircraft technicians noticed the gray-coated foursome that gathered in the blackness just beyond the cheery pools of floodlit cement.

"Thank you for coming," began General of the Army Maksimov. "You know General Major Golitsyn, of course."

The shorter general nodded.

"One cannot be too careful these days," said Donskov's division commander.

The recon commander's eyes opened wide. He understood damn well that he was about to hear something of critical importance, although he never would have believed just how momentous Maksimov's words would turn out to be. The theater commander moved close to the captain, to be distinctly heard over the grinding turbine cacophony. Maksimov's breath smelled of garlic.

"I apologize for the charade this afternoon. You certainly deserved recognition, and your regiment will be properly honored as promised, but you can be sure I did not bring you up here simply for a three-minute meeting. Colonel Leonov could have handled that sort of thing himself."

The general inclined his head toward the regimental commander, who remained silent. He's talking directly to me, Donskov realized. The others know what's going on.

"Our current locale should tell you about the extreme sensitivity of our subject tonight," remarked Golitsyn softly. "We are trusting you, Dmitriy Ivanovich, with our lives. We are all comrades in this grueling internationalist war."

Inside the hangar, an Isotov helicopter turbine spun to life. Maksimov spoke louder, and the captain strained to hear. If the desantnik officer had been a dog, his ears would be standing straight up.

"It's about the war," began the general. "How many men do you think we have lost?"

Donskov, stunned by the gravity of his circumstances, made no answer.

"Guess, comrade captain," prodded Maksimov.

"Two thousand," ventured Donskov. That sounded about right.

"As of 0001 today, 28 December, the number of battle deaths reached 11,567. For your information, our party leadership announced the grand total of only six dead and six wounded as of a year ago. So, evidently, we have taken incredible losses this past year. Or, as you and any sane soldiers here in the south realize, our party leaders have deluded themselves and the people. I have every reason to believe that they will continue to do so—*unless replaced.*"

The theater commander uttered the last words quite clearly, and let them hang in the chilly night air. Donskov shuddered. He's talking about a military coup d'état, Bonapartism plain and simple. I can be shot simply for listening to this. But he kept listening, fascinated, like a lamb frozen in its tracks by a rearing, weaving cobra.

"Who is the General Secretary of the Communist party of the Soviet Union?" grated Maksimov, his brown eyes locked on Donskov.

"Konstantin Ustinovich Chernenko, comrade general," answered Donskov.

"Very good, comrade captain, but not correct. No, not right at all. If you were aware of our general secretary's health, as I am, you would understand that poor Chernenko is a dying mannequin. The Soviet Union has no leader, and our beloved collective of leaders knows it."

"They are circling like jackals," spat Golitsyn, "waiting for Chernenko to pass on."

Maksimov went on. "Now this is all politics, and you are a fighting man, a reconnaissance captain, and no doubt unaware of all of this. It is time to become aware, because it is killing your comrades in Afghanistan, and for what?"

Maksimov's eyes bored into Donskov. "Let me speak plainly," said the theater commander, "as an old man who has seen enough lethal stupidity, some I fear of my own making. When I was a youngster, it seemed that nothing could rival the horrific carnage of the Great Patriotic War against the Nazi brigands. The sharp counter-revolutionary spasm in Hungary, and the brief flare-up in Czechoslovakia hardly counted as military endeavors by comparison to the titanic struggles around Kursk, Warsaw, or Berlin."

"So we all thought," Golitsyn added, "until we sent our men into this devil's nest, this Afghanistan."

Nobody spoke for a few seconds. The helicopter engine whined in the background.

"Here in the south," continued Maksimov, "I make it a habit to visit my fighting units. Of missions known to you, I went in with the first lift on Operation MARS, and I rode with that idiot Kurolesov during the third day of the costly Ali Khel fiasco. My staff officers tell me that, at my age, I should keep to the headquarters. I like to remind them that a rather famous old goat named Suvorov led his men over the Alps at age sixty-nine. So going to the front is a common affliction for such old war-horses. I think I owe it to our men."

Donskov nodded. He understood what Maksimov said, but he did not understand where it was going. How did this connect to that comment about replacing party authorities?

"Please understand," said Maksimov, "that as to the Afghan problem, three basic choices confront us: increase forces, maintain our present level of effort, or withdraw prudently."

Colonel Leonov piped up. "The first option is out of the question. Even a massive effort might not fully subdue the Afghans, and any objective analysis must conclude that the potential costs, both immediate and profound, far exceed the possible prize. Even without our weapons of mass destruction, we could win, but not cheaply. We all know how these Muslim bandits fight. What is there in the Hindu Kush that could justify another Great Patriotic War?"

"Worse," explained Maksimov, "every tank, gun, helicopter, and man sent into Afghanistan is another unavailable for defense against the unsleeping imperialists and treacherous Chinese deviationists."

"Exactly so, comrade general," rejoined Leonov. "Continuing the present course of defending high-priority locations, relying on special operations forces, conducting selected VDV raids and fire strikes, and building the loyal Afghan Army is not much of a strategy. True, it blocks any sort of counterrevolutionary victory, but at the cost of 2,000 dead and 5,000 wounded per year, minimum. The moral-political effects are increasingly crucial. Do you know why?"

"I'm not sure, comrade colonel," answered Donskov, feeling out of his league.

Golitsyn spoke up. "Because these losses, comrade captain, are the heart and soul of our party and motherland, almost wholly from the brave, intelligent young Slavs of Great Russia, the Ukraine, and Belorussia, the sort who flock to our VDV, Spetsnaz, and Osnaz subunits. I need not remind you that our Slavic birthrate can ill afford the subtraction of such fine young men. Meanwhile, the useless wood chips of Soviet Central Asia drop litters of children, howl to Allah, and sharpen their knives as we bleed ourselves over years, perhaps decades. We get a stalemate in Afghanistan and Islamic revolution in Tashkent. Not a fair trade, is it?"

"No, comrade general."

"There is another option, you know," Leonov elaborated. "Withdrawal sounds like defeat, but this choice offers some advantages, if we do it correctly. Yes, we must abandon any dreams of conquering Afghanistan, but we cannot do that anyway without millions of men and much of the workers' common wealth. As I said, you can forget that idea. But if a weak, squabbling neighbor under the leaky umbrella of a nominally socialist regime will do, we can have that today, courtesy of our KGB, shrewd use of a few military advisers, timely aviation support, and carefully selected VDV and Spetsnaz work. Getting the Afghans to fight each other takes no effort; we're the only reason these cutthroats cooperate at all. Pull us out, the entire hellhole collapses into anarchy, and our southern frontier is secure enough, complete with a bubbling buffer zone in which no imperialist would tread."

"It worked for the tsars for centuries," noted Golitsyn.

"And the issue is how to make it work again, how to guarantee that policy," finished Maksimov.

Donskov waited, anxious, sweating lightly despite the cold night. He could sense what must be coming. *They want me to do something. But why me?*

"Let me explain the situation in the Kremlin," offered the senior general. "There are three basic alternatives among the Politburo: Romanov, old Grishin, and this young fellow Gorbachev. Chernenko may die at any time, and one of those three will take power. Are you familiar with these people, Captain Donskov?"

"Not really, comrade general," replied Donskov weakly. His head was swimming. *Maksimov is talking about the political bureau of the party as if naming the chiefs of some clod-kicking coalition of mujahidin factions.*

Maksimov clicked his teeth once and continued. "You will have ample opportunity to gain more data from others, and as a good recon man, I know you will. Here are the bare bones. Romanov is a hard-liner, a Stalinist. He would increase forces and try to crush Afghanistan. Grishin is a tired fart, not unlike our currently expiring General Secretary. His accession means more of the same here in the south. Finally, this Gorbachev. He is an odd one, but trusted comrades assure me that Gorbachev would pull out properly, in the manner Colonel Leonov described."

"He's the least of three evils," commented Golitsyn.

"I back him," Maksimov stated, "and I hope you will also, Captain Donskov. Your colonel has already signed on with this venture. So has General Major Golitsyn."

"General Lieutenant Mikhailov of 40th Army has not," warned Golitsyn. "We had to leave him outside of this."

So the regimental commander, Golitsyn, and the theater commander himself have been involved in an antiparty conspiracy. It is absolutely unbelievable, yet it is most certainly happening. And where do I come in? wondered Donskov. Getting out did not even occur to him.

Leonov cleared his throat. "A word on the other key actors, if I may, comrade general?"

"Certainly."

"Given its head," Leonov said, "the party will hand us Grishin as our boss. So if this succession should go to the Central Committee for decision, we will have failed. That cannot be permitted. The KGB, believe it or not, stands with us in this effort."

Maksimov rubbed his forehead and spoke. "As an old soldier, I am loath to admit it, but the Chekists have deduced the material circumstances of the contemporary world order far better than we soldiers. Propaganda, moral-political subversion, chosen sabotage, and constant vigilant espionage will allow us to outguess, undermine, and defeat the capitalist-imperialist bloc. The nuclear standoff obviates the traditional military-technical correlation of forces. Our mighty armed forces, my pride and joy for more than forty years, are a muscle-bound anachronism, and Afghanistan has been our warning. A military shaped for the real international class struggle must be a desantnik army–small, ready, and ruthless. The state security organs agree, and their chairman, this smiling bear Chebrikov, sponsors Gorbachev. No doubt he has his own reasons, but I see cause for an alliance under these conditions."

"It's more than that, Dmitriy," Golitsyn argued. "Minus Chekist complicity, or at least neutrality, we cannot get to the Politburo members without excessive violence."

Maksimov completed the thought: "In any event, Chebrikov insists on army participation or he refuses to act."

The theater commander halted there. His eyes fixed Donskov. "I see, my young friend, that you are wondering what the fuss is about. If the army and the Cheka have ganged up, how can the party object?

Now I must reveal the bad news. If and when we make our move, we act against the wishes of Marshal Sokolov, our brand-new but quite elderly Minister of Defense. But Sokolov's elevation is of no matter. Even if fat old Ustinov had not died a few days ago, we would still have to buck our own service chiefs and most of our own Soviet Army comrades. Sokolov and his ilk permeate the service, they have Romanov's ear, and they are not all feeble and senile."

Golitsyn snorted. Leonov remarked, "That barracuda Marshal Ogarkov is the worst of them."

"He has been sent out from Moscow," said Maksimov. "He is not out to pasture, not by a long shot. If Romanov comes in on the army's shoulders, Ogarkov will return, and his school of sharp-eyed lackeys with him."

General Major Golitsyn stirred at that, and placed his right hand on Donskov's shoulder. "Those kind of men have no political or ideological acumen. They think like machines, they build only machines, and they trust their machines. They will try to force a military solution in the south, regardless of cost. They want to challenge the imperialists directly, not by subtle propaganda and intrigue, but by showdowns and shootdowns, like that Korean airliner that Ogarkov made into a spy plane. Ogarkov's people talk of prevailing in a global nuclear rocket war, casualties be damned. And so, they may willingly ravage all the gains of socialism to build their iron dreams, which will only serve to spur the desperate imperialists to respond in kind, with what serious consequences I can only guess. Perhaps we will get communism by returning to its primitive cave origins, if anyone survives irradiation. . . ."

Golitsyn trailed off, bitter, shaking his head. He took his hand from Donskov's shoulder.

Here it comes, Donskov realized. The moment of truth has arrived.

General of the Army Maksimov lowered his voice to a bass rumble. "So then, Donskov, to quote the great Vladimir Ilyich, 'what is to be done?' Simply this: Upon Chernenko's death, and in cooperation with the KGB, penetrate the Kremlin and insure Gorbachev's peaceful succession. You will be inserted into the zone of action as part of the 23 February ceremony, and you can anticipate more detailed orders for action within the week. Colonel Leonov will explain all of this."

Donskov started noticeably. "Comrade general, I'm not qualified—"

Maksimov raised his hand. "Surely you do not think I selected you at random for this vital task. You are eminently qualified, if only as the solitary non-GRU regimental recon chief in our deployed airborne forces. Don't you think I would prefer to employ Spetsnaz for this demanding special role? But they work for the GRU, who respond to the General Staff and the Ministry of Defense, and therefore stand against us. Your company is not the best force for the job, but it is the best *reliable* subunit available, and in this sort of work, reliability is paramount. In my opinion, you are thoroughly dependable."

Donskov's mouth opened, but nothing came out. Dependable, am I? Dependable enough to overthrow my government?

"You see, Donskov," explained Maksimov, "I know you well, though I have never met you before today. You have been thoroughly tested and evaluated. My man Golitsyn first noticed you during that strange Grenada episode, and he brought you to my attention more than a year ago, when certain enlightened circles began to consider the dark possibilities that now challenge us. Every other thing you have done in the south has been rigorously examined. The trip to Massoud, the Verskiy intrigue, your innovative Shomali train-up, the Panjsher reconnaissance to include that nasty scene at Aq Khater, Ali Khel and all that, the second Panjsher mission, and your masterful Kunar reconnaissance. I have heard all about these exploits, and I stand convinced that you and your collective have developed certain techniques of independent combat that suit you to conduct the mission that concerns us tonight."

"I'm not so sure that my company can do it, comrade general," said Donskov honestly.

Maksimov waved his hand. "You underestimate yourself. Why, I even included the story of your first Panjsher reconnaissance in my article on mountain combat in this month's *Soviet Military Review,* only to have the anecdote sliced out by nervous censors. We're not at war, they insisted. How indicative! I had written the article back when I hoped that some special method, some exact technique, could rescue us from this Afghan quagmire. Having talked extensively with my comrades in arms, and having seen the political dimensions clearly both in Moscow and in Afghanistan, I have no such illusions."

"There is no tactic that can save us down here," observed Golitsyn in a grave tone. "Dmitriy Ivanovich knows that as well as we do— better, I'll wager."

Donskov said nothing, but his eyes must have mirrored assent.

Maksimov plunged on. "Thanks to your experiences out in the mountains and valleys, you and your wolves are the element best able to handle the complicated, unique, and simultaneous subtasks that will permit accomplishment of the delicate duty I have already mentioned."

General of the Army Maksimov hesitated, exhaled loudly, and proceeded.

"Every man I asked vouched for you, and if an old soldier cannot count on his cohorts, then whom should I believe? Oh, the Sazhenevs, Verskiys, and Kurolesovs distrust you, but just consider the sources. Did you know that Korobchenko once served under my command, and that I still correspond with that old desantnik? He said you were his best. I handpicked Leonov and Golitsyn, and they have the highest confidence in your abilities. Other discreet inquiries among your subordinates have shown that they trust you implicitly."

Golitsyn concluded with this: "Even Chebrikov, the head Chekist himself, approved you by name for this undertaking, based upon voluminous and continuous observation."

So much for co-opting the company's Chekists, observed Donskov, a rather irrelevant supposition at this point. What do I say now?

The lavish praise made him uncomfortable as usual, and its very volume only reinforced an unspoken suspicion that he had been chosen as much because he was an expendable, unremarkable junior officer as for all his touted talents. Before Donskov could answer, the helicopter engine in the repair bay choked to a clanging stop, to be replaced by the lesser scream of the auxiliary power unit. Maksimov spoke again, his voice muted in tone and volume.

"We are all of us," he explained, "from the lowest fighting private all the way up to myself, a great brotherhood, privileged and damned together by our experience in the south. Our leadership has left us down here to twist in an ill wind. You, Dmitriy Ivanovich Donskov, must speak for all of us by your actions."

He grasped Donskov's hand in both of his own. "Good luck, comrade captain. I shall not be seeing you again until this is resolved."

"I serve the Soviet Union," replied Donskov. He wondered if he did so anymore, but it was too late. The die had been cast, and a prospective tsar-maker crossed the Rubicon.

Chapter Eleven

The Tower of Secrets

The bare hardwood trees and thick evergreens of the Tula field maneuver area crowded in around the 688th Reconnaissance Company command group, ostensibly out on a leaders' tactical exercise. Thanks to the energies of Lieutenant Colonel Kharskiy's regimental political section, the men had gone off on a well-deserved tour of the Tula Museum of the History of Arms, not to mention a few secretive shots of vodka or tumbles with the local ladies. This left the command collective free to train.

Four of the seven paratroopers sat on a fallen log, their broad, warmly clothed backs to the winter sun. To their right, the sergeant major squatted, his buttocks resting lightly on his heels. On the left was Senior Lieutenant Zharkowskiy, planted nonchalantly in a deep bank of dry early February snow. Donskov faced the semicircle, kneeling, squinting. The pristine snow and the desantniks' overwhites glowed dull yellow in the rays of the late afternoon sun, which filtered through the trunks and branches and cast strange, mottled flecks of light upon the small mapboard propped on Donskov's knees. It was a wide street map of Moscow.

Zharkowskiy, of course, broke the ice, at least in a figurative sense. "Welcome to the second meeting of the Military Revolutionary Committee, comrades. Soldiers of recon unite! You have nothing to lose but your heads, and what real soldier needs a head anyway?"

Everybody laughed, somewhat strained but loudly enough. When it died down, Donskov began to speak.

"Men, you know our mission is a tough one, and I thank you for trusting me on this one. I think you realize that Andrey Viktorovich's joke about the Military Revolutionary Committee is all too true. Not since Lenin's time, since the real MRCs of Petrograd and Moscow, have small bands of Communist soldiery had such crucial duties. I will restate our immediate tasks for this mission. First, to detain Romanov in his residence. Second, to enter the Kremlin and insure by all means necessary a pro-Gorbachev vote in the Politburo. Third, to secure the television tower in the Ostankino neighborhood for the use of a KGB special broadcast team. There are no programmed subsequent tasks."

The forest swallowed the ominous sentences, but not before Donskov's key subordinates heard them for the second time. This utterance did not produce the shock and dismay of the initial presentation, but looking at his platoon commanders, deputies, and sergeant major, Donskov could not mistake the gravity of their moods. Dwelling on the dangers and doubts would not help. It was better to get on with the work, to do everything possible to make Operation BERZIN a mission like any other mission. If only it were, Donskov hoped. But he knew differently.

"Reports?" queried Donskov, getting on with it.

Zharkowskiy went first. "Enemy forces vary at each of the three objectives, but invariably represent portions of the following outfits: bodyguards of the KGB Ninth Directorate, the Kremlin Commandant's Guards Regiment, MVD internal security troops, and the Moscow Militia. You are all aware that there are other forces in the Moscow Military District, but they are not proximate to our objectives, nor are they available for the sort of instantaneous response necessary to influence our combat tasks."

Zharkowskiy pointedly ignored the possible contributions of the famous show divisions, the 2d Guards "Taman" Motor Rifle Division and the 4th Guards "Kantemirov" Tank Division, the combat-ready MVD "Dzerzhinskiy" Motor Rifle Division, and four additional neighborhood MVD motor-rifle regiments, backed by squadrons of the local Air Army. While in theory such magnificently equipped units might throw back an armored ground attack, their real specialty involved staging the mass parades so beloved by the Soviets. These muscle-bound pretty boys would never even see Donskov's men, let alone catch them.

The senior lieutenant proceeded to describe Romanov's in-town apartment in the 26 Kutuzov Boulevard complex. Zharkowskiy concentrated on security aspects.

Romanov lived in a virtual fortress. Twenty-two external sentries manned set posts, patrolled with dogs, and watched from the roof. Within the structure, intruders would face eighteen roving interior guards, thirty-six static apartment wardens, and an armed ten-man honor guard, with at least two always on station at the front entrance. Other than the honor guard on detached service from the Kremlin regiment, the remainder were nonuniformed Chekists from the Ninth Directorate. The honor squad carried AKM assault weapons, and the roof men used SVD sniper rifles. The others employed pistols.

The political deputy added: "Although the KGB furnished much of this data, including the sketch I'll pass around, I've been warned that, for security reasons, they will *not* notify Romanov's guard force. All of these personnel must be considered hostile."

He passed a small hand drawing around. Donskov realized the implications of what his political deputy had just said. First, the KGB valued mission secrecy above the lives of its men. That came as no surprise. But second, and more worrisome, came the crawling tinge of uncertainty. Maybe the KGB was feeding him chosen information for its own purposes. Was the company being set up, a middle step in an even more Byzantine plot? Donskov banished the thought and focused on his trust in Leonov and Golitsyn. They wouldn't let me down. Would they?

"At the Kremlin," continued Zharkowskiy, "we will encounter three rings of security. First, on the approaches, the Moscow Militia conduct police surveillance. I have no further data at this time, other than to note that my sources mentioned both automobile and foot patrols. As an aside, I might add that the militiamen on duty *inside* the Kremlin are in fact disguised Chekists, and I have counted them among the third ring of protection."

Turning to Donskov's Moscow map, Zharkowskiy pointed with a thin stick to the northwest wall of the triangular Kremlin. "Here is our second problem. This barracks, known as the Arsenal, houses the Kremlin Commandant's Guards Regiment, about 1,800 men equipped with AK-74 automatic rifles, RPK-74 machine guns, and RPG-16D antitank rocket launchers. The unit is formed on the model of a dismounted motor-rifle regiment. They have access to a small number, no more than ten, BTR-70 wheeled armored troop transports with 14.5mm weapons, garaged beneath the barracks, and probably intended for emergency crowd control. These people guard the Lenin Mausoleum, but more to our interest, they outpost the Kremlin grounds. One battalion is on duty at all times, manning eighteen fixed squad posts and nine roving squad patrols. These mobile teams employ Alsatian police dogs. The designated sites and routes are shown in this outline."

He passed another hand-inked paper around the group. Each man studied it carefully.

Zharkowskiy explained more. A second battalion stood in readiness, with one company battle-ready on instant alert, a second on two-hour notice, and the third on four-hour recall. Finally, the third battalion was trained and rested, on a twenty-four-hour notification.

The political officer noted: "The Arsenal is currently undergoing a long-scheduled renovation, which limits ingress and egress. I have yet to determine the exact labor schedule, so I cannot be more specific."

He took in a breath of cold winter air. "The third protective apparatus consists of Ninth Directorate men, positioned around the Council of Ministers' building, the old Tsarist Senate chamber. Until recently, the Politburo held its meetings in the Arsenal, but the construction work there has caused the leadership to shift its meetings across the Kremlin to a third-floor conference center in this venerable palace. You can see"– he held up another detailed sketch, while at the same time indicating the building on Donskov's overall map –

"that our Politburo has chosen an interior room on the Arsenal side of the building. Now there are forty plainclothes sentries, sixteen sited in two-man teams inside these eight locked entrances, and an equal number split into eight roving patrols, two of which prowl each of the four floors. These people all carry AKR 5.45mm automatic carbines. The last eight are on rooftop sniper duty, armed naturally with the SVD Dragunov. I've shown all known positions and routes."

He passed around the building schematics. "During any Politburo meeting, there will also be about twenty personal bodyguards waiting in this third-floor lounge. By long-standing agreement, no armed associates may enter the Politburo chamber or its anteroom, so these characters are basically taking a break during the gatherings. Packing pistols, they might be available as a reserve force if alerted. We can count on surveillance and perhaps even active complicity from a few key Ninth Directorate men, but we must consider the remainder of the Kremlin sentinels to be threats. The niceties of KGB cooperation on the objective have yet to be established."

Zharkowskiy held up a final drawing. He moved his stick across the map to a spot well north of the Kremlin, the gigantic television tower.

Again he covered defensive forces. Along with the usual police, they included an MVD motor-rifle company, complete with BTR-60PB armored carriers. The unit occupied a small cantonment on the estate of the nearby Ostankino Palace Museum. Two of the MVD platoons spread across the nearby grounds of the Economic Achievements Exhibition. One platoon, minus its wheeled fighting vehicles, guarded the base of the television tower. They worked inside the three-meter-high electrified fence that circled the structure.

Zharkowskiy went on. "Guard duties are done rather unobtrusively before 2300, while the Seventh Heaven Restaurant remains open. Two MVD soldiers in civilian clothing occupy a post here and aid the restaurant personnel in inspecting and assisting the incoming diners. From 2300 until 0700, the platoon deploys at these two sites and dispatches a roving squad assisted by police dogs. Regular television workers pass in and out only through this gate, right near the first squad position. Since the MVD is not a participant in our undertaking, these forces are considered hostile."

"How do you assess this mass of information? Is it accurate?" prodded Donskov.

"Most of it. I see what you're driving at, however," said Zharkowskiy. "The Chekists have provided everything until now. My own investigation has been severely limited, but I have found a few helpful individuals. So far, my checking has confirmed most of the KGB data. Even the discrepancies seem to be due to administrative oversights–outdated sentinel locations or slightly incorrect weapons data. But we need to reconnoiter all of these places, and I need some local intelligence assets before I will be satisfied."

Donskov shrugged. "Good enough for now. Any questions on the enemy?"

There were none, at least not yet. It was still too early, and this "enemy" appeared to be too bizarre to prompt the usual concerns.

"Sergeant Major?" asked Donskov.

"As for our own troops, company strength stands at six officers and thirty-seven rank and file. The political deputy's auxiliaries were released to the Afghan government militia. Our attached air and artillery officers returned to their parent units. January demobs have been released, except one, that is."

Everybody but the company sergeant major laughed. The noncommissioned officer merely looked impatient and annoyed. Despite constant protestations, Rozhenko himself was the lone conscript who requested transfer to permanent cadres. His knowledge of the demanding duty facing his company played no small part in helping him decide. "If we pull this off, I can write my own discharge. If we don't, I'll be dead. So why not?" he had argued succinctly, displaying the fatalistic resignation typical of Ukrainian farm folk.

Rozhenko held up his gloved right hand and the mirth died down. "To complete my report, if I may, you are all aware that the regiment will not receive the next group of conscripts until June at the earliest. So we will go with what we have. All three platoons report weaponry and equipment serviceable."

The officers listened, already aware of most of this. Yet the familiar prebattle litany gave an air of routine to this most unfamiliar type of duty.

"Adjacent, reinforcing, and supporting units are restricted to four categories: dedicated Military Transport Aviation lift from Tula to Moscow, extensive KGB intelligence assistance, six Chekist broadcast technicians for the television tower, and a KGB promise of at least one inside man on the Ninth Directorate Kremlin detachment. That's it."

"Good, sergeant major," replied the captain. "Questions?"

Savitskiy raised his hand. "Comrade captain, any chance of scrounging some draftees? All squads are down to three or four men."

"No luck there, Igor. But that's not all bad. You know, I think we're better able to conduct this mission with a half company of veterans than a unit filled up with outright novices. Even if replacements came in, how could we possibly train them up to the proper standards? Worse, what about security implications?" countered Donskov. "We've learned our trade in Afghanistan, and so we trust each other. Try as we might, we could never recreate that environment here in a few short weeks. As the sergeant major said, we'll go with what we have, tried and true."

"I kind of expected that. Just one less thing to worry about, I suppose," answered Savitskiy.

Donskov asked, "Anything else on our troops?" No other questions were raised.

"Next," said the company commander, looking right back at the tough little 1st Platoon commander.

"Terrain and weather," began Lieutenant Savitskiy, "can be studied only conceptually at present. The city of Moscow is known to all of us as our national capital, seat of government, center of party life, and chief urban area of our country. Thanks to Young Pioneer, Komsomol, and cadet trips, all of us except the sergeant major have visited and have a rough idea of the three objective areas. Such vague remembrances, though, are inadequate for detailed planning. Extensive on-site patrolling is critical to our battle preparation, and we must take advantage of our ceremonial visit on Wednesday, 20 February, through Sunday, 24 February, to carry out thorough, directed observations. I will suggest some possible methods to arrange these vital explorations during my brief summary of terrain at each location."

Savitskiy referred to the map, his round face screwed into seriousness. He began with Romanov's building at 26 Kutuzov Boulevard, a massive edifice that once housed Brezhnev and Andropov.

The nine-story concrete-block apartment comprised fifteen housing suites of various sizes. Only twelve were currently occupied. The ground floor served as a garage and security unit quarters. The top floor was also unoccupied and appeared to provide more Chekist work space, plus at least one communications node.

Savitskiy had yet to gather any other information on the building itself or the area around it, so he could not offer any informed opinion on how, where, or when to approach this structure. Also, he had yet to pinpoint Romanov's apartment. But he had an idea of how to fill in these blanks.

"This complex," he said, "is only a block or so east of the Battle of Borodino Panorama, a fine spot for a unit political-historical education tour, which should not only teach us about the 1812 campaign, but also permit a bit of sightseeing in the vicinity."

"Noted, Igor. Precisely my thoughts," agreed Zharkowskiy.

Donskov motioned Savitskiy to press on.

"What can I say about the Kremlin?" asked Savitskiy grandly. "It is no exaggeration to call it the most famous twenty-eight hectares on earth, and surely the most secure."

Savitskiy described the objective area thoroughly. The two kilometers of red brick battlements, dating from 1485, formed a scalene triangle. Walls ranged to nineteen meters in height and up to six meters across, topped by crenellations for archers. Nineteen towers, five pierced by gates, reinforced these great barriers.

The Kremlin housed a collection of cathedrals, palaces, and government buildings. The company's particular target, the three-story Council of Ministers' building, was built at the order of Catherine the Great and completed in 1784. It had been refurbished and modernized many times. Given their scheduled ceremonial preparations in and around Red Square, it appeared that there would be little problem seeing more of this objective.

Savitskiy directed his audience to look at the city map. "What about suitable approaches? A frontal movement through the open expanse of Red Square, past Lenin's tomb, is the quickest way to get to the Politburo meeting chamber. The Chekist guards know that, and so it is also the most dangerous. Only some brilliant ruse might gain successful entry on this side. The risks would certainly exceed prudence. Discounting for the moment any attempt to enter across Red Square, there are two possible approaches for a penetration attempt. The first is through the Aleksandr Gardens to the west, which offers a direct route to our objective. Unfortunately, the palisade is especially high and solid, the Trinity Gate is heavily guarded, and the Arsenal regimental barracks dominate this wall."

Savitskiy placed a gloved finger on his commander's map, right on the Moscow River. "The approach from the south side, comrades, bears further investigation. Obstacles here include the river, the Kremlin Embankment Road, a small strip of lawn, the eleven-meter-high wall, a dry moat, an earthen slope, Cathedral Square with its three major churches, and the Great Kremlin Palace. Then there is open ground all the way to the Council of Ministers' building. The leafless trees on the lawn, the dry moat, and the slope are quite bare and offer no camouflage."

"That hardly sounds encouraging," groused Yegorov, shifting on his log seat.

"No, Kliment, it's not, unless you notice that this gate, the fifth gate, has been bricked shut since 1930. Why? Its name is the clue."

The men peered at the chart.

"The Tower of Secrets," mumbled Lieutenant Popov. "But why?"

"Well, Oleg Danilovich," responded Savitskiy, "*this* tower is the oldest of them all, and its title is no accident. The tower forms a nexus for a spiderweb of half-collapsed underground passages that crisscross the foundations of the Kremlin and old Moscow. When Grand Prince Ivan III commissioned Italian engineers to rebuild his moldering fortress, a certain Antonio Friazin designed this spire. It served to link the Kremlin into existing tunnels. Friazin's men excavated new ones as well. According to a book by a Stalin-era archaeologist named Steletskiy, one such passage lay more than ten meters deep and ran from the Tower of Secrets straight under the Nicholas Tower and out to the northeast, under modern 25th of October Street. Do you realize that such a tunnel would cross precisely beneath our target building? The book also describes other similar galleries. I am not certain how much of this underground Kremlin still survives, but it seems to me that this could be our way in."

"This is quite a long shot, Igor," observed Donskov. "But it may bear fruit. The political deputy will take it up with our KGB comrades."

Zharkowskiy shook his head. "I recommend against that, at least right away. Let me see what I can find out on my own. If there is an underground Kremlin, we should keep it our secret. It may help us carry out our key task if we encounter some sort of security breach, accidental or intentional."

Thus Zharkowskiy, typically, gave voice to what all seven contemplated.

"You don't think the KGB is playing straight with us?" queried Donskov.

"Who knows? But consider this: You believe our colonel and generals because you know them. How well do you know these state security officers you and I have met with?"

"I don't, not really," admitted the captain.

"So let's not show all of our cards, comrade captain. Let's treat the KGB like our loyal Afghan socialist brothers down south. We shall keep them informed, but only when it is absolutely necessary. Knowledge is a Chekist's currency, and it makes no sense to spend our little stash foolishly. Remember, there's no such thing as an honest Chekist," stated Zharkowskiy.

"Exactly so, Andrey." Donskov rubbed his chin and said nothing further. The blank spot in the discussion spread slowly, like blood from a belly wound.

Savitskiy broke the interlude. "About the television tower . . . " he started.

"Yes, Igor. Please complete your report," said the captain.

The television tower, at 533 meters tall the loftiest human construction on earth, stood in the Ostankino neighborhood, just south of the Exhibition of Economic Achievements. The only unusual feature was the Seventh Heaven, a restaurant 300 meters up, which rotated once every forty minutes. This place served the public from 1100 to 2300 daily. Restaurant employees stayed from 0700 until 0100. There were also nine television technical and clerical types who worked just above the restaurant level. The remainder of the facility was automated and, although accessible to repair crews, not normally inhabited. Fortunately, the exhibition park area offered ample concealed routes of advance, not to mention another superb destination for an educational indoctrination visit at the many exhibits.

With regard to weather, Savitskiy could only estimate. Meteorological norms for February and March suggested temperatures ranging from plus five degrees centigrade to thirty below zero, with an average of ten below. The average chance of precipitation was twenty percent.

"Beyond that," he sighed, "I cannot venture, other than to make one definite and patently obvious statement. The best time for Operation BERZIN is a cold night, preferably during a blizzard. Our Afghan experience shows the value of foul weather for masking a subunit's movements. This, comrades, concludes my report."

"Questions?" Donskov offered. None came.

The captain turned to Senior Lieutenant Yegorov. "Normally, we would at this point discuss ideological, political, social, and economic factors. Since Senior Lieutenant Zharkowskiy was acting as our liaison with the KGB, I have asked the deputy commander to evaluate these matters. This afternoon, Kliment Ivanovich will limit himself to a political evaluation to illuminate why Operation BERZIN is being carried out and to permit deeper understanding of the obvious and subtle constraints on our choices."

Blond Yegorov stood up. He unrolled a wide sheet of white paper, smoothed it with his gloved hands, and printed eleven names on it. They formed two groups and two solitary items.

"This is my best guess of today's Politburo. There are three factions percolating beneath the current General Secretary, Chernenko. Our mission commences upon the death of the present leader."

With a single brutal pencil slash, he scratched out Chernenko's name. "This leaves these three: First, there is Romanov, a collective of one, the wrong man. Over here we have Grishin and his old-timers: Kunaev, Tikhonov, and Shcherbitskiy. They lean toward Romanov. Finally, there is our man, Gorbachev, and his suspicious backers: Aliev, Vorotnikov, Gromyko, and Solomentsev. They do not get along. Any sort of deadlock of the two blocs produces—"

"Romanov," concluded Rozhenko. "A perfect compromise—younger, like Gorbachev; Stalinist, like Brezhnev."

"Exactly so, comrade sergeant major. Now," elaborated Yegorov, "look a bit closer at the factions. This Romanov, aged sixty-one, is the former Leningrad Party chief and now Central Committee Secretary for Armaments production. He has the backing of Marshal Sokolov and the army, except the brotherhood of the south and its vanguard, us. Despite his name, this Romanov is no relative of the former tsars, but rather a peasant by birth, reportedly corrupt, and a mean son of a bitch."

He punctuated his description with the introduction of a small photograph. It depicted a wide-browed man with receding dark hair, skeptical eyebrows, and ears flat against his head, like those of a hunting dog on a scent.

"He's a pretty one," sneered Zharkowskiy. "I heard that when his daughter married, she borrowed Catherine the Great's porcelain from the Hermitage Museum for the reception. Apparently, some rowdies smashed up these museum pieces. All in the name of good party fun, naturally."

"That story is going around," agreed Yegorov. He handed the photo to Captain Donskov, who regarded it quizzically and then gave it to the next man.

Yegorov continued. "The Brezhnev leftovers have coalesced around Grishin, aged seventy, First Secretary of the Moscow Communist Party. He is a born Muscovite, served in the army before the Great Patriotic War, and has spent the rest of his time in city political work. Reportedly, he has Chernenko's blessing, for whatever that's worth."

The deputy commander produced Grishin's picture and gave it to his commander. The boring oval face of the unremarkable little grandfather blended right into the black, white, and gray shades of the print.

"He looks like an old drunk," snapped Lieutenant Lebedev of 3d Platoon.

"Maybe, Pavel, but this particular vagrant commands the solid loyalty of three veteran Politburo men, and they represent the bulk of the main party cadres. Kunaev, of Turkic extraction, aged seventy-three, is First Secretary of the Kazakh SSR. He's a Brezhnev crony, a Central Asian 'house Muslim.' Tikhonov, aged seventy-nine, is the Premier, and supposedly almost completely decrepit. Finally, we have Shcherbitskiy, aged sixty-seven, First Secretary of the Ukrainian SSR, an insider in Brezhnev's Dnepropetrovsk mafia. These people, and indeed the majority of the inner party that supports them, would love to see Grishin take over. But if forced to a choice between Romanov and Gorbachev, they'd tilt toward Romanov. I do not yet have any pictures of these men."

Yegorov indicated Gorbachev's name. "Gorbachev, almost fifty-four, is the youngest member of the Politburo. He hails from Stavropol, down near the Caucasus. This man did not serve in the military at all, which I guess says something about his health or connections. Currently the Central Committee Secretary for Agriculture, Gorbachev also supervises Central Committee Secretariat meetings when Chernenko cannot make it. Nobody is too sure what he stands for. The KGB backs him, as do we."

The senior lieutenant showed a photograph of a cherubic, bald man with smart little eyes and a pointed chin. He passed it to the sergeant major.

"What's wrong with his head?" blurted Savitskiy. "It looks like some hooligan boxed him on his right forehead."

"It's a birthmark," Yegorov explained.

"My neighbors back home would call it a sign of the devil," remarked Rozhenko. He handed the picture to the next man.

"Gorbachev's four supporters are a diverse, quarrelsome group. Two of them hate the third, this acerbic busybody Vorotnikov, aged fifty-eight. He is the Premier of our largest republic, the vast Russian SFSR. Unfortunately for Gorbachev, Vorotnikov's ambitions encouraged him to step on Solomentsev, aged seventy-one, now the head of the Party Control Commission."

"Wasn't Solomentsev the Premier of the Russian SFSR?" queried Lebedev.

Yegorov assented with a vigorous nod. "Exactly so, Pavel, until he was muscled out by this guy Vorotnikov. Solomentsev didn't forget, either. He likes Gorbachev but hates Vorotnikov, and may vote opposite of his rival out of spite. Vorotnikov also competes with Aliev, aged sixty-one, another Russified Asian and a career Chekist from Azerbaydzhan. Aliev holds the title of Deputy Premier of the Soviet Union, under ancient Tikhonov. Both Vorotnikov and Aliev want to be Premier of the USSR when Tikhonov retires or dies, so they do not cooperate. They agree on Gorbachev but due to their personal antagonism, neither may vote that way."

"This is really complicated," grunted Popov.

"Is it any wonder our country's policies are so screwed up?" rejoined Zharkowskiy. A thin laugh rippled around the circle.

Yegorov resumed his analysis. "Lastly, there's Gromyko, aged seventy-six, the wily old fox of the diplomatic corps. His work abroad denied him any political base here, so he cannot succeed to power, but he can be an influence behind the party leader. He favors Gorbachev because he thinks the man is honest, hard-working, young, and unfamiliar with foreign affairs. Therefore, Gorbachev may be likely to heed Gromyko's advice, particularly if the old-timer can stitch together a Gorbachev majority. This elder negotiator will need all his peacemaking skills to hold Gorbachev's feuding coalition together."

Senior Lieutenant Yegorov looked briefly at the snowy ground, and then glanced up. "My estimate indicates three preliminary conclusions. One, Romanov must not reach the Politburo meeting. Lenin's rules never specified a quorum, and a Politburo ruling by nine members is as binding as one by ten. This will create a clear Grishin versus Gorbachev showdown, and Gorbachev will win five to four, if his backers bury their differences. Two, the Grishin faction can back Romanov, and Romanov might even back Grishin. None of them will back Gorbachev. With Romanov present, it's a five to five split, and the quarrels among Gorbachev's supporters may easily produce a pro-Romanov majority. Three, Gorbachev's support is very soft. If it comes down to him and Romanov, with all ten voting, who knows? I guess that's where we come in, to add the unbearable pressure of assault rifles to Gorbachev's side. That concludes my report."

"Outstanding summary, Kliment. Are there any questions?" asked Donskov.

"What about candidate members?" wondered Zharkowskiy.

"Good question, Andrey," replied Yegorov. "Candidate members may or may not be present, and if there, they may speak but not vote, of course. This parallels the usual candidacy regulations in all party organs. Three who will most probably attend are Marshal Sokolov, General Chebrikov of the KGB, and Shevardnadze, a former MVD man from Georgia. We can be sure that Sokolov backs Romanov. We trust that Chebrikov supports Gorbachev, but I am a bit leery about predicting KGB behavior. Shevardnadze is a question mark. That's all I can tell you so far."

Massive Popov rustled on his log. "Where did you get all of this stuff? A lot of it sounds like half-truths or Communist party gossip. How reliable is it?"

"My major sources were KGB," Yegorov said, "so I have yet to verify much of this information. You can bet that I will be poring over the political segments of the newspapers looking for confirmations of these suppositions, and I think some discreet interviews can also assist. You must also keep your eyes and ears open."

"Anything else?" Donskov offered. There were no takers.

The sun had become a flattened red disk, almost at the horizon. Cold hands and feet told the paratroopers that it would soon be dark, and the thermometer was dropping. It had been a long afternoon, but fruitful. The collective had discovered a lot of new, intriguing information. But Donskov still owed them his personal evaluation, and he took a few seconds to organize his thoughts before speaking. He stood up and swept his eyes across the huddled, white-suited men.

"All right, comrade desantniks," he commenced, "you have heard this preliminary evaluation of the situation. Although you can count on clarification as more intelligence becomes available, I can designate a basic task breakdown. Igor Petrovich, you and your 1st Platoon have responsibility for Romanov's apartment."

"Understood—exactly so, comrade captain," rejoined the lieutenant.

"Oleg Danilovich, you and the 2d Platoon White Wolves must force the Ostankino television tower."

Popov nodded gravely. "Exactly so, comrade captain," he rumbled.

"Pavel Nikolayevich, you know what's left. You've been with us five months, so you're ready. The 3d Platoon, plus the command collective, have drawn the main axis—the penetration of the Kremlin. The command element will back up this crucial effort."

"Exactly so, comrade captain. Count on us," Lieutenant Lebedev shot back.

I wonder if he realizes, if any of them realize, how dangerous this all will be. They trust me so much that they will commit treason with me. Well, I always wanted to be able to carry men by the force of my personality, to lead them into the great abyss and come out alive. It's happening; I'm doing it.

Donskov hesitated momentarily, then spoke. "Be assured that Operation BERZIN is not unprecedented. Far from it. Any survey of Russian and Soviet history shows numerous similar attempts. Which Russian has not heard the stories of the rampaging streltsy musketeers of the sixteenth and seventeenth centuries, or the multiple plots of the elite tsarist guards' regiments in the eighteenth century? The two most powerful Russian autocrats, Peter the Great and Catherine the Great, took power under such circumstances. Bungling noble junior officers failed to oust Tsar Nicholas I in the Decembrist Uprising of 1825, largely through lack of preparations and inattention to coordination. Yet they tried, and thereby inspired three generations of revolutionaries, including Vladimir Ilyich Lenin. Ensign Yan Karlovich Berzin, the source of our operation's code name, seized the Kremlin in November 1917 after a week of bloody fighting with White Guardist counterrevolutionaries. It's been done before. It can be done again."

He paused for effect. "This is not simply dry history. As recently as June 1957, Marshal Zhukov gathered up the resources of his armed forces to shepherd a flock of Central Committee members into the Kremlin. Delivered by Soviet military airlift, notified and guarded by uniformed officers, these delegates comprised an emergency plenum that reversed a Politburo attempt to expel Khrushchev from power. Believe me, armed components have played their role, a watchdog role, in state affairs. Indeed, our entire revolution would have failed were it not for the bold action of the workers, soldiers, and sailors of the Petrograd Military Revolutionary Committee. We, comrades, are their worthy successors."

Donskov spoke with more conviction than he truly possessed. He scanned the eager faces of his men. Did they think it could work? How could they trust him so willingly? He did not even trust himself that much.

"In our talking this afternoon, we have skirted the principal determinants of success or failure in this unique escapade. I refer to timing and discipline."

They hung on his words, their eyes locked on him.

"First," said the commander, "what about timing? This is, to a great extent, beyond our control. We must hope that we are ordered to launch BERZIN at the optimum moment, when the complicated interrelated political and military factors are in our favor. I think that the KGB controls our present General Secretary's medical care. They will choose the moment that Chernenko passes on, and we must be ready. It most probably will come at night, and it may even be sprung as a surprise, when some Politburo members are away from Moscow."

He lowered his eyes to the snow, then went on. "Timing within the mission is also important, and here we have more influence. We must be in position at three separate objectives, and we must strike in the proper sequence. If we miss our cue, we fail. That cannot be permitted, and here I must admit that I have not yet determined a way to put more of this aspect under our direct control. Right now, the KGB also dominates our tactical scheming. I don't like that. War, if this is war, does not favor coordination; it favors command. I, and by extension all of you, don't have full authority over our battle conduct once Operation BERZIN commences. We must rely on the Chekists, perhaps too much. I have not yet solved this dilemma."

Donskov brought his hands together, grinding his palms. "Discipline is as crucial as timing, maybe more so. We alone control this. As recon men, we have tried hard not to apply wanton violence against potential sources of information. Even so, we have erred all too often. You all remember."

Donskov paused, watching their jaws work and their gazes grow cloudy with bad memories. After a few seconds, they came back. The captain searched for the right words.

"In this case, we find ourselves functioning in the midst of our innocent fellow citizenry. The Muscovite populace must be protected. They are not the enemy. Yes, we want to get armed men into a critical Politburo meeting, and we will threaten mayhem. But that is as far as it goes. We have no intention of injuring the members of the Politburo, nor will we. Yet by the same token, we must not be squeamish in dealing with representatives of the security organs. We don't have time to play their games. Our job is to detain Romanov, strong-arm a pro-Gorbachev vote in the Kremlin, and get the proper word out on the electronic media. Those sentinels that block us must be killed."

Not a man blinked. They understood.

"The future of our motherland depends on us," he concluded softly.

I hope we're right, but right or not, we're going to try this, Donskov rationalized. We owe it to all the ghosts of the Hindu Kush.

They returned to the cantonment an hour after nightfall.

" . . . the Order of the Red Banner, Second Award!" trumpeted the public address system, blaring with the deep-throated, godlike voice of a staff colonel chosen specifically because of his vocal talents. The red and gold regimental standard of the 688th Guards dipped in the light, twirling snowflakes, and slit-eyed Marshal Sergey Leonidovich Sokolov, Minister of Defense of the Union of Soviet Socialist Republics, affixed the new insignia to the drooping flag.

"Good show, Leonov," mumbled doddering Sokolov. The seventy-three-year-old marshal puffed great gouts of breath. His numb, shaking fingers proved barely able to tie on the temporary streamer, which would mark the award until replaced by permanent gold lettering embroidered directly on the bright scarlet flag. A young, nimble artillery colonel from the defense minister's personal staff stood right behind, ready to help. It was not necessary this day, despite the bitter cold.

"I serve the Soviet Union, comrade marshal!" barked Leonov, tall and distinguished in his long gray overcoat, snug parade belt, and visored circular SS cap. Snowflakes dotted his light blue uniform VDV facings, golden shoulder boards, and gray coat. Behind him, just over a thousand of his Afghan-hardened desantniks stood in serried ranks, their metal-stocked AKDs at "present arms."

The marshal straightened up, his work over. He shook Leonov's hand and then slowly stepped backward, bringing his polished boots together.

"Bring your regiment to order arms and parade rest," rasped Sokolov, his voice still bearing the whiplash of command.

Leonov dropped his own salute, faced about, and gave the orders, echoed by the three battalions and the regimental support troops. Each outfit brought their AKDs down with impressive, cracking precision, a tribute to hours of practice over the last few weeks. The booming voices and crashing arms carried and echoed, reflecting from the Kremlin walls to the State Department Store behind them and then back again until they died out in the whispering dusting of snow.

Gray, sunless skies rendered the cobblestones of magnificent Red Square a dull brown on this Soviet Army and Navy day, 23 February 1985. Captain Donskov occupied his spot out in front of his Recon Company, which formed the right of the foremost grouping of the regimental support echelon, just behind the line battalions. From his position just over halfway back in the great regimental assembly, Donskov could see ahead quite clearly, an advantage conveyed by his height.

Like the rest of the 688th, the captain and his men faced the stacked boxes of the Lenin Mausoleum, and behind it the notched Kremlin parapet. The Kremlin appeared to be the color of dried blood on this cheerless afternoon. To the rear of Lenin's resting place reared the spiky Senate Tower. Behind it stretched the upper floor of the yellowish Council of Ministers' building, its squat cupola topped by a limp national flag. That's the place, all right. His heart pounded as he sur-

veyed his target, even though he and his subordinates had done everything but disassemble it brick by brick over the last few days of careful surveillance. Donskov would wager that every one of his troops,
but especially Lebedev's 3d Platoon, were also peering intently forward through the wafting, misty veil of snow. At least one company
needed no added incentives to keep "eyes front" for this ceremony.

Few citizens or tourists gathered to watch Colonel Leonov's stolid
VDV regiment receive its unit citation. The Saturday afternoon presentation had not been well publicized, and the cold and snowy turn
to the weather did not help. A few busloads of shivering Young Pioneers
and factory workers on educational political outings hung about gloomily in the permanent reviewing stands, anxiously hoping that the display would end. About a hundred babbling, sloppy Siberian visitors
shuffled and laughed, warm in their strange furs and skins. Some other
curious civilians watched from the square itself, arms folded, smoking, chatting amiably with passersby. Actually, the chain of militiamen and KGB uniformed guards almost outnumbered the spectators.
The sparse press cohort included a television camera crew and a few
print reporters, and they focused on the three solemn men behind
Sokolov: Grishin, Romanov, and Gorbachev, from left to right.

Donskov recognized all three as surely as he might distinguish
an Mi-2M from an Mi-8 or an Mi-24 Gorbach. Yes, the desantniks
had enjoyed a good laugh or two about the Politburo leader named
after an attack helicopter. Or was it vice versa, as Zharkowskiy speculated? "After all," smirked the political deputy, "the Chekists probably named both of them."

In any event, here they stood, the three principals. To the right
stooped Grishin, as gray as the day; he appeared weighed down by
his fur hat and baggy overcoat. Romanov, by contrast, stood as erect
as any old soldier, shoulders squared, massive fleshy face jutting forward, solid as the granite in Lenin's tomb. Gorbachev huddled in his
black overcoat and sported a black fedora, like some American gang-
ster. Donskov was so busy checking the trio and mentally weeding out
hovering flunkies from lurking bodyguards that he missed the start
of Romanov's speech.

" . . . well known that imperialist circles in the USA from the very beginning took an openly hostile stand toward the national-democratic revolution in Afghanistan. The criminal CIA incited misguided tribal minorities, taught torture to Afghan counterrevolutionaries, employed deadly biotoxic chemicals, and slaughtered Soviet advisers and internationalist volunteers in reckless provocations. These are the facts. Our esteemed comrades of the 688th Guards Twice Red Banner Regiment know this. They have lost friends to these hateful imperialist aggressors."

Romanov was reading his statement in front of a long, lozenge-shaped, foam-covered microphone. His low, measured tones thundered from the loudspeakers. It's all so much bullshit, decided Donskov. The rush of drivel made the captain feel better about working against this blowhard.

" . . . noninterference in the internal affairs of other states. As such, we and our Afghan socialist brothers march arm in arm, in complete solidarity against imperialism, colonialism, and neocolonialism in all their varied, virulent forms. We are compelled to render the appropriate military aid requested by a small, embattled neighbor. As the vanguard country of world socialism, we can never turn our backs on the People's Democratic Party of Afghanistan, who are struggling to implement the time-tested principles of Marxism-Leninism. The CIA mercenaries and their tired, tattered fragmentary gangs of Afghan counterrevolutionary bandits will be defeated, indeed, must be defeated. The weight of history, illuminated by the clear objective light of scientific socialism, promises no less. Long live the brave defenders of our motherland, bolstered by the indestructible ideological and organizational cohesion fostered by our wise and mighty Communist Party!"

Polite applause followed Romanov as he backed away from the microphone stand. Grishin and Gorbachev remained rooted in place, unsmiling. The crackling of wind sputtered from the speakers for a second or two. Then came the voice of the military announcer: "Citizens and guests, this concludes today's ceremony." A band struck up a bold march, and the tiny reviewing party ambled off, its older individuals stepping gingerly across the wispy snow.

It took about ten minutes for the 688th Guards Air Assault Regiment to wend its way back into the Kremlin, a train of companies stepping lively through the yawning Savior Gate, under the famous Kremlin clock, the one whose bell tolled the hour on Moscow Radio. Ragged clapping and a few unauthorized foreigners' flashbulbs marked the dreary conclusion to the awards review. In a way, it seemed a fitting postscript to Afghanistan.

There could not have been more than a dozen sightseers wandering inside the famed citadel as the airborne soldiers entered. Leonov led the long, snaking regimental column toward the Palace of Congresses, an utterly out-of-place modern concrete and glass block. The vast hall could seat 6,000, and hosted party conventions and public entertainment. Today, it served as a staging area for the 688th Guards as they waited for their bus convoy out to the Alabino barracks, the regiment's temporary home. To avoid congesting the Kremlin, Leonov had directed that the wheezing diesel buses arrive one at a time. So the men took seats in the cavernous auditorium and did what soldiers do best: waited.

Donskov elected to stand outside and evaluate his surroundings. He watched Lebedev, Yegorov, and Zharkowskiy slip out as well, pacing thoughtfully but carefully, measuring distances, estimating cover, concealment, and fields of fire while seeming to gawk. The captain simply stood on the east flank of the Palace of Congresses and looked north, toward the scaffolding that covered the facade of the Arsenal. A mountain of bricks blocked the south entrance, and that was new. They were not there yesterday. A hoist on the roof also—

"Hey, desantnik! You, Donskov!" growled a voice only a few meters behind him—the familiar sounds of Captain Korobchenko, retired. Could it be? It seemed impossible. The recon commander spun around slowly.

And there he stood, head back, great mouth open, bellowing his hearty, rolling laugh. "It's you!" gushed Donskov, without much originality.

"Of course, Dmitriy. Who in hell did you think? You know how I love a parade. The regiment looked sharp today," he said offhandedly.

He advanced and bear-hugged Donskov, nearly crushing the air out of him. It was Korobchenko, all right.

"What are you doing here, Boris? Why aren't you at home?"

Korobchenko heaved his shoulders under his plain brown over-coat. His scarf slipped and Donskov noticed that his old commander still wore his striped desantnik undershirt.

"Shit, the VDV was my home. So I went where all old soldiers try to go—the Soviet Armed Forces Museum in Commune Square. I'm a hall warden in the gallery of Heroes of the Soviet Union. Just my luck I've got the hardware to qualify. All I have to do is stand near my picture and bullshit people. And for this I get a nice two-room apartment on Peace Avenue and enough money to drink and whore myself sick. It's not soldiering, but it will do, and it beats the hell out of crunching wheat down in the Ukraine. How about you? How was the south?"

Donskov gave a noncommittal look. "About like you'd expect. About like you warned me, maybe worse. I'm the recon chief."

Korobchenko whistled. "Not bad. That's a major's slot. But hey, you're not GRU. How did you swing that?"

"It's a long story," answered Donskov. How do I tell my old company commander that my entire Afghan service might have been some sort of strange audition, only with live ammunition? Or that it ends with me trying to grab a piece of the Kremlin? And believe me, Boris Timofeyevich, even you might be shocked to hear that.

"I'll be happy to hear it," said Korobchenko, his blue eyes merry. "Do you have a pass for tonight? I've got a few bottles and some sausages."

"Captain Donskov!" someone shouted. The recon commander looked over his shoulder. It was Corporal Padorin. "The colonel would like a word with you."

"On my way, comrade corporal." He looked back at his former commander. There was so much to tell him, about Afghanistan, and especially about this latest thing, this trick Operation BERZIN. After all, if anyone could help him, it had to be Korobchenko.

"Look, Boris Timofeyevich, I've got to go. Can you give me your address?"

The retired paratrooper held up his left hand, and with his right yanked a small calling card from his pocket. "There you are. I get them from the museum, a fringe benefit. Give me a call. I'm going right home to start on my vodka and wait."

"Don't get too shitfaced," warned Donskov.

"Not at all, comrade captain," retorted Korobchenko with a mock salute. "See you tonight."

Donskov took a deep pull off the long-necked bottle. His throat burned, and he almost forgot the biting chill of the evening. "How can you drink this piss?" he asked Korobchenko.

The big man's face crinkled around his swollen nose. "Piss! This is Ukrainian pepper vodka, son. After the wild shit you've just told me, I'm sorry I didn't bring a case."

The two VDV men sat on a snow-crusted bench in Commune Square. Korobchenko had not changed his afternoon attire. Donskov, however, had switched to several warm layers of civilian clothes, a muffler, and his gray fur hat. They were alone, as the temperature had plunged to a nasty minus twenty degrees centigrade, and most pedestrians found reason to stay inside. It was a fine night for plotting in the park.

An intermittent series of automobiles whizzed by on both sides of the small square. From across the street, the glaring floodlights of the Soviet Armed Forces Museum generated a stark white light into cramped Commune Square. Barren branches cast long, lacy shadows on the fresh snow.

"A ticklish matter, Dmitriy," observed Korobchenko. "But not impossible. You know that. I don't quite understand the political reasoning, but I agree that Leonov, Golitsyn, and Maksimov are trustworthy comrades in arms, and I don't think they'd act on a whim. No doubt, more of the same old shit isn't good for the motherland. It's time for a change, and the circus in the south is just a symptom. I only hope this Gorbachev fellow turns out okay, but I don't know. No army service at all?"

"None," admitted Donskov. "But Lenin never served either. In fact, Gorbachev is a lawyer by education, just like Lenin was."

Korobchenko snorted. "There was only one Lenin. But like I said, any change might help."

The retired officer sipped a bit more of the awful pepper vodka and took a bite of a greasy sausage. "I like your conceptual battle plan, Dmitriy. You have allowed for good use of local camouflage and deception at both of the secondary objectives. In the decisive sector, the Kremlin, the tunnel idea is terrific. I still can't believe the idiots left it open."

"Open is a relative term," noted Donskov. "It's partially caved in in three spots and half awash with sewage. We won't smell very nice when we come up. The recon squad had a rough time."

"Still, you pop in through the Dzerzhinskiy Square Metro Station and pop out in the basement of the Council of Ministers' building."

"In a boiler room," added Donskov. "But I agree, it works."

Korobchenko pondered for almost a half minute. A bus lumbered past, its shock absorbers creaking. It sounded almost like the squeak of tank treads.

"How far does that tunnel go?" questioned Korobchenko.

"All the way to the river, right under the Tower of Secrets and on out to a grate beneath the Stone Bridge. The thing hooks in with the underground conduit that carries the Neglinnaya Creek under the Aleksandr Gardens. Lebedev's men made it that far. Luckily it's winter, or this route wouldn't work at all. If the river were up, we'd have to be pickerels to swim the whole way."

Korobchenko nodded a few times. "Uh-huh. Uh-huh. Okay. Refresh my memory, Dmitriy. How much notice can you expect?"

"At least twenty-four hours, and possibly more," Donskov answered. "Grebeniuk assured me of that. We need that much time to fly up from Tula and stage to the KGB safe houses, the jump-off areas."

Korobchenko clapped a gloved, meaty hand on Donskov's shoulder. "Right. Your plan is excellent, but it needs one more twist. You remember our old Chinese friend?"

"Sun Tzu? I've built my company on his ideas," replied the recon captain.

"Good. Then recall the master's words: 'Move when it is advantageous and create changes in the situation by dispersal and concentration of forces.' Now what's the key to that passage?"

Donskov came back immediately: "'*Create* changes in the situation,' of course. Make it go my way."

Korobchenko smiled. "Very well done, Dmitriy Ivanovich. You're right on top of it. Right now, you're depending a lot on the Chekists, maybe too much. Do you trust this guy, Grebeniuk?"

Donskov rubbed the back of his scarfed neck. "I don't know."

"How about the Kremlin Commandant?" persisted the older soldier. "Have you met him?"

"No," said Donskov. "Grebeniuk tells me that I can't meet with General Lieutenant Shornikov. Security considerations, he says. Grebeniuk will handle that liaison."

Korobchenko nodded once more, then swung in to face Donskov. He leaned into him, very close, his voice a hoarse whisper. "Listen, young captain, has it ever occurred to you that the Chekists *let* you find that tunnel? That it originates right near the Lubyanka, the KGB headquarters? That if a group of army thugs materialized in the Politburo, they could be liquidated by the heroic KGB, thereby discrediting the army completely and paving the way for Gorbachev's accession just as tidily as if your scheme worked out? You see, the state security may well be using all of you, from Maksimov on down, as front men, pawns in their own game. Why else use a regular recon company, no matter how unique, for tasks that would strain veteran Spetsnaz troops? If the KGB can set you up, fuck you over, and pull it off, they can emasculate the army, especially our dear brotherhood of the south. They can do what they want."

"Shit. I never thought of that," gaped Donskov. No, he told himself. I've thought of it, but my ideas never took this concrete, deadly form. *This* was how bad it could be–a complete frame-up. It had a warped, eerie logic to it.

"Now then," said Korobchenko, as if in command, explaining to his deputy commander again, like in the old days. "We must find a way to frustrate any Chekist double cross. The VDV and the Limited Contingent of Soviet Forces in Afghanistan, represented by your company, have got to play a role in this mission, a role beyond possible targets for the KGB."

"The rest of the tunnel!" Donskov rejoined suddenly. "If we entered at the river—"

"—they would not be able to predict your arrival, and you could gain tactical surprise," finished Korobchenko.

"We can pass under the Tower of Secrets and come across and then up," added Donskov. "But we need one more thing, some sort of deceptive strike, to draw off the KGB and confuse them. It must appear to be spontaneous."

Korobchenko poked himself in his broad chest with his gloved left thumb, swinging the vodka bottle up in the process. "I am your man. I told you that I am second secretary of the Moscow Afghan Veterans' Council. Yes, I joined to drink and swap war stories, but our ranks contain quite a few real hotheads who'd like nothing better than, say, a spontaneous rally for recognition in Red Square. I received a cushy job, but many of my comrades have gotten nothing for their efforts; indeed many returned to find themselves edged out of their jobs, apartments, and trade schools by those who did not fight. You saw this afternoon how little the populace knows or cares about our war service. Afghanistan veterans are a pugnacious lot who wouldn't mind taking a poke at a militiaman. What's a night in jail compared to a night in the Panjsher? You know, I can think of a dozen ex-VDV and former Spetsnaz malcontents who'd help me right now, no questions asked. You let me handle your diversionary maneuver. Send that shifty commissar of yours—"

"Andrey Viktorovich Zharkowskiy."

"Yes. Send him to me. We'll work it out, and I'll fill Red Square with a wonderful street demonstration of mistreated veterans, something guaranteed to call out the whole Kremlin regiment. I can even get a few invalid buddies to come along in their wheelchairs—our motor-rifle arm, you know? Even the goons at the Kremlin won't open fire on crippled war heroes. But just in case, I'll slip a tip to a British woman from Reuters, who can stop by to keep the Chekists honest."

"Boris, she may be a spy," objected Donskov. "I don't want any imperialists involved in this. If they get wind of the Politburo situation, they might take advantage of the confusion for their own ends."

Korobchenko shook his big head. "Don't worry. She will be there only to help my portion of the mission. The vets will be unarmed, and we need some sort of protection, if only the puny threat of world censure."

The Ukrainian gulped from his bottle, dropped it down, and eyeballed the sloshing contents. "Yes," summarized Korobchenko. "That's it. We'll draw them to the east, set off every alarm, and then you strike from the south. Like Sun Tzu said: 'If he prepares to the left, his right will be vulnerable and if to the right, there will be few on his left.' Tell your Chekist confederates that you don't want to use the tunnel, that you have chosen to infiltrate by truck or plane or autogyro, whatever. Just think of some plausible cover story, something to drive the KGB crazy. You know what will work. Make sure to mislead the snitches in your company, of course."

"Naturally. I believe I can think of something."

"Whatever you do," Korobchenko emphasized, "don't give away either your real approach or my deceptive foray. Then I'll make a show, they'll react like it's real, and you'll come in from the river."

He stopped. Both men lapsed into silence.

"Of course, the KGB may be totally straight. We might be overly suspicious," remarked Donskov.

"In that case, the plan will still work, at least from *your* point of view, and in accord with the desired political ends."

"Whichever way, some Chekists are going to die, by ignorance or by design," stated Donskov. "The KGB has either exposed their own trusting operatives in a ruthless bid to maintain this mission's secrecy, or they've set snares for us that we'll now outflank and destroy."

"Ensign Berzin lost 500 men in November 1917, but he took the Kremlin. A few dead Chekists are a small price to pay to duplicate that feat, Dmitriy."

They paused again, nearly talked out.

"So there it is," the recon captain finished. "Thanks for your help."

"Don't thank me yet," warned the retired officer. "We still have everything to do."

Korobchenko passed the heavy bottle back to his younger companion. "Suck it down, Dmitriy Ivanovich. Every little bit of courage, even from a bottle, may help."

"It can't hurt." He drank deeply. In the morning, he would have to deal again with Operation BERZIN, now new and improved—"clarified," in doctrinal parlance. For the first time, however, he began to believe that it really might come off. In fact, Captain Donskov started to look forward to the attempt.

"What's wrong with the tunnel?" asked Col. Grigoriy Pavlovich Grebeniuk, his reedy voice showing obvious annoyance. This white-haired crew-cut, thin-faced whip of a man never wore a uniform, and Donskov guessed him to be a colonel, mainly by his age. Grebeniuk neither confirmed nor denied it, and allowed Donskov to address him as a colonel. Asked his job at their first meeting, the wiry fellow merely told the airborne captain that he worked in "the central KGB apparatus."

Now Grebeniuk wheeled his black Volga sedan south down Lenin Boulevard, passing Gorkiy Park to the right, and headed for the university. This was idle driving, though. The real purpose of the trip was to permit a talk in a secure capsule, and the Volga had been thoroughly swept for electronic listening devices, transmitters, and recorders just minutes before. The colonel waited for his army passenger to reply.

"The tunnel is passable, but I'm not convinced we can get in or out without being noticed. It's a bit too sneaky for its own good, if you know what I mean. I prefer a more direct, yet subtle approach."

"Explain," demanded Grebeniuk, slowing for a traffic light.

"Infiltration, comrade colonel. We've already moved men in and out, stockpiled weapons and ammunition, and so forth, just for drills," lied Donskov with a perfectly sincere tone.

"How?" The light changed, and the sedan accelerated.

The captain explained with calculated vagueness, injecting just the right air of confidence. "Oh, we go in disguises, with fabricated papers. I've inserted men as tourists, cleaning people, and especially as laborers on the Arsenal renovation. It hasn't been too hard. With notice, I can have my sixteen-man team in position pretty quickly during the day, when the Kremlin is open. We hide out in the Nicholas and Senate Towers. Thanks to various experiments and rehearsals, it's really all somewhat systematic by now."

Grebeniuk squirmed in his seat, envisioning these desantnik phantoms zipping in and out of the center of Soviet power. Donskov could tell by the state security colonel's pronounced consternation that the bluff was working beautifully. Nothing worried Chekists more than the belief that their precious security procedures had been casually compromised, particularly by army men. If Chebrikov and his KGB henchmen were planning some treachery during Operation BERZIN, this would make them think twice and doubt their smug omniscience. Donskov guessed that there would soon be a lot of hard questions asked of the Kremlin Commandant and his men. The less they found, the harder they would search.

"My coordination role," Grebeniuk purred disarmingly, "necessitates a *complete* briefing on this revision to the plan, including a concrete elucidation of exactly how you have evaded the various sentries. I need to be certain of these material considerations to, ah, facilitate your task." The colonel spoke softly, but his darting eyes betrayed his concern. Who's reacting now, comrade?

"No problem," said Donskov smoothly. "My deputy Yegorov concocted the methods employed. He flew up with me from Tula, and is conducting some routine coordination with your chief of staff back at the Lubyanka. Yegorov will happily deliver a detailed explanation of the infiltration aspects of our current conceptual battle plan."

"Excellent," clucked Grebeniuk. "That should prove most interesting." And it's totally fabricated, you Chekist son of a bitch. We've written up an elaborate fictional account that will let you chase your tails, play detective, and interrogate the shit out of each other for some time, more time than you have. Donskov perceived from the instant he got the call to fly back up to Moscow that the moment of decision was very near.

The car crested the Lenin Hills. To the right squatted the concrete massif of blocky, stepped gray-white box skyscrapers that distinguished Moscow State University, an architectural monstrosity birthed in the closing years of the Stalin period. Grebeniuk motored steadily southwest on Lenin Boulevard, pushing toward the Ring Road that surrounded Moscow like the trench of some seventeenth-century siege force.

"Have you been keeping abreast of party affairs, comrade captain?" asked Grebeniuk. Here it comes, thought Donskov.

"I voted in last Sunday's Russian republic election, if that's what you mean," evaded the captain.

Grebeniuk braked for another light. They were almost out to the Ring Road. "Indeed. Did you happen to see our General Secretary cast his vote?"

"I saw it," said Donskov. He and his lieutenants had virtually crawled atop the officers' club television set out at Tula, watching replays of Chernenko's vote on various newscasts. They had scrutinized the still pictures in the papers the next morning, alert for details, diagnosing the old man's health like farmers estimating the day's likely weather.

"How did the boss look to you?" inquired Grebeniuk.

"Sick, comrade colonel. Not well at all." That was an understatement. Chernenko appeared to be dead already, pasty-faced, his white hair wild and wispy, his last steps unsteady, his voice unheard beneath the crisp patter of the announcer.

"The boss is no better this Sunday. By next Sunday he will be dead." Grebeniuk said it without any emotion. He turned calmly to the right, onto the great Ring Road. Was this the notification, or just a KGB colonel's opinion? Having heard far too much Chekist double-talk in the past two months, Donskov wanted to be absolutely sure.

"How do you know that?" ventured the recon man.

"Shcherbitskiy is flying to the USA tomorrow, 3 March. Vorotnikov leaves for Yugoslavia on Tuesday. On Friday, Kunaev goes to Alma-Ata in the Kazakh SSR. So those three will be gone next weekend. They have been told that Chernenko may linger on until the summer, so they have ceased hanging around the capital and have gone back to their party work."

Donskov evaluated the situation. With two Grishin bloc types gone, and the troublemaker Vorotnikov absent, Gorbachev had the advantage, four to three. It was devious, it was brilliant, and it would work.

"Under these conditions," Grebeniuk added, "your duty is simple: Enter the Politburo chamber and insure that the four-three vote occurs, or better, a four-two count if you can detain Romanov. Your firearms will prevent the fainthearted from stalling until the others can return, and your seizure of the television tower will allow our KGB propagandist cell to publicize the proper decision."

Neither man spoke for almost two minutes. A few other cars were out this sunny winter Sunday, and none of their drivers or passengers paid any attention to the black Volga. Donskov broke the silence. "When can I begin movement into the jump-off areas?"

"No sooner than Thursday. No later than Saturday. No reconnaissance after 2300 Saturday," Grebeniuk recited quietly.

Donskov cleared his throat, phrasing his question carefully. "Can you estimate the likely time of death?"

Grebeniuk responded immediately, almost cheerfully. "Certainly. 1900 Sunday, 10 March. The Politburo will meet at 2000."

You arrogant bastard, smoldered Donskov. You think you can just turn off an unwanted old man like a fucking light bulb?

For the record, the comatose Konstantin Ustinovich Chernenko expired at 1920, Sunday, 10 March 1985. The cause of death was reported as cirrhosis resulting from chronic hepatitis, complicated by emphysema. Although the dying old border guardsman held on for twenty unauthorized minutes past his scripted demise, the Politburo still convened at 2000, and Operation BERZIN began on schedule. In more ways than one, Chernenko just did not matter anymore.

Chapter Twelve

What Is To Be Done?

"Time to go, comrade captain," whispered Lieutenant Lebedev.
Donskov jerked alert with a wet squeal of rubber. He sat on a
slimy boulder, which had adhered slightly to the seat of his chemical
suit. Lucky I directed the use of these rubberized protective suits, or
my feet would have frozen solid as bricks, observed Donskov.
Instead, his warm, sheathed boots sloshed gently in the oily, stinking
water that he felt but could not see. Only the scarlet pinpoint of
Lebedev's penlight showed, bouncing through the fetid, icy darkness
under the Tower of Secrets.

How in hell did I fall asleep? Donskov shook his head. It should
have been no surprise; the captain had not slept for almost two days
as he finalized the arrangements for Operation BERZIN. The rancid
odors, frigid ankle-deep water, utter blackness, and scummy surroundings proved no match for the combination of a warm chemical
oversuit and time to kill. Always the waiting, Donskov noted.

Indeed, it had taken almost nineteen nail-chewing hours merely
to assemble the men of this understrength platoon in the smelly,
dripping sub-basement of the Tower of Secrets. Beginning more
than a day earlier, they had gone one by one onto the tiled river
embankment under the Stone Bridge, helped past the militiamen by
a series of "curious tourists" and "incidents" created by the resource-
ful Zharkowskiy. Once inside and accounted for, they had rested,
biding their time.

Now they struggled to their feet, in one of the few stretches of tunnel where a tall man like Donskov could stand up. The captain saw the glowing, telltale luminous tape on his paratroopers' fighting harnesses. His glance also disclosed a long chain of similar marks on the right tunnel wall, all the same ghoulish, greenish white color as the spectral fungus he had seen on rotting wood in Grenada.

"Ready, seven," hissed Corporal Padorin, banging his commander's shoulder. When the count hit "ready, sixteen," Lebedev in the lead would begin the tortuous movement toward the Council of Ministers' building.

Donskov made the usual checks. He fingered his equipment. He felt his AKD, silencer attached, loaded, on safe, and tied to his harness by a thin bootlace. He ran down the usual items: ammunition pouches full and ready, smoke and fragmentation grenades in place, first-aid pouch packed and closed, canteens almost full, maps and photographs up where he could get them, backpack radio hooked up and hissing soft static in his ears. He did not plan on using the radio, at least not anytime soon. His company was on a timetable tonight.

"Ready, eight," he said grabbing the soldier's shoulder to his front. Within five minutes the count had reached the lieutenant, and the movement started. Slowly, gingerly, the column shambled its way forward through the oozing, fecal muck.

While Donskov and his fifteen men got underway, three other elements also moved into position. In the storefront opposite 26 Kutuzov Boulevard, Savitskiy's 1st Platoon waited in ambush for Romanov's ZIL limousine. Two "drunks" stood ready to wander out, stumble, and roll into the street when the car appeared. Once Romanov's driver hesitated, hidden VDV snipers would puncture the tires and radiator, halting the ZIL. Then machine gunners planned to spray the wounded vehicle, followed by two volleys of BG-15 40mm smoke grenades, just to cause confusion. Thanks to the ZIL's thick armor plating and almost impervious bullet-proof glass, there was not any doubt about Romanov's survival. As for KGB bodyguards, Savitskiy wanted "to take a few out," as he put it. Maximum confusion, and hence maximum delay, seemed assured.

Out in Ostankino, Sergeant Major Rozhenko and a squad of three desantniks sat in the Seventh Heaven Restaurant, dressed in lumpy black business suits. The four toyed with steaming meals they could barely taste. Their job involved playing Ukrainian separatist terrorists. Precisely at 2015, they expected to rise up, toss a few smoke canisters, brandish AK-47s, and "capture" their fellow diners. An MVD rescue team, in fact the rest of the platoon in stolen uniforms, waited in a convincing panel truck not far away. Taking advantage of the panic, they planned to barge in through the real MVD soldiery and local police, "save" the hostages, and coincidentally grab the television broadcasting center. Then the half-dozen KGB technicians could hook up and transmit their special message.

Finally, in the broad uphill street between the Kremlin's Corner Arsenal Tower and the History Museum, Senior Lieutenant Zharkowskiy and Captain Korobchenko, retired, waited together in the gentle evening snow. Both wore dark, nondescript civilian clothes and heavy fur hats. It was a chilly night, around ten degrees below freezing. The wind blew steadily from the northeast, driving snowflakes across Red Square, which lay a couple dozen meters up the cobblestoned slope of the empty street. No cars drove here, although tanks and trucks churned this way every 7 November, on Revolution Day. The officers checked their watches and stared at the base of the Kremlin turret, at the small red and black monument that signified the Grave of the Unknown Soldier. "Thy name is unknown, thy exploit immortal. To the fallen, 1941–45" it read. The memorial served as the chosen rendezvous point for more than 200 angry Afghanistan veterans, due to congregate there at 2000 on the hour for a completely impermissible march toward the Lenin Mausoleum. These boisterous men downed drinks in nearby taverns or scooped up a last bite at home before heading down to the Kremlin to meet their friend Korobchenko.

By 1915, 10 March 1985, all of the pieces were on the board. The play commenced.

"Shit!" gasped the rifleman, tumbling to his knees. The man's weapon splashed into the foul, freezing black water. He pulled the AKD up by its dummy cord, tried to stand, and slipped again.

Donskov reached forward, snagging the crosspiece on the back of Private Tenishchev's battle harness, right between the two shining luminous markers. With an upward pull and a grunt, the captain dragged the man upright in a welter of clattering rocks and swirling water. The act caused Donskov to smack his elbow on a slanting, soggy reinforcement beam the size of a railroad tie. A bolt of pain shot up the captain's arm, but he held his tongue.

"Okay, Tenishchev?" asked the commander, almost inaudibly.

"Exactly so," the paratrooper answered quietly, bending to the front.

Donskov almost doubled over negotiating the jumble of splintered wood, mossy old rocks and bricks, and rusty iron rods. He skinned and buffeted himself weaving through the tangled debris. Donskov focused on the regular succession of glowing dots to his right. This was the last bad stretch before the Council of Ministers' building. We're almost there.

Behind him, Donskov heard more slopping, splattering, and banging. Groans and uneven, puffing breaths drifted and hung in the thick, cold air, sharing space with the awful ammonia stench of human urine. The column resembled a blind worm crawling up a twisting toilet pipe.

Another two steps, and his ankle gave way. Donskov grabbed a slippery pipe about ten centimeters across and steadied himself. A trickle of foul liquid ran onto his face; he shook his hooded head violently, and took another step. Donskov held out his arms, feeling ahead with his left hand and holding his AKD rifle in his right. His feet swished, and he bumped into something soft – the man in front of him.

"We're here," said Private Tenishchev. "Pass it back."

Donskov did so. He waited, sure that ahead of him Lebedev and Sergeant Ponomarev were pushing open the trapdoor in the back corner of a basement boiler room to free the men from the stinking tunnel. It must have been a hundred years ago that he and Ponomarev had lain in ambush at the Wheat Farm, hunting bandit rocketeers. I'll bet Ponomarev never expected that his army service would culminate in an assault on his own country's central government. But that's what it has come to. Like me, like all of us, Sergeant Ponomarev will do his duty.

Donskov checked his glowing watch: 1947. We're ahead of schedule. Savitskiy should have dealt with Romanov by now, and within a half hour, Popov and Rozhenko will take the Ostankino television center. Zharkowskiy and Korobchenko are gathering up their veterans, preparing for the march into Red Square, a gesture that should draw frantic attention from an alarmed Kremlin Commandant. And all the while, the Ninth Directorate agents must be scanning for random infiltrators emerging from the snowy night. They have no idea that we're down here, that we've shorted out the electronic sensor net intended to monitor the supposedly impassable tunnel. In a few short minutes, protected by the cloak of confusion, we'll be breaking into the Politburo room. It seemed impossible, yet here they stood, awash in the Kremlin's effluvia, on the verge of victory.

Somehow, by design, guile, and dumb luck, a bunch of recon desantniks from a line regiment had gotten this far—scant meters away from the center of Soviet power. Donskov knew that the state security people had let them do this, had permitted and assisted this escapade, but it did not diminish the VDV officer's satisfaction. The KGB let us in, perhaps even set us up, but we're doing things our way now. We've taken all of the Chekists' information and aid, told them what we wanted them to know, and now we're double-crossing the double-crossers. If we move fast enough, if we catch them in disarray, it *has* to work. This fantastic misadventure, this fever dream, seemed about to come true.

"Commander up," murmured the private to his front. Donskov stirred. Oh shit. This is what I get for congratulating myself too soon.

It took Donskov about two minutes to crab and squeeze his way through the six VDV troopers standing in front of him. When he swung past the last man, he barked his knee on a jagged rock, gashing his chemical suit, his camouflage uniform beneath, and his skin. Icy water dribbled in, mixing with warm blood. The captain barely noticed it.

"What have we got here?" he asked Lebedev. The lieutenant had switched on his red penlight, which gave a hellish cast to Ponomarev's determined face. Above, the wooden hatch remained shut.

"It's stuck," said the platoon commander.

"There's something heavy on it. I can't get any leverage, and there's not enough room for two of us," complained Sergeant Ponomarev.

Donskov put his hands up, testing. Sure enough, the door did not budge. The captain's blood ran cold, and he started to shiver involuntarily. Now what?

"Should we try demolitions?" suggested Lebedev.

"No," retorted Donskov angrily. "Do you want to bring down the whole gallery?"

Lebedev backed away.

"Sorry, Pavel," said Donskov reflexively. The captain settled a bit, at least externally. I must figure something out.

He stared at the shut opening, thinking. This screwed up everything. We counted on this entrance, built our plan around it and drilled ourselves stupid based upon one chosen ingress. And now this. Donskov wanted to wail with rage and frustration. So close—so damn close!

He tried to concentrate. There has to be a solution, an alternative. His watch shone like a little starburst, bright and cheerful: 1954. I've got about five minutes to solve this, he reminded himself. But his mind stayed blank. Nothing but the rising sense of panic, the certainty of failure, welled up to greet him.

Absently, he put his gloved, sopping hand to his face. The stinging, reeking cold made him recoil, and he lost his footing, sitting down with a loud splash. Ponomarev dragged him up. Donskov instinctively shook the beads of slime off his assault rifle, checked his backpack radio, patted his maps and photographs in their snug, dry chest pocket . . .

The map! They had reconned the *whole* tunnel. I remember more than one entrance. (You should have planned an alternate opening, dumbass, he told himself for future reference. As if there would be a future.)

The captain let his AKD hang by its string. He tore off his right glove, shoved it under his armpit, and jammed his free hand into his upper pocket. His clammy fingers closed on the documents, and he plucked them out. He knew by feel the texture of his homemade guide to the underground passage, and selected it surely, even in the blackness. In his haste, he almost dropped his packet of Politburo member photographs, but they caught in the crook of his elbow. He replaced the pictures swiftly, exhaled loudly, and turned to his prize. The officer fumbled out his little penlight. Its red glow lit the crumpled white paper, revealing an intricate spine of black lines and lettering.

"Pavel! This is it!" whispered Donskov excitedly. He put his wet, numb right index finger on the little sketch.

There, a scant seventy meters ahead on the map, was a second outlet, labeled "cleaning supplies." So they come up in a storage room a few doors down. So what?

"Let's go!" said Donskov aloud, almost tripping over his own dangling weapon in his excitement. He snatched it up triumphantly.

It took about ten minutes to grope and skid to the secondary site. Donskov led the way, his red light over his crouched head, his rifle slung, his other hand feeling the roof of the tunnel. He pressed and felt spongy, slick turf and occasionally the hard facets of suspended rocks. He tried to keep a pace count, but the tight quarters made that hard. Donskov was at about eighty-five meters, and tasting the bile of futility again, when he found it. He pressed.

The door lifted, lighter than a feather.

A weak, naked incandescent light bulb glared back at him, its fiery little heart as brilliant as a furnace to Donskov and his mole men. The commander blinked, his eyes wet with unavoidable tears from so many hours waiting in darkness. He grabbed the lip of the opening, threw over an arm, and chinned up.

The rectangular shaft of warm yellow light illuminated the captain, and it took only a few minutes to bring out the other fifteen men. Around them, in a room about the size of a one-car garage, were ranks and ranks of fat, five-liter floor-wax cans. Donskov checked his watch: 2013. A bit late, but close, he hoped. He hoped.

Ponomarev's squad waited at the far door, listening. The other sergeants checked the squads' weapons. All but the three squad leaders carried silenced AKDs. The sergeants shouldered SVD sniper rifles.

Lebedev and Yegorov already had a Council of Ministers' building blueprint unfolded atop a neat, waist-high stack of round containers. The lieutenant compared it with their tunnel chart. "Here we are," said the deputy commander. Donskov regarded it, marked his own building plan, and considered the possibilities.

"Right," voiced the captain, his mind clicking now, adrenaline flowing. "We'll use this elevator shaft, right here, to ascend. Once up in that long hall, no modification to rehearsal."

The officers nodded.

"We'd better shed these chemical suits. The heat's on in here," piped up Senior Sergeant Milyukov, the platoon's deputy commander. It was part of the original plan, but the reminder helped. The keyed-up officers had forgotten this small but vital point.

"Do it," ordered Lebedev. It took a few minutes more to strip off the streaked, waste-smeared overgarments. Donskov put on his blue beret, squaring it rakishly. The men did likewise.

"Let's go, Pavel," said the captain, his weapon at the ready.

Ponomarev's men swung open the metal door. A jangling alarm was sounding somewhere in the building, ringing and ringing. Little crimson lights, high on the dark concrete walls, winked on and off in the long corridor.

"Is that our fault?" wondered Yegorov.

"Who knows?" Donskov replied.

The squads leapfrogged down the basement hall, working from doorway to doorway. Although the bell kept buzzing and the lights flashed, they met no opposition.

The elevator doors were closed when the desantniks reached them. Right beside the shaft rose a stairway. Ponomarev put his men in the stairs, on watch. The other two squads faced up and down the dingy basement passageway.

"Where's the car?" asked Donskov of Milyukov, who was already fiddling with the opened call button panel. The sergeant snapped his head up, indicating the lights over the doors. The "3" light blinked off. A car was descending.

"Somebody's coming down," observed Lebedev.

"I'm trying to stop it," hissed Milyukov. "No luck."

Milyukov stepped back from the mass of wires connected to the sprung panel. Donskov brought up his AKD, as did Padorin and Lebedev. "You know what to do," said Donskov. The men stepped back, forming a line perpendicular to the doors.

"Clear the hall," squalled Milyukov to the squad in the line of fire. The paratroopers squirreled into doorjambs.

The elevator kept coming down. The "2" went out. The "1" lit, then went out. The last light lit, and the doors glided open.

Two impeccably dressed young Chekists stepped slowly out of the elevator, sniffing with the snub barrels of their chunky AKR carbines. Bundles of curved thirty-round ammunition magazines distended the pockets of their tailored suit coats. One told his mate: "Make sure –"

Hot 5.45mm bullets ripped into them, little hard snaps from silenced barrels. The men jerked and jumped, broken, bloody marionettes on strings of lead and fire. Donskov heard the spent rounds ricochet and pop off the distant basement wall. The pair fell, their unfired AKRs clattering and spinning uselessly away.

One's torn side spilled glistening intestines onto the cool cement. The other moaned and tried to roll over. Red, sticky roses darkened the backs of their light gray coats.

Padorin pumped another slug into the head of the living KGB man, spreading his face onto the floor. "Fucking Chekist," said the corporal laconically.

There was no time to waste on the leaking corpses. Everybody had seen much worse down south. Somebody else could clean this up.

"Into the elevator! Let's go!" rasped Donskov, waving furiously. The hallway squads picked up and ran over, jostling into the cubicle. The fluorescent light inside went out.

Lebedev and Milyukov were in the car, having jammed the door open with one of the KGB assault carbines. The sergeant cut most of the wires within the internal control panel, stranding the car in the basement. The lieutenant, meanwhile, knocked open the ceiling escape hatch and boosted himself up. His flashlight played around up in the shaft, its white beam visible through the square cutout.

"How about it?" said Donskov, looking up.

The platoon commander knelt down and looked in. "We can go right up the wall. It's like a cargo ladder—all lattice."

"Up you go, then!" announced Donskov, hoisting Padorin through the hole. Paratroopers lined up under the yawning square, restless in the dead elevator. They began yanking themselves through the hatchway, one after another. Above in the shaft, Donskov could hear the noises of rattling equipment as the men ascended.

Sergeant Ponomarev came in with his stairwell guards as the company medical sergeant went up. "It sounds like quite a show outside," he reported. His first private climbed into the hole. Yegorov and Donskov listened to the squad leader.

"I heard vehicles moving. No gunfire yet. There's shouting and running around outside, and the man I sent up to the next landing said every light in the compound is on."

"Excellent," said Donskov. "That's the deception going on, like the order said."

Ponomarev nodded briskly. "So far, so good, comrade captain."

Then it was the sergeant's turn, and he struggled up into the opening.

"You're next, comrade captain," urged Yegorov. They were alone in the dark car. Outside, the sprawled bodies waited to be found.

"I'm gone," Donskov said.

He slung his rifle, grabbed the edge of the hole with both hands, and flexed his arms. With a grunt he pushed his head through and scrambled to his feet atop the musty elevator car, brushing the taut, greasy cables.

"Come on, Kliment," he enjoined. The deputy dragged himself up, his rifle catching briefly and then releasing. Quickly, Yegorov was on his feet. Men were crawling like bulky spiders along the sides of the dim shaft, visible only by their little luminous tape markers and a few red penlights. They were on the way.

✦✦✦

It took about twenty minutes, but they cleared the shaft without incident. Once they pried open the third-floor doors, they found themselves in a nicely lit hallway that ran along the inner wing of the palace. Emergency lights flashed; bells rang steadily.

When Donskov bellied over the rim of the shaft, he got to his feet and turned left. Filth and grease stained the rich red carpet at the brink of the yawning rectangle, marking the passage of the airborne platoon. The men were already strung out, working their way down the long corridor. Donskov checked his map. This five-meter-wide passageway led right to the Politburo room. He could see a single doorway, maybe a hundred meters ahead. Perfect!

The men moved by rushes, bounding between cover. Those on the left used the series of recessed doorways to protect their paths; on the right, the soldiers sheltered behind the heavy pillars that flanked each wide window. Curtains screened the windows from the outside, but the recon troops were careful not to halt in the center of the openings. Rather, they crouched and huddled low against the solid supporting buttresses. Only a few thin-legged, flimsy wooden sideboards furnished the hall. They provided no protection at all.

Donskov moved on the right side. While halted near one of the lovely arched windows, he took a second to peek through the rich red and gold draperies. Looking up at the glowing bulbs mounted outside on the window frame, Donskov saw snowflakes dancing around the hot lights like moths in summer. It was a real blizzard out there. The commander glanced at the ground, to the grove of naked trees that separated the Politburo from the Kremlin Guards' barracks. As Ponomarev had promised, numerous lights illuminated the scene, creating an electric, bluish layer of daylight. The lamps all had fuzzy circular halos due to the falling snow. Under the blazing lights ran men, some half dressed, all brandishing weapons. They issued from the Arsenal across the way, and headed past the Council of Ministers' building, toward Lenin's tomb. Something was happening, all right.

The ringing bell was much more insistent, drawing Donskov's attention back to the red-carpeted hall. Along the top of the off-white, gold-striped walls, red blinkers winked rhythmically from gray emergency lighting boxes, spaced neatly throughout the passage.

The deputy commander slid in beside Donskov. He reported that Milyukov and Ponomarev held the rear, watching the empty stairwell and gaping elevator shaft for signs of pursuit. "Nobody behind us yet," he commented. Donskov nodded as he closely observed the progress of the lead elements.

Lebedev was moving ahead with his forward squad, almost to the door. The platoon commander halted at the end of the hall, stymied by the shut door. Lebedev glanced down at his map, cradling his assault rifle. About fifty meters behind, the captain consulted his own chart. Hold it, this room is *not* on our blueprints . . .

The burst of gunfire almost cut Lebedev in half, spinning his torn body into the velvety hangings to crack against the thick window on his right. The lead private, Semeyko, also tumbled aside, his arm broken and his stomach perforated. Every living man in the hall flattened instantly on the thick red rug, rolling behind their chosen cover. Blacks spots on the door showed where the rounds had come through.

Donskov saw it all from his safe vantage point. "Kliment, take the rear guard. Sergeant Zhivanetsyn and Corporal Padorin, follow me!" directed Donskov, on autopilot now, reacting by instinct.

Donskov had barely made it to his feet when another four rounds tore through the closed white door. They whistled around him, and he pitched face forward again, hugging the carpet, rolling left, his head flat and turned away from the windows.

Private Tenishchev was a few meters forward, propped against a door frame. He pointed up. "Camera," he said.

Sure enough, right in the corner of the window hung a big black and silver device. Donskov didn't hesitate. He twisted up and squeezed off a round, then another, right into the camera. He couldn't tell if it was hit, so he gave it a third bullet. Still no evidence of damage. Donskov waved his left arm. Nothing. He stood up slowly, quietly. No response.

"Down the inside wall, away from the windows," instructed Donskov quietly, motioning his men over. He held his finger to his lips and moved slowly toward the left side, the handle side, of the door. The bell clanged and clanged. The other riflemen did likewise, rising slowly, carefully, weapons ready.

A fusillade of bullets smashed through the door, whizzing harmlessly down the center of the hall. Donskov stood almost at the entrance. Tenishchev was just ahead of him.

"Pop the door," commanded Donskov. He waved to the two men behind him to lie prone just in front of the doorway. "Give them a magazine and I'll toss in a grenade," whispered the captain. The two desantniks crawled slowly into position.

Tenishchev lowered his barrel to the bright brass knob, backed off the long black silencer a few centimeters, and fired twice. The door swung open.

Both autoriflemen ripped off a magazine. Thanks to the silencers, the shots sounded like metallic spitting—the opening of giant zippers, not firearms. Donskov snagged the pin, let the handle spoon go, waited one long second, and lobbed an RGD-5 grenade into the room. It detonated with a sudden silvery burst, like a lethal flashbulb, and an ear-splitting crash. Donskov held up his hand. Wait.

He heard something rustling, then the thud of heavy, solid objects striking the floor. Wait. Donskov stood up. He poked his silencer in, then followed it.

Three Ninth Directorate men lay dead. One rested chin down, chewed to bits, on the floor in front of a torn-up green couch. Another had fallen on his back, arms spread wide. The third slumped on the sofa, his chest bubbling pink foam like an overflowing washing machine. A bell in the room rang and rang. An AKR assault carbine, surrounded by empty ammo magazines, lay on a shattered coffee table, still smoking. That was all.

Donskov cut the wire to the big bell with his bayonet. The shrill ringing ceased. A distant tumult of bells and whistles wafted in from outside.

The captain checked his watch: only 2101. Unbelievable. He felt like he'd been in here a few months. Mentally, he had. He scanned the building plan. Only a half a hundred meters to go, two more doors, and they'd be there.

"Let's go. I'll take the assault element now."

"What about the lieutenant and Semeyko?" asked Private Tenishchev.

"The rear squad will take care of them. Sergeant Goltsev, go. Straight ahead."

Goltsev set up carefully to open the back door of the bloody lounge. He shot it open. There was nobody there.

Ahead was a bright corridor, decorated on the solid, nonwindow side with pictures of cosmonauts and athletes receiving medals. At its terminus loomed the anteroom door. It was the only portal left. Donskov moved right behind Goltsev. Meanwhile, steady Yegorov jumped the rear guard forward to the gory room. The deputy commander began to shift the furniture to block the entranceway.

It took only a minute to reach the next door. Exterior noises were sounding fainter. Undoubtedly, the deception had run its course.

Donskov saw the camera this time, in the same corner as before. Sergeant Goltsev with his long SVD sniper rifle shot twice, disabling it as soon as he saw it. Pieces of camera rained to the floor.

"Do you think they saw us?" asked the squad leader.

Donskov shrugged. "We'll see." They hugged the left wall, well clear of the closed door.

Two from 1st Squad, four from 3d Squad, Padorin, and Donskov—it all came down to this. A glance over his shoulder showed that Yegorov was set to his rear, observing, a good deputy ready to move up and take charge if it came to that. If it came to that. . . .

"Okay," said Donskov, heart leaping like a tiger on a rope. *I hope I sound steady.* He did, mostly.

"Okay," he repeated. "Padorin and Lagovskiy, get down to spray. I'll do the door. Fire at *anyone* in uniform or armed."

Donskov moved his silencer to the bright golden brass of the doorknob, but he did not shoot. Instead, on a hunch, he opened it with a quick turn of his wrist, just like that, just like Zharkowskiy gouging out Wajid's eyeball on the point of a screwdriver. The door gaped open, a surprised mouth.

Two wonderfully turned-out guards, with gleaming white belts, sparkling belt buckles, and lovely bright black leather boots braced outside the last door, before the inner sanctum. Royal blue shoulder boards with bright gold letters proclaimed "GB." How could these Kremlin guards have failed to miss the noise of the grenade, the other shooting, the alarms? But these two were conditioned to look good and follow directions, not interpret unfamiliar phenomena. They had been told "stay here and guard the door." Orders were orders.

The handsome duo tried to bring up their AKMs, but smelly, dirty Padorin and his equally grimy partner punctured the sentinels' chests once, twice, three times apiece. They slid down almost simultaneously, gurgling and bobbing to the carpet. One left red streaks on the gold-striped wallpaper. Little dark nicks on the wall marked where the bullets had entered the massive facade that protected the Politburo members.

Donskov surveyed the vestibule. Topcoats hung neatly on wall hooks. Above, on a wooden shelf, were boxy fur caps, scarves, and a single dark fedora. That's Gorbachev's, Donskov realized immediately. One maroon sofa, a television set, and a long table against the far wall completed the furnishings of the windowless outer room. A red light glowed like an evil eye over the locked door. "In Session," it said. Nothing short of an imperialist nuclear attack would be permitted to interrupt a Politburo meeting.

Donskov looked at his wrist watch again – 2112. He edged to the closed door, trying to hear, hesitant to burst in. If he was a Spetsnaz team leader, he'd have listening systems and fiberoptic stalk cameras to sense activities inside the sealed chamber. But he had none of those things.

"Care for some help?" asked Sergeant Zhivanetsyn, proffering a stethoscope. Donskov took the implement from his aidman, exploring its earpieces, holding up the little, circular business end curiously.

Yegorov came in right then. He and his rear guard dragged the dead lieutenant and the wounded rifleman with them. We're all together now, the quick and the dead.

"We've got some people coming up behind us," warned the deputy. "I booby-trapped that middle room back there."

"Understood. Set up in here," instructed Donskov. He pondered a few seconds, then added: "It's 2115. Turn on the television and let's see what's up."

Yegorov turned the dial to Channel 1, with the volume very low. The nightly news show "Time" materialized. A pretty young blonde woman chatted away about livestock quotas.

"No luck at Ostankino, apparently," remarked Yegorov. "They haven't even acknowledged Chernenko's death, by the looks of it."

"Is he really dead?" asked Corporal Padorin calmly. Donskov's eyes opened wide. His jaw dropped. Was that possible? The commander's heart rose in his throat.

A quick glance at the Politburo "In Session" light calmed this horrific flutter. Why else would they confer on a Sunday night? Calm down, Donskov. It's working—not quite right, but near enough.

Captain Donskov scanned the fourteen living paratroopers. "Assault squad, stand by to go in. Deputy, you handle our security element. Leave the outer door open. No more killing, except to protect our party leadership. Understood?"

"Exactly so," said Yegorov. Sergeant Goltsev, Corporal Padorin, and Private Lagovskiy stood, weapons ready, waiting to go into the Politburo room. Yegorov deployed the others to move furniture and create a small barricade. The television in the corner stayed on, unheeded, its volume low.

Donskov inserted the stethoscope's earplugs. His watch showed him it was 2119, past time to act. But he wanted a recon of this final objective, if only by sound.

He pressed the disk to the door. The sound came through quite clearly. Donskov was amazed; the men were talking as if nothing unusual had transpired around them. Evidently the combination of thick walls, soundproofing, desantnik silencers, and especially the serious matter on the Politburo's agenda combined to render them oblivious to the ruckus outside. The Politburo had its own death struggle to attend to, right there in that lovely conference room. The captain's heart raced as he listened.

" . . . period of rise and consolidation of our revolution, which ended in the middle 1920s with the suspension of democratic centralism and the imposition of the Stalinist cult of personality. During this second period, the party harnessed the upsurge of the masses, liquidated the class enemies at home, and proved itself against the Fascist-Hitlerite menace in the Great Patriotic War. Socialism was built at great cost, and the Soviet Union made enormous strides as the vanguard country of the worldwide class struggle. Now we are deep in our third period, a period of party factions, disunity, dissolution, and vacillation, where 'good enough' has become our watchword. Comrades, the party is adrift. What is to be done? It has happened before, and the farseeing Lenin offered a prescription as applicable today as in his trying times: 'Put an end to the third period.' "

That must be Gorbachev, guessed Donskov.

"Mikhail Sergeyevich is correct. We have delayed this long enough. It is time to vote and move on with the political, ideological, and organizational measures that we have postponed for too long, merely to appease personal, and might I suggest, antiparty needs—"

"Hold it right there, Gromyko!" erupted a voice that Donskov had hoped not to hear. It was Romanov. How did he get here? What happened to Savitskiy? Something had gone wrong, but no matter now. Donskov did not have to strain to hear what came next.

"This ridiculous ploy has gone far enough," argued Romanov. "The choice of a General Secretary is not something to be ramrodded through in haste. When Leonid Ilyich passed on, we did not rush to judgment. When Yuri Vladmirovich died, we deliberated four days before choosing Konstantin Ustinovich. Now, with our late General Secretary barely gone from us, with three of our members away on party business, you want to choose a successor. I say wait!"

"We have waited long enough for action," retorted Gorbachev. "If Lenin waited as much as you, we'd still have the tsar."

"I see no need for a vote yet. There's always time," mumbled an old man, probably Tikhonov.

"He's right," agreed Romanov. "I move for adjournment, pending recall of our absent comrades."

"You have seen the balance and you don't like it, Grigoriy." It was Gromyko again, an edge to his tone. "The lines are clear—four to three, in favor of Mikhail Sergeyevich."

"That's tonight. You know it won't hold up! When Kunaev and Shcherbitskiy are back—"

"And Vorotnikov," said another voice, low and evil. Could it be Chebrikov? "Perhaps we should wait, Mikhail."

"Viktor," replied Gorbachev. He was in fact addressing the KGB Chairman, a candidate member. "I appreciate your caution. But the party and the people seem to desire firm leadership, not more compromises and delays. Did not you yourself refer to a mood of despair and lawlessness around the capital?"

"Haste is not leadership. The state security services remain the party's faithful sword and shield. I see no necessity for excessive speed in this vote," Chebrikov replied. The bastard! He's torpedoing Gorbachev, playing some game I can't even fathom. I wonder where we came in to this Chekist serpent's scheming? The captain's neck grew hot.

"Well then," said a distant, muffled voice. "Are we agreed to adjourn until our comrades return?"

"Maybe it is best," said another. Donskov thought it might be Solomentsev, one of Gorbachev's supporters.

He'd heard enough, and jerked off the stethoscope. It all came down to this, a captain's willingness to act. Was it courage, conviction, class consciousness, or simply the determination to play a part, to be important? Service or self? Or both? There was no time for contemplation.

"Assault squad!" he barked. The four men tensed.

Yegorov was facing him, saying something. He ignored the deputy. No time.

"Weapons on safe! No shooting!" ordered Donskov. He flung open the door and plunged in. The other three followed.

The ten men inside craned their eyes toward the camouflaged airborne troopers bounding into their space, smelling like waste and sweat, smeared in blood, grease, and gunpowder. They spread out in a ragged line, legs apart, saying nothing. Donskov glimpsed an image of Aq Khater, a frame from a horror movie. Not tonight.

For a split second, ten white faces reflected complete amazement, eyes wide, mouths agape. Then the commotion began. The

Politburo members and candidates present started talking all at once. Their speech blended together into a loud, meaningless babble. Romanov was on his feet, coatless, hands spread on the table. Bald old Marshal Sokolov, medals shaking on his great chest, shouted orders, pointing his finger accusingly at Donskov. Frail Tikhonov rocked back in his seat, almost apoplectic, swallowed by his shapeless, folded black suit with its shirt white as bone.

" . . . the meaning of this! . . . effrontery . . . who do you think . . . banana republic high jinks . . . Bonapartism . . . won't tolerate this . . . damned desantniks . . . hooligans . . . who permitted . . . Chekists in disguise" came snatches of words and phrases. Padorin, Goltsev, and Lagovskiy posed, weapons level, immobile and grim-faced. Donskov stood closest to the door, near one end of the table, where Gorbachev sat. The captain's assault rifle pointed squarely at Romanov.

"Comrades!" said Gorbachev. The noise continued. Aliev and Chebrikov stood up, pointing at each other. Solomentsev sat with his elbow on the long, oval table and his head in his hands. Grishin patted the tabletop feebly. Gromyko looked – amused, yes, entertained by the show. His slash of a mouth curled in a sardonic leer.

"Comrades!" said Gorbachev sharply. Romanov shook his fist, bellowing, his face nearly purple. "I will not stand for this Chekist intrusion on the lawful . . . "

A metallic crack, then another. Donskov was pounding his AKD's folding stock on the conference table. The wood dented; chips flew. The noise subsided.

"Enough," said Donskov flatly. The other desantniks said nothing, but the black, bottomless openings at the ends of their silencers spoke for them.

The party leaders who had stood up resumed their seats, Romanov last of all. They looked old, tired, and faintly ridiculous: wheezing Tikhonov, gray Grishin, florid Romanov, dark Aliev, nervous Chebrikov, and this spot-headed, almost baby-faced, balding man with the even white teeth and the wire-rimmed glasses.

Gorbachev cleared his throat. "As to a vote . . . "

"Long live the General Secretary!" sounded a chorus of male voices in the vestibule. "Long live the General Secretary!"

Senior Lieutenant Yegorov poked his head through the door. "It's on the television, comrade captain! General Secretary Gorbachev's selection is official! Long live the General Secretary!"

Gorbachev smiled, displaying a warm, genuine grin.

Gromyko raised his right hand. So did Aliev. Solomentsev, Tikhonov, and Grishin followed. Romanov lifted his hand limply.

Later, Soviet press organs accurately reported the vote as "unanimous."

EPILOGUE

A Traveler's Tale

When the situation has changed and different
problems have to be solved, we cannot look back and
attempt to solve them by yesterday's methods.
Don't try—you won't succeed!

V. I. Lenin

Preposterous! I don't believe a word of it."

"Jesus, Fred, you can't just dismiss it out of hand," pleaded James Mathers. "The section spent a lot of time piecing this together."

"Jim, I don't care," insisted Frederick Kingsford, deputy section chief. "Once you have some more time here in the agency, you'll quit jumping at every crazy story an émigré brings in."

Mathers slumped back in his chair, dejected. "Can't we even forward it to the interagency panel? Just float it and see if any of it checks out?"

Kingsford tilted his head. "Look Jim, let me lay it out for you. You want my analysis of this crap? Fine. Pay attention, so you won't get burned next time."

Kingsford opened the folder titled "Moscow Incidents Related to the Gorbachev Succession." He put on his horn-rimmed bifocals.

"Three things stink about this story: the wrong outfits, the wrong motivations, and the wrong people. And that's aside from your sources. The agency wants hard data—intercepts, photos, electronic signatures, or live defectors, not all this Sherlock Holmes's 'dog that did not bark' garbage. We don't have time to play with nuances in *Pravda* or odd programming changes on Moscow Channel 1, let alone this report from some British journalist from Reuters. Don't you know that Gail Fanshaw is as red as they come? She sleeps with Russians like you or I change socks. You've got to check this stuff out.

"Point one: the wrong outfits," continued Kingsford. "You're asking me to swallow that some line unit from Afghanistan just popped up to the capital for a coup d'état? Bullshit. Can't happen."

Mathers waved his hand. "This was an airborne reconnaissance company, virtually a Spetsnaz unit. Its commander must have had GRU training, probably Spetsnaz experience. The unit had returned to Moscow for a scheduled ceremony. And as I explained in the report, it seems that it was in league with certain army commanders *and* the KGB."

"See, that's where you're off base," Kingsford shot back. "The army and KGB do *not* cooperate. This is my second objection, wrong motivations. Why did these people do such things? Nobody can get into the Kremlin without the KGB's help, and why would they bring in some army unit to assure a Gorbachev succession? Why wouldn't the KGB just do it themselves, if I grant for the moment that such pressure was even employed? Look, the lines are simple. The army backed Romanov. The KGB backed Gorbachev and had the dirt on Romanov. That's it. Why would some renegade infantry company get involved in this? I don't see the connection."

"The KGB role is murky, I'll admit," retorted Mathers. "But I'm contending that these soldiers were anti-Romanov. They tried to ambush him, but got some cultural official by accident. Fred, don't you accept that there could be a dissident faction in the army, a faction disgruntled by the bungling in Afghanistan? Remember, this is an airborne company we're talking about. The Soviet paratroopers are bearing the brunt of the ongoing war effort."

"So why back a guy likely to pull out?" countered Kingsford.

"A withdrawal doesn't mean defeat. It depends on how it's handled," opined Mathers.

"No, not to a Russian, especially to a paratrooper. Romanov was the army's man, paratrooper or tanker. Soviet generals are all alike. They want more, and they want to dump it on us. Period."

"Well," said Mathers, "I think you're being too doctrinaire."

Both men paused, catching their breath. Kingsford spoke again.

"Okay. Wrong people. Let's just say that everything until now was possible. Let's assume that some wild-assed airborne unit tried to kidnap a culture minister for some reason, played terrorists to grab the Ostankino TV tower, and infiltrated the Kremlin through a sewage pipe to pressure the Politburo. Look at the name of the purported commander, will you?"

"Dmitriy Ivanovich Donskov. So what?" Mathers wondered.

Kingsford sighed loudly. He spun his comfortable leather chair around, ran his fingers across his bookshelves, and extracted a volume. He opened it, paged around a little, then stopped.

"Listen, Jim. 'Dmitriy Ivanovich Donskoy, 1350 to 1389, grand prince of Moscow from 1363. Defeated the Mongol Tatars at the Vozha River in 1378 and at Kulikovo Field on the Don River in 1380, thus earning the sobriquet "Donskoy." ' Don't you get it? The KGB is yanking our chain. This whole story is so badly fabricated that they couldn't even think up a good cover name. It would be like us planting a story of a Pentagon coup d'état revolving around Captain George Armstrong Custer. Get it?"

Mathers bobbed his head up and down. Kingsford handed back the discredited file.

"I'm telling you, I know these Soviets. You can't be too careful about evaluating stuff from Moscow. Always remember: The Russians are a conservative people. Nothing nutty happens there, not really. If you hear a story that sounds too fantastic to be true, it is."

Mathers smiled, grateful for his superior's prudent guidance. "Thanks for squaring me away, Fred. You saved me some real embarrassment."

"Don't mention it."

Glossary of Russian and Soviet Terms

AK (*avtomat Kalashnikov*)   Automatic assault rifles based on an original design by Mikhail Kalashnikov. Various models include the AK-47 (7.62mm wooden stock), AKM (modernized 7.62mm wooden stock), AKMS (modernized 7.62mm folding stock), AK-74 (5.45mm wooden stock), AKR (5.45mm carbine), and AKD (5.45mm folding stock, for air assault troops).

An-26   Antonov design bureau, NATO code name Curl. A turboprop-driven transport plane.

BG-15   40mm grenade launcher that attaches underneath an AK rifle barrel, much like the U.S. Army M-203.

BMD (*boevaya mashina desantnaya*)   Tracked airborne fighting vehicle, armed with a 73mm low-velocity cannon and a wire-guided antitank missile. The BMD-SON carries a counterbattery radar.

BMP (*boevaya mashina pekhoty*)   Tracked motor rifle fighting vehicle, armed as the BMD or, in the BMP-2, with a rapid-firing 30mm cannon.

BRDM (*bronevaya razvedyvatenaya dosornaya mashina*)   Wheeled armored reconnaissance vehicle.

BTR (*bronetranspotr*)   Various models of a wheeled armored personnel carrier, usually with a 14.5mm cupola weapon.

Cheka   Generic term for the Soviet state security service; it recalls the 1917 VChK, the All-Russian Extraordinary Commission for Combating Counterrevolution and Sabotage. Now known as the KGB.

Chekist   Member of the state security service.

Desantniks   Soviet rear area raiders, including airborne, heliborne, and naval infantry troops; colloquially, Soviet paratroopers, the vast bulk of the desantnik force.

DOSAAF (*Dobrovolnoye Obshchestvo Sodeystviya Armii, Aviatsii i Flotu*) Volunteer Society for Cooperation with the Army, Aviation, and the Fleet, a pre-induction training infrastructure that prepares Soviet youths for military service. Subjects addressed include shooting, minor tactics, flying and driving skills, parachuting, and basic fieldcraft.

DShK 12.7mm heavy machine gun.

D-30 122mm towed howitzer.

Falcon Nickname for a Soviet airman, especially a jet pilot.

GAZ-66B Light cargo truck.

GAZ-69, GAZ-69A Light utility truck, a jeep.

God of war Nickname for the Soviet artillery forces, or a soldier in those forces.

Gorbach "Hunchback," an armed helicopter; see Mi-24.

Grad "Hail," a 122mm rocket, usually fired from the BM-21 multiple rocket launcher.

GRU (*Glavnoe Razvedyvatelnoe Upravlenie*) Chief Intelligence Directorate of the General Staff; also, military intelligence in general, responsible for detection and sabotage of external threats to the Soviet Union.

Guards Honorary designation, normally won in combat, but occasionally awarded to certain elite units upon formation, as with elements of the VDV.

KGB (*Komitet Gosudarstvennoy Bezopasnosti*) Committee for State Security, the Soviet intelligence service, responsible for prevention of internal overthrow and subversion of foreign powers.

Komsomol (*Kommunisticheskiy Soyuz Molodyozhi*) Union of Young Communists, the Communist party youth organization, open to ages fourteen to twenty-eight.

Makarov PM   9mm automatic pistol.

M-46   130mm towed field gun.

Mi-2M   Mil design bureau, NATO code name Hoplite. A utility helicopter.

Mi-6   Mil design bureau heavy lift helicopter, NATO code name Hook. A heavy lift helicopter capable of lifting a BMD.

Mi-8   Mil design bureau troop, NATO code name Hip. A transport helicopter, often armed with 57mm rockets in external pods.

Mi-24 "Gorbach"   Mil design bureau, NATO code name Hind. An armed, armored helicopter, often armed with a 12.7mm four-barreled rotating cannon. Originally designed for the KGB Border Guards, the Mi-24 can carry a combat-ready squad of infantry in its cabin.

MVD (*Ministerstvo Vnutrennikh Del*)   Ministry of the Interior, which maintains an internal army organized into infantry and motor-rifle units.

Osnaz (*osobogo naznacheniya*)   Special purpose, KGB Directed Operations forces.

PFM-1   Also called "butterfly" or "green parrot." A small minelet, usually scattered by aircraft.

PKM   7.62mm squad machine gun used by motor-rifle troops.

PNV-57   Passive night vision goggles; these gather ambient light.

R-105M   Vehicle-mounted radio.

R-114D   Backpack radio, air assault model.

RBK-250   Air-delivered cluster bomb, comprised of sixty submunitions.

RGD-5   Hand grenade.

RPG (*reaktivniy protivotankoviy granatomet*)   Rocket-propelled grenade, launched from a tube with a calibrated sight. Launcher models include the RPG-7, RPG-7V, RPG-16, and RPG-16D (a special air assault model that can be broken down into two parts). The new RPG-18 is a single-shot, throwaway rocket similar to the U.S. Army M-72A2 light antitank weapon (LAW).

RPK Standard squad machine gun. Models include the RPK (7.62mm) and the newer RPK-74 (5.45mm).

RPU-14 Air assault model 140mm towed multiple rocket launcher.

Spetsnaz (*spetsialnogo naznacheniya*) Special purpose forces, GRU controlled.

Strela "Arrow," NATO code name SA-7 Grail. Soviet model 9M32M infrared heat-seeking surface-to-air missile.

Su-17 Sukhoy design bureau, NATO code name Fitter. A ground attack jet.

Su-25 Sukhoy design bureau, NATO code name Frogfoot. A ground attack jet.

SVD Dragunov "Dragoon," 7.62mm sniper rifle.

T-62E Tank with a 115mm gun. The E-model has additional armor.

T-72 Tank with a 125mm gun.

Tu-16 Tupolev design bureau, NATO code name Badger. A long-range jet bomber.

2S1 122mm self-propelled tracked artillery piece.

UAZ-469 Light utility truck, a jeep.

VDV (*Vozdushno-Desantnye Voyska*) Air Assault Forces, paratroopers and elite heliborne troops, distinguished by blue berets and undershirts with horizontal blue and white stripes.

ZU-23 Twin-barreled, ground-mounted 23mm antiaircraft cannon.

Selected Bibliography

Amstutz, J. Bruce. *Afghanistan: The First Five Years of Soviet Occupation.* Washington, DC: National Defense University Press, 1986.

Baxter, Lt. Col. William P., USA (ret.). *Soviet Airland Battle Tactics.* Novato, CA: Presidio Press, 1986.

Bonds, Ray, ed. *Russian Military Power.* New York: Crown Publishers, 1982.

Cockburn, Andrew. *The Threat.* New York: Random House, 1983.

Department of the Army. *Historical Development of Staffs.* Fort Leavenworth, KS: Combined Arms and Services Staff School, 1983.

_____. *Soviet Army Equipment, Organizations, and Operations.* Fort Leavenworth, KS: Combined Arms and Services Staff School, 1984.

Dupree, Louis. *Afghanistan.* Princeton, NJ: Princeton University Press, 1973.

Fuller, William C. *The Internal Troops of the MVD SSSR.* College Station, TX: Texas A & M University Press, 1983.

Girardet, Edward R. *Afghanistan: The Soviet War.* New York: St. Martin's Press, 1985.

Glantz, Lt. Col. David M., USA. *The Soviet Airborne Experience.* Fort Leavenworth, KS: Combat Studies Institute, 1984.

Goldhammer, Herbert. *The Soviet Soldier.* New York: Crane, Russak & Company, 1975.

Isby, David C. "Resistance in Afghanistan," *Strategy and Tactics,* No. 99 (January/February 1985).

_____. *Russia's War in Afghanistan.* London: Osprey Publishing, Ltd., 1986.

_____. "Soviet Special Operations Forces in Afghanistan, 1979–85." Unpublished manuscript.

_____. "Soviet Tactics in the War in Afghanistan," *Jane's Defence Review*, Vol. 4, No. 7 (1983).

_____. *War in a Distant Country*. London: Arms and Armour Press, 1989.

_____. *Weapons and Tactics of the Soviet Army*. New York: Jane's Publishing Co., Inc., 1981.

Jacobs, G. "Afghanistan Forces: How Many Soviets Are There?" *Jane's Defence Weekly*, Vol. 3, No. 25 (22 June 1985).

Knight, Amy W. *The KGB*. Boston: Unwin Hyman, 1988.

McManaway, Maj. William F. "Afghanistan Lessons Learned Trip." Memorandum for Chief, Firepower, U.S. Army Training and Doctrine Command, 31 March 1988.

Medvedev, Zhores A. *Gorbachev*. New York: W. W. Norton & Co., 1986.

Nyrop, Richard F. *Pakistan: A Country Study*. Washington, DC: U.S. Government Printing Office, 1983.

Nyrop, Richard F., and Donald M. Seekins. *Afghanistan: A Country Study*. Washington, DC: U.S. Government Printing Office, 1986.

Reznichenko, V. G., I. N. Vorobyev, and N. F. Miroshnichenko. *Taktika*. Moscow: Voenizdat, 1987.

Scott, Harriet F. "The Politburo," *Air Force,* Vol. 71, No. 3 (March 1988).

Scott, Harriet F., and William F. Scott. *The Armed Forces of the USSR*. Boulder, CO: Westview Press, 1981.

Smith, Hedrick. *The Russians*. New York: Ballantine Books, 1976.

Solovyov, Vladimir, and Elena Klepikova. *Behind the High Kremlin Walls*. New York: Dodd, Mead, & Company, 1986.

Suvorov, Viktor. *Inside the Aquarium*. New York: MacMillan, 1986.

_____. *Inside the Soviet Army.* New York: MacMillan, 1982.

_____. *Inside Soviet Military Intelligence.* New York: MacMillan, 1984.

_____. *The Liberators.* New York: W. W. Norton & Co., 1981.

_____. *Spetsnaz.* New York: W. W. Norton & Co., 1987.

Urban, Mark L. "The Strategic Role of Soviet Airborne Troops," *Jane's Military Review* (1984).

_____. *War in Afghanistan.* London: MacMillan Press, Ltd., 1988.

Zaloga, Steven J. *Inside the Soviet Army Today.* London: Osprey Publishing, Ltd., 1985.

Zaloga, Steven J., and James Loop. *Soviet Bloc Elite Forces.* London: Osprey Publishing, Ltd., 1985.